Sleeping With Mortals

The Story of a
New York Mistre$$

MOUNTAINLAND
publishing inc.

Sleeping With Mortals: The Story of a New York Mistress
by Cathrine Goldstein

ISBN 978-0-9745476-6-4

Printed in the United States of America

ACKNOWLEDGEMENTS

I would like to thank:

Tracy Quan; Kyra Davis; Wendy Cleveland; Michael Combe; Catherine Dyer; John Gill; Jen Howard; Michele Roberts; Dante Russo, Cadden Jones and crew; Kristen Rutherford; Tina Scala; and Susan Schwartzman.

Extra special thanks to Laura McVeety Pawlewicz for caring so very much; to Jay for all of the endless help and support; and of course, to Penelope. For eventually going to sleep.

--Cathrine Goldstein

SLEEPING WITH MORTALS:

THE STORY OF A NEW YORK MISTRESS

by

Cathrine Goldstein

Bigger breasts. At nineteen-years-old I had only two life goals, the first: to conquer the world of men; the second: to get bigger breasts. Even then I knew it would be impossible to accomplish the earlier goal without first obtaining the latter. I understood that no matter what I, Victoria Messing, was planning to do with my life in the city, I would need significantly bigger breasts to do it.

I was also convinced that men were divided into two categories: gods and mortals. You can be sure that I was only interested in the gods and what they had to offer – a life filled with riches and exotic places the likes of which I'd only dreamed of. And so, with inflated breasts and an ego to match, I began my life as a New York City mistress.

Before we go any further, let me tell you that I probably know what you're thinking: whore, tramp, home-wrecker, all the obvious labels for someone who makes a life sleeping with other women's husbands. But before you dismiss me as some callous neophyte sex slave, let me offer you some other names to ponder as well: ignorant, gullible, naïve... oh okay, let's even tag on downright stupid, shall we? During my first go at "mistressing" I was nineteen and he was forty-three; I was outmatched on every level. I'm certainly not asking you to feel sorry for me, I'm simply telling you the truth. Did I knowingly sleep with other women's husbands? Yes. Did I set out to be a home-wrecker? To ruin someone's life? Of course not. I wasn't evil. What I was, was a gold-digger – and not a very good one at that. Think Jon Voight in *Midnight Cowboy.* "Mistressing" was simply a business for me – it was a fair trade. I wanted a lifestyle that I couldn't obtain for myself, and they wanted a young beautiful woman to screw with no strings attached.

Despite my hands-on first person experience, I have still often wondered what makes a man cheat. Have you? Unfortunately, I don't have the definitive answer for that one. What I do have are some suppositions based on my ten (or so) years of experience as a coveted New York City mistress in the new millennium.

So here's my story. The sublime and the ridiculous, the glamorous and the sickening. Here's what really happens between your husband and his mistress.

I think you may be surprised.

PART I:

THE GODS OF MOUNT OLYMPUS

"Strange clouded fragments of an ancient glory,
Late lingerers of the company divine,
They breathe of that far world wherefrom they come,
Lost halls of heaven and Olympian air."

CHAPTER 1: ZEUS

"The Titans or the Elder Gods: Supreme in the universe. They were of enormous size and incredible strength. Zeus, the chief of Olympus and of the divine family is represented as falling in love with one woman after another and descending to all manner of tricks to hide his infidelity from his wife."

The instant I laid eyes on Dr. Fifth Avenue it was lust at first sight. I was still only nineteen-years-old, still living in Pennsylvania, and still flat-chested. Nonetheless, I was convinced that I would have him. He was unlike any man that I'd ever known: rich, handsome, powerful. In his office that day, I decided that he was the only doctor who could possibly perform my breast augmentation. As I rode the train back to Penn State that night, I convinced myself that it would only be a matter of weeks before I was living my new extravagant lifestyle.

I didn't care that he was most definitely married and probably already had a mistress – a Giselle Bundchen lookalike no doubt. I was sure that I could land him: Dr. Fifth Avenue. Even his name was smooth and sophisticated. I was ready for it all, up for the challenge. Bring it on, Giselle. In *Cosmo* or some such place I'd read about women like me – young, attractive, ambitious – heeding to the call of becoming a mistress, a profession far more luxurious than a common call-girl but every bit as secretive and intriguing. I wanted that. I ached for it. I would become Dr. Fifth Avenue's mistress. That was my deciding moment, on the border of Pennsylvania and New York, when I sealed my fate and set the course for my adulthood. I toasted to my new life with a Diet Coke.

I inhaled deeply; I could still smell him. He wore Armani for Men and Armani suits. His eyes were cornflower blue; his thinning, curly hair was light blonde from too much sun. His voice was high and raspy but still firm. His mustache would tickle my lip the first time he'd kiss me. I couldn't sleep... I opened my eyes and listened to the rumble of the train. I pulled out my appointment book and jotted a note to myself to call his office tomorrow to schedule the surgery. Right. I laughed. Like I'd forget.

My train pulled into the station and there was David. All six-foot-two of him. David was a sorority girl's dream: sandy-haired, built, and cute in a silly, boyish way. I rolled my eyes when I saw him. David was so very reliable, but so very boring. Frankly, I wished that he'd forgotten to pick me up – it would have made my exit that much easier. Sure I needed the ride home, but I just didn't want to see David – not that night nor any night in the future. But he didn't know that. Not yet, anyway.

David gave me a wet, slobbery kiss. As I wiped away his drool, he asked me how my day of shopping was. "Fabulous," I said. Please. It was just a little white lie. I had to make sure that he was clueless about my mission; I had no interest in before-and-after pictures of me showing up in the campus newsletter. So I let David carry my bags, I let him drive me back to my off-campus apartment, and as a going-away present, I let him fuck me that night... all the while still inhaling Dr. Fifth Avenue's cologne.

The next morning, after he farted and burped and wrapped my last clean towel around his waist, David told me about his rugby match. "We're all going out for beers and shots afterwards!" he said, truly excited, like it was something new. I had gone to countless rugby matches, but after yesterday, it all seemed so beneath me. David was wasting my time. I let out a long sigh. "Babe?" he said. "What's up? You okay?" He wrapped his arms around me and kissed me on the head. "Last night was cool. Thanks." David was a nice guy – a jock who brings flowers and doesn't ask for sex until the third date – although I gave it to him on our second. I felt bad for hurting him, but what could I do? He was in my way. I rested my forehead on his chest and inhaled him. He had a nice, clean smell – almost like Silly Putty – but he and his silly toy smell were no match for Dr. Fifth Avenue and his Italian designer scent.

David kept me tight to his chest and I felt him get hard. He leaned down for a kiss but I pulled away. "Right," he said. "Right. We have to go." His clean-shaven cheeks turned a bright pink, embarrassed by his unwarranted erection. As David dressed, I felt sorry for the both of us. I was sorry for me because that body was wasted on David, a rugby playing frat boy with absolutely no promise for the future; and I was sorry for him because he was in love with me. Truthfully, I never had any real feelings for David and I don't think that I ever could. Not even if he had offered me a two-carat Tiffany engagement ring instead of sex in his dorm room while his roommate pretended to be asleep.

Once David was gone, I jumped into a steamy shower and screamed until big, beautiful Manhattan-bound tears streamed down my face. I was free! That one meeting with Dr. Fifth Avenue had changed everything. I felt taller, more beautiful. I felt... victorious. At last I knew where and with whom I was supposed to be, and it wasn't with some twenty-two-year-old jock who drinks beer and farts.

By the time my shower and scream therapy were over, I had already forgotten all about David. I dried off in the wet towel and slipped on the same skin-tight white oxford I had worn to Dr. Fifth Avenue's office. I breathed in deeply, picked up the phone and dialed. My voice cracked as I spoke but I managed to schedule the procedure. I would have my transformation in three weeks. Three weeks was longer than I wanted to wait but I decided to be optimistic – the delay gave me time to prepare. Snagging Dr. Fifth Avenue would take some effort.

I ran from my apartment clear across campus to withdraw from school. The Registrar's Office was a blur of paperwork, different colored slips that needed signing, and people who kept asking me why I was leaving and walking out on a full four-year scholarship. I said simply, "For wonderfully personal reasons." I was the happiest I could ever remember being. That very same afternoon I packed up my things from my apartment and mailed everything that I didn't want to my mother's house. Then I took all the money from my bank account. With a duffle bag, backpack and a load of cash, I boarded the train and went back to New York City.

Admittedly, I had no idea what it meant to find an apartment in New York City. I also didn't care. I took a room that night in a dirty and overpriced hotel across from Penn Station. To me, it felt like the Taj Mahal. I gobbled a slightly stale bagel with cream cheese from the deli downstairs and I thought it was just about the best friggin' dinner I'd ever eaten. In my rapture, I thanked everyone at the deli profusely, hardly able to believe that I was finally here. An older man in a polyester suit asked me where I was from. "The West Side," I said. One of the deli guys gave me a free apple. The other one gave me a free Raspberry Snapple. Damn, if I had known that New York was going to be this easy, I would have moved here ages ago. I took my apple out onto the street and felt the excitement envelop me. The city was a glorious urban orchestra: three taxis whizzed by, nearly jumping the sidewalk; a street vendor selling books about the "true connection to God" shouted through his megaphone; a second vendor yelled at him to shut up; a young couple fought on the corner of Thirty-fourth and Seventh while a singing mime tried to pick-pocket a middle-aged woman. God, I loved New York.

Bright and early the next morning, I began my quest for an apartment. After the *Times* (hopeless) and three-quarters of the way through the *Voice* (better) I finally found a studio that I could afford. The apartment was on a low floor in an old tenement on the Lower East Side. The building was poorly maintained: it had a cracked front stoop and one feeble elevator. But for some reason, there was a part-time doorman. Nirvana. The distinct smell of fried egg rolls and Peking Duck from the Chinese restaurant below wafted up through two tiny windows.

All in all, my apartment was about four hundred square feet and I had to walk through the "kitchen," with the miniature refrigerator and miniature stove, to get to the one and only room. It was a perfect hovel for two of Snow White's smaller and nicer dwarves. (Grumpy and Sneezy most certainly would have come to blows in such a confined space.) I ran out to buy a pull-out couch even though the apartment wouldn't be ready until the following week. The delay of my move-in date meant that I had to dump some serious money on that same crappy hotel (which no longer felt like the Taj) but what did it matter? The next time I stayed in a hotel it would be The Plaza. Fluffy white bathrobes, giant bubble baths, champagne and room service.

The next morning I realized that I still hadn't called my mother to tell her where I was or what I had done. I dreaded this call, but I had to make it. My box of unwanted stuff was already en route, headed straight for her.

"You're where?" my mother asked.

"You heard me," I said. I would have done just about anything to avoid the drama that was to follow but there was just no way of stopping it.

"Oh my God!" my mother said. "My baby in New York! Just like her Mama!" I was sure I was about to get a "when I was with the band" story, but she cut to the chase instead. "Finally," she said with a lilt in her voice. "Finally you're doing something with yourself! Are you going to model?" My mother had wanted me to become a model since the age of four when I won my first beauty pageant.

"I'm just hanging," I said, avoiding all the real issues, like: "Where are you staying? Are you okay? Do you have money? Do you have any idea what you're doing?"

But those inconsequentials never entered my mother's mind. Instead, she dove into a story about her favorite night at CBGBs and asked if I would go to see if Don was working and tell him that she said hi.

"Of course," I said, "I'll go see if a man who worked at CBGBs twenty-five years ago is still there so that I can tell him you say hi."

"Great!" my mother said. I hung up the phone as quickly as possible.

Between moving, settling in, and the surgery, I used pretty close to all the money from my inheritance and my savings. Even so, I was not getting a job. I was determined to be a mistress, and mistresses are kept. That's the major perk. Even without working, three weeks went by pretty quickly. I window shopped (picking out everything my beloved would buy me), had my hair straightened and glossed, and went out to small bars in Greenwich Village at night where young NYU students would offer to buy me drinks. I'd let them, of course, but once a martini was securely in my hand, I'd lean forward (pushing together the stuffing of my miracle bra) and whisper, "I have a boyfriend." Then I'd get up and move on to the next open table and unsuspecting boy. Hey, it was a way to pass the time. But the funny thing was, I wasn't lying. In my mind, I did have a boyfriend. I was so committed to Dr. Fifth Avenue, I didn't even flirt with the tall, handsome, forty-something-year-old man in my building who was – in appearance – completely my type.

*   *   *

Afraid that something horrible happened to me, David had called my sister, Liz, seventeen times in two weeks. Liz finally broke down and told him that I had moved to the city.

"No!" I said over the phone. "Now he'll want to see me! Tell him I moved to LA. Tell him I'm dead."

"But he's a nice guy!"

"Then you date him." I hung up the phone, but not without first wrangling Liz into picking me up after my surgery. My mother, fully supportive of my decision to inflate my assets, decided the best way to help me would be to stay home to light candles and pray to the patron saint of Big Bosoms, or Titanic Ta-Tas for those of you who aren't religious.

I had to show up for the operation wearing no makeup, but I made sure my jeans and black zip-front sweater looked hot. I wasn't the least bit nervous about the surgery; I already trusted this man with my life. Sure, the night before while I was eating my individual pan pizza there was a brief moment when I envisioned the headlines of the *Post*: "Splatso for Flatso!" or "The Rise and Fall of Little Breasts! – Young woman wanting bigger breasts dies on operating table." But by the next morning, walking into his office, my fears had dissipated. I filled out the endless amount of mandatory paperwork – how much medical history could I have at nineteen? – and went into the operating room. I took off my shirt, lay down on the table, covered myself with the sheet and waited for my beloved. Moments later, he entered, looking powerful and focused, like a great warrior going into battle. I felt myself gasp and knew I was blushing. He smelled exactly as I remembered but the Armani suit was replaced with cornflower blue hospital scrubs – to accent his eyes, no doubt. He had a cap on over his blonde curls and a mask, half-tied, hanging around his neck. He smiled at me and I smiled back.

"Well," he said. "Let's get you going. How big did we decide?"

"How big do you like?" I was a woman on a mission. Dr. Fifth Avenue laughed and soon I was under. Hours later, a buxom version of me emerged from surgery to see a distraught Liz fretting in the waiting room.

"It took so long!" Liz said. "Are you okay?" I couldn't answer. All I could do was look down at my breasts and grin.

Dr. Fifth Avenue walked up behind us. "Sorry about the wait. I took my time," he said. "I wanted to make sure that she was perfect. I even closed her up myself." Liz grimaced at the expression "closed her up."

Then he turned to me. "See you in a week for a checkup." I tried to smile and nodded weakly. I felt the room spin. My head grew heavy. Dr. Fifth Avenue jumped to my side and put his arm around me to steady me. I breathed him in, deeply. "Go get a cab," he said to Liz, and she did. I put my head down on Dr. Fifth Avenue's shoulder and felt him catch his breath. I managed to look up and saw he was smiling. I threw all of my weight onto him, and gently, he half-carried me to the cab. He held the door open. "I'll see you in a week," he said, closing the door behind us. As we drove away, he was still standing on the sidewalk, watching us go.

Liz looked at me. "He was really cute. Did you notice?" I didn't answer her; I had no intention of sharing my master plan with Liz. "Well," Liz said, "I could feel the sparks between you two. Too bad he's probably married." I closed my eyes.

Two weeks and three bra sizes later, I was standing in front of Dr. Fifth Avenue's office waiting for him. I caught my reflection in a window and turned first one way, then the other, gazing at my new accouterments. They were so high and perky, I had to laugh. They were like two overripe cantaloupes popping out of the top of a grocery bag. They stretched my skin till it glistened. It looked like someone had stuck a straw into each nipple and inflated me. I sincerely worried that a stiff wind would come and take me away. Oh wait, you're probably wondering how the date was set up. In a word: quickly. Quickly, while the female nurse stepped out during my one week checkup, Dr. Fifth Avenue asked about a boyfriend and then about dinner. I said no and yes, respectively. Wham, bam, done.

That night was my first date with Dr. Fifth Avenue and I did not take it lightly. Oh, no... not I. I had spent a good three hours primping and fussing, not to mention the earlier manicure/pedicure, bikini wax and trim. I even perfumed my pubic hair, just in case. I finally left my apartment and got into a cab that raced up Park Avenue. The wind from the open window blew my hair wildly, but I didn't care. Wildly sexy was in.

We barreled down the cross street and turned onto Fifth. I took my time and exited gracefully in case he was watching. He wasn't. That meant I had to pay for my own cab. I shook off this little inconvenience, sure that from this night forward Dr. Fifth Avenue would be footing my transportation bill... and all my other bills for that matter. I had agreed to meet Dr. Fifth Avenue at his office because I thought he was working late, but when I arrived, I found the place locked down tight. For a brief second I panicked. Had he forgotten? Did I get the wrong night? The wrong time? Had I imagined it all?

Finally, in the middle of my angst, I saw him: The Phantom of Fifth Avenue. I was frozen, my eyes locked on him – he was my Svengali... or perhaps ...was I his? He stepped over a broken piece of sidewalk and then caught sight of me. He walked more and more quickly until he broke into a jog. A huge smile swept across my face, maybe for him, maybe for happiness, or maybe because I was just learning the power that I possessed. He was wearing a navy blue Armani suit and a bold multi-colored tie; he looked much too hot for early spring. When he reached me, a tiny bead of sweat trickled down his forehead. He wiped it away.

"Sorry I'm late," he said. "Patients...."

"No problem." I tossed my hair softly, fully aware that he had just blatantly lied to me. We were standing in front of a closed office – where exactly were those patients he was seeing? Ah, the hell with it. I decided to forget about the lie. There were so many more important things to think about than one itsy bitsy tiny little lie.

"You look fabulous," Dr. Fifth Avenue said. Although it was a bit tight on the top, I was wearing a white lace dress that I had worn not five months earlier to compete in a national teenage beauty pageant. Talk about improper beauty queen behavior! No wonder I hadn't won. "I mean really," he said, taking my hand. He stepped back to look me up and down. "You look astonishing." So, maybe I did win after all.

Still holding my hand, he led me to a romantic bistro on the Upper East Side ("bistro," I learned, is code for dark, hidden and private). We ate escargot and pasta, lots of bread with black olive paste, and drank two bottles of Pinot Noir. I was eating it up. All of it. The dinner, the wine... him. I was just a girl from the suburbs of Philly. What did I know from escargot? Prior to that night, my only experience with a fancy dinner out had been Red Lobster.

It didn't occur to me that I should keep certain things secret. Little things... mere nuisances really. Little things like the fact that I wasn't legally old enough to drink yet. When I mentioned this tiny little nuisance fact in passing, Dr. Fifth Avenue's face turned white as a sheet. "But you are..." he swallowed hard and asked, "over eighteen?" I watched him wrack his brain trying desperately to remember my answer to "age" on my pre-op paperwork.

"Of course!" I said as we both chugged the illegal libation, suddenly aware I was approximately as far from Pampers as he was from Depends. We finished the bottle and relaxed a bit, although in my heart I knew that I had just committed my first mistress faux pas.

After dinner and a dessert of warm berry tart with mascarpone and cappuccino, we left the restaurant and walked hand-in-hand down the avenue. I was so happy I had to keep myself from skipping. I mean, can you believe it... Victoria Messing, former freshman at Penn State, with Dr. Fifth Avenue? I grinned as we waited for the traffic to pass. Then Dr. Fifth Avenue yanked on me with the strength of a mighty Boreas wind. I was lifted into the air and spun toward him. He leaned over just as a small gust blew my hair across my face. Our first kiss was soft and gentle and... furry. The walk light turned green and he led me across the street. Dr. Fifth Avenue had such a tight grip on my hand that he was no longer holding it, but more grabbing it, like a father holds a bad child's hand.

As I tried to wriggle my fingers, I wondered if that was a game he wanted to play. I thought I remembered seeing that once: "Daddies and Bad Little Girls." Yup. I was sure of it, actually. It was one of the endless numbers of porno videos my mother had rented for me when I turned sixteen, three long years ago. "It's important that you learn how to land a successful man and keep him happy," my mother had told me that day, popping in a video. Mom would be proud.

"Can I take you to your place?" Dr. Fifth Avenue asked. I knew that it wasn't usually a good idea to bed a man too fast, but he wasn't some stupid college jock. He was a New York City plastic surgeon! If I said no, someone else would surely say yes. Then who knows what I'd miss. But I just couldn't imagine why he wanted to go to my apartment... surely someplace more, well, magical would be proper for our first time.

"My place is a mess," I said. "I just moved in. Boxes everywhere. I sleep on a pull-out."

Dr. Fifth Avenue lit up. "Oh! I'd love to help you fix up your place! It'd be like I was in college again." For the second time in three hours I chose to ignore something he said. What, exactly, was so great about college? I put his flashback-to-frat-days comment out of my mind and concentrated instead on the Mercedes Benz he was helping me into, complete with heated seats for those pesky New York winter days. As he held the car door for me, Dr. Fifth Avenue pointed toward a restaurant window. "That's my son's favorite place to eat; they have yellow plates. When he's out, he'll only eat off of yellow plates." He laughed to himself.

"Your son?" I asked.

"Oh, sorry, hadn't I mentioned him before?"

After my subtle prodding, we decided on a hotel rather than my messy apartment for the night. Unfortunately, it was the exact same hotel in which I had recently lived. An unlucky coincidence. Okay, so it wasn't The Ritz, but it was a start. I resigned myself to the thought that the better hotels were all booked by that hour of night. He checked us in, bought some apple pie – "The best in New York! You gotta try it!" – in the lobby restaurant, and we went up to our love nest.

As he lay back on the bed with a pillow supporting his neck, I slipped off my dress to reveal a white strapless bra (it was too soon to go braless), white panties, a white garter belt and flesh colored stockings. I know it'll sound vain, but I looked like a Victoria's Secret model. Really. I had done extra crunches that morning and everything. All I was missing were those ridiculous wings. Don't get me wrong. It wasn't that I thought I was so much better looking than a lot of other women – it's that I knew how to use what I had. Simply put, I oozed sex. My long dark brown hair always looked like I just rolled out of bed, my pale blue eyes batted and widened on command. And most importantly, I knew how to make a man feel like a man. So I stood, or rather, I posed for him.

"Wow!" he said. I smiled and bit my bottom lip. "Come here," he said. "Let's have pie."

Pie? Without moving from his position, he grabbed the pie from the nightstand and placed it on his protruding stomach. I walked as sexily as I could to a man balancing apple pie on his belly. The container rose and fell with his breath. When I lay down next to him, the pie almost slipped off of him and onto the bed. "Whew!" he said. He caught the pie with his razor-sharp doctor reflexes. "Got it!"

I laid my head on his chest. By now his tie was long gone and the top two buttons of his shirt were open. I let my fingers trace the remaining buttons and played with the hairs escaping the top of his v-neck t-shirt.

"I think it's so sexy you can save a life."

"Yeah?" he asked. "Well, you can too."

"Oh really?"

"Yes," he said, looking deeply into my eyes. "Mine." Obviously, he wasn't new at this. I kissed him. "You really think I'm sexy?" he asked. I tried to put the pie out of my mind.

"Mm-hm...."

"Then come here." Finally, the pie was thrown onto the nightstand and his arms were thrown around me. That night, Dr. Fifth Avenue and I consummated our relationship as man and mistress.

There is more to say about this. Dr. Fifth Avenue was my first significantly older lover, so I was surprised when he pulled off his t-shirt to reveal gray mixed in with the blonde hair on his chest. I was even more surprised at his tiny man-breasts and the fold of flabby skin that hung down around his waist. But he did have extremely strong and powerful arms, so I focused on those. Try as I might, however, I couldn't help thinking about the rest of his body. I'd never noticed any figure flaws through his suit. Obviously, Giorgio Armani was a genius. An absolute genius.

To add to this picture, Dr. Fifth Avenue wore tiny black bikini briefs, which he really shouldn't have, but at least his legs were okay, as most men's are. He watched as I unhooked my bra and he glanced at my breasts, not amorously, but clinically. I looked at them too. "No," he said, "don't worry, they look beautiful. I just want to check how they're doing." He sat up next to me and squeezed them, hard. My eyes welled with tears.

"Ow!" I said.

"Sorry." He pulled his hand away fast.

"You just surprised me," I said, putting his hand back on my breast. He kissed me again and I forgot all about the pain.

Because of his strong shoulders, Dr. Fifth Avenue could lift my entire body with one arm. We were wrapped up, an entanglement of kissing and rubbing, our bodies lying next to each other, his leg between my legs. He stroked my face with one hand and reached down to find my panties with the other. (They pulled off easily because I remembered to put them on the outside of my garter belt, another tip from dear ol' Ma.) I unbuckled him. As his body temperature started to rise, the Armani cologne engulfed me. I rolled on top of him, naked except for my stockings and garter. I kissed his chest. I moved down and kissed his belly; he moaned. I could have devoured him, enraptured by his power, his brain, his whole being. Then he held my head with both hands and gently pushed me down.

Kissing him, feeling him get harder and harder beneath me, I was falling madly in love. Who wouldn't? Here was this rich, powerful New York City plastic surgeon on top of his game who was into me. And soon he'd be in me. And then I heard... or did I? I wasn't sure if I had heard him correctly, so I paused to listen better. But I had heard him right. "Eat me," he said again.

"Eat me?" my mother asked, and I immediately regretted telling her.

"Yup," I said. "Plain as day. Ever hear that one before?"

"Not from a man," Mom said, and my mother had quite a bit of experience in this department. "Maybe suck me, or blow me or... eh...." She gave up, her inner sailor tiring of the conversation. "You know what...? It's New York," Mom said, satisfied with her assessment. "Men are more demanding there. Let him call it whatever he wants. Your job is to make him happy."

I hung up the phone in my tiny apartment which needed unpacking, decorating, and cleaning, and daydreamed about Dr. Fifth Avenue. But my happiness was cut short by a phone call from him telling me he was leaving for the weekend to take his wife and son to the Hamptons. The romance of the night before had most definitely waned.

*　　　*　　　*

I cheered myself up with a walk in the park and some mid-afternoon iced coffee. I grabbed a park bench and watched a white miniature poodle and an English bulldog, the latter obviously in heat. The poodle nipped and nipped at the bulldog, but still the poor bulldog kept sniffing her, trying desperately to mount her. I laughed out loud when I realized how much the horny bulldog reminded me of Dr. Fifth Avenue. Dr. Fifth Avenue. My mind jumped to him and the reminiscence of how we had checked out of the hotel.

He had paid the hotel bill – in cash – and for some reason, I got hot. I loved watching him handle hundreds of dollars as if it were pocket change (which incidentally, is what he called seven hundred dollars – the amount he had left in his wallet after our dinner and hotel). He struck that magical balance of making me feel like a whore and a child and that, combined with his money and position, made me feel like Superwoman. Out in front of the hotel, Dr. Fifth Avenue kissed me on the cheek while the valet hailed me a cab.

Dr. Fifth Avenue slipped me cab fare: a hundred dollars in twenties. "I hope that'll be enough to get you home," he said with a wink. I beamed at him. We obviously shared the unspoken bond of man and mistress; I had been initiated into a clandestine cult that worshipped money and sex and I loved it. The valet opened the cab door for me and I felt like a Park Avenue socialite being escorted to her car after an auction at Sotheby's. I wondered if Mrs. Dr. Fifth Avenue was a socialite. Dr. Fifth Avenue and the valet exchanged looks and money. And then a few more looks and a little extra money. I climbed into the back of the cab and pressed my hundred dollars to my breast as if it were a million. I knew he'd be the one. I just knew it.

I was lost in thought on my park bench, wondering when the gifts would start arriving, when I would move to Fifth Avenue so that he could have me closer, more readily available, when the bank account would be opened. I felt like a high class call-girl and I liked it. I was smiling when a man wearing dark glasses and a filthy, long black trench coat sat next to me on the bench.

"I want to stick my finger in your pussy," he said. I tried to ignore him. I went back to daydreaming and coffee. "Then I want to lick my fingers."

That was it. "Oh come on," I said to him. Did my fantasy have to be interrupted by such a cliché? "Try something more original. The glasses, the trench coat? You should be ashamed of yourself. Really, really ashamed." The pervert ran off. Good riddance. Tacky, uninspired perverts were something that only street hookers should have to contend with, not high class call-girls and mistresses like me.

Once night started to fall, I went home and smiled at my doorman, who handed me a dozen long-stem, dethorned red roses. The handwritten note said: "Looking forward to many more wonderful dinners and desserts. Yours, Dr. F." Clutching my flowers, I ran up the stairs and collapsed onto the couch. I inhaled them deeply, hoping they would be some exotic strain of flower which had been bred to smell like Armani for Men. They weren't. In truth, they didn't even smell like roses. They smelled like, well, nothing.

I set them on my counter, took a long bubble bath and finished off the orgasm that Dr. Fifth Avenue had started the night before. With a little training, he'd be just fine. And even if he didn't get any better in bed that was just fine too; what was an orgasm compared to my new life? Orgasms I could give myself. I took a long sip of wine, positive that he was thinking of me right at that moment. How could he not be? I had given him a blowjob that made him pass out for nearly two hours afterwards. I grinned. Not bad for nineteen, I decided. I leaned back in the tub.

Dr. Fifth Avenue showed up, unannounced, two days later. I had been working in the apartment and was covered in dust. I was wearing old, baggy sweat pants, a white tank top and had a Harley Davidson rag tied in my hair. But he didn't even seem to notice. "I can only stay for a minute," he said, unbuttoning his suit jacket. "I brought you something." He handed me a large, white shopping bag with a big box inside.

"What is it?" I asked. My first mistress present! Hurray!

"Open it," he said, smiling.

I struggled to pull the box out until finally I just ripped the bag. No time for niceties. "A cappuccino machine!" I said, holding up the box. It was an expensive coffee/cappuccino maker which did just about everything but make my toast in the morning. It was going to fit beautifully in the new kitchen of my new apartment.

"Uh-huh," he said, blushing. "Because you loved that cappuccino at dinner the other night."

"Thank you!" I said. "Do you have time to stay for one?"

"Can't. Sorry. Consultations." He walked toward me. "But let me help you—"

I threw my arms around him and pecked him on the cheek. "Thank you! Thank you! Thank you!"

"—Let me help you set it up," he said, laughing. "And you're welcome." He carried the machine to the kitchen counter, but we had a tough time finding a spot for it. The machine was way too large for my kitchen. Actually, it was too large for my apartment, but we finally settled on a tiny space just next to the sink. The front end of the cappuccino machine hung off the counter a bit – not the safest spot for steam – and the plug needed an extension cord to reach the outlet. "Be careful, though," he said, playing with the knobs and buttons. "You could bump into this when you wash dishes."

"Uh-huh," I said with a nod, trying my best to look sexy in my given state. Despite its inappropriate size, it was a thoughtful gift and I thanked him again as he buttoned his jacket.

"I really like the place," he said as he left.

"Nice," I said. I went to the window to see if I could watch him walk away.

The next time we slept together, Dr. Fifth Avenue's wife was in Miami. He stayed for a while the next morning; we drank cappuccinos in bed and did the *New York Times* crossword together. Well, he did the crossword, I only knew one answer. I felt so stupid I wanted to stop the crossword to have sex again. Sex made me feel confident. Overwhelmed by his intelligence and his knowledge, I felt younger and younger around him. I was heading back toward puberty and on my way to earning the title of dumb bimbo. And to think, once upon a time the title I thought I would hold at this age was Miss America. He thrived on my naiveté, but I hated it. Without warning, he put down the paper and really looked at me.

"What?" I asked, a little unnerved. I wondered if he was getting ready to tell me that he loved me.

"Would you still be with me if I were poor?" he asked. His voice was firm but he sounded vulnerable.

"What?" I asked again.

He repeated the question. "Would you still be with me if I didn't have money?"

I knew what I should say... all the right things. Things like, "Of course!" and, "Money has nothing to do with our relationship!" But instead I heard myself ask, "Would you still be with me if I wasn't beautiful?" He picked up his paper again. We both pretended the words had never passed our lips. They were, perhaps, the last truthful, unrehearsed words I spoke for years to come.

Dr. Fifth Avenue sent a car for me. Actually, it wasn't so much *for* me as it was to deliver me. I dressed that night, sliding a garter belt on over my La Perla stockings, knowing this was what I had been waiting for. Sure, there'd been a few glitches at the beginning of the relationship, but this was the reason young girls all over the country flocked to New York City. I was living my dream, dressing in a designer gown – which he had picked out for me – grabbing a designer clutch – which he had sent to me – and sliding into a limo to meet him at some phenomenal undisclosed place.

As I walked out of my building, I turned back to whisper a brief good-bye to it. My building and I were in complete juxtaposition of one another; I was sleek, young, shiny, with everything before me, and my building was old and worn, having seen more than it wanted to. I slid into the back of the limo, feeling like a woman. Like I had left my childhood and all that it encompassed far behind. After this night, there would be no returning. I was heading uptown in that limo and I was never going to come back. The sapphire silk gown was cut to mid-thigh and I accidentally flashed my driver a glimpse of my garter. I smiled the smile of a much older, more sophisticated woman. This night was my engagement to Dr. Fifth Avenue, but rather than a ring and a promise of marriage, I was hoping for an apartment and a commitment to take care of me. To provide for me. The driver pulled up in front of the Waldorf Astoria.

"We're here, Ms. Messing," the driver said, glancing at me in his rearview.

"Thank you," I said. Then we sat for a moment.

"I'm sorry," he said, "but I was told not to get your door until your chaperone comes to meet you."

"My chaperone?" I asked, once again feeling no more than my measly nineteen years.

"Yes, Ms.," he answered, letting his gaze fall out the window. Moments later, a shadow emerged from the building. My driver saw his cue and bounded out.

"So sorry, Victoria, so sorry," the shadow said as the driver opened my door. "Please, come with me."

I followed the shadow into the hotel and toward an elevator. He was moving me quickly through the lobby, but I was still able to soak in the grandeur of it all. I breathed it in – the chandeliers, the piano, the staircase, the awesomeness. A sign in the lobby said "Welcome, Doctors." Dr. Fifth Avenue was obviously at a convention close to home. Why and how I was there was a mystery to me. I smiled and nodded as person after person stared at me. An Italian tourist snapped a picture of me. I felt like a celebrity, and I never felt so much at home.

"People can't help but stare at you," the shadow said.

"Well, I—" I began to say, elated but slightly embarrassed by all the attention.

"I don't blame them," he said, cutting me off. "But considering our situation, it is probably best to avoid eye contact as much as you can and to walk as quickly as possible."

Our situation? I suddenly felt less like a celebrity and more like an Untouchable required to jingle a bell to warn those more worthy of my imminent arrival. The shadow led me to a top floor but when the elevator door opened, he motioned for me to stay inside.

The shadow poked his head out of the door. "Please, Victoria," he said, "come with me."

I followed him down the quiet hallway. "You know," I said trying to be polite, "I don't even know your name."

"Yes, I know," he said. Finally, he reached for a room key and opened the door. "Enjoy your stay." He held the door open for me. I walked inside.

The room was beautiful. There was a fireplace, a king-sized bed, and red and gold brocade everywhere. Champagne was chilling on a tiny table. I had no idea what I was supposed to do so I sat on the edge of the bed, careful not to crease the imported silk of my gown.

When he arrived, I was thrilled to see Dr. Fifth Avenue dressed in an Armani tux. "You are amazing," he said and kissed me full on the mouth. He reached around and started to untie the back of my gown.

"Hey there," I said, pulling away. "Aren't we heading out?"

"Out?" he asked. "I just got in." He yanked at his bowtie until it hung loosely around his neck.

"But me, silly," I said, playfully patting him. "I got all dressed up!"

"Me too," he said, "but the dinner's over. Now it's time for dessert." He leaned in toward me.

"So I'm not going out tonight?" I asked, my eyes glazing over.

"You are out."

"I mean, out... out."

"Well no," he said. "It's too close to home. And with all those doctors down there! But I thought you'd love the excitement of just being here." And he slid my dress off. So that was it. My one quick walk through the lobby was my excitement for the evening. Obviously, I'd been a bit hasty in saying good-bye to my apartment; the next morning, after another round of sex, I was delivered right back.

Over the next few months, our relationship – and all of the sex – became reliably okay. I still found the fact that he was a doctor (albeit a plastic surgeon and therefore not a real doctor, according to my mother) the sexiest thing imaginable. I loved that he had the ability to save lives; I ignored that instead he chose to lift faces. But I also knew those very face lifts afforded him a mistress and me a lifestyle of elegant dinners, limos and – when he took me out – trendy experiences like private gallery showings and late-night helicopter rides over Manhattan. He also brought me weekly gifts, this time an oversized classic Fendi bag. It was again completely impractical (it was so large it took up most of my closet) but I appreciated it greatly. It was my first real designer bag and I loved it.

I threw that thing over my shoulder and lugged it everywhere, including when I went to the deli across the street and downstairs to the laundry room.

Although I appreciated the gifts, I couldn't shake the feeling that I should be packing boxes, not loading up my current apartment. Wouldn't it be easier to move less stuff? I knew better than to ask him about it, but I had a nagging feeling that something was wrong, that the relationship was stagnating. All the initial excitement had squeezed itself down into a neat package of two or three dinners a week, followed by a gift of his choice. And, of course, there was always time for lots and lots of sex. Dr. Fifth Avenue talked about money with such a cavalier attitude that I assumed it would never be an issue between us. I assumed he would throw money at me just because he could. And I wasn't talking about a measly hundred dollars either – I meant real money. But it didn't seem to be happening.

All in all, my relationship with Dr. Fifth Avenue lasted a little more than a year. In the beginning months we ate together often, devouring huge amounts of exotic foods. On those days I was sure to eat only that one meal since lipo is not a gift that one of New York's leading plastic surgeons wants to give his mistress. My favorite restaurant was unequivocally Le Cirque, but because Le Cirque was deemed a wife spot, and mistresses weren't paraded at restaurants where their men could be caught, we went only that one time.

Confident everyone he knew was accounted for elsewhere, Dr. Fifth Avenue decided Le Cirque was okay for the night. This is another perk of being a mistress – every once in a while, when everyone else has a better place to be, you get the really great dinners. Dr. Fifth Avenue and I were brought to a tiny table in the back of the restaurant and seated. No sooner did my butt hit the chair, the manager ran to our table. He moved us to a large banquette and brought a complimentary bottle of Veuve Clicquot.

Dr. Fifth Avenue smiled at me. "This is all thanks to you!" he said, his eyes filled with joy. "We got moved to this table because you're so beautiful!" I blushed. "I'm serious!" he said. "All the times I've eaten at this restaurant, I've never been seated here. Good for you!" Okay. I have to admit his telling me about all the other times he had dined here was a bit unromantic, but the dinner we were about to eat more then made up for it. After discovering crème brulee at Le Cirque, the world seemed a better place.

*   *   *

Following dinner, Dr. Fifth Avenue and I stood in the busy coat check line. After a meal of langoustine, spaghetti alla chitarra, lobster poached in vanilla cognac, cappuccino and, of course, crème brulee, not much was going to ruin my good mood, not even the woman in line next to us.

"Huh!" gasped the sixty-something-year-old woman in her traditional winter white Chanel suit. She turned to her male companion, who had been eyeing my breasts. I couldn't blame him. My breasts did look amazing that night, especially in that strapless midnight blue dress that gave me extra lift. Dr. Fifth Avenue should have been very proud of his handiwork. In a stage whisper the woman said, "She must be half his age!"

"Oh no, my dear..." Dr. Fifth Avenue said. "She's less than half my age." I fell a little more in love.

Dr. Fifth Avenue stayed with me whenever possible and had pretty much taken over half of my "Bohemian, just like college, so-cool" apartment. What he didn't take over was the rent. Not even half of it. He kept bringing gifts, however: a running suit from his tennis club, a microwave, a cashmere bathrobe and a gift certificate for a nearby day spa. But still nothing about the rent. When I finally broke down and politely asked him why a famous New York City plastic surgeon couldn't pay the rent for this shit-hole I called an apartment, he said that he could help... sometimes. And he did. Once in a great while. But each time he opened his tight wallet he assured me that it was costing him too much. "I just can't afford it," he said, as I waved away the newly freed moths.

"Jesus," I thought, "my boobs cost $5,000. What can't you afford?" But I didn't say it. I didn't say a lot of things I was thinking. I learned to bite my tongue over a variety of issues: lateness, calling his wife from my apartment, and eating me out of house and home... including drinking all of my Diet Coke. And the gifts did keep coming, this time a membership to the gym of my choice. I was sure the presents would only increase as I proved myself to him. So I shopped around for the perfect place to work out. I found a gym much too far away to be convenient, but it had fresh calla lilies scattered around the treadmills and a fancy juice bar and gift shop. What more could you ask for in a gym?

Surely Dr. Fifth Avenue would want me to find a place I'd be happy – even if the monthly membership rivaled my rent.

I began to notice that Dr. Fifth Avenue was much freer with the money he spent on me if he was benefiting from it as well. Meaning, dinners would cost four or five hundred dollars a pop; the cars to and from dinners cost hundreds of dollars; and if he wanted to show me off to someone – like at a charity event where all the men were bringing their mistresses – then I'd get the thousand-dollar gown at the three-thousand-dollar-a-plate dinner. But otherwise I was left to fend for myself.

One Thursday night Dr. Fifth Avenue came over, starving from surgery as he always was, and had the gall to mention that I should eat something other than bread and cheese, the very things he was busy gobbling from my tiny fridge. "Well then, why don't you stock it?" I asked. He looked at me like I'd just told him Giorgio Armani was dead. But the next day he picked me up and dragged me by the hand to Dean and Deluca. He hit the pastries aisle.

"How about an apple pie for Mom?" he asked. "Does she like apple pie?"

"Sure," I said, "but I won't see her for—"

"Great! Apple pie it is!" And two apple pies were added to the cart.

That's how Dr. Fifth Avenue did everything: big, grand, compulsively. He bought me so many groceries they barely fit into my apartment, let alone my fridge. Of course, I would never see groceries again, mind you.

"Hey, Kiddo. Can I see you tomorrow around 5:30?" he asked as he kissed me good-bye. I thought about all of the things I'd rather do than give him a blowjob, watch him eat all of my food, and listen to him snore as he fell asleep to *Wheel of Fortune*. But then I thought of my mother and how she'd tell me I'd be stupid to throw the opportunity away. What the hell, I'd keep him happy a bit longer. I was really enjoying my new gym membership and could use another day at the spa. Plus, maybe I could think of another way to let him know I really needed help with the rent again, and on a regular basis. He grinned at me; he knew he'd get whatever he wanted if he called me kiddo.

"Sure. 5:30's fine," I said. What else did I have to do?

"Great!" He was elated. "Dollar Bills is having an end-of-season clearance sale. I need you to wait in the car so I can run in. Finding parking around there is a bitch." He kissed me again and went off singing *Love Shack* from the B-52's. He did a couple of little dance steps at my door.

"Sit in the fucking car…?" I slammed the door. Then I looked at the time – it was only seven o'clock. Seven p.m. and I had nothing to do. Seven p.m. and I had exhausted my social calendar for the day. Seven p.m. and he needed to get home for Sesame Street videos and dinner.

I had more and more time on my hands. I was halfway through my nineteenth year and beginning to lead a very dull life. With this in mind, I got dressed and went out to see what the city had to offer. I found myself in a bar with a young Australian model named Terrance. Terrance was breathtakingly handsome with gray eyes and tan skin; he was straight, twenty-eight, and single. At least he'd be able to stay out past seven. So I let Terrance buy me a drink and I listened to his story about being a perfume sprayer at Bloomingdales. I feigned interest for a while and even wondered if perfume spraying really counted as modeling, but I grew bored of the story, the accent, the gray eyes, and mostly of him. I started to miss Dr. Fifth Avenue and the power he flexed while we were out. What could a twenty-eight-year-old offer me? Nothing.

Just when I was about to give him the "my boyfriend's bank account can beat up your bank account" speech, Terrance said something so shocking that it actually sickened me. Never, in all of my life had anyone whispered such profanity to me. I became dizzy, lightheaded. Like an over-corseted heroine in a Victorian novel, I was woozy on my feet. How dare he? Terrance told me he could hook me up with a job. At Bloomingdales. At first I was so appalled that, in true heroine fashion, I wanted to throw my drink at him. I was nothing short of nauseated at the prospect. I mean, a job?

But then I realized how embarrassing the whole work situation would be for Dr. Fifth Avenue. If I was willing to completely degrade myself and work in a department store, then surely he would have to recognize my need for more financial support!

My knees weakened. Could I go through with it? I thought of my ever-dwindling funds. Visions of cheese and Diet Coke being devoured from my fridge danced through my mind. I downed another shot of Jack Daniels and listened carefully to Terrance. I shook my head, unable to believe that I may actually go through with it. Why, exactly, was I worried about money? I was the mistress of Dr. Fifth Avenue! One of *New York Magazine*'s picks for best plastic surgeon in the city! Clearly he needed a wake-up call, and this was the answer. I couldn't be too direct – asking for help with the rent wasn't working and I couldn't sound like all that I was after was his money. I was new to this line of work and maybe the keeper of the mistress had to be very particular about how he shared his wealth. But I had already invested a bunch of time into eating him, how much more was I expected to do, exactly?

This time, required to swallow only my pride, I agreed to let Terrance "hook me up." All too soon, I found myself working at Bloomingdales. Okay, it's like this: I knew I couldn't survive more than a day or two, so I needed to make my point and make it fast. So I went to work in the worst place I could – the food department, located in the bowels of Bloomies, churning with prosciutto di Parma and bologna. I was far from the glamorous makeup floor, and even farther from Terrance, who had outlived his usefulness. The food department, with its plastic gloves and white smock tops, was just desperate enough to make my point in a hurry. Dr. Fifth Avenue would surely be ashamed his mistress worked there; he would pluck me away like a pimento from an olive loaf.

"Food?" Dr. Fifth Avenue asked, finishing his second can of Diet Coke. "Why food?"

"Maybe so I can replace everything you eat." He looked at me quizzically. I had set the trap and I stood back, waiting for him to refuse to let me slice a single piece of overcooked roast beef. How could a woman who eats at Le Cirque slice deli meats for money? It was preposterous.

"Okay," Dr. Fifth Avenue said, as if he gave me permission. Then he thought of something. "Hey! Do you get an employee discount?"

"What?" I felt the tremor in my hands. "No!" I said. "Not for, like, three months!" I waved off the absurd question, trying to fight off impending doom.

"Well, keep the job until Christmas then. I want to buy myself this little Armani trench coat I've been eyeing." I couldn't believe it. Like my perverted sunglass-wearing friend from the park, I was a living, breathing cliché; caught in my own web of deceit. He kissed my head and left, excited he didn't have to wait for an after-Christmas clearance to buy his coat on sale.

I'm embarrassed to admit that I did keep the job until Christmas. I really had no choice – I needed the money. And I couldn't transfer out of food. I had already been trained, and it was too late to ask to be switched to another department. Besides, it would have been humiliating to be seen working at ground level. So there I was, trapped underground in my white jacket and rubber gloves; I'd played my hand too early and rather than being embarrassed by it, Dr. Fifth Avenue benefited. And what's more, with just one exception, he was the only one of us who ever used my employee discount. When we shopped together for his Armani trench coat, he told me that he was in a rush and I took too long to sign the receipt. He recommended that I practice signing more quickly.

I looked at my stint in the food department as a minor setback – a hard lesson learned in the art of becoming a mistress. But the whole scenario also left me a bit unnerved. How could Dr. Fifth Avenue let me work a job like that? How could he let me work any job? I wanted to leave – both the job and him – but I had invested so much already that I knew I needed to stay until Christmas. So I sliced and blew my way through the next three months of my life. It had to pay off eventually, right?

It was two days before Christmas. The eve of Christmas Eve. The day Dr. Fifth Avenue and I exchanged presents. I had been his mistress nearly eight months, or ninety-six days of sex, or one hundred and eleven blowjobs... but who was counting? I was ready. I had surely proven my commitment and my sexual prowess. I had also quit my job. I chose, instead, to concentrate on the future. I was sure that I was getting my own brownstone – it only made sense. That way, if I ever needed money – God forbid – I could rent out part of my building and be self-sufficient. My own brownstone and perhaps a little red... something fast...? I'd heard him on the phone with Mercedes a week earlier and I didn't think it was about a repair on his car.

Dr. Fifth Avenue was late to our present exchange, but I was too excited to be mad. He must have sensed my anticipation, because almost as soon as he walked in, he handed me my gift. Almost as soon as he did, I wished he hadn't. The box was immediately suspect – it was long and flat. What kind of car would fit in there? I tore the shiny silver paper. A keychain maybe, with attached keys? But no. I pulled it from the box and held it up: it wasn't a car. Or a brownstone. It was a white and yellow gold bracelet set with semi-precious stones. It was ugly. And finite. Okay, if not the brownstone, then at least an apartment for me to live in forever, free and clear. But a bracelet?

Come on, we've all heard of kept mistresses living in penthouses and having expense accounts at Prada. So what happened? Bracelets were "Thank you for last night," not "Thank you for the past one hundred and eleven blowjobs." I was grateful for the gift, but honestly, it looked like something for old ladies to sport at the tennis club, not for a starving nineteen-year-old former deli worker to wear on a date with her cheap aging god. I stared at it. "It's..."

"I know!" he said. "I bought you a diamond tennis bracelet first but returned it for this. This just seemed more you."

"Un-huh, more me."

"Do you like it?" he asked.

"I love it. Thank you," I said through my teeth. I plastered a smile onto my face. Then I thought of something. Maybe I was aiming too low! Maybe this was an appetizer to my gift entrée, the mere salad designed to whet my appetite for the filet mignon! Relieved, I slipped the bracelet on. I felt much better about the whole evening and smiled a genuine smile as he helped me with the clasp. Then we sat. And sat. As I waited for my additional gifts, an awkward silence filled the room. He looked around.

"Oh!" I said. I jumped up and got his present from under my tiny tree. There were no more presents. At least not for me. One hundred and eleven blowjobs were hanging on my semi-precious wrist. Dr. Fifth Avenue seemed more excited opening his present than I had been opening mine. I gave him a portable razor that came complete with a free mirror. I bought it, of course, at Bloomies. My one and only use of the discount.

"Wow! With a mirror!" he said. His voice rose as he spoke, like a little boy whose parents had just given him a puppy. "I can really use the mirror too!" he said. "I have nothing in my locker at the club." He was truly pleased. At least one of us was happy.

"Merry Christmas," he said, and we made love beside my sparsely decorated tree. While he was thrusting on top of me, I found my gaze drifting off to my wrist. I couldn't help but wonder what I was doing. He gave one final thrust and rolled off of me. "Did you come?" he asked.

"Yes! Of course!" I said. The disappointment of my Yuletide fantasy had kept me from my mistress duty of faking orgasm. His attention quickly drifted elsewhere, he stared at my tree.

"You've got a Charlie Brown Christmas tree," he said with a laugh. "You should see my holiday tree... it must be twenty feet tall! The decorator really outdid himself this year." He smiled a satisfied smile. And why shouldn't he? Everything was going pretty smoothly in his world.

After some store-bought soy-nog he said, "I'm going to Aspen for two weeks." I felt my face fall. "You look sad," he said.

"Just that you're leaving."

He perked up. "I'll tell you what... why don't you come to Vail with me next month? My wife wants to go to Aruba where it's warm. I have to go to this damned convention, so we might as well make the most of it!" I'd take it. A leftover, hand-me-down trip was better than no trip at all. I considered it an additional Christmas gift and it made me a little less glum. Besides, I'd always wanted to go to Aspen... I figured Vail was close enough.

"Well," he said, sitting up next to the tree, "Merry Christmas." I sighed. Maybe I was playing the wrong game. Maybe it all would have been much better if he had just said, "Marry... Me."

"Merry Christmas," I said. He pulled on his clothes, used the bathroom, combed what was left of his blonde hair, and walked to the door. I followed to kiss him good-bye. With one last glimmer of hope, I stalled at the door waiting for him to say, "Gotcha! Come on!" and drag me downstairs to my new Mercedes convertible. But he didn't. Actually, he didn't even do as much as say good-bye again. I had to surrender my last hopes for additional gifts. I closed the door after him and leaned on it for a moment. I was flabbergasted that I could have been so wrong, about my gifts and about him in general. All over the city, right at that very moment, mistresses were being handed keys to cars and boats and apartments. What had happened here? How could I have so monumentally misjudged everything? And what was that call to Mercedes about... and why from here...? Obviously he wanted to keep it a secret from his wife so it had to have been... Oh. Oh no. I got it. Someone did collect for his one hundred and *twelve* blowjobs... it just wasn't me. It was her. The other woman – his wife. I twirled the stupid bracelet around my wrist over and over again. She got the car, I got the toy, and I did all the work.

When my mother called, I told her about the bracelet and the trip. I left out the part about the car. Mom instructed me to go immediately to have the bracelet appraised. I did. Not bad. And that's when I learned that tacky is not a synonym for cheap. But still, I'd have to hock it before it'd be worth anything to me. Aside from the sentimental value, of course.

During our next phone call, I couldn't help but whine to my mother. "Is this bracelet really worth everything? For Heaven's sake, I worked in cheese!"

"And whose choice was that?" my mother asked. "Stop being dramatic. Don't miss your train."

I dreaded Christmas at Mom's house, but not nearly as much as any other day with Mom and Liz. Thankfully, Liz's pretty okay husband, Martin, and cutie-pie daughter, Megan, would be there. That would help ease some of the tension. So I donned the gaudy bracelet, gathered my few gifts and left for a Christmas holiday at home, counting the days until I would be gliding down the snow-covered peaks of Vail in my new ski suit.

Vail was exactly as I imagined. Yuppies, movie stars, snow, and a lot of wrinkly, tanned women who claimed to be thirty and "look great!" Causalities of the outdoors. Maybe there was something to be said for pollution – it helped preserve us New Yorkers. Despite my desire to go to Aspen, I was not a skier, so I spent my days taking ski lessons while Dr. Fifth Avenue was busy with his meetings. After the day's conference, he'd come back to our room – always eating a sandwich leftover from lunch – change his clothes, and we'd hit the town.

"Turkey today!" he said, holding out the sandwich. "Want some?"

I shook my head. "Aren't we going to dinner?" I asked, my stomach growling.

"Yes," he said, taking another bite. "But these are good. And they're free!" This was the beginning of a trend I could have done without: familiarity breeds starvation. He just didn't feel it necessary to wine and dine me quite as he used to.

One day I took cross-country lessons, hoping I would find it easier than downhill.

"Why'd you do that?" he asked that night over dinner.

"I don't know," I said. I didn't know why it mattered to him. "I thought it would be good exercise."

"So is downhill," he said. "And it's a lot more glamorous. Someone who looks like you shouldn't be cross-country skiing. Go back to your regular lesson tomorrow." This, from the man who let me slice pastrami for a thirty percent discount. What did he care if I skied downhill or cross-country? And further, I hated his tone. I felt like I had just been reprimanded by my father. I pouted and dug unknowingly into my dinner. "Good?" he asked.

"Mm-hm!" I said. "Delicious!" I had some sort of gnocchi with a decadent cream sauce. And there was also a piece of what I assumed to be filet mignon on my plate. This was my idea of comfort food – good beef and gnocchi smothered in cream. I didn't even mind that the restaurant looked like a Lincoln Log cabin built by a young Jeffrey Dahmer. There were stuffed heads of moose, deer and elk hanging everywhere, their beady glass eyes looking down at me. I was so famished I barely noticed. I took another bite.

Dr. Fifth Avenue made his move. "Do you think that one was yours?" he asked, nodding toward the wall.

"My what?"

"That elk," he asked. "Do you think that one became your dinner?"

"What?" I stared at my plate and back to him wondering if he was teasing me. I prayed that he was teasing me.

"Elk," he said. He spoke slowly and deliberately, as if he was talking to a child. "Elk. You're eating elk. Didn't you hear me order?"

"I was in the ladies' room," I said, staring at the unappetizing hunk of meat on my plate.

"I ordered you elk and sweetbreads."

I pushed the elk out of the way. I could feel the animals on the wall staring at me. I couldn't bring myself to meet their gaze or to take another bite. I concentrated instead, on the sweetbreads. "I see you like those," he said, toying with me.

"Uh-huh." I nodded. "These are delicious." I shoveled in another good-sized bite.

"You know what they are, right?" he asked, obviously having fun.

"No...." I stared at my plate again. "I don't think I want to—"

He leaned in very close. "They're the thymus glands of veal."

"The thy...ma... what?"

"Thymus glands. They're glands... you know…" He put his hand on his throat to direct me to the right area. (Despite my nausea I got a bit turned on.) "Sometimes they're from the throat. These," he said as he gestured to my plate, "are from the gland near the heart of a baby cow." I spit my mouthful into my napkin.

"The glands of a baby cow?"

"Yes. They're a delicacy. You like them... Enjoy them! I always try to get my son to eat new things too." I stared at him blankly. "Go ahead," he continued, "don't be so easily scared off."

Scared off? After everything I was still there, still expecting something better out of him. I forced a smile and thought about how much better it all was when he kept me in the dark.

All of Vail wasn't as bad as the elk and sweetbreads night. There were horse and carriage rides, steaming hot outdoor Jacuzzis dug deep in the fresh snow, loads of champagne, great dinners, and lots of skiing. Plus, I had four new ski suits compliments of Dr. Fifth Avenue, so at least I looked the part, even if I still couldn't ski worth a damn. I also liked to walk around the village at night and gaze in all the little shop windows. I fantasized that someday we might actually go shopping while a store was still open and he might buy me something. (My weekly gifts had been nonexistent since Christmas.)

Despite his ever-cheapening personality, I was pretty happy in Vail. Until our second-to-last night there. It happened while I was getting ready for dinner. I fussed in front of the mirror, changing my dress – black with no back, black strapless, black with barely any front – while Dr. Fifth Avenue was on the phone with his wife. Try as I might, I couldn't help but overhear. Really. This, I did not want to hear. I had been completely jealous of Mrs. Dr. Fifth Avenue ever since Christmas when I realized she got my new Mercedes. I preferred to pretend that she didn't even exist. Why did she need to call him? Trouble with the new car already?

"No, no," he said, "they can't do that." He was comforting her long distance. What could go wrong in Aruba? Send me there, I guarantee I won't call to complain about anything. "You'll be fine. I promise. I'll fix it all when I get home. Okay, Kiddo? Bye." There is was. That "kiddo" hurt me more than if he had just said love or cherish or adore. "Kiddo" was what Dr. Fifth Avenue called me.

Ugly thoughts began to flash through my mind. Was his wife younger than him? I mean, significantly younger? Sure she had a four-year-old child, but she could still be twenty-five... or twenty-four... or maybe even twenty-two. My youth was something I was banking on. She couldn't get everything *and* be young. That would be too hateful.

"Kiddo?" I said. "You called her kiddo?"

"Yeah? Hey, thanks for not flushing the toilet while I was on the phone."

"Why kiddo?" I asked, fighting back the tears.

"I don't know... she was upset." He paused and looked at me. "Victoria? Are you crying?"

"No!" I said. But the tears streaming down my face gave me away. "You call me kiddo! Me!" I was feeling as important in his life as a blow-up doll.

He was confused. "Victoria?"

"What?" I yelled more loudly than I meant.

"What's wrong?" He really didn't know.

"I love you!"

"Really?" he asked. This was clearly not the response I had hoped for.

"Yes." I hadn't meant to fall in love with him, and I wasn't sure that I actually had. But since I stayed through sliced cheese, a gaudy bracelet, and elk, that must mean I was in love with him. My hands were shaking and my eyes ached.

He sat on the bed, his tie dangling loosely from his neck. He held me by the arms and stared at me. After a moment he said, "I love you too. Don't you know that?"

"No," I said, sniffling. A small smile turned up the corners of my mouth.

"Then you really are stupid. Do you know that?" He squeezed my arms even tighter.

"Thanks."

He looked at me fiercely. "Couldn't you tell at Christmastime? I was like a little boy. I returned your present and bought you another. You think I have time to do things like that?" He paused again. It was clear he thought I had scored big. Then, much more softly he said, "I love you, Kiddo."

And at that, I fell into his arms and onto the bed. And that night we forgot about the town and the window shopping and the fancy restaurants. That was a night that room service was made for. We played my favorite game: doctor. Sometimes, when we were out I would make sure to address him as "Doctor" just to get the fantasy started a little early. I'd make sure someone was listening then I'd tilt my head, drop my voice and say something like, "Okay Doctor, if that's what you want." It was cheesy but it thrilled me. Inevitably, someone would nod her head. I imagined her thoughts: "Ah! That's what she's doing with him! He's an important doctor. How sexy." I loved that. If he did have a god complex, I was certainly contributing to it.

He got off on our relationship just as much as I did. One morning he let room service in while I was still naked in bed just so the attendant would see that he was fucking a nineteen-year-old. "Oh, sorry! I didn't realize you were still naked," he said to me, just a bit too loudly.

So on that night, our room service night, we fed each other's bodies and egos. He held me with his powerful arms and kissed each and every part of me – quoting its technical name and its purpose – as he worked his way up and down. And with each body part he rattled off, he professed his love to it and to me. Sometimes he'd pause to check on something like he did with my breasts on that very first night. That was my favorite part – knowing it was all real – even if we weren't. We didn't sleep until dawn.

Because he'd been late in scheduling our flight back, we were sitting in different areas of the plane. "By myself?" I asked with a whimper. "But where will you be?"

"Just a few rows back," he said. "Don't worry, it's first class, it's not large enough for us to be too far apart."

"Can't we tell people that I'm pregnant and we need to sit together?" I asked, batting my eyes. Dr. Fifth Avenue narrowed his.

"Uh, no," he said. "I'll ask the guy sitting next to me to change with you. People always like to move up, never back."

"Amen to that," I said. Once we were sitting together, Dr. Fifth Avenue studied me out of the corner of his eye. It was clear my profession of love, coupled with my pregnancy comment, was a bit more than he had anticipated.

Back in the big city, things returned to normal. He went back to gift-giving but the gifts were sporadic. The declaration of love really didn't benefit me at all, but it seemed to cut him even more slack. More and more, Dr. Fifth Avenue got in the habit of calling last-minute for a date. He said he never knew what his wife was doing until just minutes before. And as a good, dutiful husband, his wife always came first.

Having all that extra time on my hands, I had no way to avoid seeing my mother in Pennsylvania. I didn't particularly like my mother, and she didn't much like me, but we had one thing in common: we both disliked my sister even more. My sister wasn't anything like either of us. Liz was every bit as attractive as me, but she went to college, got a degree, and married young. Plus, she had what neither our mother nor I could achieve: a good, normal relationship with the opposite sex.

I traveled everywhere with a huge overnight bag stuffed with clothes. It was heavy and cumbersome, but necessary – this way I'd be prepared if Dr. Fifth Avenue suddenly became free. I thought by nine o'clock that night I was in the clear, but the call came later than expected. I stood in my mother's kitchen dripping sweat from my Tae Bo video and listened to the message he left on my home machine. His wife had taken their son to the Hamptons, late in the season, unexpectedly. The child had a date... or a play date, or whatever. His voice bellowed across my answering machine. I debated returning the call.

"What's going on?" asked my mother. The idea of an entire weekend with her was all I needed. I picked up the phone and dialed. I called his office and punched my code.

"Hi!" he said, sounding like a man who knew he was going to get laid. "Where are you?"

"In Pennsylvania."

"Can you come in?" he asked, with no regard for time or distance.

"I guess..." I said, twirling my hair. "But I just worked out. I need to shower, and the train takes two hours. I won't get in 'til midnight."

"That's okay," he said. "I'll pick you up. I'll be waiting at the information booth."

I was pissed off when I hung up the phone. I couldn't understand why I continually let my life be overturned by such an inconsiderate ox. And why I let myself be manipulated by the schedule of a four-year-old child. Dr. Fifth Avenue better make the trip worth my while.

But, obediently, I showered, checked the train schedule, and grabbed my bag full of clothes. On the train I changed into a leopard skirt, a deep v-neck black shirt and did my hair and make-up. On-lookers were duly impressed. I was still grouchy when I arrived, less grouchy when I saw him, and then livid when I realized we weren't going anywhere except my apartment.

"What?" I said as he led me through Penn Station. "You called me here just for this? Just for sex?"

"This," he said, kissing my hand, "this is the best part."

"I haven't eaten," was my only response. I understood my chosen role as a mistress required I not be demanding, but come on. At least we could go for some late-night sushi in the East Village.

"Okay," he said, thinking. He stopped for a moment. "We'll grab some cheesecake in the lobby across the street!"

And off he dragged me to that original sleazy hotel for cheesecake and then off to my apartment. After I ate half a piece of cheesecake – careful not to be gassy – and he devoured two and a half pieces – obviously not concerned about gas himself – we had sex. The sex that night made me feel worse than a hooker; at least hookers were smart enough to get paid. Afterwards, fueled by my frustration, I sat up in bed and told him that I wasn't comfortable with our arrangement. He agreed.

"I could use help with the rent," I said. "You haven't helped me in months and we always come here for... you know... and my train ticket last night and—"

"Well, you would have bought your train ticket either way," he said. "And actually, I wanted to tell you that I have to be more careful with the money I spend. Too much at one time and my wife will notice."

I sat, open-mouthed on the edge of my bed. I heard my mother's voice tell me to close my mouth and I snapped it shut, hard. I rubbed my jaw. "I don't understand. You said you'd help me out."

"I know, I know..." he said, stroking my hair. "But you need to understand. I'm a working man."

A working man. Those words played over and over in my brain. Hadn't he bragged that seven hundred dollars was "pocket change" to him? Seven hundred dollars was just about what I made in a month of slicing cheese.

"I was thinking," he said. "Why don't you go into modeling? You certainly have the looks for it. And it's good money. It can help out with your financial bind."

Uh, wasn't *he* supposed to help me out with my financial bind? I bit my tongue while he flipped through the channels and banged the remote a few times. What was I getting from the relationship? I had nothing more than a horny forty-three-year-old man who was cheap as dirt and wanted more sex than an eighteen-year-old. But how was that possible? I felt like a desperate gambler standing paralyzed in front of a tight slot machine. I was terrified to leave, sure that the next pull could be the big pay-off.

He dragged his attention from the television to give just one more word of advice. "Be careful with the modeling, though. Go to a good agency. A lot of girls only ever get catalog work. They barely make enough to pay their rent." He seemed to know a lot about the modeling business, so I wondered how many of these women he knew and how well. He had promised me that he never had a mistress before, but now, nearly a year into my life in the city, I was beginning to doubt everything I had once believed.

"How do you know?" I asked.

"Excuse me?"

"How do you know so much about the modeling business?"

"Clients." He looked away.

"Tell me," I said. "Tell me the truth."

"All right. I did have a mistress before you, but only one. Honestly—"

"Honestly ... whatever that means."

"—and she was a model," he said without missing a beat. "But she never worked. And it was short-lived because all she ever wanted to do was go to bed."

"Aw, poor you!"

"No, I mean, to sleep," he said. "I think maybe she had a very advanced case of Epstein-Barr… I hope." He shook his head and stood next to me. He put his arms around me. "But Vicki, I love you. I've never loved anyone the way I love you." I motioned to ask about his wife but he beat me to it. "Anyone, Victoria. Anyone." I couldn't help it. I broke into a smile.

He was preparing to leave at an ungodly hour the next morning. I rubbed the sleep from my eyes. "I thought your wife was away. Why the rush?"

"The doorman," he said. "What if the daytime doorman sees me sneak in to get dressed?"

"Don't sneak then."

"Oh, Kiddo, you're still so young." He patted my head.

"Not really. I'm twenty now, remember?" He ruffled my hair. "You've stayed before," I said. He didn't answer. "Whatever. Don't you even want coffee?"

"Can't. Gotta go." He kissed me good-bye while he slid into his Armani trench coat. "Modeling will be good for you," he said, looking at me. "I sure do miss your employee discount though. There's this little Armani jacket I saw in GQ." He was at the door.

"Doesn't he work for you?" I asked, making one last attempt.

"Armani?" Dr. Fifth Avenue asked, confused.

"Your doorman. Don't you help pay his salary?"

"Yes."

"Then why are you afraid of him?"

"I'm not afraid of *him*," Dr. Fifth Avenue explained. "Wait until you get married, you'll understand." I felt a lump in my throat. He left seconds later and as I lay in bed, I thought about why I was still with him and what the past year had really offered me. Sure, I didn't cash in and the gifts weren't astounding, but there were the countless galleries and museums, great dinners, and the occasional black-tie benefit. And then there was everything he taught me about the city, including the secret to hailing a cab at rush hour. He'd switched my magazine subscription from *Cosmo* to *Vogue*. He changed my lingo from "red and white" to "cabernet and chardonnay." I wore a Burberry trench coat rather than a London Fog. He brought me *The Bonfire of the Vanities*. He thought he was a "Master of the Universe," but to me he was still Zeus on Mount Olympus. He helped me become a woman. I guess that's why I was willing to stay just a bit longer.

After the wives of Manhattan were safely stowed at Lotte Berk and the Prada pre-Passover sales, Dr. Fifth Avenue decided it was time to take me to the Hamptons. It was my first time. I eagerly anticipated this, as all mistresses do: the time when it is still too cold for the wives to go to the summer house, but the hearty mistresses with a few good layers of silicon to protect them brave the elements and make the trek.

I got out of the car and stared at the house. "This is.... this is it?" I asked. I turned to him and then back for another look at the small, single-level ranch. It looked just like my mother's house. But at least my mother had a split.

"Yeah! Come on! Isn't it awesome?" He grabbed the two overnight bags.

"Awesome?" Not exactly the word I would have chosen. We were there because his wife was at her mother's. That meant we could stay the night. I wondered what happened when she called home and he wasn't there, but in the interest of my trip, I didn't ask.

I entered the modest house with the ocean "just across the street and down a little hill" and plopped down on the couch. A cloud of dust enveloped me. I coughed and fanned the air wildly.

"When was the last time your cleaning woman came?" I asked.

"Who knows," he said. "This isn't our house." And by "our," he didn't mean "mine and his."

"Whose is it?" I asked, coughing.

"It's a rental. We get a month in the summer. And this weekend is special. A bonus." He raised his eyebrows up and down. "I knew the house was empty so we could sneak in and be by ourselves."

"Wait." I was digesting this. "But what if other people show up because they think the house is empty?"

"Oh." He thought for a moment. "Nah, that'll never happen."

"Do they change the locks?"

"I don't think so." He paused. "They couldn't, too expensive. Lucky for us, otherwise we would never have gotten in! I'm hungry, you hungry?"

"Yeah," I said. I stood up and brushed the dust from my bottom. I followed him into the kitchen and stood cross-legged in the doorway. I zipped up my sweater and stuffed my hands deep into the pockets of my jeans as I watched him. He poked through the refrigerator. "Aren't we going to dinner?" I asked. "It's seven and I've heard all about the great restaurants out here—"

"Don't believe everything you hear," he said, and then to the refrigerator he said, "There's nothing here... just old ketchup. I hate ketchup. Now salsa, that has spice! Right, my little enchilada?" He wiggled his hips as he looked into the freezer.

"I heard about the restaurants from you."

"You know, you really could look Mexican! You have that exotic sensuality about you." Then, "Wait!" He turned to me with a pint of Cherry Garcia from the freezer. He had to be the oldest living case of ADD on record. "Cherry Garcia! My favorite!" He held up the container. I smiled; he looked like a happy little boy. A happy little boy in desperate need of Ritalin. "I can't believe someone left some Cherry Garcia, what luck!"

I felt my face flush. "Listen, Doc, let's not talk about your family when we're together, okay?"

"I wasn't," he said as he rummaged for a spoon.

"Who left the Cherry Garcia?"

"What?" He was confused. He liked it when I kept things simple.

"The ice cream," I said. "Who left the ice cream here if not your family?"

"Whoever was here last," he said, finding a spoon. "Not us." Again, the "us" in question was not "him and me."

"You have no idea whose ice cream that is and you're going to eat it?"

"Yes!" he said and he pulled off the top to reveal the remaining one third of the ice cream. "They don't want it anymore."

"I mean, it's got someone else's germs!"

"The germs are all frozen." He tipped the container toward me. "Want some?"

I couldn't help but look inside the container. "What is... that?" I asked, walking closer to inspect the ice cream.

"What?"

"That!" I said. "That on top of the ice cream!"

"Just some mold," he said, scraping the top. "It can't hurt you."

"I didn't even know ice cream could grow mold! I can't believe you're going to eat that," I said, turning away.

"Don't you want anything?" he asked.

Despite my nausea, my hunger pangs were overwhelming, so I was forced on a scavenger hunt. I scoured the cabinets and found a box. "Ritz," I said, holding them up.

"Great!" he said. "Enjoy!"

I reached into the opened box and pulled out a stale cracker. It collapsed in my fingers. "Gross," I said, careful not to whine. "Listen, can we go to dinner now?" Long gone were the days of Le Cirque. I would have been happy with a Slurpee right then.

"Yes," he said, "soon." He finished the mold-covered Cherry Garcia.

"It's just...."

"What?" he asked, interested now that the ice cream was gone.

"It's just you tend to eat anything that's around." I paused for a moment and thought about this. "Well, almost anything that's around." I wondered if he caught the double entendre. "Anyway, then you get full, we have sex, and you fall asleep. That's not how I want to spend my first and only night in the Hamptons." That was how I'd spent the last two months of my life – including my twentieth birthday.

"I promise, we'll go to dinner," he said.

"It's not a big deal," I said, trying to undo any damage I may have caused. "Really, I just..." I reached in for another cracker; maybe one deeper in the box would be less soggy. That's when I felt something move. "What?" A small cockroach crawled out over the top and down the side. I threw the box onto the kitchen floor. "A roach! A roach!"

"You have them too," Dr. Fifth Avenue said. "You never get worked up about them. You even named yours, didn't you?"

"Yes. Rodolfo and Mimi. But mine aren't in the crackers! And the crackers are the only close to edible thing in this entire fucking rat trap!" I stepped back, sorry I'd said it. "Look, I'm sorry, I didn't mean—"

"No," he said, "you're right. I should take you to dinner. Let me just take a shower, I'm sweaty from tennis. I won, you know." And with that he went off to shower.

I knew I was supposed to go shower with him, but I was sure he would dry off with dirty towels left by the last tenants. Small house, okay. Cockroaches, I can look the other way. But dirty towels? Forget about it. So I sat on the dusty couch and waited. I wondered what Dr. Fifth Avenue was doing in a place like this. I became obsessed with the feeling of cockroaches crawling over my skin and with the idea that I was letting him down by not showering with him. I was convinced that I was breaking some unwritten mistress rule somewhere. Unwritten mistress rules. Maybe it was time someone wrote them down.

The Rules of Being a Mistress

By: Victoria Messing

1. Be very, very young.

2. Never make them feel old.

3. Never be demanding.

4. Be independently wealthy.

5. Never wear heavy perfume, heavy lipstick, or anything that can leave evidence.

6. Fake orgasms brilliantly.

7. Repeat Rule Number 6 often.

8. Open mouth only when giving head.

9. Know when to keep your mouth shut and know when to open it. (See Rule Number 8.)

10. Prepare to do everything off-season.

I was laughing when Dr. Fifth Avenue came out of the bedroom. He had a towel wrapped around his waist. "Whatcha doin'?" he asked in his "I want to get laid" voice. Come to think of it, what wasn't his "I want to get laid" voice?

"Nothing." I hid the list in my bag.

"I was just thinking that maybe since I'm already undressed...."

When was I going to learn I needed to eat before seeing him? Despite my ravenous hunger, I knew I had to make him feel like I couldn't keep my hands off of him. I was his mistress, after all. I reached into my bag to grab my toiletries and checked again to make sure the list was buried. That's when I noticed something at the bottom of my bag: a yellow and blue wrapper. Was it...? Yes! A peanut bar! I was saved! I was careful not to share this bit of information with my fuck-buddy however, or I would never have gotten as much as a bite of it for myself. So I slipped the bar into my jeans, made a big deal out of flashing my lingerie in front of him and ran to the bathroom to devour the bar, change my clothes, and brush my teeth. All without keeping him waiting. The peanut bar managed to quell my hunger pangs long enough to climb into bed in a new, see-through black teddy.

"Wow!" he said. I was surprised he still appreciated me aesthetically; I figured he'd be used to me by now. He laid me down next to him, a rare thing for him to do, and began kissing my breasts, an even rarer thing – and odd – since he knew I had no feeling in them. But I went with it and even began to relax. I imagined that if I fucked him soon, I would still get dinner before he was too tired to go out.

No sooner did he get the teddy off me than I heard a key turn in the lock. Like a shot, Dr. Fifth Avenue was up. He moved faster than I had ever seen him move before. He pushed me and my teddy into the bathroom and he threw the towel back around his waist. I heard a strange couple enter the living room.

"Hello?" Dr. Fifth Avenue said from the bedroom, rushing to the door.

"Hello!" a man's voice said, truly surprised. "We thought we'd be the only ones out here this time of year. We're trying to get a quick second honeymoon." I could hear the girl giggling.

"Well," Dr. Fifth Avenue said, "I'm Dr. Fif... Fiffer. Dr. Fiffer. And my wife... Honey?... is in the bathroom."

"We're so sorry," said the man. "The broker told us we could have the house this weekend. We paid."

"Yes, yes," Dr. Fifth Avenue lied. "We all paid, but since it's your second honeymoon, my wife and I will go." Naked in the bathroom, my feet cold against the tile floor, I enjoyed the moments of being called his wife.

"Oh we couldn't put you out!" said the soft, giggling voice.

"Not a problem," said Dr. Fifth Avenue. I wondered if he had a tiny tent pitched in his towel. I remembered my clothes were in the bathroom so I dressed, hurriedly. I was a little glad we'd be leaving. At least I'd finally get dinner. My first night in the Hamptons ranked far below this couple's ability to pick him out of a line-up, or for that matter, to recognize him at Le Bernadine. I knew I came second. A distant second. "Honey?" he called again and I emerged from the bathroom fully dressed. He exhaled.

"Hi," I said offering my hand. "I'm—"

"Veronique-uh," he said, interrupting and adding a pretentious "uh" at the end of my fictitious name. He dressed and we made our fast pick-up and run-through of the house, and we were almost out the door when Dr. Fifth Avenue said to the couple, "Don't worry about the broker. I'll call him. Here." He left two hundreds on the small table near the door. "Have drinks on us. Happy anniversary, or whatever."

The couple thanked him as he dragged me out the door. He turned back just for a moment to let the young couple know that Veronique-uh, his wife, was French.

I was once again full of questions. French? Why French? My looks weren't enough? He needed me to be French, too? But mostly I wondered why he dropped those hundreds. He never gave me money that easily. Honestly, the money pissed me off more than anything. As we sat in the car, my mind raced with all the things I wanted to know. Was Veronique-uh his wife's name? Did I look that much like her? But I was too grumpy and too famished to ask. I was just plain grateful we were on our way toward food. If that couple hadn't walked in when they did, I would have seriously considered swallowing his cum just for some nourishment. About ten minutes into the ride, I asked where we were going for dinner.

"I thought you understood," he said. "I have to get back. And fast. What if my wife and I see that couple in public and they bring up tonight? I have to get back and call her from my home phone... at an hour that could not be realistic for me to be here and be there. I have to be able to say they were mistaken. Understand?"

Unfortunately, I did. I understood that not only was I going to be starving for the next three hours, my life was going to be in danger because he'd be driving like a maniac. The Hamptons were definitely not my favorite place.

*   *   *

"Eat me," he said again the next time we were together, and I had to wonder if he ever made this request to his wife. And if he did, what she did about it. She probably laughed at him, the very thing I was trying not to do. As I slid down on the bed, undid his belt and unzipped the Armani pants, I finally understood that if I had laughed at him, I would have devastated him. The shopping, the trench coat, Armani, it was all a cover for being raised a poor boy in Brooklyn. He needed those things to make himself feel better. Dr. Fifth Avenue was more insecure when he was naked than I was at any point in my life. Once I realized that, there was little left for me to gain from the relationship.

The relationship ended quickly after that night in the Hamptons. For some time the excitement had been replaced with misleading comfort, intrigue was replaced with complacency, but still the blowjobs remained. I found a new high: I could make a man like this – this important, this powerful – fall for me. I recognized my power and knew it was time to move on.

I took Dr. Fifth Avenue to the South Street Seaport on an unusually cold day in early May. Over cappuccinos, I watched him. His hand shook slightly on his cup, his lip quivered... he was crying. He knew what was going on, and silly as it may sound, I felt like I was breaking his heart. He did love me after all. As he lifted his cup to sip lukewarm cappuccino, I placed my hand over his to steady it. I didn't need to say much to him. We understood each other. I lifted his hand to my lips and kissed it, softly.

"Thank you," I said. "Thank you for... well, all of it." I walked away, brushing back a single tear, and I realized I truly meant it.

CHAPTER 2: POSEIDON

"Poseidon was the ruler of the sea, Zeus' brother.... Storm and calm were under his control. He was commonly called 'Earth-Shaker'."

I met Michael in the single most unromantic spot in all of Manhattan: the Jacob Javits Center, a cold, masculine building where the windows overlook the street instead of the river and the sandwiches cost twenty dollars a pop. I was there working a food show, yet another in the line of modeling jobs I had since I abandoned my doctor and my deli meats.

I noticed him across the way. He was dark and not very handsome, but he paced like an exotic animal trapped in a cage. From my vantage point, I could study him discreetly. He was about my height, slightly heavy, dressed in black from head to foot and younger than Dr. Fifth Avenue. I smiled from my glamorous cottage cheese booth and he smiled back. He had perfect, white, masculine teeth and... was it? Even from this distance I could see it. Mmm.... he had a scar, just so, over the left side of his mouth. He was nasty hot.

I couldn't fathom why I was so attracted to him when I really only liked big bosses. He was just a guy working in a seafood imports booth at a food show and I was, after all, in search of my next god. I tried to get him out of my mind. I looked around the convention center and realized that with a Sam Breakstone impersonator to the left of me, and actual cottage cheese to the right, anyone would look good. I dropped my flirtation. But when the day ended, he came to talk to me.

"Hello. My name is Michael." Did he? Did I detect just the faintest accent?

"Victoria." We both smiled again and I was lost in his scar.

"I'm going to take you to dinner, tomorrow night." His voice had a strange inflection. English was definitely not his first language.

"O-Okay..." I said, stuttering.

"Give me your address." He said it in a way that made me want to lie down right there in front of him. I fought the urge and he sensed that something was wrong. He spoke again, "I'm filling in for my manager... I own the company, well my family does, and lucky for me, my manager needed the afternoon off. Family emergency." Smile again. Scar, scar, scar. "So I'm not a model..." – he patted his stomach and laughed – "here to show food." Once he realized that I was, in fact, a model at a food show he added, "Not that it's a bad job!" Charming, quick, and considerate. Then, he leaned in really close. "I drive a Porsche," he said and he let his eyes drop as if he were embarrassed for being rich. My, oh, my.

"Which one?" I asked.

"The Porsche? Which one?"

"Yeah. Which model Porsche?" If there was one thing I knew it was cars; I studied them diligently as part of my personally designed mistress training. I definitely had the upper hand.

A huge grin spread across his face. "But that's what I'm asking you, Baby," he said. "Which one of my Porsches are you referring to?" Hook, line and sinker.

And so he did pick me up that next night, and we did go to dinner. And more dinners on more nights. And he began to call me "Bella." And always, "Baby." And I'm not proud... I felt myself get wet when he did. And we dated, heavily. Exclusively. But never on Saturday nights.

"What's up with Saturday night?" I asked one evening.

"Business," he answered without even blinking. "Man business. You don't need to worry." So I didn't. And Gloria Steinem forgive me, but I loved the idea of "man business" that I needn't worry about. In fact, I didn't worry about anything with Michael. We would drive up anywhere we wanted in the city and someone would be waiting to help me out, to park the car, and to make our evening pleasurable. I was caught in a whirlwind. We lived on vodka tonics, champagne, and caviar; we danced at Au Bar all night and were treated like the royalty of Manhattan. All of this and Michael's wife was safely off visiting her family in Sweden.

Michael had houses in Italy, New Jersey, the Hamptons and a luxury apartment in the city. I stayed in my own apartment, but he paid the rent and I never had to think about a job at the Javits Center again, let alone Bloomingdales. Our lifestyle was so busy I never even had time to fantasize about moving to a nicer place. We were constantly going and doing. When we dressed for elegant functions, we looked like a Hollywood glamour couple: his dark hair slicked back, his black eyes dancing across the crowd. He would walk me into a room exuding such power that everyone – from the hosts to the busboys – would stop to look our way.

But even with all of this, my dates with Michael became ordinary. I began to expect, well… everything. I had fast become used to expensive food and even more used to expensive cars. Michael had several Porsches and two customized Mercedes at his disposal. He also had a Lamborghini for fun, and a Hummer for our weekends of roughing it in the Hamptons. Michael had what I later learned was coined, "stupid money." That is, he had so much money he had no idea . what to do with it all. And when he gave me money I didn't save it. I just didn't care. I was too busy enjoying the insane lifestyle Michael's money afforded me to even think about the future. And please, could I really expect "mistressing" to come with a 401-K?

One Friday afternoon while I basked in the sun on Michael's yacht, I thought about what Michael did when he wasn't with me. But I didn't let it occupy me for long. Topless, I rolled onto my back and stretched like a contented cat on a warm spring day. Life was a paradise with Michael so I really didn't have any intention of rocking the boat. But strangely, on that particular weekend, not more than a month into our relationship, things started to change.

I first noticed them in the distance, down by the boat slips. There were a group of them, all dressed similarly to Michael – in black from head to foot even on this oppressively hot day. Two of them wore suit jackets. I pulled on my cover and walked to the edge of the boat to get a better look. "Who are they?" I asked the deckhand, but he didn't answer. Michael caught me staring at him and nodded to me. He said something to the gang who dispersed as quickly as they had formed. Then Michael joined me on his yacht for an evening cruise, without, of course, offering even the slightest explanation.

The next day I was lying on top of Michael on a couch in his mansion in South Hampton. The house was easily twice the size of my apartment building; it was a gated property located on a secluded street with its own private tennis courts, pools, putting green, and beach. It was worlds away from that little shack Dr. Fifth Avenue tried to pass off as "awesome." Michael was deep in conversation, the cell phone glued to his ear. I licked his scar.

"Stop it. Please. Bella, I'm trying to talk." Michael was rambling on in Italian. I licked again and playfully bit his scar. He pushed me away and I landed on the floor. He looked at me lying there. "Go swimming."

"Don't wanna go swimming," I said, pouting. Normally, I loved to swim there. My favorite pool on the property was an indoor/outdoor that was guarded by huge statues of Hercules, Aphrodite, and Poseidon. There were also some other Greek figures that I couldn't place, all complete with fig leaves. But at that moment I felt rebellious. I wanted to push Michael to his limit. He was just so cool. In all the weeks we'd been dating, I never once saw him get upset.

I moped to the kitchen to get something to eat. "Careful in there!" he said as he covered the phone. I knew what he meant. My diet. I'd always been slim but Michael liked me really thin. Skinny. He loved the way my hipbones jutted out and the two tiny muscles on the sides of my waist were the only things holding up my jeans. Considering my size, I was amazed he thought my boobs were real. What stick skinny woman has these breasts? But what did he care, he had his dream woman: a life-sized Barbie Doll with tits as soft as cement. I brought him biscotti and munched on carrots.

"I'm hungry," I said. He covered the phone again, got up, and went to the next room. That was odd behavior, even for Michael. I shrugged, figuring it was his wife. And then the doorbell rang. "Michael?" I asked.

"It's all right, Bella! Answer it!" he said from the other room. I snagged one of Michael's biscotti and opened the door. A very tall, heavy man – with a pock-marked face and a gray front tooth – was standing there, carrying an overnight bag.

"Hello?" I said.

"Hello, Victoria," he said. "Michael's expecting me. He told me you would be here."

"He didn't tell me... Who are you?" I said. Horrible images flashed before me: rape, gang rape, but I shook them from my mind. That wouldn't happen with Michael. He was too good to me. For heaven's sake, he called me 'baby.' But then again... did I really know Michael at all? We'd spent weeks together but there was always some distance between us. Fear must have registered on my face.

"Please don't be alarmed," the large man said, obviously wanting to come in. "I'm Michael's cousin, Nick."

I sighed an audible sigh. "Right!" I said. "His cousin. I'm sorry. Come in."

"I think you saw me at the dock yesterday," he said, walking past me.

"Yeah, a lot of you," I said. Then I realized how that sounded. "I didn't mean a lot of *you*... in particular... I meant a large group...."

"Oh don't worry," Nick said, chuckling. "There is a lot of me. And a big group too. Big family. We came to see if you and Michael were free for a party next week."

"Oh!" I said, thrilled to be included in a family event.

"But Michael said he was busy."

"Oh." I should have known. Nick turned back and smiled at me.

For some reason, Michael brought his cousin everywhere we went that weekend. It was strange, but I just figured it was tough for Nick to get a girl of his own.

It was hard to be romantic with Nick in the picture. But no sooner did I mention this to Michael, than Nick miraculously had a girlfriend – Cheryl – and the four of us were double dating all over the Hamptons. Cheryl was tiny, about four-foot-eleven and a size double zero. She had streaked bleach blonde hair and wore a hot pink bikini to accentuate her overly dark tan. She wasn't the type of woman I would ever choose to associate with, and I think she felt the same way about me. I had to look down (literally and figuratively) to talk to her. Conversation between us was, at best, awkward, as I did not share Cheryl's quest for "The most awesome highlights ever!" Somehow, my one-and-a-half semesters of college and my mission to become a kept woman made me an intellectual giant next to Cheryl. Despite our marked differences, Cheryl and I tried to be friendly – we were, after all, all in one boat, no matter how large.

After another couple of uneventful summer weeks, I grew to take the money, cars, boats, and houses completely for granted. Since I was alone in the mansion on Saturday nights, I rented movies and splurged on my diet. I was sure to throw away all evidence of my binges: empty bags of potato chips, Oreo crumbs, and to brush my teeth before Michael got back. He would always call me from the car on his way so I knew I wouldn't get caught. But even my hidden Twinkie binges could only keep my interest for so long. I was becoming bored. It was as if some higher power understood I needed to shake things up.

Michael's mother was an old-world Italian woman tight with words and even tighter with money. Despite the fact that Michael's family ran a thriving business, Mama wore gaudy costume jewelry because she couldn't understand wasting money on the real thing. I'd heard Michael, full of pride, tell the story of how his mother had her driver pull her car over so that she could hassle a street vendor until he gave in and sold her his Tiffany-style jewelry at half price. Then Mama and driver peeled off, heading for her mansion, leaving a poor cursing street vendor safely on the opposite side of the George Washington Bridge.

The story blew my mind. And taught me to be sure to get anything Michael gave me appraised. But amazingly, the thought of being given fake jewelry didn't affect me nearly as much as Michael's reaction to his mother.

That following Saturday afternoon as I was preparing to go get some movies, Michael slammed the phone down. He moved through the house more quickly than I had ever seen him move before, like a possessed child on speed. "Victoria. Go get your things. Now." His tone left no room for debate.

"What?" I asked, not moving. "Why?"

"My mother's coming," he said as calmly as he could. "Here. To visit. Unexpectedly. She can't know you were here."

"What, you don't want to introduce me?" No response from Michael. "What's the big deal?" I asked. "Your wife's been gone for the past three months. Do you honestly believe that your mother thinks you're just waiting around? I'm sure your father does the exact same thing whenever your mother is away," I said... unwisely.

"What?" he asked, his black eyes fixed on me. "Are you insinuating that my father is unfaithful?"

"No?" I said, more as a question than a response.

"I should hope not," Michael said. "Because then I wouldn't know what to think of you."

"And what do you think of me now?" I asked, actually curious.

"I don't have time for this, Victoria. She'll be here soon and she cannot catch you here. She is not young and I do not want to upset her. In her eyes, I was married before God. I do not want her to know any of this. It would kill her and she should be protected. She will be protected, do you understand? Besides, if she sees you here, she'll think you're just a gold-digger."

"A what?" I was infuriated. The one thing I never wanted to be accused of being was that which I so blatantly was. "Tell me, Michael, exactly how much gold have I mined from you?" Sure, my rent was paid and my lifestyle was outrageous, but where were the tangible goods?

Michael didn't answer. He left me standing there, watching him, as he commanded the cleaning staff to vacuum, dust, wash laundry, and comb the beds for stray female hairs. (We had "done it" in every bed in the house, and in every room in the house, and on every surface of the house.) I'd never seen people move so fast or work so hard. Fresh flowers were set out in the foyer, the front hall statue of the Virgin Mary was polished until it sparkled, and even the pools had some sort of smell-good softening agent added to them. They moved with such precision it was like watching the changing of the guard at Buckingham Palace. Maybe Mrs. M. actually was Queen Elizabeth. That would explain a lot. Michael stopped giving orders only to call Nick in from outside to explain to him what was going on.

Then without any warning, Michael grabbed me by the arm – not by the hand but by the *arm* – and pulled me upstairs to the master bedroom. Housekeeping was there fluffing pillows; he told them to leave and they scurried off. Michael paused for a moment and stared at me. Then something pulled his attention away. "What's this?" he asked, pointing to a vanity table. He ran his finger across the top of the vanity and held it up for me to see. Obviously housekeeping had missed a spot.

"I dunno..." I answered. "Make-up?" I was so shaken I really didn't know up from down. I rubbed my arm.

"You *dunno*?" he said.

"That's your mother's vanity?" I asked, truly clueless. "Sorry, you told me I could use—"

"No," he said, "it's my wife's vanity."

"I'm sorry," I said softly, feeling like a newly housebroken puppy who had an accident on the white carpet.

"Get your things," he said as if I was dismissed. So I did. As quickly as I could, I gathered my belongings and stuffed my Prada overnight bag (a gift from our first night together) with my clothes and lingerie. He watched me intensely. I could feel his eyes on me as I went into the bathroom to collect my toiletries. Michael followed me into the bathroom, and this time he grabbed me by both arms and pulled me to him. Hard. I let out a gasp and he covered my mouth with his. In one fast move, Michael put his arm around my waist and dropped me to the floor. He tore off my jeans and panties and fucked me so hard against the tile that my body lifted with each thrust. My head bounced against the floor. My teeth chattered. When he was done, he dressed quickly. I rolled onto my side and rested my cheek against the cool tile. "Get your things" he said again. Stunned, I did.

I hate to admit it, but the bathroom scene was a huge turn-on for me. It also petrified me a little. I was as ready to go as he was to kick me out. I think.

Once he was sure the house was magnificent and housekeeping had removed all traces of the Whore of the Hamptons, Michael drove me to the Hampton Jitney. I wasn't thrilled that another woman was the reason I had to take a bus. Especially since it was only his mother. And I was even more bothered that Michael was throwing me out after he'd just used me as he did in the bathroom. Frankly, I was pissed.

"What's going on here?" I asked. "What did we just do? I mean, that was kind of... rough." He didn't answer. "Okay, then why don't you tell me about your mother," I said. "Is that what you do on Saturday nights? Have dinner with her?" He looked at me from the corner of his eye. I watched him nod his head not as an answer but rather to check his temper. "Is it?" I asked. "Michael?"

"I told you not to ask me about Saturdays," he said, not looking at me.

"Oh come on!" I said. "Drop the tough guy act. I saw how you reacted to your mother. So you are afraid of someone."

"Afraid?" He turned to me when he spoke. "My tough guy act?" Then he forced his eyes off of me and back onto the road. He nodded again, now looking somehow disappointed in me. I knew I had overstepped a boundary. I also knew that I wasn't accurately describing how I felt. We drove the rest of the trip in silence.

I got out of the Hummer without saying a word. I looked at Michael deliberately, grabbed my bag and slammed my door. I thought he was about to say something but he didn't.

"Of course not. When does he ever say anything?" I muttered just loud enough for him to hear. Michael walked me to the bus silently. I climbed a step and then looked back over my shoulder. It was a scene straight out of a low-budget romance movie.

Michael spoke to the driver. "Take good care of her, all right? Drive carefully."

"Yes sir, Mr. M., sir," the bus driver said, leaving me, once again, utterly confused. Why would the bus driver know Michael's name? I climbed another step and felt Michael's hand firmly on my waist. I turned.

"You know how I feel about you, Bella." He said it more like a statement than a question. I stared in wonder.

"No, I don't," is what I wanted to say, but that brief moment of strength I exhibited on the way over was long gone. Instead, I told him, "We're holding up the bus."

"The bus can wait." He motioned to the driver as he pulled me back down off of the steps. The door closed behind me. I could feel people looking out of the windows at us and I squirmed, shifting my weight from one foot to the other.

"Everyone's looking at us," I said.

"They don't matter," he said, locking my gaze. "They'll leave when we're done. I asked you a question a minute ago. You know how I feel about you, right?" He didn't waver a bit. "Victoria, do not make me ask you again." I felt an audible sigh escape. He sounded so strong and so powerful. I wanted nothing more than to have him fuck me again, right there, up against the bus.

I pulled myself together and nodded. "I do know how you feel about me," I said. I searched his eyes, overcome. "And I love you too."

"Good. Now go home and go to sleep. I'll call you in the morning. Here." He handed me a few hundred dollars. "For dinner and a cab." I nodded. "Go straight home, Victoria," he said. I nodded again and he knocked on the door for the driver to let me in.

As the bus pulled away, I stared at Michael, unable to tell if he was happy or sad. He checked his surroundings before he got into the car. He popped two Rolaids into his mouth. He put his hand on his heart and rubbed his chest as he always did. I was sure Michael would be dead from a heart attack by the age of forty-two.

The next morning, Michael called like he said he would. A few hours later, seven dozen roses showed up at my apartment. I wondered why seven, but I knew he just didn't put that much thought into it. Seven dozen is probably what the florist had, so seven dozen is what he bought. Soon after the flowers, Michael arrived.

"Michael, this is an odd relationship," I said. We sat side by side on my couch. Even with my limited mistress experience I knew something was just not kosher.

"Shh... Bella," he said, putting his fingers to my lips. In my dimly lit apartment Michael looked dangerous. So dangerous, I got hot. I stared at his scar, mesmerized. He kissed me and I kissed him back. I couldn't get enough of him. I felt the weight of him, his smell overtook me. He pushed me away and held me at arm's length; I was sure that his eyes would burn right through me. I tried to get up to go to the bathroom and collect myself but he held me hard, by the wrist. "I need to go to the bathroom," I said.

"Not now." He pulled me back down onto the couch. Michael usually rolled onto his back and waited for a blowjob. I had become quite proficient, but my jaw got tired with him because he wanted so many and he took so long to orgasm. But he didn't lie on his back. Instead, he lay on top of me and slowly unbuttoned my shirt.

What was going on? Was he actually trying to seduce me? To make up for the day before? He reached inside my shirt, unhooked my bra and rubbed my breasts. His weight was heavy on me and I began to squirm beneath him. He told me to relax and stop fighting. I did. He reached down and unbuttoned my jeans. He slid them off and my panties as well. When he turned me over onto my stomach, I was still wearing my white linen shirt but I was naked from the waist down. He told me to lick his fingers. I felt him put his finger into my ass but I thought nothing of it. He did that often and I did it for him. But then he slid in a second and attempted a third. I tensed from the pain. "Hey, that hurts!" I said. I tried to roll over but he had me pinned down.

"Stop fighting," he whispered into my ear. I tried to relax. Then he shifted higher on the couch and began to slide himself into my tiny opening. Up until then, I had no real experience with men who wanted anal sex. Certainly my jock boyfriend didn't want it, and Dr. Fifth Avenue was happy with being "eaten." The whole experience was just too much and I tried to claw my way up the sofa. He grabbed my arms and held them beneath me. I had no choice but to succumb to Michael, and at once it was a mixture of intense pain and ecstasy. I was just so grateful we used lubricated condoms. Surprisingly, Michael made enough of an effort to reach around to the front to make sure that I was happy, but I could barely stand the pain of him thrusting and just wanted it to be over. I moaned in agony.

"Shhh," he said. "Bite the pillow." I did. I bit down hard, and a trickle of saliva ran down the side of my mouth. I closed my eyes and waited for it to be over. He came hard. Harder than I'd ever felt him come before. There was a huge relief when he pulled out, but I was still so sore. Again I tried to roll over onto my back, but still he had me pinned. "Now, you are mine," he whispered firmly into my ear, brushing my hair back from my face. I wanted to tell him that I'd always been his, but instead I just nodded. I felt like a branded head of cattle. As soon as he moved off of me, I rolled onto my back.

Michael excused himself and went to the bathroom. When he came back, he told me to take a shower. I let the water run down the drain for a minute while I took two Advil. After I showered, I came out to find him dressed and standing in front of the TV. He tugged his pants up at the waist and turned to look at me. "Are you hungry?" he asked. I shook my head. "Okay," he said and walked toward me. I shied slightly. He kissed me on the lips and grabbed his black leather jacket. "I have to go," he said. "Nick is picking me up." He left.

Once I was alone, I felt a strange combination of elation and fear. All I could do was pace around the room, but walking still made me sore. I wished that I had some female friends. I thought of calling my mother, or Liz. But for what? What would I say? "I have a boyfriend and he's great... sort of... but sometimes he's rough and now we're having anal sex and I don't like it." I poured myself a tall glass of Sambuca and stared at myself in my full-length mirror, wondering what I had gotten myself into.

Our relationship raged on. It had been nearly a year. I was twenty-one and had grown to accept that anal sex was a part of our lives, although I never grew to like it. I also understood my place in his life: it was to do those activities his wife didn't want or need to do. Being with Michael was like being on a roller-coaster inside a haunted house, it terrified me and thrilled me all at the same time.

"Give him anal sex as a present," my mother told me when I finally broke down and admitted what I was up to.

"Right," I said to myself after hanging up the phone. "I'm going to tell this large, mysterious man who," I had just found out, "carries a gun that he can only have the kind of sex that he wants on high holidays."

During this time, I grew more and more afraid of Michael. Although he was still calm and collected, I had seen him occasionally lash out at people with a rage that really scared me. But it was this same fear that was also such an aphrodisiac. Sometimes he would yell so loudly into his phone that the walls of my apartment would shake and the neighbors would knock. But I knew it was all an act. Michael never lost control. Not really. He screamed simply to scare people, and the louder he got, the more turned on I became. That night, I watched as he clicked the barrel of his gun into the mouthpiece of the phone. I couldn't even wait for him to finish; I straddled him, rubbing myself against him. In one quick movement he picked me up with his free arm and held me against the wall. He threw the phone hard and it smashed into a thousand little bits. I moaned as he pulled up my skirt and ripped off my panties. Then he fucked me against the wall. He jammed into me with such force that I thought he was going to puncture me. My back burned; my insides ached. When he was finished, he kept me pinned to the wall and held me tighter than he ever had before. I burst into tears.

"Shhh.... Bella," he whispered into my ear. "Everything's okay." He stroked my hair as he walked back toward the bed. I closed my eyes and prayed he would never let me go. I was shaking when he put me down on the bed. He lay down next to me and I pushed my body so close to his I could barely breathe.

"I don't think I can stand you being with anyone else," I sobbed. "I just want you to own me," I whispered, my voice cracking.

He stroked my hair and lifted my chin so I looked directly into his eyes. "I do," he assured me.

A few nights later, when he rolled me onto my stomach I told him that I wanted to hold it. "How can you hold it and have me inside at the same time?" he asked.

"Not that... *it*," I said. He realized what I wanted.

"No," was his answer.

I rolled over obligatorily and prepared my pillow. I waited, but nothing. Then, behind me, I heard that same click that had driven me crazy just days before. I turned and saw him sitting on the side of the bed holding his gun. For a second my heart stopped. Maybe I shouldn't have made such a fuss over it. I stared, wide-eyed. Who would know if he killed me? Who would even know he'd been here? Everyone we associated with was on his payroll. Including my doorman. How else would he know what I did on those nights we weren't together? I could be dead, rotting away in my tiny apartment for a week before my mother would send my sister to hunt me down. I shuddered.

"Are you cold?" Michael asked me, and I nearly jumped out of my skin. I couldn't speak so I just shook my head. I held my breath, not knowing what would happen next. Still holding the gun, he leaned forward and wrapped a blanket around me. I felt myself shrink back from him. "Bella? You okay?" he asked and kissed me on the forehead.

Of course, being me, my fears subsided as quickly as they came. I was wildly attracted to both him and the gun. I went to touch the gun, but he pulled it away, removed the clip, and cleared the chamber.

"You don't have to take that out," I said, motioning to the clip.

"Tch," was all he said. He placed the clip on the nightstand and lay back, resting on his elbow, the gun still in his hand. I was overwhelmed by his power. I ran my finger up and down the barrel of the gun... up and down, up and down, getting hotter and hotter watching him with it. He put his hand over my hand and guided me... he showed me the right way to hold it, how to pull the trigger. Then he lifted the gun and used it to stroke my face.

"You are so beautiful," he said, running the gun gently down my cheeks. I nuzzled into it. "So absolutely beautiful." I thought I would explode as he used the barrel to turn my chin toward him, to guide me to his pants. I blew him, as he wanted, and every minute or so he would lift my chin to look at me, my cheeks flushed, my mouth swollen. Still stroking my cheeks with the cold steel, he reached with his other hand to trace my mouth. Slowly he would slip finger after finger into my mouth, which I would suck and lick until he pulled it away. He smeared the tiny bit of lip gloss from my lips up across my face, and then carefully, he slipped the end of the gun into my mouth. He held my chin still with the other hand, and I froze, feeling him push the gun farther and farther until it gagged me. He pulled it out slowly and commanded me up. Still holding the gun, he rolled me onto my back grasping both of my arms over my head with one hand, while he ran the gun up and down my body with the other. He undid each one of my buttons and dragged the gun across my stomach. He took my panties down and traced the gun across my pubic bone. He moved up over me and I writhed in ecstasy as he mounted me and slid inside me, forcing my hands and the gun to be still on the pillow. He moaned quietly as I came hard. I didn't care about anything; I had lost all inhibitions. Up against my temple was something that could, in a flash, end my life. It was the biggest high I had ever felt. I came again as he did. When we finished, he dressed, loaded the gun, and put it in his jacket pocket.

"It's loaded," I whispered. He looked at me sternly.

"Bella, we should never have done that. Forget it," he patted his jacket pocket, "and this night completely." I always did what he told me, but how could he expect me to forget the best sex of my life? I was grinning from ear to ear, but he looked troubled and unhappy.

"Okay," I said, fighting my smile. But I wouldn't forget. Ever. I loved being his girlfriend, his mistress, his whatever. I didn't care that we had crossed a line.

"Do you need money?" he asked and I nodded. He left a thousand dollars on the kitchen counter, kissed me, and left.

I was on fire. I was hot and heavy into being the mistress of such a powerful man and I used it to my every advantage. "I really want kumquats for dessert," I told my waiter, and seconds later someone was sent out to find them. "I know that coat isn't available 'til next Christmas," I fussed at Burberry, "but I really want it now." The next week, I was sporting the coat. Poor Nick schlepped after us, weighed down with packages. The three of us turned heads everywhere we went, and what a sight we must have been: the model, the mystery man, and his over-sized cousin. I was loving life. A sore ass was definitely worth Michael's generosity.

We saw each other more and more often over the next two months and began having rougher sex. Each time I did something a little wild, he whispered "You're mine..." into my ear and bought me an extravagant gift. I finally found where I fit in: I belonged to Michael. Nothing we did was really dangerous or even overtly kinky, except for the times when Michael would force me to have sex with him. But considering what I was getting out of the deal, I was more than willing, so he wasn't technically forcing. For those nights, Michael set the mood by renting us a sleazy motel room in New Jersey complete with red walls, dirty bed covers, and a semen-stained rug.

One day Michael used twine to tie me, face down, spread-eagle to the bed. "Stop fidgeting," he said. "You'll make the cuts worse." After we finished, I had deep lacerations on my wrists – deeper than I'd ever seen them before, they were bloody and raw. On the car ride home I was wobbly from exhaustion, barely able to keep my eyes open. Michael helped me inside, and on closer inspection, even he was surprised at how bad my wrists looked. He bandaged them for me and kissed them, but he never apologized. Not once. The gauze bandages made me look like I had slit my wrists, so Michael told me to wear long sleeves the next day.

I nodded and leaned back on the bed. I could feel the blood rush from my face. Michael looked at me. "I think you need to eat a little more," he said, digging up a Chinese food menu. "Here," he laid the menu next to me. "I have to go, but order whatever you want." He left five hundred dollars on the bed.

"That will buy me the whole restaurant," I said and he exhaled, happy, I think, that I was still conscious. Then the room began spinning. "I'm kind of dizzy...," I said, closing my eyes. Michael looked at his watch.

"I still have a minute," he decided. "What do you want?" But he didn't wait for me to answer; instead, he ordered us nearly everything on the menu. He ordered three dishes from every column – plus every appetizer and soup they had – careful to skip anything with octopus. For some reason Michael hated octopus. It took three delivery men two trips to deliver all the food. As he answered the door, time after time, he laughed at the delivery men who asked how we could have such a big party in such a small apartment. By the time the food was all there, I was giggling hysterically. Bags were piled on my kitchen counter, on my tiny dining room table, and on the kitchen floor. There was no way to walk through the kitchen and neither of us had any idea where to start. "Egg roll, Signorina?" Michael asked throwing a dishtowel over his arm. This was the first time I had ever seen Michael play. He looked genuinely happy to see me laughing so much.

"Please!" I said as I tried to sit up. Once again all the blood rushed from my head and then boom! – I was down again. He crossed to me and propped me up as he fed me egg roll, wonton soup, and beef with broccoli.

"We need to take better care of you," he said.

"I'm fine!" I said, trying to laugh it all off. As much as I relished the attention, I didn't want to become a burden to Michael. No one wanted a mistress who needed caring for.

"Still, we have to be more careful." He kissed me on the head. This was the closest to normal Michael and I had ever been, and all it took to get us there was for me to nearly pass out from kinky sex and exhaustion.

His cell rang. Michael got up quickly and locked himself in my bathroom. "No. Absolutely not," was all that I heard. He came out moments later. "Bella, I need to go," he told me.

"Now? But we have so much food!"

"Eat what you want and throw the rest out. Better yet, give it to the homeless. Don't you volunteer at a homeless shelter?"

"No," I said. "That's your other wife."

"Bella, please. Please." He looked at me in my least favorite way. It was a cross between patronizing me for thinking I was close to him, and telling me it was time for him to go. "Get some sleep tonight," he said and then he left.

Consciously, I knew my relationship with Michael had become unhealthy. And despite our closeness, there was still a void between us. I carried with me the visible scars of our relationship but I still didn't know what Michael did on Saturday nights. I also didn't know what the constant phone calls were about and why someone in the food business carried a gun. But I never bothered to question it. Any of it. I did know that as wild as my life was with Michael, it was a small life. I had only friends he approved of, hobbies he said okay to, and food that he liked for me. Period. I wasn't even an active part of the city I lived in. Although I wanted it to last forever, I began to think about how our relationship would end. Dramatically? Quietly? One thing was certain, when and if it ended, he would be the one to do it. Because even if I wanted to, I would have no idea how to begin to get out.

I walked around in a constant state of dizziness, overcome by emotions, trying – in vain – to think straight. I could scarcely catch my breath while I was around him, but I couldn't breathe if he was away. I felt my body defy me whenever I looked at him: my heart quickened, my soul ached. The closer I became to Michael, the more I believed that I might just explode. Literally. Spontaneously combust, maybe. It was all a dream. It had to have been. I had every girly gift I had ever wanted: a Rolex and a Tag Heur, 4-carat diamond earrings, diamond necklaces, tens of thousands of dollars in new clothes, a car at my disposal. And to get it all, I was with Michael, a man so powerful he seemed to control the world. If I wanted anything, Michael would make it materialize. If someone looked at me in the wrong way, Michael would send Nick to talk to them. If it rained on me, Michael would summon the sun to appear. He made me weak.

I was also acutely aware that I was living at such a frenetic pace I would eventually burn out. Or worse. I was sore from all the rough sex and I sported fresh cuts and bruises daily. I had deep red marks on my wrists, ankles, and waist from being tied down and had developed fissures from all the anal sex. Not a pretty picture for someone who was still only twenty-one. But it wasn't Stockholm Syndrome, and I wasn't living my own version of *9¹/² Weeks*. He wasn't a sadist. Truthfully. What he was, was gluttonous. We both were. We attacked each other with such overwhelming passion that we did not know when to stop. It wasn't that he wanted to hurt me – frankly, he would have destroyed anyone who did – it's that he wanted to forget that I was a separate person. He fucked me with such force because he wanted me to become a part of him. To meld into him. He was a spoiled little boy who didn't realize his toys would break if he didn't care for them. I truly believed this man owned me and everything around me so there were no lines to be drawn. The more he did, the harder he branded me, the more he marked me, the more I wanted. I would have fallen on my knees before this man, and I did, many times. He was my god, and fucking him became my religion.

I needed to occupy myself on those long days – and sometimes nights – that I was away from him. I wanted something to do, maybe even a second career. But with Michael as my boyfriend I couldn't work just any job, which meant I needed to model. That was the only option for Michael M's mistress. But how could I model when my body looked like it did? Every inch of my body (except my face – Michael loved my face too much to touch it) had a bruise – some freshly purple, some that lovely fading yellowish-green color. My face had become drawn from the late nights and the constant dieting. Despite having become a pro at covering up the bruises, I knew no make-up artist would want to work that hard. I pushed the thought of modeling away for just a bit longer.

One day, Michael told me that he needed to disappear for awhile. He called me from the airport to let me know that he was on his way to Italy and wouldn't be back for about a month. He told me the rent was paid and Nick would be by to bring me some money. When I asked why he was leaving, he wouldn't answer. "Behave, Bella," was all he said, then, after a pause, "Don't worry." Michael's last words to me before he hung up the phone were, "Wait for me, Bella. It will be one month." I did.

When Michael came back from the mysterious trip, he seemed older and worn. He was even more distant toward me. I knew I should be changing as well, that I should be growing as a person – that I should want more from life than to be manhandled by the god of the ocean – but I couldn't even imagine my life without Michael. He was my life. His first night back we made love like husband and wife. That night there were no pillows, no ties, no ropes... nothing between us at all, except the condom Michael insisted on wearing. At times I had to look away from him for fear I might melt. But each time I did, he would gently bring my gaze back to meet his... stroking my face, my hair, my mouth. My body felt like it was levitating, I pushed myself as close to him as possible. That night he made love to me as if he was going to war; he devoured me as if I was his last meal; he looked at me as if he was saying goodbye – forever. As I lay beneath him, I knew our relationship would never go any further than this one magical moment and there was nothing I could do about it. I told myself that I should want more. Even my original plan to be a mistress involved more than this; it involved being my own person and establishing a future for myself all on a man's dime. Instead, all thoughts of anything but Michael left the moment I met him.

Michael stayed distant from me over the next month. He'd become quiet and moody. The doormen at restaurants and clubs seemed twice as attentive, but we hardly went out anymore. On the rare occasion we did, it was all arranged days in advance. There was nothing spontaneous. Our evenings out were strictly to entertain me. We went to private clubs filled with our friends, but Michael – who normally loved to lead me around the dance floor – would only stand with his back to the wall and watch as I danced. I chatted away as we sat in a banquette in the dark, deserted VIP room, but Michael would only nod, downing shot after shot of Johnnie Walker Blue. Michael arranged to have a private movie showing for the two of us, just Michael and me in the entire theatre. Well, the two of us plus Nick; Cheryl was long gone. I was overwhelmed by this romantic gesture. He even bought me popcorn, with butter. Something was definitely going on. I just couldn't put my finger on it.

Michael had replaced his latest Porsche with a Ferrari Testarossa and wanted to try it out. It was maybe two in the morning and even the George Washington Bridge was quiet. We sped across and onto the Jersey Turnpike heading for, I imagined, a sleazy motel. The Ferrari raced faster and faster and so did I. I never worried, not even when Michael drove like a demon – he maneuvered that car with the same confidence and expertise that he maneuvered me. He drove like a professional. So I sat back and sighed with every downshift – completely caught up in the roar of the engine.

We hurried down the turnpike in our quarter-million dollar chariot. Soon, there were flashing lights behind us. Michael looked in his rearview, nodded, and said, "I'm sorry, but I need to go a little faster now." He pushed the car to what seemed even its limits. Faster and faster we raced until we reached liftoff. I glanced at the speedometer to see we had left double digits – and the flashing lights – far behind us in a cloud of beautiful Italian dust. Finally, we glided off an exit and drove directly to what I assumed was a large private resort.

We stopped at an enormous gate and I strained to see beyond it. When I finally realized what I was looking at, I had to hold back a chuckle. I just couldn't believe my eyes. We weren't at a resort. Or a hotel. We were at Michael's home. His real home.

I never knew he lived like this. I never knew anyone lived like this. Michael's mansion may very well have dwarfed Notre Dame. Why the hell did we spend so much time in cheap motels and in my cramped studio? It was obvious that Michael had more money than I ever realized. He had more money than God.

"Wow," I whispered. Even in the pitch black of night and from this distance, I could see its enormity. It was white, with majestic columns flanking a porch and a driveway the length of any short country road. Thanks to the many trees lining the property, the house was invisible from the street, but flood lights were everywhere, placed strategically between the trees and along the path to the front door. There were smaller houses on the property as well: a guest house, groundskeepers' quarters, a stable complete (he told me) with Arabian Stallions, and a twelve-car garage. His estate must have been half the state of New Jersey.

Michael stopped at the gate momentarily and with a loud buzzing, the huge gate unlocked and opened. The flood lights flashed on. Dogs began barking but were quieted by a man dressed in black carrying a rifle across his shoulder. Slowly we drove deeper into the compound, then we stopped at another, smaller gate. That gate opened quickly. We were about to enter a fortress. A fortress that I could never escape by myself, in a state I didn't know, with a man I had just then, finally figured out.

I couldn't believe I'd been so stupid. The money, the attention, the private movie theatre… the gun. But he made such an effort to hide his businesses from me – to protect me from it all – that I just never caught on. And you know what? If I had figured it out earlier, it would only have made me want him all the more.

Michael parked the car in a garage attached to the house and told me to be quiet. I got out of the car without saying a word, but my breathing was loud and hurried. I tried to calm it as Michael led me through a maze of doors, each with its own security code. My heart was racing and my head was spinning. Michael took my hand and led me toward a staircase. I walked past a dining room with an enormous baroque chandelier and toward another staircase with a smaller, matching chandelier.

We went up the staircase, and Michael led me to a room. Before we stepped inside, I heard another man's voice. I froze, but Michael held my hand fast. He answered the man in Italian and took me to a small room at the end of one hallway. Only once we were inside did Michael turn on a light. After my eyes adjusted, I looked around at a very normal room. It looked like a teenager's room, complete with photos of cars on the walls. Cars! What car could this man possibly covet? Michael told me to get undressed but to keep my panties on. He gave me a t-shirt that hung to my knees and said, "Of course I'm perfect, I'm Italian!" He stripped to his white boxers and tank top and we climbed into the small bed together. It must have been a room that he kept for a nephew I'd never heard of. There was just so much I didn't know about him.

I wondered how we could be there. What about the staff, what about his wife?

Michael got up for a second, went to the bathroom and spoke to an intercom on the wall. I tried to decode the Italian; I thought he asked for a six a.m. wake-up call. Michael climbed into bed and put his arms around me. I could feel his breath on my neck. I was filled with questions, but I didn't dare speak. I tried to calm my breathing but it just seemed to accelerate. "Shhh... Bella, go to sleep now," he said into my ear.

I closed my eyes, but the whole experience was too much. I would never sleep. I could tell he was wide awake too. I squeezed my eyes tightly and rubbed his arm. I tried to let him know that I understood and that it was all okay. All of it. I would love him no matter what. Hell, I loved him even more now that I knew. He was more powerful than even I had ever realized, and power, to me, was the greatest aphrodisiac in the world.

He must have understood me because quickly and silently he rolled me onto my back and took my panties off. Without saying a word and without even looking at me, he slid inside me. He moved slowly, seeming unsure of how I felt about him, but my body answered his with unbridled eagerness. He drove his rhythm faster and faster and harder and harder until he completely overpowered me. Then, quite unexpectedly, long before he was done, he stopped thrusting and looked at me. Really looked at me, just as he did that time in the Hamptons, when he decided to claim me as his own. I didn't know what to think. I wondered if he was trying to figure out what to do with me, if I had become a problem. Moments later, as quickly as he had stopped, he started again, still holding me captive with his gaze. Then he fucked me – really fucked me – declaring ownership with every push.

When I came, he covered my mouth with his hand and forced my head to the side. He left his hand there, pinning my head to the pillow while he finished. When he was done, he moved my head back, gingerly, so I would look at him. He lingered there, holding me, my entire body swallowed up by his one arm. He stroked my cheek and smiled a small heartbreaking smile. It was the one of the most controlled lovemaking sessions that Michael and I ever had. After we were through, I must have drifted off because at six, when the wake-up call came, I woke to find Michael had coffee waiting for me.

I smiled at him and sat up in bed. He smiled back at me and kissed me gently on the lips. Then, for some reason, I did something I'd never before done with Michael: I took the lead. I put both of my hands on his face and held them there. I felt his entire body tense, ready to break away. But he didn't. He relaxed. I reached up and ran my fingers through his mussed-up hair. He held his breath, just watching me... feeling me. He closed his eyes. Time stood still as I let my hands run purposely across his scalp. He grabbed my hands in his and lingered for another moment, staring at me. Then he kissed me. Finally he released me, and shook his head as he pulled away. He got up and grabbed his cell.

As I drank my perfectly delicious coffee with fresh cream, I let myself imagine what it was like to be Mrs. Michael M. I allowed myself to fantasize on this one particular morning because I was in such an exceptional place. Once I went home, fantasy over. It had to be. I couldn't do that to myself, to torture myself over something that could never happen. I was his mistress, and that's all I would ever be. But on that one morning, I imagined lying in a much larger bed, the servants popping champagne and preparing fresh croissants and strawberries for our breakfast, his first wife left far behind somewhere in Sweden. I imagined spending the day riding our champion horses, galloping across our estate, stopping for a picnic under an elm tree beside a stream where he'd fuck me –

hard – riding me like one of his horses. He would keep the riding crop in his hand, snapping it every so often; the sound pulsating through my body, needlessly reminding me of his absolute power. He would speak only to say, "It's you, Bella, it's only ever been you." And then he would fuck me – harder still – whispering "Shhh…" into my ear as he wiped back my tears. Sure, that was pretty close to how our life was, but if he married me, he would have a piece of paper that proved that he owned me. God how I wanted that.

Michael was on the phone so I drank my coffee without speaking. When I finished, I got up, dressed, and he led me downstairs. And that's when I saw them, there, in his living room – the same living room we had walked through only a few hours earlier – dozens of roses, fruit baskets, candies, and wild flowers. An entire florist's inventory sprawled across the foyer, growing up the staircase and taking over the top floor. We had to step around the flowers to make our way down. What was going on? Did the servants bring these out every morning when Michael descended the stairs? Who were they all for? It made no sense, but I was wise enough not to ask. As Michael hurried me out a side door attached to a small garage, I noticed a card on one bouquet: "So sorry. Deepest regrets. Signed, Highway Patrol." I knew it was time to go home. We climbed into a black Mercedes with exceptionally dark windows and started a silent trip back to Manhattan.

When we got to my apartment building, Michael leaned over and kissed me. He said nothing of the flowers and nothing of the night. As I started to get out he said, "Bella… sometimes people misunderstand situations." I nodded and left wondering who he thought had misunderstood, the police or me.

Michael and I had a fight. Well, more accurately, I had a fight with Michael. We had been together over a year and I was tiring of being the fuck buddy. The fantasy of being his wife and living in that house made my reality more hateful. I wished something more had come from our night at his mansion, that there would be some confidence confided in me. I wanted to be more to him than ever before, but still he kept me at bay. I imagined if things remained as they were, I would be Michael's mistress until I was thirty and then he'd dispose of me. Maybe literally. All I knew was it was time for more. I was also in an exceptionally grumpy mood.

I knew when I was overstepping my boundaries with Michael, but that night I didn't care. While I was getting dressed to go out, I kept playing our relationship over and over in my mind. I was twenty-one, and what was I? I was still treated like a toy, even though I knew his feelings for me ran deeper than that. Why wouldn't he show them? Act on them? Take the next step, whatever that was. I was his party girl, and I was beginning to feel like my mother. I hated that feeling. I had successfully avoided my mother for most of my time with Michael. I would have been too embarrassed to explain the cuts and bruises I was modeling. "What are you doing, Victoria?" my mother would always ask. And what could I tell her?

"Gee Mom, the usual. You know, some good-natured S&M with Tony Soprano."

My mother's call caught me by surprise. I needed to vent, so I told her how Michael still kept some distance between us and how I was tiring of it. I waited for a response, listening to my mother suck down a Camel. My mother didn't just smoke her cigarettes, she didn't inhale them, she sucked the life out of them... like she sucked the life out of anyone who stayed with her long enough. Finally, she said, "Well, he's just busy, Vicki. Go shopping, you'll feel better. Oh! Speaking of which, I saw this outrageous little dress on Mary Hart the other day! I just kept picturing it on you, especially now that you're so beautifully skinny—"

"Mom, he's here," I lied. "I gotta go." I hung up the phone angrier than when I had picked it up.

Admittedly, I was out of sorts from the conversation with my mother when Michael picked me up. But it was his suggestion of dinner on the Upper East and Au Bar afterwards that pushed me over the edge.

"Can't we do anything new?" We were heading uptown in his newest Porsche, the Carrera convertible.

"What would you like to do?" Michael asked.

"I don't know. Go to a museum? A play? Something except eat and drink."

"We're eating first," was his answer. Then he said, "Let your hair down. I don't like it up."

"Fuck you," I said. I was testing him and we both knew it. Hell, even bad attention was better than no attention.

"What did you say?" Michael abhorred cursing. Especially from me. He found cursing morally objectionable. Go figure.

"You heard me." I was on fire, my heart racing, my palms sweating. I was being a bitch to a man who carried a gun, who led a secret life, who was.... well... anyway, I felt alive. I felt brave, and daring. "Fuck you," I said with resolve. There. I had thrown down the gauntlet and there was no turning back. I would never be a virgin to him again. I wanted to shake Michael to his core, to affect him the way he affected me, so it was his lack of response that really set me off. I jumped out of the car at the next red light and began walking in the opposite direction. He got out of the car.

"Get in," he said, but I ignored him. I just kept walking, absolutely thrilled I made him get out of his car. "Get in!" he said again. I giggled at the idea that I had made Michael M. raise his voice. Michael M. M&M - like the candy. Hard outside, melty inside. Wisely, I kept that thought to myself. I heard the car move behind me.

"Shit," I said. I lost. I pushed it too far. He wouldn't bother with me again that evening; I'd proven I was trouble. He was going to let me walk home, in heels, and I deserved it. I was stupid enough to get out of the car without cab fare.

But Michael didn't leave. Instead, he came after me. He threw the car into reverse and backed up the entire block. The car jumped the sidewalk just in front of me and blocked my way completely. "You could have killed me!" I screamed. People on the sidewalk began to watch. There was, after all, a shrieking woman and a silver-gray Porsche blocking the sidewalk on Fifty-first Street.

Michael didn't answer. He hated a scene even more than he hated confrontation. He took my arm, led me to the car, and pushed me in. He locked the car and me in it. I could have opened the door but he was making a point, so I stayed. Besides, I got what I wanted; I got my reaction. He walked around to the driver's side of the car, unlocked it, and got in.

Michael turned the car in the opposite direction and once again I realized that I had no idea where we were going. Silently, he drove down the East Side, past my building and across town. I didn't recognize the area; it certainly wasn't the way to any restaurant or club that I knew. Michael didn't stop for a light until we got to the meat packing district on the West Side. He found a secluded spot.

Michael pulled the car over and immediately a she-male approached us. She looked in the window, gave me the finger, and walked away. I laughed at the attempted solicitation, but Michael was staring dead ahead out the windshield. After what seemed an eternity, he turned to me and spoke.

"You embarrassed me tonight, Victoria. Don't ever do that again. Ever." I knew I was supposed to nod in agreement but instead, I snapped at him.

"I'm sick of this," I said. "All of it. I'm madly in love with you but I don't know who you really are. You devour me but keep this huge distance between us, and you... you treat me like I'm for hire but don't pay me! I'm tired of it! Nick... the mysterious trips... your mansions... the police department! Come on! I'm not stupid."

"Then stop acting stupid," he said. "Shut up right now."

"No! I will not shut up! I'm not some dumb little old-world girl from Italy or Sweden or wherever who's just grateful to be in your presence. Man, your wife must be brain-dead." He grabbed me by both wrists and held me hard. "You're hurting me," I said. And his dark eyes turned cold. I tried to fix the situation. "I shouldn't have said anything about your wife."

"No," he said. "Forget about her. This is between you and me. This has nothing to do with anyone else." And I smiled at him. I couldn't help it. It's what I wanted to hear. At that moment I was clearly more important than his wife or anyone else in his life. He pulled me closer and squeezed my wrists harder.

"Ow," I said, pleading.

But he didn't let go. He stared at me and spoke. "Don't ever get out of the car again unless I tell you to. This is not a joke. This isn't about having a tantrum."

I knew I should back down, but I was too hot, both sexually and emotionally. I wanted to know how far he would go. When I was with Dr. Fifth Avenue I would get turned on because he could save a life. That night, I was even more excited by the idea that Michael could take one, even mine. I started to giggle, uncontrollably.

"Are you listening?" He took both of my wrists in his left hand and put his right hand behind my neck. He forced my head back – hard – to look at him. "Are you listening?"

I didn't want to answer. I wanted to push every button he had. I wanted to make him as crazy as I was. He yanked my head even farther back and my teeth slammed together. Then and only then did I get scared. But I still couldn't bring myself to say anything. He stayed so cool, and I wanted to push, push, push. No one could stay that way, that unaffected, forever. Not even him.

He took his hand from behind my neck and raised it to the seat next to my face. He was positioned to slap me, but I wasn't worried. He loved my face too much; there was no way he would ever leave a mark on it. So I was victorious. I had pushed him into action and he was left with nowhere to go.

I had never, in all my life, ever felt like I did at that moment. I was with my lover – the man I adored and feared, the man who unquestionably owned me – and I had no idea what was going to happen next. Pure lustful fear radiated throughout my entire being. Even my scalp was tingling. Michael squeezed my wrists tighter. I began to lose feeling in my hands and I began to get wet. I desperately wanted to kiss him so I leaned forward, but he shook me by the wrists.

"Listen. You are going to listen to me," he said. "This is not something you can fuck around with. Your life could be in danger if you do not do everything exactly the way I tell you. Do you hear me?"

I heard the uncontrolled laughter explode from my mouth. I honestly hadn't meant to let it out, but I didn't know how to stop it. It started somewhere in my stomach and crept up across my chest and out into my shoulders. Finally, my mouth twitched and a long, loud laugh came pouring forth.

Wham! I felt a slap across my face. Michael had hit me. Hard. It was the first time I'd ever been hit and I was stunned. I didn't cry or complain, I just shook free of his grasp and held my cheek. I looked at him, wide-eyed and awestruck. I loved him.

"I didn't want to do that but you need to listen, now. Do you understand?"

"Yes," I said, nodding. Intellectually, I understood that I should want to get away from him, but neither my body nor my heart wanted to go anywhere. I told myself I couldn't leave because there was nowhere for me to go, that I was in a bad part of town and there was no one to help me except for a few she-males who were all busy themselves. But I wasn't kidding anyone. Least of all myself. I wanted a rise out of him, no matter what the cost. And the cost, well frankly, it turned me on even more.

I held my face and looked at Michael. At that very instant I was overcome with lust like I'd never felt before (it surpassed even the night with the gun). I ached from wanting him so badly. My cheek still stung, and I said, "I'm sorry."

He seemed to understand me. He undid his belt and I leaned over and blew him until I couldn't take it. I tried to mount him but there wasn't enough room for the two of us, so he pulled me out of the car and bent me over the fender. He took me from behind as a small crowd of she-males looked on, shouting supportive comments like: "You go, girl!" and "Mm-hm! That's what I'm talking about! You do him good!"

I came fast; he pulled out moments later, right before he came. Not knowing what else to do I stood there, bent over, feeling him drip down my ass while he got a rag out of the front trunk. I was well aware of my naked ass exposed on the street and felt the sting of my cheek. Michael wiped himself off of me and then slapped my butt, telling me to pull my skirt down. I did, and then I stepped out of my panties which had dropped onto the filthy street. As I went to put them into my bag, Michael grabbed them and walked over to one of the she-males. I was tousled and worn, but captivated by Michael. He borrowed a lighter, and set the panties on fire. The she-males gathered 'round like Girl Scouts at a bonfire. Someone let out a sincere "Ooh" as the panties burned. We were all under Michael's spell. All that was missing from our New York campfire story were marshmallows. One she-male looked at me intently with big, soft cow eyes and we exchanged a brief smile. I wondered what she had gone through that night. After the panties burned, Michael kicked the ashes around and the ladies applauded.

"Good thing they were only a thong, girlfriend!" one said, and they all laughed.

"If you ever want a real woman, you come see me, honey!" another said.

Michael put me into the car. I sat carefully, trying not to wet the seat, and he drove me home.

That night, I replayed the entire scene in my head. I iced my cheek but didn't change my outfit. I knew I shouldn't have liked what happened. I should just want to forget it. But the truth was, I loved it all. I climbed into bed dressed, and masturbated. I fell asleep as soon as I brought myself to orgasm.

I saw Michael on and off for the rest of that year. We never again mentioned that night and I was sure never to ask him too much about himself. The rough sex kept up but every time he forced me, I wanted him all the more. I was an addict and Michael was both my drug and my supplier. I spent years of my life as just another piece of property that happened to belong to Michael M. But somehow through the haze, I knew as long as I was with Michael I was a prisoner, unable to grow or develop as a woman. I would always be who he wanted me to be and nothing more.

Late in the year, Michael went back to Italy and the relationship petered out. I was sure he went to his wife. I understood the break-up was the best thing for both of us, but I was just devastated. I knew that by letting me go he felt that he was protecting me. I knew that it was the right thing to do but it took me many months – and many sleepless nights – to get over it all: his money, his power, him. I missed Michael for years to come, and I knew that, despite it all, Michael was the one man I would ever actually love.

CHAPTER 3: HADES

"Hades was the third brother among the Olympians, who drew for his share the underworld and the rule over the dead. He was also called the God of Wealth. He had a hat which made whoever wore it invisible. It was rare that he left his dark realm to visit Olympus or the earth, nor was he urged to do so. He was not a welcome visitor."

After Michael, I had to completely rebuild my life. I didn't know how to start or where to turn. For a solid year after he left, my body still ached for Michael and because of Michael. And life without Michael's wealth was just depressing. I felt like a nobody, like no one knew that I existed and even if they did, no one cared. And my lifestyle... oh God. After just one week, eating Lean Cuisine from Jack's 99 Cent store and shopping at Lord of the Fleas ceased to be campy and turned just plain sad. I would walk by our old spots and hyperventilate: The Plaza, Au Bar, the countless restaurants, the private clubs. I'd close my eyes and pray that I would see him. That he would be back in New York and we'd pick up where we had left off. But then I'd open my eyes and nothing. Michael was gone.

I had to force myself to spend my time in more constructive ways than moping and swooning. Although Michael was generous enough to pay my rent for a few months after he left, what I needed was to make money. I couldn't go back to the Javits Center – it would remind me of him – so I couldn't book any more trade shows. That meant I needed to change modeling agencies. I did, but I still stuck with a lower-end agency. I just didn't have the desire or the energy to go chasing after a better agent. Ironically, I eventually found myself to be a coveted catalog model, the very thing Dr. Fifth Avenue had warned me about. I modeled cars, hats, clothes, anything that would pay the bills. I sent the clippings home to my mother who was thrilled. "There!" she said over the phone, "Didn't I tell you to become a model! Now you're actually doing something worthwhile and cashing in on your looks!"

*   *   *

During the height of my second-rate modeling career, I met John, a fifty-plus, highly placed, fast-talking, New York garmento. John was at least 6'3" with gray, wavy hair and black eyebrows. He had a deep voice and a smile that made most women smile back, me included. My booker had told me John was looking for a catalog model for his ads in the trade papers. Dressed in jeans, a white t-shirt and high-heeled boots, I was off to snag a job. What I found was my next boyfriend.

John's only noticeable shortcoming was that he liked them young. Really young. And usually that meant that he liked them stupid. At twenty-two, I was older than John liked, but I could still lie about my age effortlessly – at least for the moment. Despite John's requirements, I knew that twenty-two was prime mistress age; three more years, however, and I'd most definitely be over the hill.

John made no excuses that he liked his mistresses to be babies – and "babes" – or that he got them by calling modeling agencies and setting up go-sees. I didn't care. It took the guesswork out of finding my next boyfriend. By now, I was pretty experienced with older men and had learned how to handle myself in the city. During my months away from Michael, I fought off my depression by trying to convince myself that there would be someone better out there for me. (I don't think I really bought it.) So I had put myself back into mistress boot camp and groomed myself to be the perfect companion to another wealthy, high profile man. That meant being poised, witty at dinners, beautifully dressed, and most importantly, an expert at fellatio.

Since Michael, I knew to ask around and learn all that I could about my potential men. Across the board, John got rave reviews. He was a two-woman man: one wife, one mistress. He had current and negative blood tests, good cars, and was supposedly very generous. The darker side of John was that he was rumored to have made his fortune by owning a multitude of sweatshops in Vietnam and China. Since the jury was still out, I chose not to think about that. All I wanted from John was a straight married man/mistress relationship with normal sex. I was still recouping from Michael and had no interest in falling head over heels – or in getting involved with anything kinky – ever again. I needed to protect myself.

*   *   *

On our first date in mid-summer, John picked me up in his Bentley complete with driver. Well thank heavens! I had been genuinely worried that I would never do better than Michael's entourage of cars. I smiled as I glided into the back seat; the car was cool and smelled like a mixture of new leather and some sweet cologne I couldn't place. We went to Marylou's on Ninth Street for dinner and had a quiet table in the garden in back. We laughed and talked and John commented on how beautiful I looked and how he loved that I didn't pluck my eyebrows. Please. I spent fifty dollars a month on eyebrow maintenance and that didn't count gel, brushes, filler, or a tip. But what was a girl to do but to thank him and tell him how handsome he looked as well.

Over a shared dessert of melon sorbet, John laid his cards on the table. "I'm married," he said. "I will always be married, to my wife, so if that's not okay with you—"

"I'm eighteen. I'm just here for some fun!" I said with a laugh. Two lies in eight words. Wow.

"Great! I'd like you to be available to travel and not to sleep with anyone else while you see me. In return, I'll take good care of you and I will not sleep with anyone else either... except my wife, of course." He sipped his wine.

Okay... our date had turned into a job interview. Should I have brought references? The horny plastic surgeon? The kinky importer/exporter? "Fine by me," I said.

He kissed me. I closed my eyes and inhaled deeply. That was it, Kourous for Men. That was the sweet smell in the car. He smelled terrific. Even better than Dr. Fifth Avenue. I lingered for a moment.

So this was okay. I was moving on without Dr. Fifth Avenue hurling lightning bolts or Michael drowning me in a tidal wave. I just had to hope that John and his yummy scent had an equally tantalizing bank account. When I opened my eyes, John was staring at me with a big grin on his face. Hot diggety dog. If he was this happy with me over a measly dinner, imagine what I'd get for my blowjob expertise! Plus, John was big in the world of New York businessman – as in, the cover of *Forbes* big – so his choosing me proved that I had become quite a commodity as a mistress. We finished dessert, feeding each other, and went back to the car.

I was pretty content sitting in the back of the Bentley, holding hands with my coverboy. The car rolled along. I had no idea where we were headed, but I was sure that it would be fabulous. So when the driver pulled up in front of a rundown apartment building on the Upper West Side, I was confused. I just assumed that it was a hot new club I hadn't heard about yet. John didn't say anything as we walked to the front door. I looked around for a bouncer but there wasn't one. Heck, there wasn't even a doorman. There was, however, a group of guys hanging out on the front stoop, popping in and out of the lobby. "Hey," I said as casually as I could, thinking that maybe it was a rave and these guys decided who got in.

"Hey, Mama," one said. "Why don't you leave Daddy over there and come play wit' us for awhile."

"Yeah, Baby," another said. Together, they reminded me of Lenny and Squiggy.

I turned to John. "What is this place?" I asked, but John didn't say anything. He was too busy enjoying the attention I was getting. Two guys wearing Yankees' hats joined the group to add creative sound effects to the already offensive catcalls. "What are we doing here?" I whispered, knowing that this would never have happened with Michael.

"You don't have to whisper," he said with a smile. "It's our place."

"Our place?" I said, looking back over my shoulder at the boys.

I had no idea what John could possibly mean by "our place," but I followed him to an elevator and up three stories. He led me to a back apartment and unlocked the door. I stepped inside. Good Lord. I didn't know what I expected to find, but I knew it couldn't be much worse. Maybe twenty or so cats eating the dead body of his last girlfriend would have been worse. Maybe. But this place? This was what a man who had a chauffeur-driven Bentley called an apartment? John scurried to a corner and turned on a lamp as some unidentifiable creature scurried in the opposite direction. Things did not improve with light. The room was far worse than any dive motel room Michael and I had ever shared. I would have worked three real jobs – and all of them in deli meats – to be sure that I never had to live in a dump like this. This was our apartment.

There was a run-down galley kitchen complete with peeling paint, a missing handle on the hot water, and two champagne glasses adorned with generic flowers and faux gold rims. One had a pink lipstick stain on it. Fascinated, I walked to them and touched one. "Oh, my last girlfriend bought those," he said.

"No kidding?" John was making such a bad impression I figured the poor thing probably paid for them herself. The rest of the apartment went downhill from there. Since it was a studio, I walked from the kitchen directly into the bedroom. He didn't even bother with a couch. The bedroom consisted of an old bed frame supporting a king-sized mattress. The mattress was bare. Better it than me.

"Take your jacket off," John said like an adolescent anticipating his first kiss. I looked around in earnest for where to drop my jacket and decided on a lone – three-legged – kitchen chair. It was better off covered.

"What is this place?" I asked. I heard the demand in my voice so I covered it with an enormous fake smile.

"Our love nest," John said, jumping onto the bed. Wasn't he worried about catching something? "You can stay here if you like!"

"What, and get bugs?" was what I wanted to ask, but I said nothing. I only nodded.

Okay, there was obviously only one reason that I was there, so I figured I might as well get it over with. The sooner it was over, the sooner I could go somewhere else. Anywhere else. And there was another reason that I was willing: I hadn't had sex since Michael. I still needed to purge him from my system and I hoped having sex with another man would do it. I unbuttoned my shirt and laid it carefully on the bed trying to avoid direct contact with the mattress. We had sex, and I was amazed at how easy John was to please. Woman on top (I barely needed to touch the bed!) and straight sex worked best for John. Halfway through the encounter, he reached up and grabbed my breasts.

"Firm! Are they real?"

"Of course they're real. I'm just young." Somehow this answer satisfied him. Unfortunately, he was the only one who was satisfied that day... or at any other time for that matter. I never had an orgasm while I was with John. Never once. Though I didn't care. Sex that satisfies him is the obligation of a mistress, but where that satisfaction occurs, well, that may need to be negotiable.

*   *   *

Later that night, after the Bentley dropped me off in front of my building I heard an odd noise coming from under one of the cars on the street, the faintest of cries – a mewing to be exact. I looked under the car and sure enough, hiding next to a front tire was a tiny, solid black kitten. He couldn't have been more than a month old.

"Hey!" I said, reaching under the car. "You're going to get hurt. You need to get out of there." But the kitten just hissed at me. I reached farther. "Come on, I'm trying to help you." The kitten arched his back and hissed again. I had to laugh at the chutzpah of this four-ounce ball of fur. "All right," I said, "your decision. But you're going to get squashed when this car moves." No reaction from the kitten.

A couple walked by staring at me. "There's a cat under the car," I said. "Really. I'm not talking to myself. You want a cat?" The couple hurried away.

"You know," I said to the kitten, "they could have been a mommy and a daddy for you. Now you're stuck." The kitten mewed again. "What, me? Oh no way. You got the wrong person." I squatted next to the car. "You'd be a huge hassle. There'd be fur everywhere, a litter box, you'd scratch up my shoes. No way. Sorry, Charlie. But you need to get out of there." The kitten sat down. "Look, I'm on my knees here. And I'm wearing Prada. I don't think you fully understand the magnitude of this gesture. Come on out." The kitten didn't move. "Fine. Play it your way. I've dealt with tough guys before. I'm going now. Take care of yourself, okay?" The kitten stood back up, he was shaky on his legs. "I know you must be hungry. And scared. But I know my limitations and that's good, right? Trust me, you'll be much happier out here than you would be with me." Just then a taxi barreled by. "Look, you need to go someplace safe! Well, see you."

I headed to the deli to grab some tea. I couldn't help but look behind me. Sure enough, my little friend poked his head out. "Good!" I said. "Now go home!" But he just sat there. He watched me walk into the deli for my tea. I came out with three tiny cans of gourmet cat food. "Okay, look," I said to the kitten. "I'll feed you this one time, and then that's it. I asked the deli guys and they said no one's asked about you. So where do you come from?" I opened the top of one can and the kitten gobbled it up. "You were starving, weren't you? I know what that's like. Here." I opened another and he gobbled it up as quickly as he did the first. Then he threw up. "Okay, whoa! See, that's why you're not coming home with me. Slow down." He did. When he finished the third can, he waddled over to me, purring. "You're welcome," I said. "Now take care of yourself." I started to walk away, and this time the kitten seemed to cry because I was leaving him. "What?" I asked. "Okay, here's the deal. I will come out tomorrow morning and if you're still here, I'll feed you again." He waddled closer. "Look, you're probably covered in fleas! There is no way you're coming in with me." The kitten looked at me with the saddest blue eyes I had ever seen. "Fine. Just for tonight. Then tomorrow I'm taking you to the Humane Society to get you adopted." The kitten hissed as I approached. "Oh they're nice there. Come on." I scooped up my new friend.

I had already taken Charlie to the Humane Society for a check-up when I got a call from Dr. Fifth Avenue. (Charlie and I struck a deal – the first sugar-daddy who happened to be allergic to cats and Charlie was out.) Dr. Fifth Avenue still checked on me periodically; he claimed that he was interested in my career but mostly he asked about my love life. We spoke only once while I was with Michael. "Those Italians can be so hot blooded," he told me that day. "Watch out for yourself." But since Dr. Fifth Avenue found out that I was alone again, he made a resurgence. "So, who ya seein'?" he asked.

"Just somebody," I said, watching Charlie settle into his new bed for a nap.

"What's he do?" Dr. Fifth Avenue asked.

"Some garmento."

"Names, please!"

"But just between us," I said, "because he's married." We shared a laugh. Then I let it drop. "John K." I sat back, smirking.

"Wait a minute... John K.! *The* John K.! You have to be kidding me!" Dr. Fifth Avenue was truly impressed. A barrage of questions followed. "Where did you meet? How rich is he? What kind of cars does he drive?" And most importantly, "What's he like ... you know, in bed?" I savored his interest and admiration. Then he said it, "He's the president of my tennis club you know!" Oh. I didn't know. Eventually my men would have to overlap, I just didn't expect for it to happen so soon. Hopefully, my past life of slicing deli meats would remain a secret. Dr. Fifth Avenue kept going, tripping over his words, "Do you know that his picture is painted on the wall of the Palm?" Yes, I was already privy to that very important piece of information. Dr. Fifth Avenue was stunned. Then he gathered his wits. "I can't believe I had you before John K.!"

"Hold on there. You had me?" I could be demanding with Dr. Fifth Avenue by then, I had passed him up.

"You know what I mean, be a sport. Hey! I just leased a Chrysler convertible for the summer, want to have lunch Thursday?"

A Chrysler? Oh no. But then I thought of John's love nest, and that, coupled with my complete lack of affection for John, made lunch with Dr. Fifth Avenue sound like a hot prospect. Besides, my relationship with John seemed to be backfiring – the more time I spent with him, the more I missed Michael.

"Lunch, I guess," I said. "But oh! I can't... I—"

"Have a date?"

"Yes, actually."

"Well then, how 'bout after?"

I glanced at my watch. "Got another date?" John asked as we sat at lunch on Thursday. I did have another date, with Dr. Fifth Avenue. And soon. The date was really no big deal, but I couldn't wait to break free from John. I don't know what it was about John that made me so uncomfortable. So unhappy. Every time I was with him, I just wanted to get away. What's more, it was a Thursday in July, the last day of the week that married men in Manhattan were free before they go off to join their loving wives in the Hamptons. It was prime wining and dining time for all of us mistresses, and I decided that I couldn't waste the entire day on John.

I stared at the menu and tried to find the item not with the least amount of calories or the least amount of garlic, but the item that took the least amount of time to prepare. Found it: tomato and mozzarella salad. Already prepped, waiting to be drizzled with balsamic vinegar and whisk! Gone. I glanced anxiously from my menu to John and nibbled on the corner of my lip. I had begun this nasty habit of lip biting just about the same time that I started dating John. Completely unaware, I would gnaw at my lip until little layers of skin peeled off, leaving sore red spots behind. I had to wear lip balm before lipstick and then lip gloss just to cover up the damage. And most of my men were fundamentally opposed to lip gloss.

I stared at John. How could a man own and operate a large clothing company but not be able to pick an appetizer? He felt my stare. "How about tomato and mozzarella?" I asked. But just as John began considering my suggestion, the unthinkable happened, a business acquaintance of John's walked through the door and spotted John and me. In the world of man and mistress, this was never supposed to happen. Suddenly, this intruder had an unimaginable amount of power over John. That is, the intruder knew not only that John had a mistress, but who that mistress was. It made John extremely vulnerable.

Knowing this would require energy I didn't have, I accidentally bit my lip and winced from the pain. John glared at me and raised his eyebrows. It was show time and I had better perform. Problem was, I didn't have the time or the strength to entertain two men. Heck, I barely had the patience to be witty and fun for one. But there we were, man, mistress and intruder, all in our assigned roles: John, nervous and needing to look important; the acquaintance, smiling wider than I thought was humanly possible; and me, bosom inflated and ego deflated, wanting only to escape.

"Bob!" John said, "Bob! Over here... sit down." And Bob did. A few introductions and poof, they were full into business/tennis banter. I scanned Bob up and down. He wore the generic New York independent businessman wardrobe: dark pleated slacks, loafers, and a three-button cashmere henley in whichever color they felt best accentuated their eyes or their tans.

I fidgeted, looked at my watch, played with my fork. John looked at me – making sure that Bob would hear – and then asked, "Got a go-see?" There. Now Bob would know that I was a model. It was of utmost importance to these fifty-plus-year-old men that their female companions be models, as if one-third their age and beautiful wasn't enough. And so the competition was off. Bob explained that he was Bob Meters of Meters Copy Machines.

"Oh," I said, smiling, "how wonderful for you."

I listened as John lied about how well business was going for him. I knew that he was lying because I had already seen four different drivers in the short amount of time that I'd been around. One of them told me it was because John never paid them. John and Bob continued on and on over salads and right through cappuccinos, competing like schoolboys on a playground, and it was mostly for my benefit. Why, I don't know. All I cared about was how much my boyfriend had and how much was being given to me. Like I gave a damn who won the last tennis game or golf game or whatever. It was such an odd dance we all danced – with such intricate choreography. Unless – then a strange thought entered my head – was it possible that John didn't understand the rules? Did he think that I was with him just because I liked him? Was he trying to impress me? Maybe if I waited long enough, he would give me his Varsity letter jacket next spring! I nearly spit my cappuccino at the thought.

Sitting there, I found myself waxing philosophical. I couldn't help but wonder why any of us were there. What did I really get for my little performance? And more importantly, why did they risk their wives and families for lunch and sex? Could marriage be *that* inconsequential? Did cappuccino taste that much better with a twenty-year-old sitting next to you? And even better with an eighteen-year-old at your side? All I wanted was for my god to share his wealth and I made no secret of my objective. What was it that they wanted?

The attention came back to me. Bob asked what I did besides, "Obviously model." What could I say?

"I'm a not-very-successful gold-digger-slash-mistress. I'll flop on my back for any rich man who might pay off. Speaking of which, do you have lots and lots of money?" Uh... no. So, instead, like a properly trained little puppy – I mean, mistress – I said, "I date John." There it was, succinct and applauded.

"Oh well! Good for you!" Bob said, impressed. "A lot of women want that job, I can assure you!" Really. Well, whoever she was, she'd better have a strong stomach to handle that apartment.

Bob and John raised their overgrown and horrible eyebrows at each other and nodded their little nods. They exchanged their secret men's club approval of me. I was Max in the land of the Wild Things. Everyone raise your cappuccino cup! "Cheers!" Clink, smile, clink, smile, clink.

John droned on and on. I was sure that he was consuming all of the air around me, his big mouth opening and closing widely. I was transfixed. While I stared at a piece of half-chewed biscotti rolling around on his tongue, I forced myself to remember what I was getting out of the relationship: a chauffeur-driven Bentley Monday through Friday in winter months, and Monday through

Thursday in summer. Plus rent. And clothes. Unfortunately they were only clothes from his collection; oh, how I missed my shopping sprees at Gucci with Michael. Despite the obvious but small monetary gain, something was wrong... but what? It kept escaping me. It wasn't John exactly; I didn't much like him but for the most part he was who he claimed to be. And judging from Dr. Fifth Avenue's reaction, John would definitely raise my stock as a mistress. So what was it?

John smiled at me with a big green wad of lettuce stuck between his front teeth. I'm sure Bob noticed it too but I was the one who would end up swallowing it when John kissed me. My stomach flipped. I pushed myself to focus on the Bentley and John's other good qualities. What were those again? Oh yes, John was easily manipulated. For example, my rent was $1100 a month but I told him it was $1700. This was my discreet way to get an extra bit of spending cash.

The waitress came to take our dessert order. What was cappuccino and biscotti? I had no time for the formalities of dessert. I had to go; it was dangerously close to time for date number two. More importantly, I was just so sick of John all of a sudden. Grossed out, really. So, what else could I do? Quietly, I whispered an offer into John's ear. Bob didn't hear what I said, but he witnessed the exchange, and that alone would create enough gossip at the club to turn the mere president into a god. Even if it was only the god of the Underworld. John politely declined dessert and made his excuses. He jumped up, paid the bill, and left the copy machine man wondering what exactly I had offered, because there is only so much you can do during sex ... right?

Luckily, John was an innocent and I hadn't offered much. All I had to do was go through with it. We got into the Bentley and I slid the partition shut. I undid his pants and blew him, careful not to let him mess up my hair. In the interest of tidiness, I swallowed and then fumbled with my empty Altoid box. An Altoid would have been nice. Under the guise of rushing to prepare for a dinner party, I had the car drop me off at Grace's Marketplace on Seventy-first Street. I kissed John goodbye – he gave me a closed-mouthed peck on the lips – and he promised to call on Monday.

I watched John's car pull away from the safety of Grace's window wondering which study that I had read was right, the one that said semen had very few calories or the one that said it was loaded with them. Lost in thought I turned around and bumped into a woman who actually was shopping for a dinner party. She was chatting away, pushing a little boy in a stroller. They both seemed blissfully happy. "Sorry," I said.

"No problem!" the woman said. She smiled and so did the child. The little boy told me that his name was Nathaniel. I realized that I was standing so close to them that Mommy could probably smell John on my breath. I backed off. All right, the woman wasn't a virgin, but still. Then, just as she asked me to hand her a loaf of pumpernickel, I was startled by a knock on the window. I turned. There was Dr. Fifth Avenue, staring in, his head sandwiched between two loaves of onion sourdough, his blue eyes looking maniacal through the glass. It was just as well. Mommy wouldn't want me touching her pumpernickel if she knew where my hands had just been. Dr. Fifth Avenue pointed to his watch to show me it was getting late.

I walked outside, looking back at the woman and Nathaniel. The boy reached up with all his might to place the loaf of pumpernickel on the counter. His mother waited eagerly to applaud him for his victory while the rest of the line shuffled and mumbled in frustration. Dr. Fifth Avenue looked in to see what all the fuss was about.

"New mothers," he said, shaking his head. "They think that everyone in the world has as much time as they do."

Of course I knew better – even Liz had been frazzled when Megan was that age – but I didn't say anything. No matter what I said, he would know better. Almost immediately I regretted my decision to see him. I thought about turning around to pick up a little treat for Charlie – some whitefish salad, maybe. But I stayed. We walked in silence for a few minutes. I could still taste John in my mouth. "Glad you were free for lunch!" he said, sounding truly happy.

"Yeah." We ducked into a BBQ place not far from Grace's.

"The food's outrageous here!" he said. "Wow, do I have a craving." I read the sign: BBQ for two, all you can eat, $8.95. How outrageous could it be?

I ordered an iced tea and watched Dr. Fifth Avenue devour a plate of ribs. I pushed the lemon around with my straw, but I couldn't even find the strength to take a sip. I hadn't seen Dr. Fifth Avenue since our break-up, but he picked up right where we'd left off. I wondered if he would notice that I had changed. For one thing, I had lost ten pounds since he last saw me. Or maybe the scars on my wrists? They were slightly raised and still a light red; completely obvious. But seeing them would require him to pay attention to someone other than himself. Come to think of it, John never noticed them either. Or if he did, he never mentioned them. He probably just didn't give a crap. I saw changes in Dr. Fifth Avenue, however. He had significantly less hair and he seemed to have found the ten pounds I lost. His hands were beginning to look old as well, spotted even... or maybe... was it? Oh. It was just BBQ sauce from the feast. After some small talk he got to his point.

"Tell me about John," he asked.

"What's to tell?" I wasn't being coy. It was an honest question. Dr. Fifth Avenue squinted his eyes and after some thought I did have something to say. I leaned over the table like a conspirator and he joined me, rubbing his hands first in a wet-nap and then together, in anticipation. It all spilled out. "Well, to start, we go to this horrible apartment on the Upper West Side. I hate it. I feel like a cheap hook—"

"An apartment! Good idea. Any idea how he hides it from his wife?"

I felt like crying. I was not engaged in mistress espionage, and it wasn't my job to steal John's trade secrets. But I didn't cry. Instead, I moved my iced tea aside, made sure that no one was looking and kissed Dr. Fifth Avenue. I pushed my tongue all the way to the back of his mouth and rolled it around until I was certain that I had deposited some of John's cum.

"You taste great!" Dr. Fifth Avenue said. I smirked and added Sweet 'n Low to my tea.

John and I went to LA. Finally, I was sure, my patience would pay off. At last I would be living the high life again. We stayed at a five star hotel in Beverly Hills, I shopped on Rodeo Drive every day, and any drug I desired was available to me, from amphetamines to X and everything in between. Our evenings were spent in secret little nightclubs where waitresses walked around with endless trays of cocaine, all for our snorting pleasure. Everything was available and the drugs were always free. Unfortunately, I just wasn't a big druggie. Sure, I'd experimented, who hadn't? But nothing really turned me on. Weed was nice, but coke made my nose and esophagus burn. I tried X just to see if it would improve my sex life with John. Something had to improve my sex life with John. Ah, if only X could have marked the spot. Well, at least it made masturbating more fun.

I was doing all right in LA. I was pretty much living the coveted mistress life and I was able to keep my brain off Michael, for at least part of the day. The rest of the time I longed for him. Besides shopping, I slept late, ate by the pool, and lay in the sun on the balcony of our suite. So why did I feel so unfulfilled? Okay, so I really didn't like John, but still, that shouldn't have mattered. And stupid as it sounds, I missed Charlie. He had moved from his bed up to mine and I missed falling asleep to his purring. I called my doorman every day to make sure that he was feeding Charlie. I was falling into a dangerous situation – I was becoming a cat woman pining over a lost love. I needed to change my ways.

One day I argued with the maid. "I have to make the bed!" she said from the hallway.

"Come back later when I'm gone," I said to the door.

"No, now! I need to make the bed!" She was angry.

"Later!" I yelled back. She must have left because I heard nothing else. Fifteen minutes later, the phone rang. I wasn't allowed to answer it but by the third call I was so pissed off I picked it up. I figured if it was Mrs. K. I would pretend to be housekeeping. "Hello?"

"Hello," said the calm voice of a much older woman. "This is Peggy from housekeeping. I understand that you wish to sleep late every day," she emphasized *every*, "but my staff needs to do their jobs. Mr. K. is a very good customer and I need to be sure that his bed is made."

"Well then," I said, matching her calmness, "make it around me. Believe me, he'd rather I was in the bed than not." For a second I actually cared that John wanted me in his bed.

"I'm sure that's true," she said, still being polite, "but we're not in the habit of making beds while people are in them. We're on a schedule, and Mr. K.—"

"I think I know what Mr. K. wants more than you do." I loathed her complete disregard for me. "I am the guest here," I said. "I am sleeping. You can make the bed when I say you can make the bed."

"Look," she said matching my tone, "Mr. K is the guest here. He's the one paying the bill. And he'll be the guest here long after you're not – if you know what I mean."

"I know exactly what you mean, and I'll have your job for it!" I screamed into the phone. "I don't know who you think you're talking to – Peggy – or what you're insinuating, but I am Mrs. John K.!" As soon as I had said it, I knew that I shouldn't have. But what could I do? It was abundantly clear that in this hotel, mistresses carried as much clout as hookers.

"I'm terribly sorry for the misunderstanding, ma'am" she said, hanging up.

I wasn't sure that she really believed me, but I didn't care. I was wide awake and furious. My mind was reeling. Why were wives treated so much better than I was? What difference did one stupid little platinum band really make? I did everything their wives did (and often much, much more) except vow to "love, honor and obey," and frankly, in the case of Michael, I did even that. Why was Victoria Messing crap under housekeeping's shoe? Why did I have to pretend to be married; why didn't I demand respect for myself as is?

To make myself feel better, I thought about taking the car to Rodeo Drive early that day. I went every afternoon to walk up and down, back and forth, with the express purpose of finding myself that perfect little something. One day that would be a bag, the next, a pair of shoes. But it wasn't like I had free reign on Rodeo Drive. As a mistress you have to be careful not to push the finances too far or you will quickly be replaced by a newer, lower-maintenance model.

Given the funk I was in, even Rodeo Drive didn't excite me. I called the concierge and asked what else there was to do because I was, "So sick of California I could explode!" Laughing, he told me the Beverly Hills Mall was nearby. The Beverly Hills Mall? Mall? He had to be kidding me. The day was going to be a complete disaster. A mall? I was a New Yorker! We didn't go to malls. Granted, it probably wasn't going to be filled with oversized people eating diet frozen yogurt, but still. It was a mall. Beverly Hills or not, I had my standards.

I swam off my aggression instead. For lunch I ordered grilled seafood over salad. I did my best to scribble an undecipherable "Mrs. John K." when I signed the check just in case Peggy was checking up on me. After lunch I went back upstairs and climbed into the newly made bed to watch Oprah. When it was over, I toyed with the idea of calling housekeeping to remake the bed. Instead, I got dressed and went to the bar to wait for John.

I was looking forward to seeing John – I needed to be on good terms with the boss of my enemy. When he picked me up I fawned all over him. All the petting and kissing and flattery elicited a big dopey grin from John, and that made it obvious to everyone watching that John was crazy about me. As I patted John playfully on the chest, I glanced around in the hopes of spotting Peggy. (It never dawned on me that I had no idea what Peggy looked like.) I poured it on for her: smiles, hair tosses, kisses, and squeals of delight whenever John put his arms around me. How dare she judge me? That night, an overly attentive John and I went dancing where I laughed off my stupid day by drinking a vat of margaritas and fucking John in the bathroom of the club. The next morning he told me that our evening was one of the best nights of his life. I told you he was easy.

On our fifth day at the hotel, John walked in and repeated the routine of the past four days. Immediately, he flicked on MTV.

"Again?" I asked, tired of MTV, California, and John. I clicked off the TV.

"You're acting like my wife," he said. I was only a little sorry for my faux pas. I stormed into the bed and threw the covers over my head. I bit my lip, hard. Naturally, John thought it was an invitation. I didn't care. I was so bored, sex gave me something to do. After I blew him, I swallowed and looked up at him.

"Is that acting like your wife?" I asked.

"Uh no... no, it isn't."

My unhappiness coupled with our afternoon delight worked in my favor – John took me shopping that evening. Guess where? You got it, the mall.

I approached it timidly, not knowing what to expect. My senses were alert, I tried to stay sharp. I brought bottled water and Skittles in case we got lost. Come now, we have all heard the urban legend about the New Yorker who goes to a mall and never returns! Supposedly she loses her co-op, her ability to know downtown from uptown and most importantly, her fashion sense. I was terrified. Cautiously, with John leading the way, I walked into the belly of the beast.

Immediately, I spotted a frozen yogurt kiosk. "Ah-ha!" I said, pointing. All around us was a cacophony of sound – happy, peppy people were talking over equally happy, peppy music. The music was piped in from every corner of the building, obviously the work of some diabolical designer impostor. John took one look at me and laughed.

"It's not going to hurt," he said. "Come on!"

"Are you sure?" I looked at the many identical stores, all lined up in a row. Huh. It was good design work. No need to push through hordes of angry New Yorkers or to dodge renegade cabbies to go from one store to another.

"Victoria, come on! I'll buy you something!" he said in a lovely sing-song voice. What? Actual clothes? Not just samples from his showroom? Well Hallelujah! If John was willing to branch out of his own line… well then, when in Rome, right?

Of course, out of the entire mall he bought me only one thing: a big red sweater with large appliqués on it from Dolce and Gabbana. It looked like it belonged on a high school cheerleader. Come to think of it, that's probably exactly what he wanted it to look like. There would never be an appropriate time or place to wear that sweater but at least it was stupidly expensive. The salesgirls flirted with John while we checked out, but I didn't care. I was too busy looking for exit signs. Then we escaped… nearly unharmed.

We flew back to New York a couple of days later and somehow I found myself preparing for another date with Dr. Fifth Avenue. I had no idea why I was seeing Dr. Fifth Avenue again, but if one sugar daddy wasn't enough, why not try two? Surprisingly, the relationship with Dr. Fifth Avenue intrigued me. There was suddenly a new dynamic; Dr. Fifth Avenue and I both had reason to keep our dates secret.

I took a deep breath, looked in the mirror, and thankfully, I liked what I saw. That was a relief because John was making me feel old. I had tried to make plans for my "nineteenth" (i.e. twenty-third) birthday on the plane ride home, but instead of planning an exciting trip to Rio, as I had hoped, the whole ride was quite depressing. John kept toasting to the "old lady" and even enlisted a flight attendant to lend an attentive ear to the story of how this was going to be my last year as a teenager. Unfortunately, in first class you can get pretty much anything you ask for. Except sleep. All I really wanted was some sleep. And then, on that chatty and somewhat sad ride home, John snuggled up to me to take a nap. He put his head on my shoulder. I rubbed my temples.

"You smell great," he said, "like pineapples. That face wash you use. Sometimes, when I can't fall asleep at night, I pretend I'm lying next to you. I smell the pineapples and I know everything's okay."

So he fell asleep but I was wide awake for the rest of the trip. What the hell did any of that mean? I went back over his words again and again: "I know everything's okay." Was he telling me that he needed me? Me? That was a whole different kind of relationship. A much more important one. A much more intimate one. A much more lucrative one. Had I sold John too short? Did he have real feelings for me? I looked down at him resting on my shoulder. I could probably get past all my ill feelings for him if I really tried. He was handsome. And successful. And well-known. I kissed him on the top of his head.

Halfway into Manhattan, in the back of the Bentley, John leaned toward me and said, "I want to ask you a favor."

"Uh-huh...?" Despite my improved mood, I knew this wasn't a good way to start a conversation.

"When it's over between us," he said, "promise me you'll never date my son."

"Excuse me?"

"Shh, shh," John said in a hushed voice as he motioned to his latest driver. It was okay that the driver knew I blew John, but not okay that he heard John didn't want to share me with his son. What would happen to John's "father-of-the-year" award then? "My son," he said. "He's only three years older than you. Promise me you'll never date him."

I felt the anger well up inside me. So he was as big a dick as I thought he was. He had no plans for anything long term with me. "Oh, I promise," I said. For the rest of the ride I sat stiffly, staring out the window, with John next to me, perfectly contented.

I was still pissed at John as I finished dressing to see Dr. Fifth Avenue. Charlie wove in and out of my legs as I tried feebly to keep my nipples from popping out of the top of my leather bustier. I was wearing tight white jeans that barely allowed me to breathe and high fuck-me shoes that made it hard to keep my balance. I hoped Dr. Fifth Avenue hadn't planned any romantic strolling around the city, but I was pretty sure that the only exercise I would have to worry about was fighting him off. I clasped the bracelet around my wrist and stared at it. It seemed so long ago that he gave it to me. I had been so young back then, so optimistic. Everything was exciting and new. But by this point, with the single exception of Michael, the men were all the same, the food was all the same, the sex was all the same and there was never anything new. Correction, this night was new. We were going out on a double date.

Meet our dinner companions: Merv and Jenny. That is: Merv and Jenny! Merv and Jenny (!) were average New Yorkers and extremely plain. He was in finance and she was... oh who the hell cared. But God, was she perky. And annoying. All through pre-dinner drinks she pulled her shoulder-length blonde hair up into a ponytail – careful to smooth all the strays – and then let it drop back down. She did this over and over. At the bar and at the dinner table. I tried to be friendly with her but my attention was pulled back to my nipple, which must have popped out again because Dr. Fifth Avenue and Merv were both staring.

"Oh for God's sake," I said as I readjusted to make the nipple less conspicuous. Jenny also noticed my nipple but she wasn't so appreciative; she rolled her eyes and arched her back. Poor Jenny. Not only was she flat but she was also in the uncomfortable position of dining with a woman she hated. But don't worry about our little flat-chested, hair-pulling Jenny; she had spunk. Caught with the devil as her dinner companion, she decided to make the most of it; she tried to flirt with Dr. Fifth Avenue. That's when the evening finally became interesting. I looked up from my appetizer salad.

"I just love Bulgari jewelry!" Jenny said leaning forward and opening her bright green eyes until they were nearly as round as my boobs. She pronounced it "Bull-jar-ee." And everyone had already decided that I was the stupid one at the table. Amateur. Believe me, by the age of twelve I knew the proper way to pronounce all major jewelry companies – and that wasn't one of them. Dr. Fifth Avenue and Merv smirked at each other and I felt a little bit sorry for Jenny; she was clearly out of her league.

"Uh, listen, I think it's pronounced Bulgari," I whispered to Jenny. "And you'll never get it from him." I nodded to Dr. Fifth Avenue and smiled at her.

"Thank you," she said, smiling back. I twirled my gaudy bracelet and she mouthed an "Oh!" to me. We shared a laugh.

After finishing the surprisingly pleasant dinner, Merv pointed to my breasts and asked Dr. Fifth Avenue if he "did those." Jenny jumped to my rescue and pulled Merv away, but not before Dr. Fifth Avenue happily took full credit.

"I can make hers match if you'd like," Dr. Fifth Avenue said, pointing at Jenny. Her cheeks flushed hot pink. I shook my head and we walked to the car. On the way, I overheard Merv tell Dr. Fifth Avenue that he wouldn't waste the money on boobs because he was through with Jenny.

We all climbed into Merv's convertible – a Chrysler – can you believe it? Chrysler must have been running a leasing special for any man who was cheating on his wife that summer. Couldn't Jaguar have run the same offer? I tried my best to get Jenny to sit with me in the backseat, but there was no way that was going to happen. These men had just paid for a meal, they were going to get some payback. So there we were, in the Chrysler; Merv driving, Jenny sitting shotgun and Dr. Fifth Avenue and me scrunched in the back. Merv decided to take us all for a little spin since it was such a beautiful night and the air had that first fall crispness to it.

I leaned back, inhaled deeply, and watched the city whiz by. My lungs felt clean and fresh. They even hurt a bit from the shock of the cold weather. As I let my hair blow freely in the wind, I wondered what other twenty-two-year-olds were doing. Probably going to football games, or studying hard, or making out with their college boyfriends. Mmm, that was the one part of college I actually liked. Snuggling under a blanket at a cold night game, anticipating that first kiss. Then I had the jarring revelation that twenty-two-year-olds were already finished with college. At least their undergrad work. Over these past few years while I ran around with man after man, my classmates had graduated and started their careers. I sat back up. Big deal, I told myself, trying to convince myself that it didn't matter. I started my career before any of them. I looked over at Dr. Fifth Avenue.

I felt his hand on my knee. Even a convertible couldn't shield me from my horny date. I still had to deal with him. Without so much as a word he leaned over and popped my breast out of my bustier. Just like that. I didn't even see it coming. And although he had no business doing it, I was a tad impressed with his speed and dexterity. He started licking my nipple. I let my gaze fall back out of the car and watched the buildings grow closer as we ran up the FDR. Then he bit me, accidentally, I hoped.

"Ow!" I said, pushing him away. There was only one sensation I could get from the damned fake boobs – pain. I rubbed my nipple and realized that everyone was looking at me – Merv in his rearview, Jenny turned in her seat, and Dr. Fifth Avenue from the other side of the car. Dr. Fifth Avenue looked as if he had been slapped in the face. And he should have. I had broken one of the cardinal rules of being a mistress: Never, under any circumstance, do you let your benefactor think that you are not completely excited by his touch. Heck, you should orgasm just from his stare. I needed to remember to add this as an addendum to the list of rules that I had compiled all those years ago.

Although I wasn't his mistress any longer I still knew what was expected of me; I needed to right my wrong, and fast. Laughing, I pulled Dr. Fifth Avenue to me, kissing him playfully. Naturally he took that as a go and mounted me, fully clothed, in the back of the car. I could feel his tiny penis harden. Thank God he had to dismount at the exit. Even with the magical night air, I couldn't breathe with him lying there, holding me down. Dr. Fifth Avenue and Merv exchanged looks of approval because my actions had forced Jenny's head into Merv's lap. Sorry, Jenny. But thankfully, that gave Merv a reason to drop me off.

Dr. Fifth Avenue and I got out of Merv's car and watched it speed away. We were standing on the street in front of my building when he kissed me, mostly with his tongue. I backed off. "Can I come up?" he asked, leering at me. My stomach burned. He still had a tiny bulge in his Armani suit.

"No, sorry. My sister's visiting," I said. Little lie.

"Lisa, Liza...."

"Liz."

"Oh yeah, I remember her from your..." He pointed to my breasts. "She was hot too. In a totally different way. Classy."

"Yeah, well thanks." It was the perfect ending to the evening.

"You know what I mean," he said, kissing me again.

I turned and walked into the lobby. I couldn't get away quickly enough; the stench of his cologne was suffocating me. Why did I still feel the need to entertain Dr. Fifth Avenue's horny advances when John was my boyfriend? From the safety of my lobby, I watched Dr. Fifth Avenue hail a cab. He was beginning to move like an old man. He looked back over his shoulder as he got in. He didn't look happy. In the distance, a thunderstorm was brewing. I saw a lightning strike and wondered if I had angered the gods. I ran inside... fast.

CHAPTER 4: HEPHAESTUS

"Hephaestus: The God of Fire. Among the perfectly beautiful immortals, he only was ugly. He was lame as well. The working man of the immortals. A kindly, peace-loving god, popular on earth as in heaven."

Despite the no-sex night, Dr. Fifth Avenue kept on calling. I saw him occasionally over the next few months but I was never sure why I did. Out of habit, probably. I knew why he saw me, though. To him, nothing had really changed. We were pretty much the same, only now he had a rival. A rival he respected. What's more, Dr. Fifth Avenue felt that he had the upper hand: he knew about John but John didn't know about him. In some weird way, I think he enjoyed this more than when he had me all to himself.

Sometimes after playing tennis with John, Dr. Fifth Avenue would show up unexpectedly at my apartment. He must have already talked to John and known that John wasn't coming by. Dr. Fifth Avenue would barge in carrying his racket and sporting a just-showered, post-tennis glow. I hated the surprise visits and told him so, but that never dissuaded him. Once, I even threw a plate of steaming spaghetti past him and into the sink just for emphasis. He picked up a piece of the spaghetti and ate it. "It's overcooked," he said, making a face. He grabbed another piece and juggled it until it cooled off.

"Shut up!" I said. "Just shut up! You don't know everything!" I pulled at my hair. He thought my tantrum was cute; he never took me seriously. I was a child, a pet, a thing less important and not as real as him. He offered a piece of the overcooked spaghetti to Charlie who was wise enough to run away.

We both knew that the main reason Dr. Fifth Avenue stopped by was to get John updates. And all I ever had to offer was that I was never going back to that horrible uptown apartment. Dr. Fifth Avenue would listen intently and nod his head in empathy, both of us knowing I'd go back the very next time John called.

Of course the other reason he came by was to try to get laid. He wanted to prove to John that he was worthy of John's company and what better way to prove his worth than by fucking the same mistress?

That weekend, with both my men away and still missing Michael, I found myself depressed. Not knowing what else to do or who else to turn to, I called my mother.

"Hello?" My mother was asleep.

"Hey, Mom. I was wondering if I could come home tomorrow."

"Are you sick?"

"Yes," I wanted to say, "sick of my lifestyle." Instead, I said, "No, not really, I just have a free weekend. And I'm a little blue." I knew I'd be sorry for saying it.

"What do you have to be blue about?" my mother asked. "You have all these rich men fawning all over you and you lead a life that most women would kill—"

"It's just that time of the month. Just hormones." I couldn't stand one more second of my mother's clueless summary of my life.

"Whatever. Sure," my mother said. "Of course you can come home."

I got off the train in Philadelphia and watched the people in the station. Most looked happy to be there, like they were returning home after a long trip or meeting up with a loved one they hadn't seen in ages. I walked by a young couple locked in an embrace. He held her face while he kissed her softly, again and again. I traced my own lips, imagining Michael, the only man who ever really kissed me like that. Even if it was while I was tied to a bed. I forced my eyes away and found a cab.

When we pulled into my mother's driveway, I could see cigarette smoke seep out from around the front door. I grabbed my overnight case – complete with the extra outfit – and rang the doorbell. Much to my surprise, Liz answered the door.

"Oh, hi," I said.

"Oh, hi."

"Is Megan here too?" I asked, hoping to see my niece.

"She's at a sleepover," Liz said. She stepped aside to let me in.

"Well is Martin here?"

Before Liz could answer, my mother greeted me with a hearty, "See! You can always come home again! Both my babies are depressed, and both came home to me." I was immediately sorry that I was there, but I was also curious about what perfect Liz and her perfect life had to be depressed about.

I could stand only one night of watching *Pretty Woman* and eating microwave popcorn while I listened to Liz yell at her husband over the phone. They were obviously in the middle of an enormous fight. I had no idea they ever fought, and it was uncharacteristic of Liz to lose her composure in front of anyone, even her mother and sister. Maybe especially her mother and sister. I tried to imagine John and his wife fighting like that but I just couldn't picture it. I stared at the television through the haze of smoke; I couldn't believe how much John looked like Richard Gere. About halfway through the movie, Liz slammed the phone down and Mom began to cry over the plot. It was too surreal for me.

After a fitful night's sleep, I took the earliest train I could. Going home was supposed to be a refuge but for me it fueled my desperation. I wanted to call John and end it, mostly because of the apartment on the Upper West Side, but I knew that I couldn't. Almost all of my modeling work came from him, and without John or the work, how could I pay my rent? Besides, I would miss the Bentley too much. But I would have to make some changes. First of all, I would simply refuse to go to that apartment ever again. And I'd insist on getting some clothes that weren't his label. I wanted a real designer: Gucci, Prada, Armani, Ralph. I missed them all, and I was sure they missed me too. And I needed some money. Real money. Ask as I might, John had no interest in giving me a spending account. He threw some cash my way once in a blue moon, but he also gave me a song and dance about not giving me too much money or his wife would notice. If women only knew the truth. If wives only understood that they have their husbands financially castrated, and if girlfriends only realized that they were never going to cash in – then all women could ban together to rule the world. Men would be put on allowances and given sex only when deemed appropriate. "*And I think to myself, what a wonderful world.*"

I sat at my tiny table, staring at my suitcase, paralyzed with indecision. Charlie sat on my lap and I rubbed his head. I tried to cross my legs but banged my shin on the iron base. "Goddamned piece of crap!" I rubbed away the pain. Charlie jumped down and ran to a sunny spot near the window. I wanted new furniture. Hell, I wanted my new apartment. This apartment was only supposed to be a starter for me, but it was four years later and I was still in the same place. I had even celebrated my twenty-third birthday here, alone, while John was in Israel with his family. The only significant change that had occurred was that my closet was overstuffed, thanks to Michael. God, did I miss Michael. Despite the fame and titles that my other men held, Michael was really the only one who had offered me an outrageous lifestyle. The others just wanted to see how little – money, effort, gifts – they could get away with.

It was Sunday morning and I was starving. I should have been on the Rivera dining on exotic fruits and freshly brewed coffee. Instead, I went to my tiny fridge and looked inside. Coffeemate, relish and ketchup. I checked the coffee can… empty. This just wasn't how it was supposed to be. I went to the deli to bum my free breakfast, and on the way, I bumped into that tall, handsome man from my building.

"Hi!" he said.

"Hey," I said. I needed caffeine and I just wasn't in the mood to be neighborly.

"Where you going?" he asked, obviously wanting to start a conversation.

"That way…," I pointed to the deli.

"Oh, for breakfast?"

"Mm-hm," I answered, still walking.

"Let me get it for you." I stopped in my tracks. He was extremely handsome, but what could he be worth if he was living in the same building as me?

"Thanks, but no," I said. He looked devastated. "The guys never charge me for my bagel and coffee in the morning."

"Oh!" he said, "I can understand that!" I smiled at him.

"Um, well, I'm running late," I said. It was a very small little lie.

"Me too," he said. "Gotta get to the office. Patients waiting." So he wanted to make sure that I knew he was a doctor. I mean, patients on a Sunday morning?

"Okay then." I made a bee-line for the deli. He shook his head and we went our separate ways.

Monday afternoon John called. It was an odd time for him, he usually called by eleven to tell me what was going on for the week and when he was free. Before he could say anything, I broached the apartment topic. "Listen, John, I need to talk to you about something. I just don't like going to that apartment on the Upper West Side. I'm sorry, but it's how I feel."

"No sweat," he said. I was expecting more. He always seemed so attached to that apartment.

"Really?" I asked, only half-believing that he was okay with it.

"Yeah, sure. I was going to suggest a change of scenery myself. Your place really is nice."

"Oh," I said. "You're kidding...?" I was careful not to sound too thrilled. "So, when do you want to come by?" I tried to sound like I was interested in seeing him but the truth was that I needed some cash and I had to clean before I could possibly let anyone in.

"Don't know yet. Have to get my schedule. I'll call you back in a bit."

"Oh. Okay. Well, talk to you later!" I hung up, relieved.

But John didn't call me back that afternoon. Actually, he didn't call me the entire next day. Just in case of a surprise visit, I cleaned the apartment that morning anyway. When I hadn't heard from him that next night or the following morning, I wondered what was going on. I went to the gym and when I got back, there was a message from him on the machine.

"Hey! Sorry I've been out of touch. So crazy here. Fashion week's coming up. Anyway, want to meet tonight? Maybe have a romantic dinner in and then hit a few clubs? Say...seven? Sound good?"

Good? It sounded great. We hadn't been out clubbing since California and a "romantic dinner" sounded like he was once again trying to impress me. His voice sounded younger and happier too. Like it did when he told me about the pineapple smell. That was more like it; maybe we could start fresh.

That afternoon I went shopping for some new placemats at Bed, Bath and Beyond and a moderately priced bottle of wine at a nearby liquor store. I took my time getting dressed and decided on a micro mini with a sequined top. I teased my hair and smeared my eyeliner. Then I slipped into mega-high stilettos. Seven o'clock on the dot. I waited to open the wine. I leaned back against the couch trying to look sexy but not mess up my outfit. Seven-fifteen, no John. I rearranged the couch pillows and resumed my pose. Seven-thirty, still no John. I ran for the bathroom and when I came out, I saw there was a message.

"Hey! It's me. Where are you? Seven o'clock, right? Dinner's waiting."

I couldn't believe it; he'd completely forgotten we were meeting at my place. How typical. He hadn't paid any attention to me or my speech about never going uptown, ever again. Oh, screw it. I'd go if it meant a much-needed glamorous evening out. It would take too long to call him back, so I grabbed my bag and the wine and took off for the Upper West Side.

I buzzed from downstairs. "It's me! Sorry!"

"No problem," he said. "Come on up!" He buzzed me in. I was laughing as I rushed to the elevator and up to the third floor. Talk about star-crossed lovers. For some reason, the prospect of this whole night made me giddy. I was so happy to be out and feeling like me, I almost forgot that it was John I was seeing.

I knocked on the door and whispered my sultriest, "It's me." I heard him run to the door.

"What's the matter, you forget your key?" he asked as he opened the door.

"No silly," I said, banging his chest with my purse. "I never took a key, remember?"

"Victoria!"

"Who were you expecting, our dinner delivery?"

"Uh, no..." he said, keeping me in the doorway. "I'm just surprised you're here."

"How could I pass up an offer of dinner and clubbing with my favorite guy?"

"Right! Yes. Of course." He was stammering. "Um, Victoria, when did you get that message from me?"

"This afternoon." Had he lost his mind? "When you called... can I come in?"

"Sure..." he said, not moving.

"Come on!" I said. "Let me by." I couldn't believe that I was actually trying to get in to that apartment. "Wow!" I said, looking around. "Look at what you did here... just for tonight?" The apartment smelled of fresh paint. All the dishes and glasses were put away, there were fresh sheets and a comforter on the bed, and the kitchen had been restored to usable.

"You did all this for our dinner?" I asked, wide eyed. He'd had it renovated over the weekend. He must have finally realized that you can't take a woman like me to a dump. I was surprised and touched by his gesture. I gave him a heartfelt, "Thank you," and kissed him softly. I pulled away when I noticed the suitcases leaning up against the wall. "What's that?" I asked, pointing at the bags. Then the thought crossed my mind. "Oh my God," I said, my mouth dropping open. "No way. Did you? Did you leave your wife?" I turned to him, awestruck.

"What?" he said, "No! Of course not. I told you on our first date that I would never leave her."

"Well then, what's with the suitcases? Why are they here?" Then I got excited. "Are we going on a surprise vacation? We'll need to get someone to watch Charlie..." He looked away. "John?" He couldn't look at me. "John....? Please. Tell me what's going on." I shifted my weight uneasily.

"They're uh... they're not mine, Victoria."

"Yeah. Well now I see one of them has a Snoopy decal stuck to it. So whose are they?"

"They belong to... I met someone. Someone else."

"What? And those are her bags?" He nodded. "When were you going to tell me? You invite me for a romantic dinner and an evening out and you were just planning on dumping me?"

"I...uh—"

"And why would you get rid of me? I'm the perfect mistress!" I said, realizing how ridiculous I sounded.

"It was just time for me to move on, I guess."

"You guess? What was all that crap about smelling the pineapples then?"

"Excuse me?"

"You know what? Who cares. I was planning to leave you anyway, what with this trashy apartment. So what is she, eighteen?"

"Nearly," he answered, not the least bit embarrassed.

"Let me guess. She's a dancer. Bright blue eyes. Just off the fucking turnip truck. Here from Kansas."

"Iowa. But you're right about the rest of it."

"Please. You don't even like blondes!"

"I made an exception."

"So why did you insist I come here? To see her stuff?"

"I didn't."

"You called and called back. And when you asked where I was, I came right over. Explain that!"

"I sort of called the wrong number. Twice. Debbie is leaving her apartment and moving in here. Horrible roommate situation."

"You called the wrong number? You meant to call her?" I was floored.

"Actually, yes."

"And when were you going to tell me?" I asked, seething.

"I tried the other night, but then... I figured the best thing would be to call every now and again, and after awhile you'd just figure it out."

"Weren't you afraid that I'd come to the office and make a fuss?"

"No. You're too smart for that."

"Wanna bet?" I asked, absolutely furious. Why did I care that John was leaving me?

"Don't bet with me, Victoria. I'm still going to cover your rent for the next three months. That's my security. And I'll still call you for jobs when they're right for you."

"But let me guess. The rest of your ad campaigns are going to be starring a buxom blonde."

"Something like that," he said, looking straight at me. "I'm sorry, Victoria. I just think it's for the best."

"Will she get the Bentley?" I asked, as tears welled in my eyes. He didn't answer. "The Bentley...?" I said in a tiny, cracking voice.

"She's never even seen one before. I mean, how cute is that?" he asked, his face lighting up from new love. He had never, in all our times together, ever looked at me like that.

"Whatever," I said. I picked up my purse. "I'm so out of here." I stalled at the door for a minute. "So, uh, what will you do, mail me the rent check?"

"Yes," he said and I slammed the door.

I needed to be more careful in the future. The whole night could come back to bite me in the ass. Hard. If John told that story around the club, I could be ruined. There were many yet unconquered gods who played tennis at John's club. Not to mention that Dr. Fifth Avenue would most certainly find out. Oh God! There would be pity visits from Dr. Fifth Avenue who would just assume that he could come back. I was mortified. And pissed. And broke. I'd spent my last twenty on cab fare, assuming I'd have the Bentley take me home. I turned back and knocked on the door.

"Yes?"

"It's Victoria. Can I have cab fare, please?" He opened the door and gave me a twenty. I stared at the twenty until he handed me an additional hundred. And then one more. He obviously didn't mind throwing money at a problem to make it disappear. "Thanks," I said, turning away.

"Victoria," he said as I turned back, "I am sorry."

I took my micro mini covered ass, stuck my tail between my legs and slunk home to drink the bottle of wine. Alone.

Over the next few weeks I really had nothing to do except find my next boyfriend. I had no interest in chasing after men in conventional places like the grocery store; how many gods do their own food shopping? And I refused to become a groupie trying to slip in backstage at a concert or a game. The next man would have to come to me. I figured the best way to pass the time was to work out. That way, when Prince Charming came my way, I'd be ready. So I spent endless hours on the treadmill, determined to look better than ever. Since I had to pay my own way at the gym, I worked out at the local YMCA. Unfortunately, the chance of finding a stray god at the Y was slim to none.

Then one day, as the fates would have it, I met Ivan, a successful author who worked out at the Y simply because it was next door to his apartment. Ivan gave me a great amount of modeling work through his connections as a former garmento, and really made me laugh. The only problem with Ivan was that he was so unattractive. Not unattractive in a sleazy way, he was just not very handsome. Or sexy. He was a redhead with sensitive skin who always seemed to be fighting some kind of rash... and losing. Ivan had been that geeky little boy on the playground who was beaten to a pulp, so he over-compensated by being a very masculine man. This, I appreciated. Besides, after Dr. Fifth Avenue, Michael, and John, who was going to look good? I gave him a chance.

Ivan remembered the little things: to send flowers, to hold the door and to give me money on a regular basis. He understood how tough it was to "be in the arts" and considered himself my personal benefactor. Lord knows where he got the idea that catalog modeling was an artistic endeavor, but I wasn't going to correct him. Or complain. Ivan was forty-five, married (but having trouble), with a best-selling book about past-life regressions on the market. He was smart and thought that I was smart too. And best of all, he was extravagant when it came to gifts and dinners – more so than both Dr. Fifth Avenue and John put together. He wasn't that daring when it came to locale, so we would often go to the same little bistro in Chelsea, but the food was fabulous and they treated us wonderfully. Ivan told me that since he had some degree of celebrity he had to be extra cautious. Fine by me. I had his direct office number and called him whenever I needed to talk. He always took my calls.

We worked out together every day, and sometimes Ivan would make me laugh so hard that I had to send him away or risk falling off of my treadmill. After our workout, we would go back to my apartment and fuck, still sweaty from the gym. He thought I was being sexy by skipping the shower, but the truth was, I'd hidden as many of my designer bags as I could in my towel-dried tub. I didn't want to deter Ivan from buying more. Eventually, he gave up asking if he could shower at my place. It was hard for me to get hot for him, so I learned to close my eyes and fantasize about Michael. Ivan was a sensitive lover and pretty tuned in to the female body but I just couldn't relax and enjoy; I couldn't shake the feeling that I might catch something from him. I learned that a couple of mid-day Bellinis would help loosen me up. In all ways.

Ivan was very dramatic. He never asked me about the scars on my wrists – which by now had faded into two thick, raised, white lines – but he knew that they were there. One day he kissed them and held them to his heart. I was sure he thought I had tried to commit suicide. I felt a little bad about it but I let him think whatever he wanted. I mean… it was all working for me, you know?

What Ivan lacked in attractiveness, he made up for in generosity. I was way out of his league and he knew it. I only needed to complain once about my uncomfortable couch and miraculously, the next day a new sofa bed was delivered, complete with new bedding. Ivan was exceptionally good with home furnishings. A new rug followed, and then a chair we picked out together at ABC Carpet and Home. Even my tiny little place was starting to look, well, nice. As a writer, Ivan could take huge chunks of the day off, and we spent a great deal of time shopping. Since his first business had been the garment business, he liked to keep up on the latest trends and fashions. He always brought a large wad of cash with him and bought for me freely. He used every excuse in the book to buy me whatever I wanted. Within reason, of course. "Hmmm," he'd say, "that Dior bag is something I could copy for next year's line." We both knew that Ivan never made purses and that he would never go back to the garment business, but he felt the need to excuse his purchases. Excuse away, I would say.

Ivan asked me to move in with him.

"Hey, Victoria," he said that morning while we were working out.

"Yes," I asked, running along beside him. I sipped the gourmet cappuccino he had brought for me.

"I was thinking…"

"What?" I asked. A drop of my sweat fell into the tiny sip hole on the lid.

"I want to give you a key."

"To what?"

"To my apartment."

"What?" I stopped dead on the treadmill.

"To my apartment. It's right next door, and we can actually shower there! And well…."

"Ivan, I've never even seen your apartment."

"I know, I know," he said, slowing his pace. "And I'm sorry about that. Really. It's just, well, you understand my situation."

"Better than you think," I said. "So what's changed?" I began to jog again. Although this was coming out of nowhere, I had recently been afraid that Ivan would do something rash like leave his wife for me. Then what would I do? I did not want to be Mrs. Ivan. I chewed on the plastic lid of my cup.

"Oh, don't do that," he said. "You'll hurt your teeth." I stopped and stared at him. "Sorry," he said, "it's a habit. Fatherhood. You go ahead and chew on anything you'd like." He smiled at me, trying desperately to recover. "Look," he said, now unable to make eye contact, "I just really, really like you. And I know it's not the penthouse on Fifth Avenue you're always talking about, but it's nice."

I thought long and hard about how to word this one. "What are you actually offering me, Ivan?"

"Well, me, I guess. If you want me." There it was.

"You? As in, all of you?" I wanted to be perfectly clear.

"Well, no. I can't do that. I'm married and I need to stay that way. At least while my son is so youn—"

"I can understand that." I broke into a run. "So then, what? A place to crash closer to the gym?"

"It's nice, Victoria."

"Okay then, so a nice place to crash. Why haven't we gone there before?"

"Because I needed to see where we were going before I invited you in." I stopped my run. I felt sorry for him.

"And where are we going, Ivan?"

"Hopefully, to my place," he said, smiling. I smiled back.

I accepted Ivan's offer of an additional place to crash with less enthusiasm than I'd accepted Dr. Fifth Avenue's cappuccino maker. At least I knew what the cappuccino machine offered – really good coffee. That is, when I remembered to buy coffee beans, and milk. But what was Ivan offering?

Ivan's apartment was nice, although I flinched when I saw the décor. I was afraid he was going to expect us to spend our time naked under matching his and hers kimonos while we drank green tea and chanted through all the positions of the Kama Sutra. His apartment was on the twenty-second floor of a beautiful doorman building. The lobby was painted a warm salmon color and the apartment was an off-white, decorated with Asian and modern furniture. He had a carved divider against one wall with an antique kimono thrown over it, and a wall of windows with an incredible view looking uptown. He had at least three strategically placed Buddhas and cushions on the floor of his living room. I knew Ivan was a yoga devotee, but before I saw his place, I was able to forget that facet of his personality. After, there would be no escaping it.

I had to take Ivan's key or risk losing him for good. And I couldn't afford to lose Ivan. It had become a very difficult situation.

"Make yourself at home!" Ivan yelled to me from the kitchen. I heard the champagne cork pop. I hated the phony vibe I got from Ivan's apartment; my apartment may have been miserable, but at least it was real. I walked into one of the three bedrooms; it had Buzz Lightyear sheets and curtains. "Not that one!" he called. I stepped back. "Sorry," he said, walking over to me with two glasses of Dom Perignon, "but it's my son's room." He pulled the door shut. "This one's my home office," he said, opening a door to a room crammed full of books and papers. It was the polar opposite of the rest of the apartment. "And this one," he said, opening a door slowly, "is our room." And by "our," he did mean mine and his.

"Nice," I said, looking at the platform bed, fur rug, reading nook, tall armoires, and the two red lava lamps by the bed. I couldn't think of what else to say. "Ivan," I finally asked, "what am I doing here?"

"Hopefully, making use of that," he said, pointing to the bed.

"No, really. I mean, what about your situation?"

"My situation is far away," he said, taking my hand and leading me to the bed.

"Are you asking me to move in?"

"Yes."

"Full time?"

"Yes." I had a pain in the pit of my stomach like no pain I had ever experienced before. I finished off my glass and reached for his. "Here," he said, pulling a large square box from the closet. It was wrapped in gold paper with a matching gold bow. "For you. Welcome home, I guess."

I knocked back his glass as well and opened the box slowly, trying to shake the haze from my brain. Ivan had given me a large globe.

"I want to give you the world, Victoria," he said.

"Oh. Well, thank you."

"Welcome home, Victoria," he said. "Welcome home." As he held me, I cried tears of complete sorrow. There I was, being offered an out, and all I could do was wrack my brain to come up with a way to stay in. My gaze fell on a Lucky Cat near the window. That was it.

"But what about Charlie?" I asked. "Surely, you won't want a cat here in your beautiful place."

"Well, no—"

"Then I hate to say it, but I'm stuck."

"You could just give him up, you know."

"Give him up?" I said, my eyes once again rimming with tears. "No. That won't happen."

"Okay," Ivan said. "But my wife's allergic. To just about everything in the world. I can't have a cat here."

"I thought your wife was far away."

"She is. But she comes in to shop some days and we use the apartment."

"So then, how can I move in?"

"Well, you'll need to keep your place. And keep your stuff there. But you can bring a bag with a few things that you can take back with you whenever I need you to. I was going to get you a new bag as a gift, but you seem to have a lot of them in your closet already." And he'd never even seen the overstuffed bathtub. So once again I'd be required to carry a bag of my personal items back and forth with me. I'd clearly joined a specific nomadic tribe of mistresses.

"So how would anything really change, Ivan?"

"What do you mean?" he asked me. "You'd be living here. Except when my wife needs the place."

"Oh," I said, terrified that I would now be required to spend every night having sex with Ivan in his Shagadelic room. "Thank you for your lovely offer. I'll be happy to spend some time here, but I'm sorry that my situation won't let me make full use of it." And there it was. My love for Charlie had given me my get out of jail card. Whew.

"So, what are you doing?" Ivan asked me one day as he rolled over next to me. I stared out at his glorious view. I had been staying at his place on and off for about a month and I had taken to it – with its stocked refrigerator and bar – pretty well. I was actually back to enjoying my time with Ivan. He lit us a joint.

"Goody!" I said.

"Not so fast," he said, pulling the joint away. "First tell me, what are you doing?"

"Uh, lying here… What do you mean what am I doing?"

"I mean bigger picture. What are you doing?"

"About what?" I asked, pulling at his arm with the joint.

"Patience!" he said. "About your life." He gave me a drag.

"Oh, that," I said, inhaling. "Who knows, who cares."

"Well you'd better know," he said. "What about your future? You can't model forever."

"I don't want to model forever," I said, inhaling again. "Actually, I never wanted to model at all. It just sort of fell on me."

"Well I can understand that. You're so beautiful."

"Thanks. But you don't have to be beautiful to be a model. Just tall and skinny."

"That you are," he said, rubbing my back. "But really, if you're not into modeling, then what?"

"Then what, what?" I asked again, letting the nice buzz overtake me.

"What are you doing with your life?"

"Waiting for my knight in shining armor to buy me all of Manhattan!" I said, waving my arms dramatically in the air.

"Victoria," he said, "that's not a plan."

"It's not?" He was becoming the definition of a buzzkill.

"No. Come on, what was your reason for moving here? To the city? Did you want to act, write, conquer the business world?" I burst out laughing. "Well, clearly not the business world, but you must have some sort of ambition." He was getting worked up.

"Must I? I'm Gen X, babe. Haven't you heard? We're allergic to ambition."

"That's ridiculous," he said. "Victoria, come on." He was getting angry. "Tell me what you want to do." I just shrugged. "Victoria, what do you want?"

"I want to be taken care of, all right? By a rich married man who adores me. I want a penthouse on Park Avenue and a shopping account at Bergdorf and fancy dinners and a chauffeured town car!"

"Well that's not a plan!"

"Sure it is!"

"No, it's not," he said.

"First you tell me that I have to tell you my plan and then once I do you tell me it's not good enough. If I want to feel inadequate, I'll move back home with my mother." I was up on my elbows now; my nice buzz was beginning to fade.

"Shh, shh," he said, stroking my arm. "I didn't mean to upset you. All I mean is, that's not a realistic goal."

"Why not?" I asked, pouting.

"For one thing you're way too smart for that. For another, where are you going to get a deal like that? I don't know if you've had any experience with other married men, but it doesn't work like that."

"Of course it does," I said. "That's why women become mistresses."

"I thought a woman became someone's mistress because she falls in love with a married man."

"What?" I laughed so hard I snorted. "Of course not, silly! It's a career choice. Just like anything else."

"Victoria, I have to say I'm surprised at you."

"You are? Why?"

"Because I didn't know you were so insensitive."

"*I'm* insensitive? You fuck me in the same bed you fuck your wife."

"I don't fuck you," he said. "I make love to you. And if I knew the only reason you did it was to get your rent paid, I may have thought differently."

"Oh come on," I said, snuggling up to him, "that's not the only reason." There was all that shopping too. "It's the pot talking. Be a sport."

"I understand," he said. But he was still visibly upset. "Victoria?"

"Mmm?" I asked, lying on my back taking another long drag.

"Have you... what I mean to say is, were you ever anyone's mistress before?"

He wanted to know if this was, in fact, my career choice. If I liked what he was offering, I needed to do some damage control. I sat up like a bolt and tried to shake my buzz.

"Anyone's mistress? Of course not!" I said, sounding as traumatized as I could. "How could you even think that?"

"That's what I thought." He settled back.

"Just you, Baby, just you." I traced the outline of his bicep. He held the joint for me.

"Let's forget all that other stuff we said, okay?"

"Okay." Truthfully, I already had.

"Hey," he said, getting closer to me, "what do you say we go have some extravagant five-course lunch somewhere and then spend the afternoon shopping. Totally wasted!"

"Sounds perfect," I said. But an unwelcome thought crept back into my head. "Ivan?"

"Yeah?"

"That idea that mistressing can't be a career choice, do you really think that's true?"

"What do I know," he said, kissing my stomach, "I'm wasted." I got dressed to go shopping.

It was my twenty-fourth birthday and, surprisingly, I wasn't dreading it. I was looking forward to seeing Ivan and hoping for a nice dinner out and some expensive jewelry. Long gone were the expectations of a car or a brownstone. I understood that I would have to go higher on Olympus for them. Much higher. As in, Donald Trump, higher. I rolled over in bed and thought about what I wanted to do that day. Charlie suggested a morning nap, so we fell back to sleep and I dreamt about future shopping sprees with Ivan. By this point, shopping was for sport and sheer greed. My tiny closet was jammed full and I had an extra clothes rack in the middle of the studio. I had shoes and a bag from pretty much every significant designer.

At three o'clock that afternoon I called Ivan; I wanted to know where we were heading that night so I would know how to dress. I tried his line but Ivan's secretary told me that he was busy and despite my insistence, I couldn't get through. On my birthday? I was a little peeved. I decided to keep myself occupied by going to get a manicure when Neil, my daytime doorman, buzzed to let me know I had some packages. I ran downstairs and was greeted with a variety of flowers and boxes. "Just pile 'em on!" I told Neil, as he filled my outstretched arms. I struggled to carry them all upstairs and finally dumped everything on the floor, hoping there was nothing breakable. Charlie chased the ribbons and Mylar balloons. I picked up the three flower arrangements before he could eat the flowers, placed them on my table and read the cards.

The first card said only "Happy Birthday!" and came with two dozen long-stemmed red roses. It was from John. A handwritten note inside said, "Two dozen for your twentieth!" I laughed, realizing I had never told John my real age. I couldn't imagine why he was sending me flowers but my best guess was that his secretary had a list of pertinent birthdays for the year. It was probably too much to keep track of who was in and who was out. Or quite possibly, knowing John, they were meant for someone else.

I left the roses in the box and moved to the next – a bunch of deli flowers with a rumpled "Happy Birthday" card attached. On the back was scribbled, "Can I see you tonight?" with a new cell phone number – Dr. Fifth Avenue. Although I still spoke to him occasionally, I couldn't imagine wasting my birthday night on him. Thank God Ivan was taking me out.

The last arrangement had roses and carnations with a balloon that said, accusingly, "Happy 24th!" It was from 800-flowers, or FTD or some such place. Figures. The card read: "Ha-p B-Day! Luv, Martin, Liz and Li-tl Megan." Dear God.

"When is Megan ever going to be old enough to be Big Megan and when will Liz ever learn to write out an entire f-ing word?" I asked Charlie in my best Westchester preppy voice. I hunted down a knife to pop the offensive balloon. Liz would be the one person clueless enough to announce to the world how old I really was. She wouldn't want *me* telling all the PTA mommies that she is really 30-ish, and not mid-20-ish, after all.

I moved on to the boxes. The first was a pretty black sweater from Mom, with a gift certificate to Bloomingdales. The very place I was a cheese-slicer not that long ago. Poor Mom. Always so close.

The next box was a beautiful silk, flesh-tone nightgown from Victoria's Secret. It was from Ivan. The card read: "Why don't you slip this on and tell me some of my Victoria's Secrets." Oh my. I really thought a best-selling author could do better than that. What an odd choice of gift coming from Ivan. Sure he had given me plenty of lingerie, usually from La Perla, but we had always shopped for it together. He must have been setting the mood for later that night. I suddenly needed a margarita.

I took myself out for a giant strawberry margarita. The only patron at my local Mexican joint, I threw myself onto a bar stool and watched the barback prep for the huge crowd that came in later for the pick-up scene. I ordered the jumbo-sized margarita with extra salt. "Salt on strawberry?" the bartender asked me, frowning.

"It's my birthday!" I answered and he backed me up with a second. The strawberry was sickeningly sweet. The margarita spilled over my hands and onto the bar. I licked my fingers. "This is so good," I told the bartender, who laughed at me.

"Go easy," he said. "Don't want to be partied out by tonight."

"Never!" I said and gulped some more. After just one of those margaritas I was pretty well wrecked, but I managed to plow through half of the second. I decided it was time to head to the nail salon for my manicure, so I jumped off the stool and felt the floor come at me, fast. I steadied myself against the bar and hobbled to the door swaying left then right, obviously shit-faced.

"Hold on there, birthday girl!" the bartender said as he ran up next to me. "Come on back, let's have some cake and coffee."

"Okay," I said, smiling at him. In an attempt to maintain some dignity, I tossed my hair as he helped me back to the bar. Even in my drunken stupor I saw him shake his head at me. This was probably the earliest he ever had to babysit a drunk. "You know," I said, once he had propped me back up on my barstool complete with a mug of fresh hot coffee, "I have all sorts of men fighting over me."

"I'm sure," he said, drying some glasses, back behind the bar in his safety zone.

"Really rich ones too," I said, rolling my r's. "Old men, mostly. I'm a mistress."

"Oh," he said.

"If you knew how difficult a profession it is to break into, you'd be more impressed," I said. "It's like being an actor... tough to break in."

"Hold on there one minute," the bartender said, now looking at me. "What do you know about being an actor? Are you one?"

"Nope," I giggled loudly, "a model. But hate it." I finished the sentence dramatically. I blew on the coffee to cool it down and took a sip.

"Let me tell you," he said still facing me. "I am an actor, and it's a hell of a lot of work. I trained for years to get fairly good at it. And I work my butt off every day, so don't say you know what being an actor is like, okay?"

"Okay," I said, shrugging. Then I really looked at him. "But if you're an actor, why are you a bartender?" I was sincerely confused.

"Because acting doesn't pay a lot at the beginning." He dried the glasses feverishly.

"I get that," I said, finishing my coffee. "My first boyfriend didn't even pay my rent! I had to work at Bloomingdale's." I leaned over the bar and whispered the last part. "In deli meats."

"That is bad," he said pouring me another cup. "Maybe you do get it." He poured himself a cup as well and we toasted to our respective – although perhaps not entirely respectable – professions.

Once I sobered up a bit, I managed to make it to the local nail salon. Everything the nail technician said that afternoon was immensely funny, even though I didn't understand a word of Korean. I giggled straight through my blood-red paint job. I gave her a nice tip and headed out.

When I got home, I had messages on my machine. "You have six new messages!" my answering machine said. My machine always sounded so excited that I had messages. Like it was rooting for me and my social life. I played them back. Beep! Mom, wishing me a happy birthday and asking if the sweater fit — glad I opened the box before playing the message.

Beep! Dr. Fifth Avenue asking about the evening and telling me he would call back after surgery. Beep! My credit card company telling me that I was past due.

"Well that's rude," I said to the machine. "And on my birthday."

Beep! My booker, telling me I missed a go-see. Beep! Dr. Fifth Avenue again. I couldn't figure it out, where was the call from Ivan? I played the last message, hoping it was from Ivan. It wasn't.

"Hello, Bella. How are you? This is Michael. I know it's been a long time... a very long time, but I wanted to wish you a happy birthday... although I'm sure that you have many people doing that. And I wanted you to know that I was thinking of you. And that... it's always been you, Bella." I slumped down on the floor, staring at the machine.

How? How could he call after all this time? I began to shake and covered my mouth with my hand. My stomach felt violently ill. I tripped over Charlie, but I made it to the bathroom just in time to throw up the jumbo (and a half) strawberry margaritas. I flushed and dropped to my knees, clutching the toilet as if it were the only thing keeping me from dissolving into complete nothingness. It may very well have been. A flood of memories overtook me. I remembered how I felt looking into that bathroom mirror the first time we had anal sex. The moment when he first told me that I was his. I remembered his breath, his smell, his arms, that scar. I closed my eyes and forced myself to concentrate on Ivan. But how could Ivan possibly stand up to Michael? And why was Michael calling me now?

I was overcome with the feeling that Michael may show up at any minute. It felt like he had never left, like he was in Italy for a month and was simply returning home. I jumped up, my head spinning and splashed ice-cold water on my face. I ran around trying to straighten up the apartment. I gazed in horror at all the new furniture. How could I ever explain it all? Eventually I realized how ridiculous I was acting and tried to pull it together. I stopped and sat down with a large glass of water. I tried to steady my breathing as I sipped. The phone rang again and I nearly jumped out of my skin. I answered it, dazed.

"Hello?" I asked, hoping and not hoping it was Michael.

"Hey, there." It was Dr. Fifth Avenue.

"Hey back."

"Whatcha up to?" he asked, doing his usual bad impression of a 1970's DJ.

"It's my birthday," I said, trying to regain my composure. The vomiting had left my head much clearer. "Thank you for the flowers."

"Yeah, listen. My wife took a long weekend away, want to do dinner?" I checked the time – five o'clock. I didn't know what to say.

I stalled. "I need to answer the door now. Can you call me back in ten minutes?"

"Oh. Okay." When I hung up, my heart was thumping so hard I thought it would jump clear out of my chest. I didn't know what to do, so I picked up the receiver, checked for the dial tone – twice – and called Ivan.

"I'm sorry," his assistant said. "He's left for the day."

"For the day? Okay, thanks."

"Do you want to leave a message?"

"No, thank you," I said, remembering that no matter how accessible he usually was, Ivan was still a married man. I hung up, more confused than ever. Why had Ivan forgotten all about me, and more importantly, why did Michael call? I sat, stupefied, trying to imagine why Ivan was ignoring me. But I couldn't focus. I couldn't think of anyone but him. No – I needed to concentrate on Ivan. He was, after all, my bread and butter. I convinced myself that Ivan's son was sick – not anything horrible, just a bad cold – and he needed to stay home. I decided Ivan was trapped in a suburban nightmare with my four-carat diamond and sapphire studs. That idea satisfied me well enough because truthfully, I just didn't care. It would be so easy to throw Ivan aside when Michael rides in on his tidal wave. I took another deep breath just as the phone rang again. I stared at the phone for four solid rings, paralyzed and terrified. Finally, on the fifth ring I approached and checked the caller ID. It was Dr. Fifth Avenue. Again. I answered the phone, trying to sound normal.

"Well?" he said. "What time?"

"What time, what?" I asked, perplexed by the whole evening.

"Dinner," he said, irritated that he had to work so hard for this one evening.

"Okay, where?" I asked. I had no idea what I was supposed to do. But it was my birthday, I hadn't seen Michael for years, and Ivan was missing. So I shut my eyes tightly and willed Dr. Fifth Avenue to say "Le Cirque." Instead, I knew that it would probably be some unknown, trendy spot. The ultimate oxymoron of Manhattan dining.

"It's a surprise," he said. "Just look hot."

I hung up the phone, bothered by his demand that I "look hot," but even more bothered by the idea of a surprise dinner, since I knew what that could potentially mean. Once, on a day trip to the island to buy ski clothes, we went to another surprise dinner – Taco Bell. Like my apartment, Taco Bell was, "cool!" and "hip!" and he hadn't eaten there, "like, since, college!" At least my lifetime ago. And like my apartment, I could have done without it. We dined on our taco and chalupa specials alongside a woman with a tight white T-shirt that said "Baby," with a large arrow pointing downwards, nearer to her crotch than her belly. It was certainly not the cosmopolitan dream I had envisioned when I became his mistress. But on that day, I smiled, pretending to enjoy myself. And he was happy. Back then, that was enough to make me happy too. So I undid the top button of my skin-tight black lycra pants and bit into my taco.

I erased all of my messages except Michael's and decided, with resolve, that I would have a good time with Dr. Fifth Avenue. It was my birthday and I was twenty-four, not nineteen. I didn't want tacos and I didn't want to eat dinner next to anyone wearing anything less than Ralph Lauren… Black Label. That was that. On that note, I looked through my closet, deciding what to wear. I took inventory, first by designer, then by color. Most of my designer dresses were from Michael and I thought wearing something from him would make the evening even more confusing and difficult for me. Finally, I narrowed it down to a full-length sheer black dress with a plunging neckline and no back or an Armani silk slip dress also in black. I was tempted to go with the full-length but knew I would never have the strength to pull it off. That dress required mega-confidence and Michael as your dinner date. I decided on the slip, took a steamy shower, brushed my hair back off my face, and did neutral make-up with shiny lips (Dr. Fifth Avenue no longer deserved kiss-proof lips), all the while keeping an ear bent toward the street for the roar of a Ferrari.

I was finishing my lips when the doorbell rang. Startled, I dropped my lipstick, missing my dress by millimeters. "Shit!" I said as I walked to the peephole to see who it was. It was Dr. Fifth Avenue. I was so disappointed I wanted to cry. I seriously considered feigning some horrible illness just so I could stay home and wait for Michael. But waiting around would kill me. I needed to get out. And maybe I would run into Michael somewhere.

"Just a minute!" I yelled as I raced about trying to compose myself. I grabbed the lipstick off the floor but couldn't find the cover. I threw the lipstick straight into my bag – my little Chanel bag – a move I was sure I would later regret. But that was nothing new for me. I regretted most of my decisions. I needed to head Dr. Fifth Avenue off at the door. I told myself it was to avoid conversation about my new furniture, but truthfully I was terrified that Michael would show up to find Dr. Fifth Avenue in my apartment. I grabbed my coat and bag complete with rogue lipstick and opened the door.

"Who ya hiding in there?" Dr. Fifth Avenue asked, irked that he had been left standing in the hallway for so long. He tried to look around me. Charlie hissed at him. I turned back to Charlie.

"Go lie down. Mommy will be home soon." Then to Dr. Fifth Avenue I said, "No one." I hit him playfully on the chest. We walked to the double-parked Mercedes and headed uptown. I was thankful he didn't ask about John, and even more thankful that the Chrysler was long gone.

I wondered if he would notice how agitated I was. He didn't. He was too consumed with his own happiness, and he was extra-animated that night. He was singing along with Billy Joel, wiggling in his seat, rocking back and forth to "Only the Good Die Young." A melodic voice was not one of the many gifts he was blessed with. I laughed despite myself.

"It's nice to see you smile," he said. I wondered if he knew it was over with John.

"Thanks," I said. "Where are we going?"

"I told you, it's a surprise! But man, do you look hot!" He wiggled more and more fiercely. Dr. Fifth Avenue never really looked like he was dancing, more like he was having a seizure. I was genuinely concerned we might crash. At least someone seemed to be enjoying my birthday. I crossed my fingers and prayed we were heading for Le Cirque and crème brulee... I wouldn't even mind if they forgot the birthday candle.

But, alas, there would be no Le Cirque for me on that birthday. As we blew past the entrance, I looked longingly out the window, waving as we went by. Goodbye all you beautifully sculpted animals, lit up like little versions of the night sky! You who welcome hungry wanderers, offering refuge and sustenance from the brutal world of Madison Avenue in mid-winter. My, how a custard deficiency made me wax poetic.

We reached our destination, a very different Midtown restaurant: Ferrier. I stopped in my tracks, the restaurant was packed. I wondered how he could risk it. More importantly, I wondered what the chances were that I might see Michael. Dr. Fifth Avenue didn't even seem to notice the crowd; there were too many hip people to include any of his and his wife's friends. This restaurant was for the young mistress. I had asked him once, long ago, if he was worried about being spotted by a patient when we were together. He told me that was the least of his concerns.

"What I do," he said, "requires much tact. My patients are much more concerned that I might out them in front of their dinner companion than I ever am that they might out me." He pulled me inside.

When I could finally focus and make sense of the hullabaloo, I saw the restaurant was staffed by model and actress wannabes and filled with Wall Street men, hoping to land a wannabe. There were also various other trendy people, a few artists and musicians and the token dead-beats, the out-of-town wealthy husbands and their voluptuous wives who had learned about this place by reading the review in their suburban issues of the *Times*.

I felt all eyes on me when I walked past the long bar – after all, people watching was the chosen sport of the night. "Who is that?" or "Isn't that Tom Cruise?" they would ask each other as person after person walked by. It was all so odd. I was one of the youngest people there but I felt as if I had completely outgrown this scene. The bar people all looked at me at once. One stockbroker type winked. I cringed.

"Wanna stop at the bar?" Dr. Fifth Avenue asked.

I shook my head and kept moving. I overheard some comments, some "wows" and some laughing; someone mentioned our age difference. Why? I don't know. It was New York. Half of the women in this city are with geezers twice their age. Still, I felt my shoulders begin to creep upward and a pain in my neck. My arms tightened. I had also begun to lose circulation in my fingertips whenever I was tense. This was one of those times.

We were led to a table by the next Elite up-and-comer, and Dr. Fifth Avenue ordered his favorite wine. I scowled at him. Not even champagne for my birthday.

He realized what he had done. "Sorry!" he said. "Your birthday! Should I have ordered champagne?"

"Not a problem."

Naturally, he took the better chair so he could people watch, and I was left with my back to the door, staring at him and the hallway to the bathroom. That meant that if I wanted to occasionally check if Michael had appeared, I had to crane my neck a full 180 degrees. Dr. Fifth Avenue loved his seat. He looked past me as person after person walked in. What a waste of an effort to look great. I gulped my water, waiting eagerly for something stronger to arrive.

We were recited the day's specials by a husky-voiced young woman whose breasts rivaled mine. While she spoke, she suspended a short pencil between the thumb and middle finger of her left hand, and used her right hand to turn it, point side up, point side down. Point side up, point side down. Rather then listening to what she was saying, I stared hard at her breasts, wondering if hers had feeling. She seemed surprised that it was me and not my date who was ogling. Surprised, but not offended. She leaned over me to point out something on the back of my menu. She caught my eye and smiled. It was the same smile I had given to countless men. I smiled back just as Dr. Fifth Avenue looked up. He cleared his throat. She tucked the pencil into her skin-tight silver sequined dress and walked away.

"Wow! She was into you!" he said, leering after Ms. Breasts. "Did you notice?"

"Not really." Of course I'd noticed, and I was flattered. She was almost unbelievably beautiful – as in, it's hard to believe that she's real – beautiful. She could have been Beyonce's twin. The attention felt great. Maybe I still had something to offer, even if it required that I play for the other team. I looked in her direction to see if she was still watching me. She glanced back and then disappeared into the kitchen.

"Talk about every man's dream!" Dr. Fifth Avenue said. "Hot lesbian sex!"

"It's my birthday," I said. He nodded his head and shut up. We went back to our menus.

I tried to focus on dinner choices as the wine was poured. That's when the deejay cranked the music to an ear-damaging volume. Try as I might, I couldn't concentrate with Madonna banging through my brain. At the very least, I wanted something spectacular for my birthday dinner. But who could decide with all that noise? Oh Lord, I was getting old. Then, just when I thought I couldn't be any more uncomfortable, the restaurant came to life, as if on cue. Ferrier suddenly morphed into a circus and I was caught under the Big Top. Our maitre d' grabbed the microphone.

"Ladies and Gentlemen! Welcome to the greatest show on earth!" the Ringmaster shouted. "To amaze you, for your viewing pleasure, watch – as the Fat Ladies dance on their tables and chairs! Can the tables hold their weight? Who knows? Wait and see!" Voluptuous Long Island and New Jersey wives climbed onto their chairs. "Now our acrobats, the wait staff! They join in the merriment with both glamour and ease! And later, folks, you'll see the Strong Men carry the Fat Ladies home after their third cosmopolitan kicks in! What a feat! These same men have been fucking their size two mistresses all week! Will they have the strength? The endurance? The stamina? Come one! Come all! To the greatest show on earth!"

It was a very different Cirque than I had hoped for. I was happy to be lost in my glass of Perrier at Ferrier. But then, the Ringmaster came by. "Dance!" he said. With that, Dr. Fifth Avenue grabbed my hand. He stood up and danced over to me.

"Come on," he said, moving his arms and wiggling his hips. He looked like a horny hula doll bobbing on a car dashboard. Like a ringer at a limbo contest, he pushed his pelvis forward as far as it would go. I couldn't blame him. If I had a body part that small I'd probably do anything I could to make it look bigger too. Oh wait... I already did.

I didn't want to dance, but Dr. Fifth Avenue had me up out of my seat and pressed his tiny member against me. He slid easily against the silk and I felt him get hard.

"And now...In the center ring!" the ringmaster shouted in my head. "Here's Victoria with... you guessed it! The one, the only... Bozo the Clown!"

"I don't want to dance," I said and Dr. Fifth Avenue resigned himself to wiggling alone, watching the Fat Ladies and the model wannabes cut a rug. Ms. Breasts was standing in the background watching my every move. Best I could tell she took my reluctance to be about him and not about the dancing. She started moving, slowly, sexily... swaying her body, bending deeply at the bar. My body moved in response. Soon the music ended and she disappeared. I sipped the horrible wine, suddenly in need of a drink.

"So, what are you up to?" Dr. Fifth Avenue asked twenty minutes later when he sat back down. There was sweat on his brow.

"Well," I said, giving him as much of my attention as I could, "actually, I made friends with an author." Dr. Fifth Avenue looked at me blankly.

"Friends?" he asked, raising his eyebrows.

"Yes, friends."

Dr. Fifth Avenue gave me the most patronizing smile I had ever seen. "No man wants to be friends with you, Victoria." His answer turned my stomach.

"Really?" I asked. "Well he's brilliant, and he thinks I'm smart... and I'm learning a lot from him. He's offered to send me to college. His treat. Just for fun to expand my mind." I had no idea where any of this came from. "So, I picked out some classes that I want to take... I'll probably start this spring."

"Classes?" Dr. Fifth Avenue asked. "You mean like dance classes?"

"No," I said offended by his amazement and angry that he wasn't buying my lie. Besides, did he really have the gall to suggest that I needed dance classes?

"Well, what then?" Dr. Fifth Avenue asked. "What kind of classes would you take?"

"College classes. You know, literature, science, I don't know. To finish my degree. Maybe business." I felt like I was instigating something.

He looked at me with genuine surprise. "Why?" he asked.

"Why, what?" I said, trying to remain calm. Sip, dab, stare.

"Why college classes?" Sip, sip, look around. "There's your friend," he said, pointing in Ms. Breasts' direction. I didn't want to drop the subject. I wanted to know what he meant.

"Because I want to finish my degree," I said, standing my ground. The lie had begun to have a life of its own. "And why not?"

"I didn't think you had that kind of money. That you could just, you know, throw it away on whatever." He let his body move up and down with the beat. Well, sort of with the beat.

"I just told you that my friend is paying for it," I said. "Thanks for paying such close attention." And then it dawned on me. Watching him only half-listening to me, I finally understood. Mistresses are kept just poor enough – in every way – so they can't run off on their men. It's like keeping a puppy hungry and being the one to offer it food. If I got an education it would be a direct threat to Dr. Fifth Avenue. Who knows what I would learn? Who knows what I would realize I was capable of? And what use would I be to him if I were educated? His face scrunched up into a scowl. I felt like I had disappointed my father.

"Even if he wasn't," I said, "I don't consider getting an education throwing money away."

Dr. Fifth Avenue looked me straight in the eyes for the first time all night. "Maybe not for someone average... but you! You're so beautiful. What do you need an education for?"

I felt the anger well up inside me and my cheeks flush. I stared back and said, "Maybe to prove that I'm not stupid?" I heard the vulnerability in my own voice. I waited for him to say that I didn't need to prove anything, but I should have known better. Those Armani suits were his way of proving to the world who he was: poor boy made good. I stared at him wide-eyed. "You think I'm stupid, don't you?" He took a sip of wine. "You do, don't you?"

He looked over his menu at me. His voice was soft and sympathetic. "Well, you do make it hard to think otherwise." He smiled at me, a broad, calm, pacifying smile. "Now, go ahead, order something you really want. It's your birthday!"

I slumped in my chair. Happy Birthday to me. I downed my entire glass of that wretched wine. He ordered another bottle.

After our mediocre meal was over and while we were finishing off our second bottle, Ms. Breasts presented Dr. Fifth Avenue with the check and me with her number and a note. "Call me. I get off at 11:30. Tracy." I was fascinated by Tracy. I couldn't imagine why a woman would get implants for another woman. No woman would like fake breasts; they're too obtrusive and hard. And you only go through a major surgery for a man, right? No woman would expect you to alter yourself physically for her. I considered calling Tracy just to ask. I threw the slip of paper into my bag.

"Whatcha got there?" Dr. Fifth Avenue asked.

"A number."

"Are you gonna call?" he asked, bouncing in his seat.

I sighed. "She just wants the name of the guy who cuts my hair," I said. Then I tired of all the mendacity. "And if it were more, why the hell not?" I asked. "Why shouldn't I call her? What is the big deal about two women getting together for more than just friendship?"

Dr. Fifth Avenue began speaking at break-neck speed. He told me precisely what the big deal was, and he had quite a lot to say on the subject. I shook my head, wondering how I ended up at dinner with Howard Stern.

When I finally got home, I ran to pee and sitting there, I made the decision to hang Tracy's number on my fridge. Tracy proved that there were some options for me, that I didn't have to be a slave to a man. I never expected to actually call her but I wanted to remind myself that I could. I went to my bag and pulled out the slip of paper. Wouldn't you know it, the open lipstick had smeared her number completely. I rubbed at it with a tissue but it just made the smudge worse. I rubbed harder and harder until I had completely wiped the number away. Why couldn't she have just used a pen instead of that damned pencil? So I wrote my own note – "Tracy at Ferrier" – in pen, and hung it on the little fridge. There. I smiled. There was my option. I was determined to make twenty-four a better year than all the others.

PART II

THE LESSER GODS OF OLYMPUS

CHAPTER 5: EROS

"Evil his heart, but honey-sweet his tongue. No truth in him, the rogue. He is cruel in his play. Small are his hands, yet his arrows fly far as death. Tiny his shaft, but it carries heaven-high. Touch not his treacherous gifts, they are dipped in fire."

The next day I woke up with a hangover, blurry from confusion and wine. I was angry that Ivan hadn't called me on my birthday and out of sorts over Michael. But I was even more pissed that I'd spent my birthday with Dr. Fifth Avenue. It was as if I was trapped in a one-act play with only two other characters and they just kept reentering. My very own version of "No Exit."

I spent that very confusing morning in bed with Charlie, wondering why it now mattered to me that Dr. Fifth Avenue – or people in general – found me smart. What did I care? I had walked out on a free education and I wasn't exactly in a profession that required a Mensa membership. My mother's philosophy was that education was only for men and ugly women. But there was a part of me that secretly envied Liz, who had a Master's Degree in psychology, and I'd always wondered how she felt about our mother's opinion.

Mom had only a high school diploma herself, but my father, who died young, had been educated. He held an MBA from Cornell and a law degree from Stanford. They found each other at a small bar in the East Village one night in the early seventies and were completely attracted to each other, mostly because of their differences. My mother was the quintessential party-girl everyone loved (she assured me), and my father was a corporate attorney whom everyone feared (he assured me). Compared to my mother and her flightiness, my father was straight-laced and conservative. Because of him we're named "Elizabeth" and "Victoria" rather than "Sunshine" and "Moonbeam," or worse, if we had been boys, "Jack Daniels" and "Marlboro Man." When Liz came along, they settled down. My mother became a suburban homemaker reading the tabloids and preparing Jell-O for our dinner, while my father retreated to his office six days a week and worked so hard he dropped dead of a heart attack at forty-one. Neither Liz nor I got to know him very well. But neither of us felt like we were missing anything either. At least I didn't. That's just the way it was. Mom assured us that it was the man's job to go out and make a life for the woman and sometimes that resulted in tragedy. She saw my father's death as an occupational hazard. I accepted that idea much more willingly than Liz, who cried herself to sleep for years after his death. Me, I slept fine knowing that in choosing my father, my mother had provided well for her family. I always found it interesting that my mother never remarried. I've often wondered if that meant that somewhere inside her, she actually loved my father.

Years later, as I bounced from therapist to therapist, several of them would insist on the boring old cliché that I was dating significantly older men because I was searching for a father-figure. I assured them that I was simply attracted to older men; I coveted their lifestyles, especially their money and success. That, of course, led two of my therapists to ask me out.

Twenty-four brought with it the brutal realization that without Ivan (or John or Dr. Fifth Avenue or especially Michael), I was broke. The income I received from my men covered surface expenses but I never managed to stash anything away. Being a mistress had its costs. There was the gym membership – even a Y in Manhattan was pricey; regular haircuts and color treatments; the occasional blow-out; make-up – usually Chanel or Mac to keep up with the latest trends; waxing – bikini, leg, and eyebrow; regular manicure and pedicures; facials; body polishing for glowing, soft skin; lo-cal foods; teeth whitening procedures; all those at-home creams and potions for face and body; pricey anti-cellulite cream; self-tanner; and visits to specialty gyms to tone those trouble spots.

When I ran through my options, I panicked. Michael had left a message, it's true, but would I really see him again or was that phone call just a fluke? Sure, Dr. Fifth Avenue was around for the occasional dinner, but he never offered any real financial assistance and, frankly, he was becoming more of hassle than he was worth. Besides, even he would eventually stop calling if he never got sex. And Ivan was, well, M.I.A. The only viable option to help lessen my money crunch was to find a new man, stat. Until then, I had no choice but to work more. So I spent that next Monday on hateful go-sees for Bridal Week, which was coming up at the end of the month. Bridal Week – a bit ironic, no? With much effort to look like a happy young bride, which meant adding a lot of extra pink blush to my sallow cheeks, I booked the second-to-last job of the day. At my earlier go-sees they all seemed to say the same thing to me: "Your look is great! But you just don't seem like a bride to me." Well, no kidding. I was glad to be done.

When I finally got home that evening, I lit some lavender candles and climbed into my tiny bathtub. I marveled at how the phone didn't ring when Dr. Fifth Avenue had family night at home. Lying there, I began to wonder what I was doing wrong. Why was I forced to pound the pavement looking for modeling jobs when I had devoted years into fucking several high-powered, wealthy men? Their wives weren't out schlepping a portfolio up and down Broadway. Next year would be my twenty-fifth birthday, and I would be too old to book a lot of jobs. Even more terrifying, I'd be too old to be the mistress of certain men, men like John. I needed to cash in, and cash in fast. I had to find the better boyfriend, the bigger god. But where?

It had been so easy to go from man to man these past few years, but would it always be? I had always likened myself to a pro-athlete; once I was too old to play the game, I would retire to a luxurious lifestyle in the South of France. Unfortunately, I had no signing bonus or multi-million dollar contract stashed away. My work was totally of-the-moment with no long-term safety net. Despite the warm water and the permeating lavender scent, I began to get stressed. Then the phone rang. I lifted myself a bit and perked my ears. My head was sure that it was just my mother checking on my weekend plans, but my heart thought otherwise and started thumping. It wasn't my mother, though I couldn't make out who it was over the sound of my own quickening breath. But it was definitely a man.

I jumped out of the bathtub and ran, naked, toward the phone. As soon as my feet hit the tile floor my legs flew out from under me. I landed hard on my tailbone and slid onto my back. I pushed myself up slowly and walked around the apartment in circles.

"I'm okay, I'm okay," I said to a worried Charlie as the still unidentified voice droned on into my machine. I couldn't hear a word he was saying because my ears were ringing from the fall. But I could tell the tempo was too quick for Michael and the voice was too deep for Dr. Fifth Avenue. That meant it had to be Ivan. I tried to focus and read the caller ID but my eyesight was blurry. I grabbed for the phone but Ivan had already hung up. I star-69ed the call, but it was unavailable or private. "Shit!" I threw the phone. Who could I call? I had only office numbers and a few cell numbers. I had no idea where Ivan was calling from, and Dr. Fifth Avenue wasn't available until Monday. If I had known Michael's latest number, I would have caved in and called him ages ago. I grew hysterical as I crawled across the floor looking for the phone. I found it and called my mother... obviously, I was terrified.

"Mom, I fell."

"What do you mean, fell?"

"Coming out of the bathtub... I slipped, my eyesight's funny and I have a headache. I feel like I'm going to throw up."

"Oh, Jesus Christ. I knew this would happen with you living alone. You must have hit your head. Call an ambulance." My mother took an extra long drag on her cigarette.

"I didn't hit my head." My call waiting beeped in. "Mom? I feel better, sorry. My other line beeped through. I'll call you later."

"Maybe it's one of your doctor friends. What good are they if they can't help you when you're sick?"

I clicked over to the other line. "Hello?" I was crying.

"Victoria? What's wrong?" It was Ivan.

"I fell down – I can't see! I feel like I'm going to throw up!"

"Did you hit your head?"

"No." I stammered like a wounded child.

"Then you'll be fine. It's probably your central nervous system that got a little shock. It'll wear off."

"Can you come over?" I sniffled.

"What? No, Victoria, I'm away."

"You didn't call me on my birthday." Obviously I wasn't that sick.

"I'm sorry. Victoria...?"

"Yes?"

"I don't know how to tell you this, but—"

"What?"

"I won't be around much anymore."

"Why?" I asked, feeling so lonely and tired that my heart actually ached. "Are you moving?"

"Sort of."

"Where? What's going on?"

"My wife and I are giving it one more shot." There was no apology in his voice. "I'm giving up the apartment and moving to the Island full-time."

"Tonight?"

"We have a child, Victoria," he said. His answer was definite.

"Can't you come see me? I fell. I'm sick…."

"No, Victoria, I can't be your friend anymore."

"Why not?"

"My wife," he said, "she's pregnant. And I owe her, well, everything. We had fun, Victoria. Besides, I was just a career move for you anyway." And with that it was over, at least for him.

"You fucking jerk!" I screamed at the dial tone.

My sight was still blurry from the fall and my tears, and I was beginning to freak about my whole situation. I wrapped myself in a towel to try to stop shaking. I snuggled Charlie but I just couldn't stand being alone in my little apartment any longer. I ran to the buzzer and called my doorman.

"Jim? It's Victoria in— Yeah. Listen, I hurt myself and I was wondering if that guy… cute, tall… is he really a doctor?"

Jim insisted that the doctor would come to me. Not even six minutes of sitting on the couch, fretting, and the doctor was at my door. Even with blurry vision I could tell that he was at least as tall as John and even more handsome than I remembered.

"I heard someone needed a doctor?" he said. I stared at him and forced a smile. I was still in my towel and my face was red and puffy from crying. All my usual defenses were down.

"I fell," I said.

"Can I come in?" he asked. "Jim knows I'm here. I promise you can trust me. And besides, you have that attack cat there!" Charlie ran to the bed. The doctor looked at me and blushed slightly. "Do you have a bathrobe?"

"Yeah, bathroom."

In an instant he had the robe for me. I let my towel drop to the floor and he cleared his throat. I slipped into the robe. We sat side by side on the couch and as I explained my symptoms, my sight slowly returned to normal. When I could finally focus, I saw that he had salt and pepper hair and was more handsome than all of my boyfriends put together. Even John. I smiled. "Better?" he asked.

"Oh, yes," I said nodding. "Better than I ever imagined."

"Excuse me?"

"Nothing. I was just scared," I said, rethinking my position on him.

"How about some tea?" he asked.

He made me wait on the couch while he found his way around the little walk-through kitchen. Sooner than I wanted, tea was made and finished.

"Can I sleep tonight?" I asked, assuming he would leave soon.

"Yes. There's no danger of a concussion. But..."

"But? But what...?"

"Don't be alarmed. Sorry. I was wondering if you'd like to watch a movie with me?"

"A movie? Okay." I was happy for the company but hesitant to get involved with someone who wasn't an Olympian. But a movie was just a movie and an on-call doctor was worth something, especially since I had no health insurance.

Over a movie and mushroom pizza in my little apartment, the doctor told me he lived in the penthouse of my building. "Sure, this building has a penthouse," I said, tilting my jaded little head. But it did. So, that night I learned something new about my building, and about its handsome penthouse tenant – he was a proctologist. Naturally, his profession made me think of Michael and I even considered asking him a few questions about how to make certain areas feel better. But no sense spilling too much information or ruining the moment. He was, after all, my knight in shining armor, if only for the evening.

Finally, the doctor confessed that he had been asking about me for quite some time. "Really?" I said, picking the mushrooms off of my third piece and feigning complete surprise. Of course I knew, I just never paid any attention. I never thought he was… well, good enough. I fed Charlie little pieces of the melted mozzarella.

"Yeah," he said, looking down and struggling with his words. "I even like it when you go to the laundry room with your hair all piled up in a thing on top of your head." He mimed the action with his words. It was just fine by me that he didn't know the word "scrunchy."

I felt my robe fall open slightly but didn't bother to close it. I wasn't sure just yet what it was I wanted from him and figured I might as well keep him tempted. He did his best not to notice. "I asked Jim to tell everyone in the building that I was a doctor. I figured, eventually you would get sick and we would meet up. It just took a little longer than I hoped."

Much to my surprise, I agreed to see the doctor again, and much to his surprise, I didn't sleep with him until our fourth date. Our dates weren't overly exciting – Italian food one night, a movie another. On our second date, he gave me a bottle of Chanel No. 5 with matching bath accessories. It was thoughtful but I exchanged it for Coco. He was obviously courting me, but he was doing so in a very mundane way. That worried me. I began to think that he might be clueless about what I expected, things like lavish nights out and extravagant gifts. Not to mention that my rent was coming up fast and I was left to pay it all on my own pretty much for the first time since Dr. Fifth Avenue. After some hinting, we eventually made it to a club, but we were expected to wait in a line to get in. This, of course, embarrassed me and made me crave my dates with Michael all the more. Once we finally got inside, I discovered that the doctor was a fairly awful dancer, especially in comparison to Michael who could shake my world both on the dance floor and off. I thought it best to avoid doing the club scene with the doctor ever again. I think he was relieved. Strangely, it didn't dawn on me until our third date, while we were standing in a movie line, to ask about a wife.

"A wife?" he said, horrified. "What makes you think I have a wife? I'm out with you!" An unmarried, older doctor was not my original game plan, but what the hell. It wasn't as good as winning lotto but it was close to winning the daily number.

On our fourth date, he let me into his apartment with great expectation. I was pleasantly surprised. The apartment was big, it was the entire top floor of the building. That was a relief; I just couldn't imagine why a doctor was living in my half-way house... half-way to demolition, that is.

I looked around. Happily, I stumbled upon a picture of him posing next to two antique corvettes. "Nice picture!" I said, perking up.

"Thanks," he said. "The cars are part of my collection. It's sort of an obsession of mine." Whew. I felt so much better knowing that he had a fleet of good cars. I nosed about some more, hoping to discover additional hidden treasures. Unfortunately, what I found was that the apartment was really nothing special – except for a beautiful terrace. On closer inspection the terrace was actually a converted roof area but who gave a shit? It was still called a terrace in my book. "Nice huh?" he asked, delivering wine.

"Mm-hm," I said. "This would be a great place for—"

"A Jacuzzi! I know. I've been meaning to put one in."

"Well then why don't you?" I asked, sipping my Shiraz. An outdoor Jacuzzi in the middle of downtown Manhattan would be a nice thing to cool off, or warm up in. But try as I might, I couldn't imagine the two of us naked, huddled up on the roof of my building. Somehow, the idea made me want to burst out crying.

That evening was something of an out-of-body experience for me. I tried to be interested in him but I just couldn't shake the feeling that he was going to be a hugely disappointing boyfriend. I tried concentrating on his cars but I just didn't believe that they were really his. And how many make up a collection exactly? He was so far beneath the usual caliber of man I dated that I actually cringed when he touched me. I didn't even want to commit to the evening, never mind to something more. But I pushed myself. I needed someone to get me over my hurdle.

Under my sweater and black pants I was wearing an emerald lace bra and thong, a gift from... oh who remembers. Fancy lingerie is the most prevalent expensive gift a mistress is given – for obvious reasons. It is also the one gift that is more for the giver than the give-ee, and unfortunately, it is neither returnable nor hockable.

With my usual routine of half-stripper and half-virgin, I undressed to my bra and panties and watched him as he unbuttoned his shirt. His blue eyes matched his shirt exactly and his chest hair was gray. He was handsome. Then he slid his jeans off to reveal white boxers which he seemed to fill out well. Unfortunately, I discovered that boxers are misleading. It seems tiny members may be – along with high MCAT scores – a requirement for medical school.

"You're so beautiful," the doctor said as I lay back on his bed, one knee bent, my arms lifted above my head. In that position, I knew that I could rival any *Playboy* centerfold. I also knew it was my time to get what I wanted from a man. After that – once he had "had" me, my power waned. I lifted my butt and then wiggled back down. I patted the bed. He let out a soft, "Oh my God" and climbed in next to me. It was now or never. He slipped his arm behind my neck and I sat up. He sat up next to me and whispered, "Are you okay?" as he brushed the hair off my face.

"Yes," I whispered. "Sorry, I'm just a little preoccupied."

"Now?" he said.

"Always," I said, looking at him with my best doe eyes. "I just, I just have some things going on that have me under a great deal of stress. And being here, in your beautiful apartment reminded me."

"Why should anyone as gorgeous as you be stressed?" he said, kissing my neck.

"Thank you," I said, "and you're right." I pulled myself together visibly. "I'm sorry I brought it up. Especially here. I don't know if I should tell you this, but I've been anticipating being here, in your bed, for awhile." I let my eyes drop and felt my cheeks flush. Take that Eleanor Duse. "It's a special thing for me to get this close to someone. Rare."

"Me too," he assured me, moving his body closer. I could smell his cologne as his body temperature rose. Issey Miyaki for Men.

"I was just so happy for a moment and I felt so relaxed. Then the emotion came pouring out. Please forget I said anything," I said, trying to lie back down. "Please." But he held me up and put both his arms around me. He looked me square in the eyes.

"You can tell me," he said.

"No, this is my problem. Please...."

"Victoria," he said, kissing me gently on the lips, "please tell me. I'm your boyfriend. If you can't talk to me, who can you talk to?" I felt the adrenaline rush overtake me as I moved in for the kill.

"But I don't want you to think horrible things of me. Promise you won't."

"Of course."

"I was supposed to get some work this week – modeling – but the guy who hired me turned out to be such scum! And he wanted me to go out with him tonight... which meant, well, you know what that meant... and I couldn't, I just couldn't." I let a giant tear fall as I buried my face in his chest.

"Good for you, you stood up for yourself!" he said, holding me.

"Yes, but now I don't know how I can possibly pay my rent!" I sobbed in his chest.

"Is that all it is?" he asked, laughing.

"It might be funny to you!" I said. "But I'm terrified!"

"Oh, Victoria, don't worry about that. Please. Let me help you out."

"What?" I asked as innocently as I could.

"I'll take care of your rent for you. For as long as you need."

"But I couldn't let you. I've never..." I stopped short on that thought. Too far. I fixed it, quickly. "I mean, it would be too much."

"How much could you possibly pay here?" he asked. "Besides, I make plenty of money. Let me help you out. It would make me happy."

"Really?" I said, lifting my head and reading his face.

"Absolutely," he said, kissing me.

"How would we even do it?" I asked, making sure that he wasn't just pacifying me with an empty promise. "What? Would you write me a check?"

"How's cash?" he asked, rolling out of bed and going to a dresser drawer. "What's your rent here, $1300 a month?"

"$1100" I said, not wanting to be caught in a lie since he might very well see my rent bill someday.

"Well here's thirteen," he said, counting out hundreds. "That way you can buy some food too. You always seem so hungry on our dates." I smiled a big, beautiful smile of victory.

"Thank you so much," I said, wiping tears from my eyes. "You don't know how you just saved me. Now," I asked, my tone changing notably, "is there anything I can do for you?"

The doctor kissed me, long, passionately, and hard. A little too hard. My head was forced into the pillow. I grunted and tried to move. I wedged my arms between us and used all of my strength to push him off of me. He picked his head up and smiled, pleased with himself. He looked just like Marmaduke the Dog, big, clumsy and dopey. He kissed me again in the exact same way.

Deciding he was looking for more passion, I attacked him. I rolled out from under him – happy to be on top – and kissed him up and down his chest. He liked it, but I sensed that he was definitely looking for something more. Quickly, he moved me next to him and ran his hands down my body. He rested them between my legs, touching me, again too hard. The next time he kissed me, my lips went numb. I knew they would be bleeding soon; I still peeled layers of skin off of them every day. I pushed him back, and unfortunately, he took it to mean I wanted him to go down on me.

He slid my panties off and I braced myself for the pain. For the doctor, oral sex was a wet, slobbery war, and I was its casualty. Finally, he was ready for intercourse but there was no way I could even imagine enjoying it anymore. I was trapped. My $1300 dollars was sitting on his dresser. I'd have to finish what I started if I wanted to walk out with it.

He was rough straight through intercourse. But this wasn't anything like Michael rough. Michael rough was "I know this is brutal, but it's a game we play because I control you completely" – and hell, I enjoyed every minute of it. This was just awkward, juvenile sex. His last girlfriend must have been a tank. I thought of calling her, maybe she'd share her survival strategies with me. That is, if she survived. His forceful thrusting gave me a headache. He reached around and put his hand under my waist. He lifted me up and slid his hand down onto my ass.

"No!" I said. "Sorry. No anal sex." I left it at that, with no explanation. He was disappointed but he got over it and finished conventionally. When we were done, I was bruised from head to toe, and while he basked in the afterglow, I healed. I couldn't wait to get out of there but I had to put in a certain amount of post-coital time or it would all be too obvious.

"Wow!" he said when he was finished.

"Yes, wow."

He rolled over and looked at me. Maybe he was sizing up the amount of damage he'd caused my face. He smiled a big, contented smile.

"So, what do you think? Do I have movie star potential or what?" As far as I was concerned, he didn't even have porn star potential. I ignored him and looked over at my money wondering if I could get more out of him, and even if I could, if it was worth having to do this again. "I guess by now you've figured out that I like things a little differently," he said. He looked shy and insecure; his mop of hair was tousled like a little boy at recess. "And I don't want to scare you off, but since we're both being honest tonight...."

"It's okay," I said out of obligation. "Tell me." What else could he want? Would I have to come to bed in full armor?

"It's not just anal sex that I like—"

Here it comes, I told myself. I played my game, now I'd have to play his.

"I also like, you know, vibrators... butt plugs, oils...." It was his shopping list for the week.

"Oh," I heard myself say. I wondered how far I would have to go in my quest to pay rent.

"I'd like to take you shopping," the doctor said. Well that was more like it! Ladies and Gentlemen – we have a winner! He went on like he was asking me to the prom, fidgeting with the sheets. "We can get lots of stuff together."

"Shopping?" I asked. Ivan's sudden disappearance had left me with S.A.S.W. Severe Afternoon Shopping Withdrawals.

"For toys."

"Toys like for my niece?" The hurt little girl act had worked so well on him before, I thought that maybe it could get me out of this scenario as well.

But the doctor just laughed at me. So it was to be Dr. Ass and me shopping for anal plugs and lubricants. For leashes and whips and vibrators. Not quite my idea of an ideal relationship. It was clear I'd underestimated him, this would be the hardest $1300 a month I had earned to date.

The next time I saw him, I managed to escape the shopping trip, but no sooner did we hit the sheets than he wanted up my ass, literally. Aside from his roughness and complete lack of lovemaking skills, I had another little problem to deal with. The sex that I had with Michael left me with bleeding anal fissures which Dr. Ass would surely notice, considering it was both his chosen profession and his chosen point of entry. I just wasn't ready to answer his questions. Heck, I hadn't even erased Michael's last message from my machine. So once again I refused.

"Victoria," he asked me that night as we lay back in bed, "how old are you?"

"Twenty-one." The young bit seemed to be working for me. "How old are you?"

"Forty-eight," he said, "and that's old enough to know what I want. Sweetheart, you're going to have to learn to do this eventually."

"Why?" I asked, putting him on the spot.

"Because I like it. And, you're my girlfriend. You should want to make me happy."

"I do," I said, sounding as young as I could. "But that scares me. I'm not ready."

"All right, sweetheart," he said, closing his eyes. What an amateur – he hadn't even tried bribing me with options, like offering me pot or large amounts of wine to help with the pain. Even if he had, I wouldn't have gone for it. Anal sex was only for Michael. I made up an early call time and left as soon as possible.

Normally, I took the stairs back down to my apartment but I was just too sore. I waited for the elevator, dabbing at my bleeding lip while he stood in the doorway waving good-bye. Thankfully, the elevator came quickly. I hobbled on to find another passenger – and not just any passenger – the building gossip, a prudish, elderly woman with her two Pomeranian dogs. She must have gotten on the elevator just when I called it up. Shit. If our rat trap had been a co-op, one look at me leaving his apartment with unbuttoned clothes, smeared make-up, and blood dribbling from my lip would have gotten me tossed out on my over-used ass. She scrunched her face up into a taut little prune. She held the dogs tightly to herself. I smiled at her; she gasped. She whispered something into the larger dog's ear and he barked at me. The little one nipped at me. I looked closely at the two growling dogs. Clearly, they were better cared for then I was.

Dr. Ass disappeared the next day. I thought maybe he had run because of my dislike for all things anal, and I was happy for the break. I kept track of how many times I had to fuck him for the same $1300 and it was quickly becoming too many. But I felt like I couldn't walk out on him because next month's rent was right around the corner. I hated the position I was in. Two days later I got a call. Dr. Ass was in the Hamptons, and, naturally, there was a wife after all. I had never seen her because she loathed the city and stayed in the Hamptons as much as possible. He was playing me as much as I was playing him. Both of our innocent acts had run their courses.

"But don't be angry," he said to me. "It's not a real marriage. We haven't had sex in over two years."

"Gee, I wonder why."

"What do you mean?" he asked. When I didn't answer, he explained his situation. "I needed to come out here because she has the flu and she's upset. I have to help her. I'll be back in a week or so."

So there it was. That was his shtick. He liked to save women. He became a doctor to rescue damsels in distress. I imagined his wife feigned illness whenever she wanted her husband back. She probably prayed for a serious disease.

"Don't bother coming back for me," I said. "I'm gone." With that, I had the excuse I was looking for. Finally, I had a plausible reason to dump Dr. Ass on his ass. Although I was painfully aware that my money situation was extremely tight, I just couldn't stomach having to see him again. I had one month's rent; I cut my losses and escaped.

During my two-week love affair with Dr. Ass, Dr. Fifth Avenue called frequently to ascertain that I had really stopped seeing John. He was devastated. I thought maybe I should take him out to help get him over the break-up. Softly, through a cracking voice, he asked me for the particulars. Obviously news didn't travel as fast at the tennis club as I was afraid it might.

I had nothing going on in the man department. Ivan never even showed up at the gym again, and Michael... well Michael finally left another message, this time to let me know that he was out of the country. (It only took me another couple of weeks to get over that message.) All that was ahead for me was a hateful week of Bridal which I had to get through.

I showed up for work on Monday in jeans and a cream-colored cashmere cardigan. I shared the dressing room with two other women, neither of whom came from big agencies either. Paula was about twenty-eight with enormous (real) breasts, whose entire portfolio consisted of her work in Japanese *Playboy*. Mandy was a bigoted Southern bitch, about twenty. Mandy took one look at me, rolled her beady little brown eyes, and said, "Ugh." That was the only thing she said to me the entire time we worked together. On the fifth day of a six-day week, my agency called me.

"They don't need you anymore."

"What? Why?" Despite my hatred for both modeling and brides, I was doing a good job with the show.

"Their answer? They've decided that you're just not right."

"After four days? How is that possible?"

"Who knows," my booker said. "If you ask me, this business sucks."

Later that day, I learned from Paula we were all fired because the designer had hooked up with some newer models who were willing to finish the show for half of the usual rate. If they had told my booker the truth, the designer would have been required to pay us for the full week. So the blame befell each of us older models. My booker was right; this business sucked.

That night, I consoled myself by getting naked and throwing on the luxurious cashmere robe I saved for special occasions. Charlie snuggled down onto the cashmere, purring. I started early on an entire bottle of Shiraz, ordered Mo Shu Pork and Peking Duck and thumbed through the new *Vogue* I had lifted from the showroom. While I waited for the delivery, I tried to figure out precisely how broke I was. It wasn't pretty. New York was just such an expensive place that even if I cut back on luxuries like professional hair coloring and waxing, I still spent way more in a month than I could ever earn modeling. As I poured myself another glass of wine, I wondered where I could learn how to get more out of my men. I had already fucked some really good catches and yet, despite a closet full of clothes, I had nothing to show for it. I had sixty-seven dollars in my bank account and although I had the $1100 from Dr. Ass for rent (the other $200 was long gone), I still needed to pay phone, electricity, cable, and credit card bills. I was broke and knew I would soon be approaching desperate times.

I was already a little drunk when the buzzer rang. I tied up my robe and stood at the opened door. Charlie waited for me on the couch. The very young delivery guy got off of the elevator and walked the wrong direction down the hall.

"Down here!" I whispered so I wouldn't disturb the neighbors. He turned and picked through three bags to see which one was mine.

"Thirty-four dollars and sixty cents," he said, handing me my bag.

"Excuse me?" I asked, stunned. "You're kidding! You must have given me the wrong order." I tried to hand the bag back.

"No," he said, "your order."

"But all I have is Mo Shu Pork! It can't be thirty-four dollars and sixty cents." I said this slowly and deliberately in case the problem was a language barrier.

"Mo Shu Pork and Peking Duck," he said just as slowly, no doubt thinking the same thing. "Plus soda."

"Shit, I forgot." Those drinks were expensive.

"Thirty-four dollars and sixty cents," he said with resolve.

"Yeah, yeah I heard you," I said as I got my wallet. But when I looked inside there was only a twenty. I began digging through my wallet and then opening and closing a few kitchen drawers hunting for a forgotten stash. The delivery guy looked at his watch. "Hold on a minute," I said. "I'm just looking for more money." But I had no more money. And I wouldn't have any more money until I got paid for those past few days of work. That could take weeks. My agent would give me an advance (although he'd deduct ten-percent for fronting me) on Monday but I'd still have to survive the weekend. I couldn't get any more money from the cash machine because they required me to maintain a fifty dollar balance. Thirty-four dollars was just about half of my life savings. I was about to spend half of my life savings on Chinese food. Wow! Food was too expensive. I swore never to have to pay for it, ever again. I was Scarlet O'Hara waving my twenty at the gods of Mount Olympus. "As you gods are my witnesses, I'll never pay for my own dinner again!" I was frozen in the kitchen, clasping the money. I'd lived on cereal straight from the box for my dinner every night that week and I was in need of some real food. I could send back the Peking Duck and pay for the Mo Shu with the twenty, but that would leave me with no money at all for the weekend. And I had absolutely no food in the house. Not even peanut butter. I was desperate. "Look," I pleaded with the delivery guy, "just come in for a minute. Give me a second." I dialed Dr. Fifth Avenue's number which was completely ridiculous but I had to try. Naturally, Dr. Fifth Avenue wasn't reachable, it was Friday night. I buzzed my doorman who assured me that he too was broke until his next paycheck.

"Okay," I said, walking back to the delivery guy. "I am in an embarrassing situation here. I have no money, but I didn't realize that when I called. Do you think you could give me this food on credit tonight? Please? And the next time you deliver, I'll give you an extra tip. Honestly."

"Thirty-four dollars and sixty-cents," he said again.

"Yes, I know how much it is," I said, trying to remain calm, "but I don't have it."

"No money?" he asked.

"Exactly," I said, somewhat relieved that at last he understood. He grabbed the bag back from me and turned to the door. He muttered something at me in Chinese – which I'm glad I didn't understand – and then in perfect English he said, "Don't call anymore." He opened the door. It was time to try a different approach. He was a man after all.

"Listen," I said, twirling the belt of my bathrobe. "Can't you help me out... just tonight? Please? Buy my food for me tonight and I will give you a giant tip next time."

"No," he said.

"I don't think you understand," I said, tossing my hair and putting my hand on his shoulder. "I'll give you a twenty-dollar tip next time!" He looked at my hand and I pulled it off his shoulder.

"I don't need twenty dollars," he said, his patience tested. I felt my hunger pangs grow more and more violent.

"Okay," I said, near tears, "that was my stomach growling. Didn't you hear it? I'm starving. I need food." I considered grabbing the food from his hand and kicking him out the door. I thought about breaking into Dr. Ass's apartment and scouring for food. Then another, better thought occurred to me. "How old are you?" I asked, in my best Marilyn Monroe voice.

"Twenty-three," he answered, his voice questioning me.

"And what's your name?"

"Mee-han," he said, wondering why he was still at my apartment.

"Hi Mee-han, I'm Victoria. Are you married, Mee-han?"

"No. Lady, I need money!"

"Yes, I know," I said shifting my weight from one side to the other and leaning against the doorframe. "It's just, I don't have any... but I thought, maybe... do you like models?" I asked, swallowing my last bit of pride.

"Sure," he said, suddenly interested, "everyone likes models."

"I'm a model," I told him, again trying the hair toss.

"Yeah?" he asked.

"Yeah," I said. "Have you ever dated a model?"

"No!"

"Well I'm not asking you on a date," I said, shooting him down, "but I do have a proposal for you."

"What's a proposal?" he asked, clutching my bag.

"An idea. Come back in for a minute. Please." He did. "Look, you're a young guy, not married, you like models. I'm a model and I am very hungry; you have my food and I have no money."

"Yes....?"

"I'm offering you a deal. I'll let you look at these," I motioned to my breasts, "my tits, for one minute and you give me my food, free and clear. What do you say?"

"Yes!" he said, without a moment's hesitation. "Here's the food!" He threw my bag at me and placed the other two bags on the floor.

"Wait a second," I said, "slow down. There are a few rules. One, you don't touch me. Two, you don't touch yourself, and three, you never mention this to anyone or to me, ever again. Okay?"

"Sure!" he said, ogling my breasts. He salivated and swallowed. I couldn't believe I was actually about to do this. I made sure my blinds were closed, then I took my bag of food and placed it securely on my table. I had him stand up against the door and I walked to the other side of the kitchen, wedging myself safely between the food and him. He was grinning from ear to ear. I breathed in and opened the top of my robe, first a little, and then all the way, until it was completely open, exposing my breasts entirely. I didn't want him reneging for partial view. I counted to sixty.

"One, two, three—"

"Not so fast!" he said, his eyes wide, taking in every bit of my breasts. I slowed down.

"Fourteen, fifteen…" I went on counting as his eyes moved up and down and side to side. He tilted his head to the right, and then to the left. I looked back to see that Charlie had buried his head under the pillow out of sheer embarrassment.

"Thirty, thirty-one, thirty-two," I said wondering if I could have gotten away with just thirty seconds. He took a step closer and raised his chin. He looked down his nose at them, smiling. Then he bent forward to get a smidge closer and view them at eye level. "Sixty!" I said and closed my robe tightly.

"Wow!" he said. "Next time I bring you Chef's Delight!"

"There won't be a next time," I said, closing the door behind him. I felt a little bit sorry for him when we were done. He could go to any peep show in the city for far less than thirty-four dollars and sixty-cents to see a whole alphabet of breasts – many significantly larger than my C cups. Oh well, that was that and it was done. For both of us. I chuckled to myself as I tore into the food. I stuffed in a bite of well-deserved Peking Duck and sunk down in front of the television.

The next morning, Charlie and I awoke to the sound of garbage trucks outside our window and the smell of leftover Moo Shu. It was enough to make me want to vomit. Actually, in retrospect, all of the previous night was enough to make me sick. It was Saturday morning and I still had only twenty dollars to get me through the weekend. To add to my ever growing nausea, I decided that the Chinese food night was a clear sign that it was time to consider an additional line of work. A third job, so to speak. I dragged myself out of bed, fed Charlie, splashed water on my face, threw on an old Gap baseball hat and a pair of distressed sweatpants and dragged myself to the gym. On the way, I bummed my usual breakfast off of the deli guys across the street. I walked slowly on the treadmill, sipping my coffee, surrounded by scantily-clad women pumping their heart-rates and their vitamin waters. Finally I began to jog, trying to keep up with my own caffeine-induced palpitations. I pushed my brain to think of possibilities for employment. Gym trainer? They probably weren't hiring non-athletic night-owls who lived on caffeine. Perfume sprayer? I cracked myself up at the thought – me, standing in the middle of Bloomingdales, threatening Dr. Fifth Avenue with a spritz as he shopped with his new girlfriend (and him running back to ask if he could use my discount).

"Excuse me, is this taken?" asked a voice next to me.

"Ivan?" I turned so fast I nearly gave myself whiplash. Maybe he had come to apologize and resume paying my debts. But it wasn't Ivan, it was just some guy – too young to be of any real use. "What did you ask me?"

"This treadmill... are you saving it for anyone?"

"No," I said, turning away.

"Okay... but, is this yours?" He pointed to the towel I had left on his treadmill.

"Sorry." I reached over to grab it. I was running pretty fast by now but I was still able to notice how cute he was in a wannabe rocker sort of way. He was wearing a Hard Tail wife-beater which showed off his great biceps but barely covered his many tattoos. He wore a Hendrix hat backwards and was nicely scruffy. I let myself daydream for a few moments that he was actually a huge rock star who was about to fall madly in love with me and offer me everything – or at least some small island somewhere. Rock star at the Y. Maybe not. I forced myself to concentrate on work.

Mistress wasn't working out so well but I wouldn't give up on it. Instead, I considered myself something of a specialist in between positions. I simply needed a corporate recruiter who would call whenever there was an available man for me. Until then, I needed something else to do. What else was I qualified for? The only real marketable skill I had was for the business which took place between the sheets. That was a line, albeit a fine line, that I did not want to cross. I punched up the machine faster and faster until I was panting. Sweat streamed down my face and stung my eyes.

A woman walked by, warming up on the indoor track. She was gorgeous... and more importantly, she looked just like Tracy. Tracy from Ferrier... on my birthday. Tracy whom I never called. Tracy who never had the opportunity to satiate my bi-sexual curiosity. Wow. She really looked liked Tracy. Was it possible? Here? How serendipitous.

"Tracy?" I asked. She didn't hear me. "Tracy?" I asked again, still running. I wasn't sure why I wanted her attention. I guess I wanted to explain why I never called. Why I had acted like a man. Truthfully, I didn't know why. Sure, I had an excuse – I had smudged her number – but I could have tracked her down through the restaurant. I tried one last time: "Tracy!" I yelled and lost my footing. I grabbed the handrails fast, just as I went down into a full split. Not the most graceful move but at least I didn't fall. Everyone on the top floor of the Y stared at me. Everyone but the woman who clearly was not Tracy. I shut off the machine and pulled myself up. The rocker wannabe leaned over.

"You should be more careful. You could hurt yourself like that." I glared at him.

But my chance sighting of the Tracy look-alike gave me an idea. Tracy was a gorgeous woman with similar assets and she was working in a restaurant, as a hostess or something. Maybe that was the answer for me. Temporarily, of course. Just until I found my next man and mistressing paid off big. But I couldn't work at a restaurant, exactly. No way. I just could not serve Dr. Fifth Avenue and John with their new mistresses. That would be too much, enough to make me cry, or more likely, to offer them each a blowjob under the table. I thought back to my past men regretting how I took the chauffeur-driven Bentley for granted while I had it. No restaurant. I needed somewhere less conspicuous. And forget about working anywhere I might be seen by Michael. I couldn't even begin to imagine what that would do to me.

That night, after a disastrous date with a coke-addicted attorney I had met at the gym, I walked home from the Upper West Side. On the way I passed a nightclub full of the bridge-and-tunnel crowd. Surely none of my men would ever be seen in a place like this, full of big-haired women hanging all over men ordering Seven and Sevens. It was the safest work environment I could find. See, since abandoning the deli counter, I had been known to my men strictly as a model. Dr. Fifth Avenue was the only one who knew differently. But I couldn't get away with a job like that any longer (thank God). No one of merit was interested in saying that his mistress worked at the Gap (thank God). But this club... this I could very well get away with.

I walked to the doorway of the club and passed a group of badly dressed women waiting behind velvet ropes to get in. One of the bouncers was enticing the ladies by offering admittance to the first one who would show him her most hidden tattoo. Not surprisingly, he had many takers. Thank goodness it was a fairly warm night. Woman after woman rolled down the top of her skirt or jeans to show off the tattoo on her lower back or upper ass. The bouncer concentrated hard on the task at hand; he inspected each tattoo closely, running his fingers over the ones he liked best. Braille tattoos perhaps? A huge horny group was forming outside the club so I pushed past them all, the bouncer, the crowd and the tattoos. Once inside, I spotted a security guard and managed to corner him long enough to get some info even though I was not willing to prove to him that I had no ink. He told me who to talk to and what to say. I did.

Twenty minutes later, after an in-depth quiz, Michigan hired me. "What garnish goes on a Manhattan?" he asked. "What does a margarita take?" Bam, bam, bam, I knew every drink in Mr. Boston's little book. Thank heavens I liked the occasional cocktail, who knew they would ever offer more than a hangover? I was now, officially, a cocktail waitress in a club. I was to start the next night, trailing. My uniform, I was informed, was black short shorts up my butt, fishnets, heels and a black bra.

"Can you supply that?" Michigan asked.

"That's all I own!" I said, laughing. Michigan didn't find me funny, so I said a simple, "Sure, I can supply that," and thanked him for the opportunity. I offered my hand to shake but Michigan just grunted some unintelligible response and walked past me. Eventually, I learned that it wasn't necessarily me who Michigan didn't like, it was women in general. Unless, of course, they were offering sex. Confused? Me too.

Trailing meant nothing more than being a glorified busboy. I made no tips for the night, and I had to follow around the snotty waitress who was training me. The waitress could tell me to do whatever she wanted: clean her tables, empty the trash. And at the end of the night, if I was lucky, she'd throw me ten or twenty bucks. Ten or twenty bucks. I hauled my ass around a club all night for ten or twenty bucks. When the shift was over, I dropped into a chair and reminisced about my nights clubbing with Michael. I saw a half-finished bottle of Veuve Clicquot at another table and hobbled over to grab it. I took a huge swig of the warm champagne and nearly burst into tears. I fell into another chair, dramatically. How did I go from being Michael's mistress to this? I didn't have an answer. I was somewhat unfulfilled when I was with my men but so devastatingly desperate without them. I promised myself this was only temporary; I could survive this for a very limited time. I couldn't rely on flashing for food forever and what would happen when the rent was due? I dragged myself home.

The next night, donned in micro black shorts that would have made Daisy Duke proud, stockings, heeled boots, and a black miracle bra, I was on my way. The whole evening was looking up – the place was crawling with men – and I had the potential to make money. I was like a fat kid working in a candy store.

"What can I get you?" I asked. I smiled and stood there, one leg out, weight on the other, my left hand balancing a tray and my right hand on my hip.

"Uh... uh..." the table said. College boys. No good.

I worked hard and long hours. The club was three levels and I became so good at my job that I could work both the top two levels of the club – the upstairs and main floor, at the same time. It was a terrific workout and the money was good as long as you could handle the second-hand smoke, the bleeding toes, and the swollen ankles.

It's temporary, I told myself as I delivered cosmo after cosmo, night after night. That became my mantra: "This job is temporary; you will quit soon." I repeated it under my breath as I garnished and delivered, sauntered and leaned. With a tray full of drinks, I walked to my victims, placed a glass down, and bent strategically over it, topping it off expertly. That night, someone bumped my arm and a few drops of a Red Devil splashed onto my customer's hand. "Sorry," I said. "I got your fingers all wet." I offered him a napkin.

"Not a problem," he said. "I'm new in town. You look like someone who knows the city. Would you mind being my tour guide tomorrow night?" I heard murmuring from his table companions. They turned to each other and whispered like little boys plotting to hit the one girl on the playground with their dodge ball. I was intrigued but not stupid. Surely, to ask how much being a tour guide paid wouldn't be a good idea. Some of the other cocktail waitresses at the club turned tricks; I didn't want to be mistaken for one of them.

"Sounds fun, but a girl's gotta work. Bills, dinner..." I filled his friend's martini glass.

"Well, could I buy you" – deliberate pause – "dinner?" he asked. His friends laughed and hit each other on the arm.

"Funny!" I reached over, grabbed his tie and dropped it into his drink. His very red drink.

"You bitch!" he said. "That's imported silk! From Italy! My girlfriend gave me that for Christmas. I told her I was working late tonight. How do you expect me to explain this?" I shrugged. His face turned as red as his drink. Still muttering at me, the group got up, paid their exact bill — nothing more — and took off. Out of the corner of my eye I spotted an animated red-tie talking to Michigan. He was waving his tie around and pointing at me. As far as I was concerned, the bastard deserved it.

I didn't get away completely unscathed. I had to pay for the drink. And I had to listen to the wrath of five-foot-two Michigan for about ten minutes. Plus, I had delivered several trays of drinks to Red-tie and his friends, all for no tip.

I had worked at the club for a couple of weeks and I hadn't been out with a man for about the same amount of time. I was quickly growing tired of it all. My days were always the same — sleep until eleven, when Charlie would wake me up by licking my face, feed him, play with his cat dancer for a few minutes, and try to go back to sleep. On some days I would have a go-see and I'd drag myself out to that, but those days were few and far between. My nights were standard — get there by four-thirty or five, set tables with candles, get a pep talk from the twenty-two-year-old manager and start trolling for tips. I worked almost every morning until four, and before I could leave, Michigan had to count out my money. That meant an extra half hour or so because he was busy getting a blowjob from some nameless tramp — male or female — who had wandered into the club that night. Michigan had to be a drug dealer. What else did he have to offer? Drugs were the only feasible answer.

Every night it was the same: I leaned against the door frame that led directly to the main office and listened to Michigan's pre-orgasmic sex sounds. I tried to guess if it was a man or a woman he had with him. It's harder to know than you might think. Definitely female, I decided as I waited, tray posed on hip, hoping this girl would be good enough to finish him off quickly. I was exhausted.

"Yeah, Baby... good... that's it...." He gave a litany of instructions as I stared at the fingernails on my free hand. I chipped at the peeling red paint. "Ooh... ohhh... that's so good... faster, faster!"

Oh come on. I wanted to give the girl lessons. This was the longest blowjob in history. Longer than the ones I used to give Michael. Oh, Michael. I wondered if he was still out of the country. The wall was holding me up and I looked at my watch, five-fifteen. Legally, we'd been closed an hour and fifteen minutes.

"Come on," I said, whining to no one in particular. Twelve hours of this shit was enough. I didn't care if I interrupted. But just as I raised my hand to knock, I heard Michigan finish. His voice was so high and squeaky – like a little girl – I had to stifle a giggle. Seconds later, the door opened and I peeked in to see who the blowjob girl was. I should have known: the same woman who'd been sitting bare-assed on the couch hours ago, twirling her panties over her head like a lasso. Various strange, drunk men would walk by and lift her skirt higher and higher – and she would laugh – until, of course, she was completely exposed. And then all the men just stood there, gawking. That puzzled me. Really. I mean, it wasn't like the pussy was doing magic tricks or anything. I understood the fascination with "Match Girl," the woman who would get completely naked, place matches in three strategic areas of her body and light them. (She had to split the base of the match on the top two areas and keep her pubic hair really short.) Match Girl I understood. Bare-Assed Blowjob Girl? She escaped me. So, assuming that you needed to possess a great deal of testosterone to fully appreciate her, I just shrugged and walked by, delivering my drinks. The crowd had become exceptionally thirsty.

I was still waiting as I saw Blowjob Girl wipe her mouth. She already had cum beginning to crust up on the edges of her lips. So much for condoms. She staggered out the door and past me, her skirt pulled up around her waist. Michigan was standing in his office doing up his pants, laughing at her. I had to say something. "Hey, your skirt," I said and mimed that it needed to be pulled down.

"Wha...?" said Blowjob Girl.

"Your skirt...." Blowjob Girl turned around and barfed all over the floor in front of Michigan's office. All that bobbing up and down must have been too much on top of the twelve or so margaritas. The vomit smelled so bad I put a bar rag over my mouth. Michigan came out of his office, stepped over the vomit – and the girl who was now on the floor – and went to the bar. He lit a Marlboro, demanded a Patron – straight up – from Steve the bartender, and told him to call a busboy to clean up the mess. Steve was pissed.

"No busboys now! It's five-thirty, boss," he said to Michigan. "No bouncers, no staff, no one except those of us closing and poor Marta in the bathroom." You could tell from the way he was mopping the bar that he was furious.

"Then tell Marta to come clean this up." I grabbed Michigan's attention while I could. I handed over charge slips, register tape, and whatever cash I owed. I sat wearily on a bar stool, my feet throbbing. "Everything looks in order here," he said, looking at me. "What do you say you give me a kiss good-night?" Was he kidding? But this little scumbag set the schedules and I needed to make money. I closed my eyes and leaned over to kiss him on the cheek but he turned to catch my lips. He tasted like tequila, cigarettes, and cheap perfume. It made *me* want to vomit. I waved to Steve who was stuck cleaning up the puke, and got out while I could.

On the ride home, I cracked my window and breathed in some early morning air. Between the cab's foul odor and the smoke I had worked in all night, the cool air felt great. I hated blowing what precious little I had on a smelly cab but at this time of night, I had no choice. The cabdriver glared at me in the rearview and turned his heater on. I pretended not to notice.

I was working on average six nights a week, which meant my entire life was consumed by this ridiculous job. I no longer had time for beauty treatments and upkeep. Even the gym had been replaced by the staircase I ran up and down, night after night. Three weeks in, I decided it must be near quitting time, so I checked my bank account. I'd been throwing in everything I could, eating dinner almost every night at the club and surviving on bananas and no-name yogurt for lunch. The only thing I splurged on was Charlie's food, which I bought at a pet store rather than the supermarket. My life had become dull; I was doing nothing for fun, and getting dressed-up meant pushing past my Manolos to throw on my skimpy club outfit. And skimpy it was. The longer I worked there, the shorter my shorts were getting. I was now working in the equivalent of a string bikini bottom, and many of the women who had been there longer sported a thong. It was obviously a direct correlation, the skimpier the outfit, the better the tips.

I broke open my checkbook and feasted my eyes on all my hard work. Fifteen hundred thirty dollars after bills. And rent still had to be paid. What? I looked again. Fifteen hundred thirty dollars. How was that possible? I had worked twelve hours a night for almost a month and I barely made enough to keep living in my dump. I didn't know how, but I was going to make some changes. Charlie meowed at me. "Shut up!" I said, throwing the checkbook across the room. "At the very least you could have been a dog. Then we could go to a park and I'd have a chance to meet a guy. Some big-wig walking his German Shepherd or something." I pulled a pillow over my head. Charlie jumped up next to me and tried to nuzzle under the pillow with me. I rubbed his head. "I'm sorry Charlie," I said. "Really. I'm glad you found me." We went to sleep.

A couple of nights later I met Joseph, the Banana King Drug Lord of South America. I knew immediately who he was and what he did, and by now I was smart enough to recognize a bodyguard when I saw one. I also made no judgments on his chosen career... who was I to judge?

Joseph was short, as South American Banana King Drug Lords tend to be, and fairly handsome. He had full, shiny hair and an average face, a thick body, and a cell phone attached to his waist. I cut through his entourage to bring him a drink, and he asked me out for the very next night. After playing hard to get for about ten seconds I said yes.

Joseph was a bit of an unsophisticated choice for me. Once upon a time Michael would have protected me from a man like him, but at this point, Joseph was my best option. Oh how the mighty had fallen. I gave Joseph my number and discovered later that he had called it while we were still at the club – obviously checking to see if it was real. We flirted unabashedly and I thought nothing of ignoring the rest of my clients as I sipped Cristal and chatted the night away. His English was horrible so I had a mostly one-sided conversation. I hadn't been this on since John. I talked and talked, patted him on the arm and leaned in attentively any time he said anything. It was more like a date than a night at work, and God did I need it. The more Cristal I drank, the closer he got to me.

By two o'clock, he had his arms tightly around my waist and if anyone asked me for anything he would put up his hand and say, "She's mine!" The other cocktail waitresses glared at me as they carried their trays, empty and full, back and forth to the service bar. What did I care? He was my ticket out of there. And Michigan loved it when we made friends with the clientele – it was great for business. I was so sure that the Banana King Drug Lord was the one, I didn't even stop him when he slipped his hand in the back of my bikini and let it rest on my ass. Finally, I was back – if not on the right track, at least I was heading in the right direction. Joseph was going to have a huge payoff. By the time last call was announced, I was beaming from champagne and attention. Then the club closed.

"Oh," he said. "I have to go?"

"Unfortunately," I said, wiggling free of his grasp and grabbing my tray.

"But you... you go too?"

"I have to close up." The ball was in his court.

"I see you tonight?" he asked.

"You see me tonight." I was already planning outfits. I stalled as much as I could while he collected himself. "So, did you enjoy having your own private waitress all night?" I asked, looking for a tip. I needed it. I had spent all of my work hours flirting.

"Very much! But wait," he reached for his wallet. "You work tips, no?"

"I work tips, yeah."

"Well, wait." He called over a senior member of his entourage. The man leaned over to whisper in Joseph's ear. "Sorry," Joseph said giving his attention back to me, "my English...."

"No problem." I hoisted myself up to sit on the bar.

"I would like you have this," he said, handing me first a one hundred-dollar bill and then four more as the older gentleman guided him.

"Good?" Joseph asked.

"Good," I said. I hopped down and left to check myself out.

I felt no guilt about calling in sick that next night. As I dressed, I was surprisingly grumpy, even though I was glad to be going out. That was nothing new. Going all the way back to Dr. Fifth Avenue I was often downright nasty while I prepared to go out. I never knew exactly why. Something about preparing to be on show and not drawing a performer's respect – or salary – really bugged me. I was a champion dog being groomed for Westminster, but I knew once the judging was over, it would be back to the cage for me. The irony is, I made myself into that dog.

I guess I'd always thought being a mistress would be a lot less effort.

That's what this date was about. A South American Banana King Drug Lord would surely understand how to treat a woman. Heck, he had given me five hundred and all the Cristal I could drink just for my scintillating conversation, and he barely spoke English. I stared into my closet. That was it – I'd wear low clingy black pants with a black gauze shirt open to my navel. You could see my nipples faintly through the shirt, and you could see the outline of my breasts when I turned in either direction. I smudged coal liner around my eyes and filled in my lips with a light pink. I looked like a hungry, wild animal... which was exactly what I felt like. Charlie meowed at me in disapproval.

"Yeah, I know, buddy," I said, "but if we want to keep on eating, I need to go." He understood. He rubbed against my leg and hopped up on the bed to wait for me.

Joseph really didn't know the city, so I made the plans for the evening. I decided on a new French bistro on the Upper East Side that I'd overheard two women at the club discussing. I was dying to try it and this was as good a time as any.

I told Joseph I'd meet him on the street corner and there he was, waiting on the sidewalk as my cab pulled up. Nice. I could tell the evening was going to run oh-so-smoothly, even though there were no fancy cars escorting me to and fro. I slithered my way out as he paid my fare. I kissed him on the cheek and we walked hand-in-hand into the restaurant. We were seated at the best table in the house and immediately brought several appetizers, olives, and the house burgundy. Joseph and I shared steamed mussels in Vermouth and drained two bottles of wine. We were having a pretty good time considering our language difficulties and the fact that Joseph's bodyguard sat at an adjacent table, staring at us. He continually stopped our waitress to see what she was bringing to Joseph. He dug his fork into every course and overturned the beautifully prepared plates. He took an enormous bite of my quail. I glared at him. This wasn't *The Godfather* and I was pretty sure no one had followed Joseph to New York and into this random kitchen to poison our quail. But the bodyguard had his job to do and so did I. I turned my back on him and threw everything I had at Joseph. I decided on the, "It's-not-something-I-normally-do-but-I-would-make-a-beautiful-and-phenomenal-mistress-for-you" routine, which meant I had to do my best to seem vulnerable. Men always found this character the most endearing. Men are, after all, men. The woman he saw at the club, the tough, bar girl who let him put his hand on her ass, she wouldn't be back for a few months. The point was to let him know what was there, and then to make him fall in love. I pushed my quail back and forth on the plate.

"You don't like it?" he asked.

"I do," I said, letting my face flush. "It's just, a little too difficult to cut." So Joseph rose to the occasion, cutting through my quail, feeding me piece by piece. And that's how we ate most of our dinner. By the end of the meal, he held my hand tightly. I couldn't help but get a bit dizzy, he reminded me so much of Michael. I smiled at Joseph and we ordered another bottle of wine. After the meal, I had Joseph's leftovers packaged for Charlie. I realized that this was probably a turn-off, but I considered it nonnegotiable. Charlie had never tasted quail. But just in case, I opened my shirt a bit wider.

After dinner, Joseph and I stumbled down the street. His bodyguard ran after us, trying to keep both of us upright. Joseph slipped, and I laughed so hard I had to squat down on the corner of Madison and Seventy-third. It was all I could do to keep from peeing.

"Fucking drunks," the bodyguard said under his breath, picking both of us up.

While we attempted to stroll further down the street, Joseph professed his love for me. "My wife," he said in broken English, "she no understand me."

Even through my drunken haze, I was astonished that such a lame line was universal. I chalked it up to too little language and too much wine. But I wasn't fooling myself; I was sober enough to know that I had become a shade desperate, and drunk enough not to realize that I was buying it all.

"You and I," he said, "we love at first sight!"

"Yes, darling!" I said. I threw my arms around him with the high hopes of becoming Joseph's well-kept New York mistress. He pinned me against the nearest wall and licked my face and neck. He reeked of Burgundy and his breath was hot. His bodyguard stood watching as people walked by and gawked. The

PDA made me squirm; I didn't want to be spotted behaving like this by any old boyfriends. I tried to rub away a burning sensation in the pit of my stomach. I didn't much like having a hot-blooded, married man whose wife lived permanently outside the city. There were no boundaries, no friends who could catch us. He opened my coat and slipped his hand into my blouse but I drew the line. "Un-uh," I said. "Not on the street." I pushed him away and we parted awkwardly that night – awkwardly because he assumed he was getting laid. Eventually Joseph conceded and promised that he would be back.

Joseph did, in fact, come back. In the month he was away, he left countless messages. Day after day I would hear, "I looove you, Victoria!" pouring from my answering machine, his voice filling my tiny apartment. I never believed him, of course, but the messages made me smile. He sent roses twice, chocolates once, and a thousand-dollar gift card to Saks. He also sent a five-hundred dollar gift card to a sporting goods store. I pondered that one for a while, not sure if I was regifted or if he was telling me that I needed to work out more. I didn't know which one was better… or worse. It was an odd courtship.

Upon Joseph's return, I found myself at the Marriott Marquis on Broadway, climbing into bed with the Banana King Drug Lord of South America. Just your typical Saturday evening. I was excited, and ready. This was the night to sleep with him. I had spent another month working in that disgusting club and my finances were beyond embarrassing. Things were so tight I'd even considered ordering Chinese food again. I was ready to be a mistress again. So ready, I would have gone back to any of my old friends just to get out of my current situation.

When I entered the hotel that night, I felt my heart flutter. I knew I was going to be greeted with a plethora of gifts from South America, lots of hugs and loud declarations of love. Even so, despite my excitement and my anticipation, something just wasn't feeling right. For one thing, Joseph didn't even meet me in the lobby, let alone send a car for me. Instead, I was greeted by that same older man from the club – the one who tipped well. I gave him a cheerful smile but he was stoic. He showed me to Joseph's room and I noticed that he had a strange gait, almost a limp. He opened the door and stepped aside. I looked in and saw Joseph's bodyguard sitting in a chair, reading. He grunted to me while the older man spoke.

"I saw you at the night club. I see you tonight. I will never see you again."
Then he walked away. What? What an odd statement. Was it a warning? I had no
idea who Joseph really was and I had to get a grip on reality. It was me walking
into that hotel room with a relative stranger, just me. I had to get past the idea
that Joseph was really Michael, and I couldn't expect Michael to come running if
things got out of hand. One thing was for certain, I was not having sex in front
of Joseph's bodyguard. Or with his bodyguard. I was also sure that Joseph, like
Michael, must carry a gun.

Suddenly, I became uneasy. I thought about bolting, but to where? For
what? I rubbed at the burning feeling in the pit of my stomach and wondered
about the older man's limp. Did Joseph make him lame? Had he crossed Joseph
somehow? Was I being overdramatic, or too careless? I decided that I had to
take my chances. We were in a reputable place filled with tourists and families; it
wasn't like we were in some cheap motel off a deserted highway in the middle of
nowhere. This was Times Square, the place where some of the greatest
opportunities in the world happen. I stepped in to find Joseph standing in the
middle of the hotel room in his boxer shorts. He was on his cell phone, yelling at
someone in Spanish. He motioned for me to come in and for his bodyguard to
leave. We did. I was instructed to put my bag down and to get into the bed.

"Are you kidding me?" I asked, but he just waved me away. He was a
different Joseph than I remembered, and I wasn't sure he knew who I was. Did
he think I was just brought in off of the street for him? I sat in the bodyguard's
chair, determined to get to the bottom of it all. I thought about the old man's
words, and once again I considered leaving. Even if there was no danger, Joseph
could turn out to be a one-night stand and what would that do for me? Then
again, why would he have invested so much effort into me already if I was
nothing more than a quick fuck? He was probably just stressed from a bad day
of exporting bananas and other cargo.

Joseph got off the phone. "Why do women always make things so difficult?"
he asked with an even heavier accent than before. He took my hand and led me
to the bed. Yes, he was a very different man than I remembered him to be. What
happened to the laughing? The statements of love? The really good wine?

I remembered that Michael was sometimes like this, closed off and focused
on business, so I undressed to my bra and panties and got into the bed
determined to be a phenomenal lover and get my just rewards: a nice little

penthouse on Fifth Avenue – on a street close enough to rub it in Dr. Fifth Avenue's nose. Joseph didn't say another word as he slipped my panties off and rolled me onto my stomach. It all happened so quickly I barely had time to react.

"No anal sex!" I said.

"No," he said. He slipped a pillow under my hips to make me higher for entry. I made sure he had a rubber on and then we had fast, non-descript sex, in the traditional, bent-over-a-pillow way. The only thing he said to me the entire time he was in me was, "You are a big momma, aren't you?" It was dreadful. I felt fat, ugly and used.

When he was done, I rolled over and slipped my panties back on. He got right back on the cell phone. "If you don't mind," he said, "I need to work now."

"That's it?" I said, wishing I had gone to work myself. "I think you're mistaken, I'm not a call girl!"

"What means call girl?"

"A hooker, you know, a prostitute. I'm not a prostitute. I'm a mistress. And I was planning to be your mistress, damn it, not your whore!"

He covered the cell phone. "Let's go to breakfast in the morning then." I could tell he was cornered, and that he had no idea what the word "mistress" meant. He just wanted me to leave.

"Where?" I asked.

"Here. Downstairs at eight. I have a... an eleven o'clock flight."

I packed up and crawled home.

Overly eager to fix a horrid night, I showed up the next morning nearly an hour early in my best Princess Grace-at-breakfast look: impeccable make-up, a white shirt, dress jeans and boots. I marched right up to his room. He was leaving, just then, for the airport. "Joseph?" I asked, approaching him.

"Victoria? Oh! I have an earlier flight... my son... he's sick... I need to go." Lie on top of lie on top of lie. And he had just been lying on top of me a few hours earlier.

"Fine. I'm coming with you," I said.

"To Venezuela?" He looked panicked.

"To the airport." I was determined not to leave our night as it was, although even I was beginning to lose faith in the possibility of long-term love here. We went downstairs, got into his limo, and headed for JFK. The long trip was boring as hell and we quickly ran out of things to say. We settled on discussing a map we found in the back of the car.

"So this is Queens?" he asked, pointing.

"Uh-huh," I said, unhappy beyond belief. We finally got to the airport and I walked him all the way to his gate. I understood that it was over. That mysterious older man from last night was the only one telling the truth; neither he, nor Joseph, would ever see me again. But I wasn't giving up without a fight. I pretended that we still had something special.

At the gate Joseph said a loud, purposeful, "I love you! I'll call you when I land!" He followed with a giant, thrown kiss, and then he started off.

"Wait!" I yelled after him. He froze in his tracks. I could see his body tense and his shoulders creep upwards. He turned back, reluctantly. "I have to get back," I said. "Is your car still here?"

"No."

"Then I need money to get back." I had officially given up on the chance of a future but I had no interest in being stranded at JFK. At the very least he was going to pay for my transportation – even if I had to make a show out of it.

"Oh," was all he said. People were staring at him waiting to see what he would do. After humping me on the street corner on our first date, I was surprised he could be embarrassed by a conversation.

"I need money to get back to the city," I said. "Did you expect to leave me stranded here?" I heard someone grunt and shake her head in disapproval. He reached into his pocket and pulled out a twenty. "Twenty?" I asked in disbelief.

The grunter offered an "Mmm-uhnnn..." in disgust.

He stalled. "I'm not so good with your money. This is what I have."

The grunter could no longer contain her feelings and she stepped up to help. "Twenty dollars to get back to Manhattan?" she asked, her voice booming through the terminal. "Mister, what country are you from? Give the girl at least fifty to get back. At least."

"Thank you!" I said.

"You know it, girl," she said. "Man shouldn't be disrespecting you like that." She turned back to Joseph. "You know what else? The girl's skinny as a stick! You throw in a few extra bucks so she can buy herself a taco or a burrito or something." With that she turned and walked away, and I was sixty dollars richer.

Honestly, I'd been hoping for at least a couple hundred so I'd have enough left over to buy myself something; I needed to console myself after my first one-night stand. He was the Banana King Drug Lord of South America and after last night I was owed way more than a measly couple of hundred bucks. But there I was, happy to pocket my sixty. And he was gone.

I concentrated on the money in my hand. If I was lucky, I'd have about ten dollars left when I got back to the city. Ten dollars. Ten dollars was laundry or cheap Mexican food or a rental movie and a bag of popcorn. Any of which would be a fitting ending to the night and day of the ten-dollar whore. Crestfallen, I walked to the nearest cab and hailed it.

"Going to the city?" I heard a middle-aged man ask from the opposite side of the cab.

"Why, yes," I said, puckering my lips into a smile. So with minimal effort that consisted only of some small talk with a handsome stranger in the back of a cab, I was able to pocket that sixty bucks after all.

I woke up early the next morning still pissed about the way I was treated. I cleaned my tiny kitchen and threw out everything that sounded even remotely South American. Obviously the bananas were the first to go – whish! – down the chute they went. Two cans of Del Monte Tropical Fruit – goodbye! The fridge also had some leftover sweet and sour which was suspect but I didn't want to be rash... I might be hungry later on.

When I was done, I sat on the kitchen floor, rubbing Charlie's belly. What was I doing wrong? Maybe it was time to make some radical changes in my life – to get a real job, but doing what? What was I possibly suited for? I was qualified for nothing. Even if I finished school, what good would that do me? College offered too many useless courses: art history; the history of the theatre; where were all the real classes? Where was: "How to Cash in as a Mistress 101" or "Honors: The Rules for Being a Successful Gold-Digger?" College was never the answer. A better man was. And I needed to find him – fast.

My body was really starting to take a beating from my stupid job and I wouldn't be able to burn both ends of the candle much longer. I also missed go-see after go-see because they were held too early in the morning. My entire life was that club and I was perpetually tired and cold. Every morning, while I waited for Michigan to count me out, my teeth would chatter uncontrollably. Where was the glamorous lifestyle that I dreamt of when I rode the train back to school all those years ago?

I was so lost on that particular morning that I broke down and called my mother for advice. I bit my cracked lip as I dialed. I winced.

"How did it go with Joseph?" she asked.

"Not so well."

"What do you mean not so well? What did you do?"

"Frankly, way too much."

"What?"

"Nothing," I said. I tried to think how to word this correctly. "I just don't think he's Mr. Right."

"Mr. Right?" my mother said. "Your men are all married! You're not looking for Mr. Right, Victoria. I don't know who you think you're kidding." I was surprised by my mother's brazenness, but she had a point.

After I hung up the phone, I lay back on my couch and wiggled my feet in the air. I wished I had gotten way more than sixty bucks from Joseph and could go drown my sorrows on a shopping trip. I let my gaze drift to the coffee table and the telephone number of my cab companion from JFK. I couldn't bring myself to call him. Why, I don't know. For the first time in my life, I wished that I stood for more than the pursuit of money. I wished that I had an activity other than fucking rich men. I wished that I could find more rich men to fuck. I wished I were more like Liz, confident, successful, secure. I wished I were more normal... or maybe less normal. I wished I had stayed in school and was working a real job, able to pay for my own Chinese food with actual money. I wished I had some talent or some skill. I wished I were an artist like she was.

I had seen this woman once, maybe a year earlier. We were shopping in the same dumpy store in the East Village and as soon as I laid eyes on her, I wanted to be her. I decided on the spot that she was an artist, probably a painter; she had random, multi-colored paint splotches all over her faded jeans. She wasn't as classically pretty as I was — whatever that means — but she was just so cool, so together. Everything I'd always wanted to be. You see, I never really felt like I fit in anywhere. Half-Jewish, half-Catholic, too pretty to have women friends and apparently unable to have a real relationship with a man, I was pretty lonely most of the time. Or maybe those were all just excuses I gave myself because I hadn't yet achieved anything with my life. All I know is it was frighteningly easy for me to fall under the spell of someone as seemingly unaffected and glamorous as that woman.

I was so captivated, I even tried to run into her again — another dozen or so times — but it never happened. On that particular afternoon I watched her pick out clothes: fringe jackets, super low denims, hot black pants that looked amazing on her. She stood outside the tiny dressing room and accessorized, pairing the clothing with scarves, denim jackets, belts. I stood silently and watched as she modeled an Indian print top that tied around the neck. For some unknown reason, she didn't like it. Once she chose another blouse from the rack stuffed full of batik shirts and tie-dye skirts, I snagged her castaway top and darted back to my own dressing room. I pulled the shirt over my head and tied it around my neck. I stared into the mirror, waiting to be transformed into my new alter-ego, a direct descendent of the goddess Lakshmi. Oh my. I hadn't realized it, but the top was stuck around my stupidly large breasts. I had to tug and pull to get it all the way on, leaving white deodorant stains smeared down the sides. I stared in the mirror again but my hope of looking like this glamorous goddess faded quickly. Instead, I looked like a stripper bursting out of my pasties. Plus, my implants made me look as wide as I was tall. I pulled the top off as fast as I could, but it got stuck again. I grunted as I pulled it over my head. Thank God the music was loud.

Back in my own clothes, I caught a glimpse of her at the counter. There she was again with her paint splotched jeans and her nipples that showed through her unwashed, wrinkled T-shirt. I stared hard at her breasts, envious that she didn't need to wear a bra.

As she exited the store, I snuck to the counter to watch her through the window. That's when she did the most incredible thing: she went to Starbucks to get coffee. There's nothing better in life than strolling around New York City with a cup of coffee. Lucky for me, because I was friends with the deli guys, this activity was free. With the intensity of a stalker, I watched her exit Starbucks, wondering what phenomenal place this feminine marvel (with coffee!) was heading next. God how I wanted to be her! I wanted desperately to have a purpose, a reason to get up in the morning. A reason to grab coffee "to go" as I rushed somewhere, anywhere. A reason for being. I was interrupted by the loud voice of the saleswoman.

"You gonna take those or what?"

"What?" I asked.

"The shirts. You gonna take them?"

I looked at the boring white shirt in my left hand and the stripper's top in my right. "Yeah," I said, "this one," and handed over the boring white shirt. I felt the saleswoman staring at me. "What?"

"That'll be thirty-eight," she said and I handed her my overused Visa card. I looked out the door. Where was my new friend going next? "You're wasting your time," the saleswoman said.

"What?" I asked again, now annoyed that she was continually interrupting my fantasy. "What's wrong with the shirt?"

"Not with the shirt, Sweetie, with that girl. I've seen her in here with a guy. Her husband, I think. Gorgeous. Dead ringer for Lenny Kravitz."

"Oh, I'm not...." The saleswoman sneered at me. "Yeah, well, thanks," I said, grabbing my shirt. What did I care what a random stranger thought of me? I barely cared what I thought of me. Besides, she was only accusing me of a lesbian crush. I've often wondered if I'd be happier as a lesbian, to take men right out of the equation. But then I always get caught on the same damn thought: who would pay the bills? It was just too complicated.

Back on my couch, I let my feet flop down and felt the blood rush into them. They were tingly with pins and needles. I needed to start living in the real world. I spent too much time fantasizing and imagining how life could be. Joseph was a prime example of that. He – and his entourage – gave me every sign our relationship would never be any more than a one-night stand, but I ignored them. Let's face it, the only truthful thing about me was that I played at everything. My men became my creations. They weren't sleazy assholes who were cheating on their wives! Oh no! They were merely misunderstood saints – albeit rich saints – hidden inside very confused exteriors. It was my job to save them, and to be rewarded handsomely for doing so.

I sat up on the couch and shook my head. To start cleaning up my mess, I grabbed a pen and an old scrap of paper and began to make lists. Charlie swatted at the pen as I listed what I wanted versus what I had, and then weighed what I had versus what I went through to get it. Maybe if I saw it clearly written out before me, I would be able to make some sense of it all.

Chapter 6 – "Ares"

"Ares figures little in Mythology.... He had no cities where he was worshipped. The Greeks said vaguely that he came from Thrace, home of a rude, fierce people in the northeast of Greece. Appropriately, his bird was the vulture. The dog was wronged by being chosen his animal."

Sleeping with married men, which had started as an alluring vocation – a good way to get fancy dinners, pay bills, and enjoy the finer things in life – had become an inescapable reality. I was sure that there was an enormous sign on my back, visible only to married men, that read: "Will fuck. Won't ask questions." My back? Sure. The sign was sprouting from my cleavage.

To this day what surprises me the most is the percentage of men who are actually willing to cheat. You have to admit, it is a bit daunting. It does make one leery of marriage. No? You think I was responsible? You think if I wasn't offering, they wouldn't cheat? You think I twisted their little peckers 'round and 'round till they fell under some magic spell? I merely said yes to the man's existing offer; he wanted me, and he was willing to cheat to get me. He was already down, wounded and vulnerable. Although I have often wished that I did, the truth is that I never really made the kill, I just moved in for the feast.

Meanwhile, back at the old club... I was like a zombie on that one particularly vulnerable night, shuffling from table to table. The music from the live band crashed through me... hurting my ears, assailing my body, nailing me to the floor. It was all I could do to walk. That's when I spotted a man sitting at the bar, staring at me. He would watch me and then turn back to sip his single malt. He was neither particularly handsome nor out of place, but for some reason I felt that he may have something to offer me. With a huge amount of effort I managed to smile, but he just turned away. It bugged me that he didn't take the bait. I decided he was a peeping Tom who just liked to watch from afar.

Finally, after another grueling hour and a bachelor party to serve, Tom at the bar finished his drink and approached me. I adopted my "I'm-hot-as-hell-so-don't-fuck-with-me-pose" and waited for the come-on. Instead, he was very cold. He handed me his business card: "D.C.'s Model and Talent."

Then he spoke. "You should be a model. You're too beautiful to be working here."

"Ooh…" I said, nodding at him. "The model line. Sure."

Undaunted, he finished his thought. "I'm not an agent, but call that number. Tell them that I spotted you at a club and you want to enter the Model and Talent Search they sponsor." He turned to leave.

"Thanks," I said, "but I never really considered myself a model type." I was still with my second-rate agency and still doing the occasional job, but I didn't owe Tom any details. And I certainly wasn't going to waste my precious time with another man who was full of shit.

He looked around the club. "Obviously, you don't consider yourself a model," he said. That did it. With more spectacle than a threatened cockatoo I tossed my hair, raised my eyebrows and puffed my lips. I mean, how dare he think that I didn't think that I was a model type. Wait… huh?

"But, nevertheless," he said, "it'll be worth your phone call. With that mouth and that body, you could do very well." He left me standing there, puffed up, holding his card.

I tossed the card onto my tray with plans to throw it out immediately, but then... I didn't. I stashed it in my pocket. Maybe I would call. Maybe it wasn't the world's most pitiful pick-up line. Maybe Tom was legit. Maybe. What else did I have going on? I'd never given modeling a fair try, so maybe there was something to it. Maybe it was a way out. I was so tired of being a really good cocktail waitress. Sadly, I had become a super-efficient serving machine – a kind of superhero at "Le Club"– able to part thick crowds of grabby drunk men with a tray full of martinis in one hand and five bottles of Corona (with lime) in the other.

*   *   *

About a week later, I had a meeting at D.C. Model and Talent. I was skeptical simply because it sounded too good to be true, but when did that ever stop me? Naturally, I put reason, thought, and intuition aside. Off I went.

As soon as I walked through the door, I was greeted by a pretty blonde woman named Jan. Jan was about twenty-eight with an amazing body and gorgeous hair. She was the quintessential all-American woman, the perfect cheerleader type. She was every frat boy's/every football player's/every beer drinking man's dream. Jan smiled and I instantly recognized her from a television beer commercial. "Yup, that's me," she said, rolling her eyes. "That's my claim to fame, the middle girl in a beer ad. Girl number two. But I guess it's better to be 'Weis' than 'Er,'" she joked.

Jan and I discovered we had a lot in common. Over the next hour or so, we sat in a tiny office huddled over a small conference table drinking Diet Cokes and swapping New York war stories. I was so glad to finally have a woman to talk to – or anyone to talk to for that matter – that I probably spilt more than I should have. Then Jan finished off her second Diet Coke and adapted a much more serious tone. "I guess congratulations are in order," she said as she shook her can and drained the last bit of soda. She looked away.

"For what?" I asked.

"Your cover?" she said, surprised I didn't know.

"My what?"

"Oh. You haven't heard yet. You were selected as the winner of Dorian's – Dorian is the owner of the magazine – Dorian's magazine's Cover Model Contest."

"But," I said protesting her statement and still assuming that we were the best of friends, "he hasn't even seen a picture of me! How could I have—?"

"You're just that beautiful," Jan said, resolved. And that's when I realized that this was all an elaborate sales pitch.

"Jan, listen," I said, trying to recapture the tone of our friendly chitchat. "I've lived in this city a long time. I know when someone is bullshitting me (at least this time I knew). What's up here?"

"All right," Jan said, sitting back in her chair and suddenly becoming very cold. "Dorian did pick you for his cover model." Then she leaned in and whispered. "I just don't know if you understand what that means."

"I don't think I do." I crossed my arms.

Someone knocked on the door and we both jumped clear out of our seats. Jan sat back, rearranging herself. I felt like the principal had just caught us lighting a joint. We looked at each other and Jan exhaled. A middle-aged woman with a fake tan, deep grooves on her face, and bright orange lipstick stuck her head into the office.

"Dorian's on the phone for you, Sweetie!"

"Okay, thanks," Jan said, picking up the phone. I tried to be nonchalant but I listened to every word of her conversation. Her voice and body language changed considerably; she sounded much younger and more playful, like a voiceover for the Playboy channel. "Yes," Jan said, purring into the phone. "Of course I will... when haven't you been able to count on me?" She raised her eyes to meet mine. "Well, she's right here, right now...," she said, finishing the conversation in a whisper. She was smiling when she hung up the phone.

"Look," Jan said in what I assumed to be her normal voice, "this is between us, because if he," she gestured to the phone, "finds out that I told you this I'm fired, got it?" I nodded. Jan looked toward the closed door and then lowered her voice once again. "I work for Dorian," she said, "in a couple of capacities. Yes, I'm a model, but there are other things that are asked of some of his models. Me, for instance, and you included. Just keep him happy. You really don't need to have actual sex with him. And whatever you do, don't tell him that you live in the city, he'll think you're more accessible to him."

I got a cramp in the pit of my stomach. "The man at the bar—?"

"A scout," Jan said, finishing my question. "He scouts for Dorian's models. I don't know what else to tell you. I see Dorian once a month or so, we have nice dinners and long talks and he represents me. Sometimes, as a favor, we get a hotel room after dinner. He's all right," she said shrugging. "If it weren't for Dorian, I don't even think I'd have an agent. No real agency would ever pick me up. And," she said, "I have a fiancé... in Jersey. He's great. He has a boat."

"That's nice," I said, not knowing what else to say. "What does your fiancé think about your trips to the city?"

"Work," she said, "he thinks they're only for work. And they are. Modeling work can consist of a lot of different things. Besides," she looked away now and I saw in her profile that she was younger than I had originally thought, "he's engaged to the 'Weis' girl. All his friends are jealous. He knows how lucky he is."

"I'm sure," I said, feeling old beyond my years.

Jan said one more thing as we stood to leave. "My fiancé and I will probably set the date this summer."

"Congratulations," I said, never really knowing if Jan had told me about her fiancé because she was explaining that I was her replacement or because she needed to prove that she was better than me. Or maybe she just needed to feel better about herself.

I met Dorian for dinner that week, intending to change his ways and land myself a magazine cover based on my looks, not my blow-job expertise. Even so, my decision to go to dinner was last minute. Frankly, I was famished and needed a meal. Charlie was also pretty sick of his not-so-gourmet dry food, so I promised I'd bring him leftovers. Seeing that our options for food that night were Dorian or more "titty Chinese," I called Jan to get the particulars on dinner. That was that. I agreed to dinner and only dinner. I would see Dorian professionally, and I would wear something I already owned. There would be no investment except a bit of time.

The darker – and perhaps even more truthful – side of my decision to see Dorian was based purely in desperation. I desperately wanted a different life and I desperately wanted out of the one I already had. Maybe (I hate to say this but...) my mother was right. Maybe modeling was my ticket up, or out. The more I worked at the club, the deeper in debt I seemed to get and tips were quickly becoming a scarcity thanks to the twice-weekly Ladies Night specials Michigan was running. Being one myself I hate to say this, but for the most part, women just don't tip worth a damn. And they're nothing short of evil when their husbands leave anything over ten percent. Take the night before my dinner with Dorian, for example. Some woman's husband tipped me a twenty (a twenty – not a hundred) for delivering him a beer and she was furious. Believe me, Hell hath no fury like a woman whose husband spends money on another woman. She came after me, trying to pry the money out of my hand (good luck) yelling, "You are disgusting! You are nothing more than a useless piece of shit who should die and get trampled on by the customers!" True story. "Who do you think you are?" she raged. "You look like a slut with your tits hanging out. You are absolutely gross! You'd better not ever go near my husband again!" Her hot drunk breath burned my face. The floor came to a standstill while she stood there, hollering at me. And this was a husband I hadn't slept with. When she was through, I managed to keep the twenty but Michigan wouldn't let the bouncers throw the bitch out; it seems some male patrons found the whole scene rather entertaining. I was fed up. The only consolation was that very late in the evening her over-sprayed 1980's hairstyle got too close to a burning candle... and yes, it is funny now because no one was seriously hurt. Well, at least she wasn't. I make no promises about her poor husband whom she dragged out of the club by his hair.

Dinner with Dorian was nothing exceptional, but I ate everything I could get my hands on: bread, appetizer, entrée, coffee, and two desserts. Not to mention a little more than my fair share of a bottle and a half of a white burgundy. My goal was to make the dinner sustain me for a while – I figured it worked for snakes. I also asked for a veal chop to take home to Charlie; I told Dorian it was for my lunch the next day. Dorian stared at me while I ate, but to his credit he only mentioned my appetite once, and only to ask if I wanted more. I was pleasantly surprised, but I was also 5'9" and my size four clothes hung loosely on my protruding bones. What was he going to say? After dinner, Dorian suggested that we go back to his office to discuss business. Going back to the office meant any of the following three things: one, it was away from home and wife, two, it didn't cost anything, and three, it was private. (Of course it may also mean all three of those things combined.) Since he was a gentleman through dinner I agreed to it, but I proceeded with caution.

Dorian's office was in a trendy downtown hotel. As I followed him on and off the elevator, around a corner, and through an opened door, I held my breath. I knew going to a hotel was risky, but once I saw that we were in an actual office, I relaxed. I reminded myself that a lot of legit businesses in Manhattan were based in hotels.

I looked around while Dorian played the messages on his answering machine. "Hi, I want to be a model." Beep. "Hi, I'm calling about your Cover Model Contest." Beep. "Mr. C., we're calling in regard to your late bill." Erase. The walls were covered with pictures of models on various magazine covers – *Elle*, *Vogue*, *Mademoiselle* – none of whom, I was sure, were Dorian's.

After a brief trip to the men's room, Dorian returned to show off his office. It seemed like a legitimate office to me, but what did I know. Michael had had an office in the meat packing district that consisted solely of an answering machine in an abandoned building. I smiled and nodded at the photos as Dorian went on and on. My face lit up at the picture of last year's cover model. This year it could be me! Yippee!

I sat tightly wedged against one arm of the leather couch. Dorian was a large, heavy-set man, so when he sat down next to me I was lifted into the air. I liked sitting higher than him; it was like being on an adult see-saw where I was always on top. The restaurant had been dark, so this was my first opportunity to really see what Dorian looked like. He was balding, with razor-burn on both of his cheeks and a large gap between his front teeth. So he wasn't *People* magazine's "Sexiest Man Alive," but I wasn't there to sleep with him and for the moment, he seemed nice enough and was keeping it professional.

While we talked, Dorian downed four shots of Jack Daniels, on top of the wine and the three or so whiskey sours he had had with dinner. So maybe not so professional. Then he leaned across the couch and rested his hand on the cushion between us. He was sweating so profusely his hand slid off the couch and he nearly toppled over. I hoped the near-collapse would signify the end of the evening, but Dorian and his drink were both left intact. "Let me cut to the chase," he said, slurring.

"Please." I could have used another drink myself.

"I don't need a girlfriend," he said. "I have plenty of those. And I don't know what Jan told you…"

"That makes two of us." I was completely entertained by his attempt to try to form words.

"But I need a cover model who, appresh...appreee...appreshigate...." He couldn't get it out. He was sweating from every visible part of his body – I didn't even want to think about the non-visible parts – and his face turned a dark purple. I thought that he might keel over. Then what would I do? If I called 911, the police would ask me who I was and what I was doing there and, uh, what was I doing there at eleven o'clock at night? Not to mention how bad this would look to my future boyfriend, the future Mayor of New York!

But Dorian didn't die, and he sobered up enough to make his list of demands. "I don't need sex," he said, "but a blowjob would be nice." He laughed. "Nice, but not necessary! I'm a married man. Uh, I mean, a *business* man." Yeah, that's what he was.

"Uh-huh," I said, nodding along and wondering when blowjobs stopped counting as sex.

"The cover is yours if you want it." His eyes glazed over.

I had to ask. "But you've never even seen my book, my pictures?"

He attempted to stand. "That's why I need you to step on the scale for me."

"Excuse me?" This scenario just couldn't get any weirder.

"The scale—"

"I'm five-nine."

"Nice," he said, barely able to stand, "but I need to weigh you too. Now strip to your bra and panties." He didn't slur a word. It seems that this scenario could get weirder after all.

"What?" I stood and met his gaze. "What did you say?"

"You heard me, I want to... I mean, need to weigh you."

"I'm a size four," I said, looking at my clothes. "A small size four."

"That's good." He let his eyes run slowly up and down my body. "But I need to know what you weigh."

"Like 114 or so." I hadn't been on a scale for ages but last I checked I was 120 and my size fours fit just fine.

"It's just a part of the business. Besides, I like it," he said, with a big greasy, gap-toothed smile. "Now strip and hop on. I might need to remove your bra and panties too. Sometimes I get a false reading."

"No. That does it. No way. Absolutely not."

"Then you can kiss your cover good-bye," he said, sobering up fast.

"Fine by me!" I said, incensed. "I didn't believe you anyway!"

"Why are you so pissed?" he asked, sounding legitimately confused.

"Why do you think?" I asked, grabbing my coat and Charlie's dinner. I left.

"You bitch!" he screamed after me.

When I reached the lobby, I was completely relieved and insanely upset at the same time. I could feel my heartbeat throbbing in my neck. This was my real, honest-to-goodness (or maybe dishonest-to-badness?) life, and it seemed I could only eat dinner if it involved being naked. I mean, whose life was like that except mine? Why couldn't I catch a break?

My bus pulled away seconds before I got to the stop. I shivered as I walked the four blocks to the train. On the walk I wondered why this night and this request bothered me more than most. I stepped onto the six train, and asked myself if it would've been better if Dorian just wanted a blowjob. At least I expected that. Then I asked the scary question: would I have done it? Would I have dropped to my knees before a complete stranger just for a magazine cover and the promise of a break? I really didn't know the answer to that one. So maybe the evening was for the best. Maybe Dorian's request was so outrageous it saved me from myself.

Dear God! Who had I become? At what point did my life start losing all of its niceties? Sure, the man/mistress relationship consisted of sex for money at its primal core, but it was covered by rules, sugarcoated by appearances, blurred by conversation. Being a mistress meant being the other woman in a man's life – not the disposable hooker who gets fucked and then left out like yesterday's trash. If only Michael were around, he would have destroyed Dorian, but where was Michael? Intellectually, I knew that wasn't the question I should have been asking. I should have been asking why I was allowing these situations to happen. I needed to step up. I no longer had my very own god to save me. Michael wasn't coming back. I needed to make some changes. The train pulled into Astor Place. It was my stop.

I spent that night like so many others, rubbing Charlie's tummy while I soul-searched over a jar of peanut butter and worked on my list of notes which had morphed itself into a journal. I dug around with the spoon, picking out bits of peanut from the extra-crunchy store brand. I had nothing to show for all of my twenty-four years except some random jewelry that I'd long since hocked and a couple pictures in trade magazines. Sadly, one picture I never showed anyone because I looked like a badly made-up drag queen. I'd now lived for nearly a quarter of a century, probably close to one-third of my life, and I had accomplished nothing. I had to change my ways before another twenty-five years passed and I looked back to see that I had amounted to nothing more than being a broke cocktail waitress at a sleazy club. And even that option wouldn't be around forever. Who wants a saggy ass and wrinkled décolletage delivering drinks? I needed a way out. I needed to be rescued.

PART III

THE LESSER GODS OF THE EARTH

Chapter 7: The Amazons

"Aeschylus calls them 'The warring Amazons, the men-haters.' They were a nation of women, all warriors."

I was back at work and more determined than ever to find a man. The right man. Men who could take lives and men who could save lives were all that I had time to find attractive. And I needed to find this life-taking/life-saving man within two weeks. It was my new plan and I wasn't screwing with it, but all of the added stress made me even grouchier than usual. On Saturday night, I nearly bit Libby's head off for moving in on one of my tables. Libby was a beautiful African-American woman who had been at the club six months longer than me. By nightclub standards, we were career cocktail waitresses. Libby wasn't intimidated by me or my pissed-off attitude; in fact, she stared me down smack in front of the customer. "Shut the fuck up and mind your own business," were her exact words. Later, she told me that she was there because one of her regulars was sitting at my table.

"Then tell him to sit in your station." I began to walk off but Libby followed.

"Hey, you know what you need?" she said to my back.

"Let me guess," I said, turning to face her.

"You need some advice." Huh, not the answer I was expecting.

"Really?" I sounded as angry as I could, in a voice as tough as I could make it.

"Yeah," she said, laughing at me. Libby always seemed to be laughing at me.

"So? What's the advice?"

"Get a man. Get a date. Get laid."

"I'll keep that in mind, thanks." Then for some reason I said, "Well's just a little dry right now, you know?"

"Why?" she asked looking me up and down, not letting it go. "Where are you getting your men?"

"Um…" I looked around, blushing. She stared at me in wide-eyed horror.

"From here?" she asked with pure disgust in her voice. "No wonder."

"Well I didn't plan to!" I said in my own defense. "I came here expressly because my type of man wouldn't be caught dead in here! Then it just happened."

"You need to stop that and fast," she said, shaking her head. "Sometimes my outside men come visit me here, but never the other way around."

"Well then, since you know everything, where do I get them? These men who are so great?" If she had all the answers let her share them.

"Where? *New York Magazine!*" Libby said like it was common knowledge.

"Yeah, sure."

"Just try it," she said. "I've used them for years. The men in that magazine understand what it means to be a man."

I was skeptical, but could my new Prince Charming really be just one little personal ad away? "Do I run one or answer one?" I asked. Libby turned and waved me off, laughing as she went. She had disappeared into the crowd. How about that. My guardian angel appeared to me as a gorgeous female in a push-up bra and thong. How jealous most men would be. I looked for her over the crowd, turning myself in a full circle like a cat chasing her tail. A man at the next table rubbed my thigh.

"Hey! Babe! Are you as stoopid as you look?" The entire table laughed – all men, of course. "You tink you can handle a drink ordah, or you too busy tryin' to fig'uh out how to walk forwards?" He stood and pointed at his feet. "Left then right," he said. "Left then right." He used his hands to mime gigantic breasts that bobbed while he walked. The personals were sounding better by the second.

*   *   *

Retired Physicist, 82 – Kind, caring, owns homes in South Beach and Scarsdale. Looking for tall, leggy girl 20-25 who loves fine dining, furs and having a good time.

Send pictures – full body and face. Bikini pic helpful.

Helpful for what? An early grave? Next.

Looking for Love – 40ish, jet-setting businessman looking for the perfect female companion, early-20ish (max!), to help pass the time on those endless flights to Europe and back.

Must love travel, four-star hotels, exotic food... and being spoiled. Pic a must.

Xavier was an Englishman who sold men's suits to Barneys. Not at Barneys... to Barneys. I was sure to clarify that.

He loved the headshot I sent him. "Are you as sexy as that photo says you are?" I could hear him panting through the phone. "The way you've raised your eyebrow just so. And all that hair... those lips! You better be as sexy as your picture."

Hoping his pluses would outweigh his apparent minuses, I agreed to meet him. In addition to having money and offering travel opportunities, Xavier lived out-of-town, so not that much would be expected of me. Plus, there was no way an Englishman would be as hot-blooded as the Banana King Drug Lord of South America. This was good. Xavier was promising a very nice lifestyle which I would only have to pay for once a month or so. Huh. I sounded remarkably like Jan.

I met Xavier for lunch at a small bistro on Lexington Avenue and learned that he had two children at home. So, after a shared bottle of Shiraz with lunch and a kiwi tart for dessert, we took a walk to FAO Schwartz to get Furbys. I picked out two for my niece and handed them to Xavier. While he stood in line, I did a little more shopping. I picked up a Glitter Hair Barbie, a beautiful wooden doll house and a very expensive Madame Alexander doll. Hell, if he was footing the bill, I might as well take care of Megan's birthday and Christmas too.

Oh, and I added a couple of high bouncing balls for Charlie and a giant bag of cinnamon gummy bears for me.

"Anything else?" he asked as I handed him my finds. He knew he couldn't say no to me, his ad promised that he would spoil me. Besides, compared to what I was expecting him to buy for me, this was child's play.

"Sure!" I said, not taking the hint. "Here." I put a jar of green slime and a teddy bear wearing an FAO sweater on the counter. I smiled, planning our next stop – Barneys. I thought Barneys was an extremely considerate suggestion on my part seeing he probably got a considerable discount.

I knew that this wasn't proper mistress behavior. We'd only gone to one store and I had already proven to him that I was expensive and high maintenance. But I didn't care. It was time a man proved to me that he was worthy of sex; not that my sex was worthy of gifts.

While an unhappy Xavier paid, I thought back fondly to my shopping sprees with Michael and Ivan. I sighed and pulled myself together, vowing that I would make Barneys even better. Good for me! That's the go-get-'em (all of 'em) attitude! Unfortunately, Barneys was scratched due to an emergency work engagement, so after quick kisses in the cab goodbye, I was home.

I sat in my tiny apartment, pissed. While Charlie played with his new toys, I dug my hand into the container of green slime and let it roll back and forth between my fingers. It felt great. It was sticky and smelled like plastic. When I squished down on the slime it farted. I laughed so hard Charlie came over to see what the fuss was all about. He didn't seem to get it. Then I stopped laughing. There was no one in my life who would laugh with me. Not one single person who would find slimy farting sounds as funny as I did. No one to call and say, "Listen to this!" I was alone and it was my own fault. I had made love and sex into a business and everyone had gone home for the day. They had closed up shop until regular business hours resumed, and regular business hours were pretty fickle – some days, open all night and other days, closed for vacation. I squished the slime again – slime I'd only bought to aggravate a man I was supposed to be seducing. I cupped my hands and let the slime leak through my fingers and fall to the floor.

*   *   *

Xavier came back to town and we headed to dinner at a Russian caviar restaurant on Madison Avenue. As we climbed the stairs, I could feel his eyes on my skirt. I turned around deliberately. He smiled.

A pretty Russian hostess who barely spoke English showed us to a small banquette, opposite a roaring fire. I slid in, admiring the detail of the upholstery, thinking that it was too bad that it would be under my ass all night. It would have made nice curtains. There were portraits of great Czars on the walls, piles of desserts, a giant samovar and lots of couples – some feeding each other, some necking. The guy next to us had his hand up his date's blouse. She was giggling. This was obviously a place you take your date in an attempt to get lucky. Heck, if you were really lucky, it might happen right in the restaurant. I made a mental note not to place my bag on any surface in the ladies' room. The restaurant smelled of fresh, strong coffee. I sat back on the soft couch and inhaled deeply.

Dinner was remarkably okay – we drank ice-cold vodka, ate blintzes topped with sour cream and Beluga caviar, and listened to the live band playing Russian folk music. The musicians wore bright red and yellow puffy sleeved costumes, and the more vodka I drank, the more they looked like a mutant strain of giant exotic songbirds.

Through dinner I learned more than I wanted to about Xavier. More than I wanted because I just didn't care. I know it sounds cold and selfish, but I wasn't getting any younger. There was only one thing I wanted to know from Xavier, or from any other man for that matter: how much are you willing to give me and what will I have to do to get it?

I feigned interest in his story about how he got started in his business while I got bombed on vodka. All through his story I thought about my past lovers and – with the exception of Michael and I guess Ivan – their miserly ways. It just didn't make any sense. How could a man think that it's okay to have a mistress and not take care of her? I mean, really take care of her? What could possibly be in it for us? I pushed Xavier's hand out from under my skirt. I drank some more and listened while he told me he had his two sons out of wedlock. Somehow, that was supposed to be more appealing to me than a long-term marriage. I downed another shot of Russian vodka.

Imported Russian vodka is strong. So strong, in fact, I thought I could send Xavier telepathic messages to buy me things. I concentrated on his full eyebrows, his small round face, his enlarged pores, his clean-shaven cheeks, all the while mentally telling him: "Send Victoria to Europe. Buy Victoria an apartment. Victoria gives great head." As soon as I sent this last thought, Xavier reacted. Figured.

Xavier finished his ninth or so shot and threw the glass clear across the room – missing a waiter's Ushanka by mere millimeters – and into the burning fire. The glass smashed into a million little bits. The man behind the samovar, not three feet away, glared at us. I shrugged, but Xavier smiled, pleased with himself for honoring the age-old, time-honored tradition of assaulting a harmless fire.

The Russian hostess ran to our table. "I've told you a half a dozen times, Xavier, stop throwin' the fuckin' glassiz! I don't care who you are fuckin' tryin' to fuckin' impress tonight!" She stormed away, cursing us out in her Russian-by-way-of-Brooklyn accent.

Xavier wasn't the least bit embarrassed. "Twat," he said nodding to the hostess as she complained to the manager. I still hadn't spoken a word since my fruitless telepathic communication attempt and I knew it was probably time. I tried, but the vodka had made my head too fuzzy. I even opened my mouth to form a sentence. What I was trying to say, I had no idea. But it was definitely something. Maybe. I sat back; the loud, happy Russian songbirds were beginning to annoy me.

Xavier leaned across the table and took a bite of my potato pirozhok. As we drank and drank and drank some more, I grew increasingly sullen, but Xavier became downright chatty. He talked about his wife, whom he'd finally married, and their nonexistent sex life, then again he talked about his business and the "asshole buyer" who was making his life miserable. I could barely keep my eyes open. Finally, he turned his attention to me. He began by promising this and that, but even drunk as I was, it was something in his promises, in the way that he said them, that made me suspicious. Things like, "I'll scurry you and those luscious lips to London tomorrow!" and "Would you like to go to Hawaii, Vicki?" And then, when it came time to pay the bill, he had to split the charge between two separate credit cards. How many vacations was that ten-dollar credit line going to offer me? I just couldn't buy what he was selling... and Lord knows I wanted to buy it.

As I enjoyed a last blintz, I became slightly more lucid. Xavier needed to become a better liar if he wanted a mistress. It was all so obviously an act that even I couldn't fall for it. But, then again, somewhere out there was a wide-eyed eighteen-year-old who'd be more than willing to buy it all. It would all be new to her. Heck, it wasn't so long ago that I would have been willing to buy it. All the way back to, let's say… the beginning of this evening.

Resigned to the demise of our relationship, I had one last shot of lukewarm vodka and ended the date. Xavier didn't give up so easily. He called again and again, always around two in the afternoon, wanting phone sex. He would whisper my name and orgasm almost as soon as I said hello. I changed my number – a hard thing for me to do because of the possibility of another call from Michael – but I knew if Michael wanted to find me, he would.

Tall, Wealthy, Masculine, Blue-Eyed, Distinguished Entrepreneur – Seeks classy gal to help me through those lonely nights. Non-smoker.

Must be: A beautiful, head-turning, young gorgeous female with a fantastic body who is also compassionate.

Looking for that one girl I can make my queen. Must send picture and include true age. Measurements a plus.

He may have potential, but where was the direct promise to spoil me?

Lonely, Attractive, Nice Old Guy – 65+++ Big Bucks. Seen it all.
Hoping to find smart, good-looking lady, any age for future and fun. Willing to spend.
Picture of you please...

Excellent! Honest and to-the-point. Can you believe it? I actually submitted.

The next week I received a phone call. I played the message. "Hi, this is Gary. You submitted your photo and a note to my father's personal ad: Lonely, Attractive, Nice Old Guy. He wanted to meet you and was very excited at the prospect, but unfortunately, my father passed away three days ago. I just wanted to let you know out of courtesy – you see, my father was a very courteous gentleman – and also to let you know that I would be interested in taking you out in his place. Of course, you understand, this wouldn't be a date, just a type of memorial for my father... well, something to remember my father by and to honor his memory with. I, of course, am a happily married man with three children and another one on the way..." Erase.

"Tall, Wealthy, Masculine, Blue-Eyed, Distinguished Entrepreneur..."

The "Distinguished Entrepreneur..." was a diamond district guy. I met up with him at a tiny French restaurant downtown, the kind of place you swear you'll return to but can never find again. The "Distinguished Entrepreneur" was tall, about six-foot-three, with a big barrel chest, a ruddy complexion, a white beard and a rim of white hair around the sides of his head. He was the spitting image of Santa Claus. In other words, he was the perfect man for me. I could hardly wait to sit on his lap. I closed my eyes and imagined Christmas morning and an enormous sack full of diamonds.

Santa and I had a nice, comfortable evening together. After my third glass of merlot, I was willing to buy any story Santa was selling. Even the one about how he had fallen in love with his wife because she was a nurse who worked with orphaned children. Why not? He went on with a slight tear in his eye. "But now, sadly, she has pulled away from me. Some mental problems are isolating her." I tilted my head in sympathy.

Sitting there, sipping my after-dinner brandy, I let my thoughts go. I saw myself lying by the fireplace in my gorgeous Fifth Avenue penthouse playing with the diamond necklace Santa had just given me – the perfect match to the earrings that he'd given me the week before. After our weekly visit, he would proclaim his love for me and disappear, leaving me to count my diamonds and my blessings. By the time we began wrapping up our evening I felt somewhat cherished, respected even. I cozied up to the feeling. Finally, I thought I'd found a man who understood. Or perhaps I was just so broke – as in "maybe I should order some Chinese food" broke – that I was reading way too much into the relationship way too early. The best part? Santa would dote on me without the additional accessories – the cuts and bruises – that went along with being

Michael's mistress. This could very well be the beginning of a beautiful friendship. I drained my last sips of espresso.

By now you must be wondering what it feels like to knowingly choose a boyfriend who has a wife. The answer is, you just don't think about it. Really. And if you ever do, you get past any pettiness or jealousies by considering it an ego boost, that is, I win. I trumped the wife. If he were happy with her, he wouldn't be with me. It is a literal game of survival of the fittest. Whoever looks the fittest in her jeans, wins. Believe me, if my body hadn't looked like it did, ain't none of those men woulda come arunnin.' No one's claiming it's a perfect system, we're dealing with men here. Wives end up screwed; mistresses, fucked.

There's also a real difference between sleeping with a married man and being someone's mistress. In fact, I've always had a complete disdain for women who just want to sleep with married men, who won't go the extra mile and make the commitment. Who simply follow some primal urge, rather than learning the art of seduction and manipulation. It's completely trashy. It conjures up images of cheesy toner companies with female receptionists and male bosses; of frizzy blonde hair that bobs up and down and long hot pink fingernails that scratch his thighs; of greasy comb-overs and Subway meatball-hero-stained ties and polyester pants around his ankles while secret blowjobs transpire by the copy machine. They make the rest of us look bad. That's why I chased Joseph all the way to JFK; I made the effort. Anyone can sleep with a married man, but being a mistress requires great skill.

What about finding a man who was willing to cheat? For the most part, every married man I'd ever met was more than happy to cheat on his wife. I know there were exceptions – Liz's husband, Martin, for example, and an occasional man at the club. But they were rare. And if that's the way it works, I was better off as a mistress. 'Tis better to cheat with than to be cheated on, I decided and left Santa, happier than I had been for a long time. I looked forward to our next date, Italian food.

The following Tuesday, Santa took me to his favorite Italian restaurant. Just as I was about to walk in, he pointed to a spa next door. "I hope you don't mind... I took the liberty of booking us massages after dinner. You'll love it!"

Mind? I didn't mind at all. Not one little bit. Especially since the appointments were for after dinner. Like a starving stray, I left Santa on the street and followed the scent of fresh marinara sauce straight into the restaurant. When he caught up with me, he led me to the bar to relax with a few glasses of burgundy before dinner. I hadn't eaten yet that day, so the wine went straight to my head. While he told another story, I ate as many breadsticks as I could to mask my hunger pangs and to stay upright.

After dinner, we strolled next door. Even after the osso buco and homemade pasta, I was still a bit tipsy when I walked into the beautiful Asian spa. Between the wine and the heavy food, the massage would surely put me to sleep. I knew Santa wouldn't mind, he kept telling me that he wanted me to relax. What a guy. I went into the women's locker room and threw on the soft waffle robe and cushioned slippers waiting for me. I floated out, humming. For a brief moment while I was changing I considered liberating the slippers – they were amazingly comfortable and mine were tattered and full of holes. I decided against it. No sense in making a bad impression; Santa would clearly buy me anything and everything I wanted.

A stressed out employee came running toward me. "Hurry! Hurry! Mr. Diamond waits!" she said, scurrying me into a large massage room. What an odd personality to be working in a calm spa environment. I decided not to let it ruin my good mood. Good moods had become rare for me.

I walked into my massage room and was surprised to see a long curtain separating, I imagined, two massage tables. Did Santa decide to cut costs by getting me a semi-private room? I tossed off my robe and climbed onto my table. The two tables must have had something to do with the feng shui of the room. I wasn't going to worry about it. I lay face up and saw handrails suspended above my table. That could only mean one thing: I was getting a deep tissue, walk-on-the-back, shiatsu massage. Oh. I was about to have a woman who weighs no less than me jump up and down on my back. Great for the boob job, not to mention my slightly queasy stomach. I rolled over anyway, deciding to be a good sport.

A minute later, my masseuse opened the curtain and there was Santa, lying on the parallel table. He was face down. He lifted his head to smile at me.

"Isn't it great!" he said, beaming. "His and hers massages!"

"Great," I said, now understanding his generosity. My massage began and moments into it I realized that not only was this massage painful, it wasn't the least bit relaxing. I had to keep a constant watchful eye on Santa who was desperately trying to catch a glimpse of any body parts my masseuse exposed. "Ow!" I said when the masseuse put her elbow into my shoulder blade. Santa lifted his head.

"Relax! You too tense!" my masseuse said.

But I couldn't relax. Instead, I watched Santa sneak peeks at my breasts every chance he could. My head was throbbing from the wine. I was relieved when it was finally over. I slid my hands down my breasts to make sure they were still intact.

Still naked, I asked my masseuse for my robe; she threw it onto my table. I slipped the robe on, careful not to expose anything more for Santa's viewing pleasure and slid into my ultra-comfy slippers, deciding then that I would liberate them after all. I started to leave, but my masseuse blocked the door. "Mr. Diamond, you wait for him." So I did. She was right. In my zeal fueled by hunger and desperation, I was starting to forget all the rules of being a good mistress. I sat on my table and took a deep breath to relax. I watched as Santa rolled over onto his back. With the massage oil covering his body, he looked like a great humpback whale, broaching. His sheet fell away, and Santa was naked. Wow, that sure killed my Christmas spirit. Of all of us there, I was the only one it seemed to bother. I looked away, grateful that his stomach was so large it camouflaged any erection he may have been sporting.

"Come here," he said when his massage was over and everyone had left. He lay on the table and held out his arms. I was trapped. Even in the dimly lit room he looked nothing short of revolting. What could I do? I didn't want to storm out on Santa Claus! No sense in getting on the naughty list so early in the game. I had to be creative. I had to have him think that I wanted him without offering him anything. I turned my back to him and let my robe drop down just to the top of my butt. I glanced at him over my shoulder. I wiggled myself around and held the robe up just over my breasts. Then I pretended I was going to let the robe drop, but instead, I pulled it back on.

"Not yet," I said, praying that this little posing session would keep him happily diverted. I tried to make my escape, but Santa grabbed my belt and pulled me to him. I smiled at him, wanting to leave, wanting this to be over.

Santa reached into my robe and stroked my breast. Thankfully, the room was dark so he couldn't see my surgery scars. Whenever I knew the twins would be on display for anyone but delivery men, I always covered my scars with Dermablend. Since Dr. Fifth Avenue had closed me up himself, the scars were more noticeable than if he had let his assistant – who normally did the stitching – finish the job. It was no one's business but my own that I had a little help. Obviously, I wasn't expecting to bare all for Santa so soon. He pinched my nipple, sat up and licked my breast. I closed my eyes. When I just couldn't stand anymore I pulled my robe closed, laughed off the incident, and went to get dressed.

After a quick shower where I soaped and scrubbed my breasts twice, I met up with a fully clothed, visibly pissed Santa. He had been waiting for me for twenty minutes and he was still horny. I thanked the ladies at the club, paid little attention to the mood of my date, and walked out. Santa hailed a cab for me. I knew I'd blown it and the relationship was over before it started, but I also felt triumphant, like I had survived some major life challenge. Okay so he licked my boob; it's not like I could feel it anyway. I waved to him from my window and, reluctantly, he waved back. The fact that he called to see me again stunned me.

For our third date, Santa and I went to the Upper West Side to pick out some bedding. Whose house it was for and when we would use it was still to be determined.

The young salesman stared at me and back to Santa and then back and forth again. "Is he your father?" he whispered while Santa was engrossed in plaid versus stripes.

"What do you think?" I asked. I let my weight slump to one hip and my belly-button ring show. "Do you really think I would buy bedding with my father?"

"Wow! I mean... no!" said the salesman, caught up in the straining fibers of my too-low-cut sweater. "He must be really rich!" I winked at the boy while we checked out. I owed him something, he had made me feel beautiful and powerful, two feelings that I hadn't felt for a long time. I was still smiling on our sleigh ride – Mercedes, SL-Class – to the sushi restaurant. I switched the radio back and forth a couple of times.

Santa snapped at me. "Can you just pick one?" he asked. "I mean, if you're going to do something, then do it. Don't start to do it, or say yes and then stop." He shook his head. Apparently, he wasn't over our last date after all.

"Okay," I said, giggling. "Sorry." What was going on here? Wasn't Santa supposed to be jolly? I figured he was still horny, but come on, hadn't this guy heard of masturbation? I looked at him again. Oh yeah, he certainly knew what masturbation was, that's how he survived high school. I fixed my lime green sweater in the passenger side mirror. The sweater was cut so low you could see the entire top of my breasts, right down to my demi-cut bra. I adjusted to make sure my nipples weren't showing.

Santa glared at me from across the car. "Are those yours?" he asked.

"Are what mine?" I asked back.

"You know. Your tits."

"What kind of question is that?" His old, horny, crotchety act was wearing thin. "Of course they're mine." As opposed to what, "loner breasts" I kept for the weekend?

Over tuna handrolls in the East Village, Santa mellowed a bit. After two shared bottles of sake, he confided he was looking for a replacement for his last girlfriend who'd abandoned him for rehab. The bitch. The job description for this coveted position went something like this: "What I'm looking for," he said, taking a sip, "is what I had with Sharon, before. She dated, I understood that, but we lived together. She would party with her young friends and then come home to me. On good nights, she would be so wasted that she would throw all the covers off me and attack. I gave her money for her lifestyle and she was my girlfriend."

"And where was Mrs. Claus through all of this?" It was a stupid question, but I had to know.

"I told you, she has some mental issues," he said, looking away.

As I devoured a salmon skin roll, I decided that Santa must have had his wife committed to get her out of his way. I imagined poor Mrs. Claus locked away in some rubber room while Santa enjoyed turning their bedroom into his own "rubber" room. It was too much for me. On top of all that, I just couldn't bring myself to do anything with Santa. It would be difficult just to close my eyes and give him a blowjob. Maybe if he dangled some diamonds in front of me. Maybe… but he wasn't going to. Santa was stingy. And I don't think even my wildest Michael fantasy would get me through sex with him. He simply repulsed me. Not to mention that I was legitimately worried he may have contracted some STD from his last girlfriend. I quickly ordered and ate two extra eel rolls, finished my sake, grabbed some sashimi to go for Charlie and told Santa that it was over.

When he dropped me off I felt both relief and terror. I was still broke, still waitressing, and I still had no way out, but Santa seemed like too high a price to pay for a few measly dinners and maybe some jewelry. Honestly, I think Santa was just as happy to see me go as I was to get out; I don't think I was his dream either. He was lucky; his elves could make him the perfect girlfriend. But me? It was time to grow up and stop believing in Santa Claus.

Since I didn't have the money to run an ad myself, I became proficient at answering them. I always sent a phenomenal picture of myself – a headshot for semi-wealthy men and a full-body shot for extremely wealthy men. I never asked for a picture in return. Some were surprised, others just grateful. After Santa, I answered a couple of other ads but a lot of them sounded phony. I had heard that people – especially young men – sometimes ran gag ads to see who was pathetic enough to answer. Seeing that I was definitely pathetic enough, I was extra careful who I mailed to. If I didn't hear back from someone, I forget about it. I didn't need to waste time obsessing over rich teen-aged boys laughing at me and whacking off to my picture.

My third attempt with the personal ads was a veterinarian:

Animal Doc Seeking Animal Lover: Vet seeking woman to spend quality time with. Me: successful and generous. You: attractive and kind. Non-smoker please. Vegetarian a plus. Photo a must.

Well, what could be wrong with him? He loved animals, rescued strays, donated his time to shelters. He was successful and generous. Plus, think of the free veterinary visits! He just might be the perfect man. Surely, even Charlie would approve.

"Indian food?" I asked my vet over the phone. "Wouldn't you rather go somewhere... um... better?" "Expensive" was the word I was looking for.

"They have a great menu," he said, sounding a little disappointed.

"Okay," I said, reconsidering. The vet was a vegetarian and Indian food was the logical choice.

Thinking about it, I was sure that I could be a vegetarian too. What was some granola and vegan pizza compared to a warm, passionate, caring, wealthy man? Besides, Charlie and I could always sneak a couple of double cheeseburgers while our vet was off saving Manhattan's four-legged population. How noble a profession! So much more so than, say, Dr. Fifth Avenue. I cursed my lowly beginnings with an immortal plastic surgeon. How selfish to be a doctor only concerned with money. How far I had come in both compassion and appreciation! What growth! Bravo for me!

I was relieved to find the Indian restaurant was rather upscale. I stood by the maitre d' waiting for my vet. I had never seen him, but he had my picture – he would have to find me. I looked at my watch – right on time – which could only mean that he was late. Huh. Maybe there'd been a furry emergency. Or his wife held him up. Then, out of the corner of my eye, I noticed a man sitting alone at a table, staring at me. He sipped his soda and stared straight at me. "Are you sure that man isn't waiting for someone?" I asked. The maitre d' reconsidered, approached him, and sure enough, he was my date. It was an odd beginning, but I went over and started the evening with high hopes.

"Wow!" he said. "You're even more beautiful than your picture!"

"Aw," I said, sliding into my seat, "that's sweet. Thank you!" I ordered a club soda with lime in an attempt to look more worthy.

"What about me?" he asked. "Do you think I'm attractive?"

"Ye... Yes," I said, "but more importantly, I think what you do for a living is wonderful! You must be a very special man." Truthfully, the vet was pretty awful looking, but I wasn't the least bit surprised by his appearance. He was mousy, with oversized glasses, thick brown hair that fell into his eyes and full lips, full in a very different way than mine. If he had been handsome, he would have been too good to be true, and he certainly wouldn't have been running a personal ad.

"And what do you do?" he asked. "I bet you're a model."

"Yes," I said, wishing my drink was there. How could I explain what I do?

"I knew it!" he said. "I'm dating a gorgeous model! Score!" He pounded his fist on the table. I wished I'd ordered a martini.

"Why didn't you know it was me?" I asked, truly curious. "When I was waiting over there, by the maitre d's stand. You have my picture, do I look that different?"

"No, no, not at all. It's just...."

"What?"

"It's... well, frankly, the way you're dressed." I looked down at my outfit. I was wearing a long flowing skirt and peasant blouse. I thought a vet would appreciate the hippie look.

"What about it?"

"I didn't think it was you standing there. I was just hoping... expecting a little bit sexier outfit. I mean, since you're so sexy in your picture."

I wanted to curse, but I was good and held my tongue. All I actually said was, "Oh." I was proud of myself for not cursing, goddamnit. My drink finally arrived. I grabbed the waiter's arm. "Could I please have an Absolut tonic?" I kept his arm. "Quickly?" He understood. He smiled and took off for the bar.

"But you look nice!" the vet said, oblivious to my exchange with the waiter. Maybe he was trying to apologize for being such a dick. I relaxed a bit and flipped through my menu. I was about to ask him for recommendations when I noticed him looking at my blouse.

"It's vintage," I said.

"What is?"

"The blouse? That you've been staring at... it's vintage. Circa 1968."

"Before you were born, huh?" he asked.

"Yes," I said, and that was, in fact, the truth. He stared even harder. After a few awkward moments, I closed my menu. "Is there something you want?" I was beginning to get a little embarrassed for both of us.

He pushed his soda aside and leaned in over the table. "You have really nice breasts. Do you think there's any chance I'll see them before the night's over?" He asked this with a straight face and all before I had a chance to order.

"No," I said, standing. "No, I don't think so." The waiter arrived with my vodka tonic and I drank the whole thing down, still standing. When I finished, I placed the glass back on the waiter's tray, thanked him, and glared at my vet. I wished I had something witty to say to him, but instead I just walked out, grateful that I hadn't worn any of my usual sexier outfits. I would have hated to serve as fodder for his late-night jack-off. Huh. Now it made sense, "Animal Doc Seeking *Animal* Lover" – I finally caught the double entendre. I was through with the personal ads.

"Hey Libby!" I said the next time we worked the same shift. "Those personal ads suck! I had one bad experience on top of another."

"That's what men are," Libby said, matter-of-fact. "One bad experience on top of another. That's why you have to make them pay."

"But you can't always get even," I said, fed-up with Libby and her pearls of wisdom.

Libby just shook her head. "Honey, I don't mean pay in that way." I felt my face go white and despite myself, I took a step backwards. "Well, don't worry yourself about it, I'm not contagious."

"No, I know, I didn't mean—"

"Relax," she said, "and come here." Libby led us to a small bench near the upstairs bathrooms. We were pretty much out of sight and we could actually hear each other. Libby flopped down wearily and I sat next to her, rubbing my ankles. She lit a cigarette. I was surprised that Libby was talking to me – let alone offering advice. But that night there was no animosity between us. We were just two exhausted cocktail waitresses, sitting on the same small bench, both rubbing our throbbing feet. She flicked some ashes with her ring finger in the exact same way that my mother did.

"Look," she said after she took a long drag on her cigarette. "You know how they always say that there are two types of women? The one a guy fucks and the one he brings home to his mother?"

"Yeah," I said.

"Well I think it's the other way around. That there are two types of men, but only one type of woman: smart. Too smart to let them know any different. The two types of men are those you date for fun, and those you date for money. Never," she emphasized this staring straight at me, "ever, cross the streams."

"That's what I've been trying to do," I said, hearing the whine in my own voice. I was relieved to have a confidante other than my worn-out, overstuffed journal. I leaned in to reveal my trade secret. "I've been a mistress for a lot of years now," I whispered. Libby giggled while she blew out a puff of smoke.

"A what? A mistress? Well how's that working for you," she asked. "Haven't seen you quit the club."

"Well neither have you," I said, matching her bitchiness.

"Why would I?" She became very serious. "This is my office." She sat back and smiled at me. Her face softened as she spoke. "Look," she said, "many years ago I started as an escort. I got dressed up, went to functions – sometimes nice places – like benefits at museums. I went to a lot of dinners for awards and such given to scientists and computer geeks. Guess it's true what they say, that they can never get a date." She shrugged and went on. "Then I just got tired of fighting off the advances. Some of them expected more, a lot more, and I was supposed to deliver. You know how it is." I nodded. "One day I mentioned it to someone at the service and they more or less told me that I could do better – you know, financially – if I went along for the ride. So I did. It was really no big deal. It wasn't *Pretty Woman* or anything. I didn't cry through it. It was just kind of nondescript and quick. He was a horny computer geek and I was the beautiful girl of his dreams. Later, when I picked up my check the woman at the service said that the guy had requested me again for a 'similar function' next week. That was code for I fucked him and he wanted me to do it again. I didn't care so I said sure. Then I looked at my check and realized that my agency had taken a huge percentage of the profit for my work. That's when I said no way. I had the guy's cell number, so I called him direct. Next thing I know I'm working for myself, my own boss. I came here to have a home base, an office. I tell my new clients to meet me here so I can scope them out, and sometimes my regular clients come here to arrange a meeting or to introduce me to a friend. Last year, I made over six figures. Well over six figures. And I only pay tax on what I make here."

"What?" I asked, my eyes widening. "Six figures? Just from that?"

"Yup," she said. She stood triumphantly and stomped out her cigarette on the floor. She grabbed her tray and slung it on one hip. It was the same pose I used whenever I was closing a deal. "Victoria, think about it. I can hook you up to get you started. I'm overbooked these days. You know where to find me." She looked at me long and hard and said rather sweetly, "We all end up flat on our backs eventually, so what's wrong with a little security? I'm not telling you it's the greatest thing in the world, I'm telling you that it is no different from anything else. And it's the closest thing to a guarantee you can get when you're dealing with a man. Look, you already know what it's like to be a mistress," she said, mocking me.

"What about—"

"What? A wife? Wives get used up when they're young, cheated on when they're middle-aged, and fucked over in divorce court. Money will never fuck you over."

She handed me a business card. I scoured it for tell-tale signs.

"Well, it doesn't say 'Libby Bene, Whore' if that's what you're looking for. But it has a cell number. If you call, I'll know you're interested."

"Thanks," I said as she just stared at me. "I... I...." I had no idea what else to say.

"You... you...." Libby smiled her big beautiful smile and laughed at me. "Relax, Victoria. I was just giving you some woman-to-woman advice."

"Well, how would I... even get started? I mean, besides with your help." I was truly overwhelmed by our conversation but lucid enough to realize that if I did go for it, I didn't want Libby to take a cut of my profits as a finder's fee.

"You an actress?" she asked.

"Model."

"Even better. Ask your agent if he knows of any 'available men' – he'll understand. It'll get you started. Then the guys tell their friends about you and before you know it, you're in business."

"Oh," I said.

She leaned down. "Look," she said, "that's the guy from the other night. The one in your station. He's one of mine. That's why I moved in on your territory." I looked in the direction of the tables.

"He's not so bad looking."

"There's a variety. You learn to be choosy. Most of them have wives that won't give them blowjobs. It's amazing what a man will do to have his dick sucked, huh?" Libby laughed and shook her head. "Fucking assholes," she said, under her breath. She caught me staring at her.

"Yeah, well, see you later!" she said, laughing off the anger. Then Libby sauntered off to her client and her six-figure lifestyle, leaving me to think about all the blowjobs that I'd given away for free.

Chapter 8: Silenus

"Silenus was a jovial old fat man who usually rode an ass because he was too drunk to walk. He is shown by his perpetual drunkenness."

I met Lenny while I was doing extra work on a soap opera. I got booked for the job because one of the New York soaps was casting for model types who could act. To my agency, the fact that I was able to read meant that I had acting talent.

I walked into the casting office on the far West Side and was surrounded by other young women all in mega-high shoes, holding scripts and reading through their parts. I signed in, picked up my sides, and started reading them over. I looked at the girls, most of them actresses waiting for a break. I wondered if any of them were so broke that they were considering becoming an escort. The room looked like a casting for a Noxzema commercial; I was surrounded by the epitome of American youth, fresh-faced and full of hope. The girls were all around my age but they all seemed so young and so healthy. They looked nothing like me; my lifestyle was clearly starting to wear on me. One by one the girls each disappeared into an office, then walked out moments later. I was next. I pulled my sleeves down to cover my wrists and went inside.

Inside a very large office, a man instructed me to stand against a wall to be measured. I passed the height test easily, and I did a pretty good read of my script. The next week I found myself on the set of the soap opera with five other women, all dressed in identical black dresses with our hair slicked back in tight buns, like castoffs from the Robert Palmer "Addicted to Love" video.

My only line for the day was "Cold beer?" which I delivered with enthusiasm to one of the older, established actors, Lenny, aka Spike Jansen. Within an hour,

I had a date. Spike called the next day and asked if I was ready to go out. "Where?" I asked. Hello Rainbow Room!

"I don't know... how about the ferry to Staten Island?"

"Okay," I said, not sure if he was joking. I certainly couldn't imagine what the lure of Staten Island was. But I went with it – he was Spike Jansen after all. Maybe he was preparing for a scene?

Dressed in jeans and a fitted leather jacket, I met Spike at the dock downtown. As soon as he said hi, it was obvious he was slurring his words. He also had trouble walking, which meant the boat ramp was going to prove to be a challenge. So, wisely, we opted for dinner on the island of Manhattan instead. We found a nearby trendy-looking restaurant and after an uneventful two hours, Spike was so drunk he could barely stay upright in his seat. Drunk as he was, he still managed to sign a couple of autographs for the women sitting in the booth next to us and to kiss me full on the lips. His kiss was gross, but the autograph signing made me a little hot for him. And he was Spike Jansen! In the flesh! Millions of adoring fans would give their right arms to be where I was – sitting opposite Spike. After dinner we parted ways, agreeing to meet that coming Saturday for another date.

Saturday night, dressed in a new Betsy Johnson dress and heels, I entered Spike's apartment. "Nice place," I said, "but isn't it weird that I'm here? I mean, where's your wife?"

"No wife," he said, looking at me sideways. He must have thought that I was hinting. Sure, he didn't wear a wedding band, but none of my men did. If he wore a ring and I didn't, it would mean that he was married... but he wasn't married to me.

No wife? Well, wow-wee. Not my first choice, but I could handle it. A soap star of my very own! No more club, no more debt, oh the things that I could get! I felt a pitter-patter in my chest. Maybe I could get out of my shit-hole apartment and into this palatial place. I looked around greedily. It was clear that Spike had money. Lots of money. Seems neurosurgery/drug dealing paid well in Great Maple Forest. The apartment was loaded with an elaborate home theatre system, remote control blinds on the windows, a sub-zero fridge, and a top-of-the-line espresso machine.

I dropped my jacket and turned dramatically to show off what I had on underneath. Hell, I would have dropped my underpants at that moment. Sadly, Spike didn't seem to notice. Come to think of it, I'm not sure that he would have noticed if I had dropped my drawers. I walked toward him and threw my shoulders back. I smelled my own faint smell, a mix of unscented deodorant, soap, and excitement. I smelled yummy... sexy, earthy, and wild. I made a little grunting sound. Nothing. Nothing, because Spike was, in fact, tottering again. I sighed. He wasn't just tottering, he was shitfaced. I was dating Dudley Moore as "Arthur." Seducing him was going to take a considerable amount of effort.

"Are you buzzed?" I asked, patting him on the chest.

"A little," he said, leering.

"Well, how can a brain surgeon-slash-drug dealer run his empire if he's drunk?" That would surely wrap him around my finger.

"Oh, I'm not really a brain surgeon or a—"

"Yeah, I know," I said. "It was a joke. I was trying to show you that I watch your show. You're terrific by the way." Never hurts to add an ego boost complete with a hair toss.

"Oh. Yeah. So, where do you want to go to dinner?"

"I thought you were making the arrangements." How could we get into a decent restaurant at this hour on a Saturday night? Unless... could Spike be so well connected that he could get us into any place we liked? Well then, I vote for the Skybox at Tao!

"There's a restaurant downstairs..." he said, slurring slightly. "We could go there."

"The Chinese place?"

"It's good food."

"Oh, okay. Great!" I said, wishing that he had made a little more effort. I reached for my jacket and Spike kissed me again. His breath reeked of alcohol. I pulled away and looked at him; he could barely meet my eyes. I wondered if I was wasting my time. Yes, I also liked a spirit or two to pick up my spirit from time to time, but how could you have a relationship with a man who was perpetually drunk? But there was no way he could be a soap star and be a drunk.

No matter how handsome he was. It just wouldn't be possible. He must just like to party. With that thought in mind, I kissed back.

Spike stopped for a minute and smiled. "What do you say we go to dinner later?" he said, smooth like honey, or in his case, thirty-year-old scotch. He patted the couch. "Why don't you come over here, you gorgeous creature, and let me prove to you just how beautiful you really are." Nice, right? The thing was, I'd seen him deliver that exact line – in that exact way – to Scarlet Long, the tramp of Great Maple Valley.

I wasn't planning on sex so soon or with someone so drunk. But I understood what I wanted really didn't matter; of the two of us, he was the hotter commodity. Millions of women had crushes on Spike Jansen and I was going to be in his bed. Then who knows...? Maybe he would be the man I had waited for! The man of my dreams! But truthfully, I really wasn't that gullible anymore and I wasn't pinning my hopes purely on Spike's charm. There was another important factor here, Spike was a celebrity. That had to make him trustworthy.

Sure that I wanted something – or for that matter, anything – with a soap star, I took Spike up on his offer to slip into one of his shirts. I sauntered past him on the way to his over-sized bathroom, feeling a tad like my little show was doing more for me than for him. I slipped off my dress, thinking that maybe Spike could get me a full-time job on the soap. I paid no attention to the voice in my head telling me that I wasn't an actress. What good would reality do me now? As I unhooked my bra and covered my scars, I imagined our picture on the cover of *Soap Opera Digest*. While I threw his shirt on over nothing but my panties, I thought about our little Proctor and Gamble, Ivory Snow babies. Actresses were always talking about their break, and I was convinced that I was finally getting mine. I walked from the bathroom back to the living room. Spike was sitting on the arm of the couch, sipping whiskey – in a proper soap opera pose. He would sip and grimace, sip and grimace, with one arm cocked just so and the other arm fully flexed. I stopped for a moment to look for the camera.

"Hey," I said. "Your pose, that's great!"

"Pose?" He finished his drink. Then I realized that this was Spike at ease. "Wow," he said, "you look great."

I did. I was wearing an aqua-marine colored shirt that hung mid-thigh and made my skin look even shinier than usual. I tossed my hair and walked on my tip-toes to the couch. I stood strategically, still stretching to make my legs look longer. I lounged back on the couch in my *Playboy* pose and noticed a small bag on one of the couch pillows.

"What's this?" I asked.

"Oh, just something," he said. I looked at it again. I had never seen such an oddly packaged condom before.

"What though?" I fingered the bag.

"Something... bad," he said. "Very, very, bad. Are you a bad little girl, Vicki?" he asked.

"It depends on what you have in mind," I forced out through my clenched teeth.

"Well this," he said, waving the little bag, "is special."

I grabbed the bag. It wasn't a condom. "Is it... blow?"

Spike laughed at me. "Blow? No! Crystal meth... Much better. I confiscated it from some Cuban drug lords a couple of weeks ago."

"What?" I couldn't tell if he was kidding. "You mean Spike did, right?"

"Isn't that who you're here for? Spike Jansen, at your service." He bowed grandly and lost his balance. Even through my disgust, he was still charming. "Come on," he said, regaining his composure. "I want us to take a hit... then you can sit on my face." He was salivating, staring hard at my panties. He stuck out his index finger and tried to slide my panties to the side. Okay, even Spike's charm had officially worn thin.

"What?" I asked. "You want what?" Images of soapy clean Ivory Snow babies danced out of my head.

"I want to—"

"I heard you. But the answer's no."

"Oh, I get it, 'Members Only,' huh?"

I shook my head, let out a huge sigh, and in one grand gesture I grabbed my things and went to the bathroom to change back into my clothes. Looking into the bathroom mirror I had to chuckle. Members Only? Good Lord. "Good for you, Vick," I said to the mirror. "For once, good for you." I wasn't being a hypocritical prude here. I had certainly experimented with a few mind-altering substances before. Partying was one thing. Taking drugs to get through sex or just because he wanted me fucked up – well, that was quite another. And he was so fucked up himself, did he even know who I was? Besides, I knew that this was going to be just another one-night stand. Spike may not have had a wife, but he was married to his addiction. It would take Aphrodite herself to break up that marriage. Fully dressed, I came out to find Spike reclining on the couch. He crooked his finger for me to come to him. He didn't even realize that I was halfway out the door. He patted the couch.

"Oh God," I said, rolling my eyes. I walked to the door.

"Where are you going?" he asked.

"Home," I said, and I marched out. In one final dramatic act, I asserted my independence and left without asking for cab fare. But I did snag a twenty from under his keys on the table in the hall.

Spike's doorman was shocked to see me so soon – obviously many, many other women took Spike and his crooked finger up on his offer. My behavior had become odd, I was chasing after men but leaving before they had a chance to prove themselves. I had seen four men recently but I didn't sleep with any of them.

On the ride home, I secretly hoped that Spike had the worst case of blue balls in the history of mankind. But it never worked that way. Spike Jansen had a list of woman at his disposal, and he was probably too drunk to get it up anyway.

The next day, still feeling pretty good about myself, I called my mother. "Well, you've slept with so many other men, what difference would it make?" Mom asked, blowing her signature smoke ring. I could smell the smoke through the phone.

"It wouldn't," I said. "But I didn't want to."

"If you didn't want to," my mother coughed, "then you should never have gone there to begin with. I can't say I'm not disappointed. I was looking forward to watching your boyfriend on the stories." I hung up the phone. Less than an hour later, Spike called.

"Look," he said. "I have lots of problems right now... issues. Things you couldn't even begin to understand. My brother is sick and the show accused me of having a relationship with an underage actress. But my drinking is not out of control. Actually, the union says that the show has to allow me to go to rehab three times and so far I've only been once."

"Okay," I said, not sure what I was supposed to say.

"And one more thing," he said. "I wasn't trying to give you – in particular – a hard time."

"I know that," I said, and I did.

"I mean honestly, it could have been any one of those six actresses on the set that day. You were just the one who said yes."

"Aren't I always." I hung up the phone.

Following my night with Spike, it had become painfully clear – even to me – that I was not on the right path. I needed to get a life.

Three years later I saw a sobered up Spike at a bagel shop on the Upper East Side. I hate to admit it, but he still looked great. When were all the years of drinking and drug use going to take their toll? He ran up to me as if all of this had happened yesterday. "Hi!" he said. "Hi... It's Spike." Every woman in the bagel shop turned to him, their suspicions confirmed. "I mean Lenny!" He laughed. "Remember? We—"

"Yes, yes. I remember," I said, surprised that he did. I really didn't want to get into this at ten a.m. in a bagel shop on the Upper East Side, but as I looked around at a bunch of gawking Upper East Side mommies with their babies in tow, I knew I was getting into it. How could I escape? A swarm of teen-aged girls buzzed around us. One gawking mommy stuffed a bagel into her crying baby's mouth, not taking her eyes off Spike for a moment. Another accidentally gave her baby a coffee cup rather than a bottle. Spike had his audience.

"I just wanted to say that I'm sorry. For all of it," he said. "For everything. Really." Then he walked to me, stroked my hair, smiled at me, kissed me softly on the lips and hugged me... for a long time. A really long time. It may have been a minute or longer that I stood there in Spike's arms, unable to move. He even shed a tear. Then Spike walked away. It was a beautiful scene, complete with a grand exit. In one sweeping motion we all turned to watch Spike walk out of the bagel shop. I stared after him, dumbfounded.

"Plain with cream cheese," the voice from behind the counter said softly. I stood there, trying to figure out what had just happened. "Plain with cream cheese!" the voice repeated. I snapped out of it and picked up my bagel. The teen-age girls were pointing at me now, trying to get the courage to talk to me. I had to be someone if Spike Jansen hugged me! I tried to pay for my bagel. "On the house," said the chubby, middle-aged bagel maker behind the counter. The eight or so girls walked up behind me.

"Really?" I asked the bagel maker.

"Mm-hm," she said. "Any friend of Spike Jansen is a friend of mine."

"Thanks," I said, caught up in the mayhem Spike had caused.

"He's so hot," the bagel maker said, still staring out the window after Spike.

"Amen," said a starved-skinny mommy sans stroller who joined our little crowd. They both turned to me.

"Is he... is he as good in bed as he looks?" asked the bagel maker, desperately wanting to know.

"Yes," asked the mommy in a whisper. "Is he?" Her sleeping baby woke and began to cry. She grabbed the stroller and rolled it toward me, wedging me into a corner, deliberately blocking my way.

"Well?" asked the bagel maker holding her breath. I knew what they wanted, and since there was little chance that either of them would ever be in Spike Jansen's bed, I gave it to them. I leaned in close to the two women, the mother covered her baby's ears. I felt the girls close in on us.

"Better..." I said.

"Really?" asked the mother, her eyes wide with anticipation.

"Let's just say," I said, raising my eyebrows, "I felt things with him I never knew I could. If you know what I mean." The mother gasped. The bagel maker clapped her hands in excitement. There. I gave them something for my free bagel. And it wasn't completely untrue.

"I knew it!" said the bagel maker. "Scarlet moans so loudly when he makes love to her! Did you see them yesterday?"

"And what about Crystal?" asked the mommy who had now forgotten to cover her baby's ears. I smiled.

The two women were deep in conversation as I walked off. I couldn't believe that Spike remembered who I was. It was only those two thwarted encounters three years earlier and he was wasted. Then it struck me; Spike didn't remember me. He merely recognized me. Maybe he was back in AA and needed to make amends. He probably thought I was some random woman whom he, Spike Jansen – neurosurgeon-slash-drug dealer – did something to offend at one time or another. He was right. Two years after our bagel shop encounter, I heard on the news that Spike Jansen – aka Lenny, the actor – was found dead in his Manhattan apartment of an apparent, perhaps intentional, drug overdose.

The night before my twenty-fifth birthday, I dreamt I was back in my old bedroom in my mother's house where a huge dragon was ready to attack me. He was pretty much your typical dragon, fire blazing from his nose, talons big as watermelons. I was frightened by him, but I was also clearheaded and I knew exactly what I had to do. In one breath, I jumped out of bed and grabbed the sword that just happened to be hanging on the back of my door. I screamed at the dragon and took a huge swing at him, but I missed. Nevertheless, the dragon backed off and began to get smaller. Each time I swung and missed, the dragon shrunk in size. Eventually, he was so tiny I took him into bed with me and went back to sleep. I woke up perspiring, my hands shaking, but feeling strangely content. I went to the bathroom to splash some cool water on my face and that's when I saw it: my first gray hair, the physical manifestation of the fact that I was no longer young. I dug through my scalp frantically, looking for other grays. Thankfully the little bastard was an orphan, but it didn't matter; I sunk to the floor and I sobbed. And sobbed. That one little gray hair completely overwhelmed me. All at once I felt a combination of exhaustion, regret, and terror. I was starting to get old. What was I going to do? I was certainly nearing the age when I needed to stop wondering what I was going to do with my life –

and actually do it. Yet there I was, clueless, desperate and gray. Twenty-five was going to be a rough birthday for me.

On my twenty-fifth birthday, I didn't worry about Le Cirque versus Ferrier. I didn't worry about balloons or flowers or even who knew how old I was. It was a quiet day. I started it in my tiny bathtub, in my tiny apartment, gently blowing bubbles off of my hand. Charlie tried repeatedly to climb into the tub, but finally gave up. He curled up on the bathmat, waiting for me. As I sat there I wondered about, well, everything. I had to get more out of life than this ... there had to be more. Where was my man? Where was my money? Where was my Fifth Avenue penthouse? My brownstone? "What the hell am I doing wrong?" I screamed from my bathtub. My neighbor slammed his door. "Fuck you too!" I yelled and then slipped underwater to hide. I felt the bubbles gather on my head. I came back up and they tickled my nose.

In order to properly celebrate my milestone of twenty-five years, I started to panic a little... okay, I started to panic a lot. I sat up in the tub, hyperventilating. What was I going to do with the rest of my life? My childhood opportunities were quickly disappearing. Think, think... I racked my brain for answers. I could always go back to Dr. Fifth Avenue and be his mistress again but why would I do that? What was in it for me except a cheap boyfriend and a lousy lover? What was the point? Then I sat up and forced myself to answer the real questions: Did I really want an entire life of no husband, no children, no real job... no real life... exchanging blowjobs for handouts? What kind of life was that?

The water began to get chilly and I looked at the prune-like fingers on my hand. I imagined myself an old woman with wrinkly skin. Where would I be then? Oh God, *what* would I be then? I had always believed that I would be set as an old woman, that I'd be filthy rich, living on Fifth Avenue and going to the theatre daily. I believed I was exceptional and that I was on a special life quest, but so far all I had achieved was a high school diploma and big boobs – not the criteria for someone on the path to enlightenment, but rather, the path to the nearest lap dance and pole. I couldn't imagine why I was worrying about the distant future. I should have been concerned about how to cover my new gray hair, not contemplating my life. But for some reason as I sat there thinking, the previously devastating gray became somewhat, well, inconsequential.

I thought about Liz and how I'd watched her give her life over to her husband and her child. She used to be so amazing. For years I was secretly jealous of her: she was popular, together, and happy, a high school cheerleader and honor student, on the Dean's List all through college. Once she was even arrested for throwing a wild party on campus! Of course, the charges were dropped and she kept that indiscretion a secret. But I didn't even think the old Liz existed any longer. The new Liz squashed the old Liz under the wheels of her Lexus SUV long ago, on her way to Megan's soccer game. New Liz's entire self-worth was built on being Mrs. Martin Dunne, mother to Megan.

Who was right, Liz or me? Was the right choice to be married and risk losing it all, or was it never to be married and risk never having anything? Those were deep thoughts for a woman whose only ambition was to be supported by a rich boyfriend. But this feeling that maybe there is more to life than this kept creeping up on me. I hated twenty-five. I sunk back underwater.

CHAPTER 9: TYPIION

"Even after the Titans were conquered and crushed, Zeus was not completely victorious. Earth gave birth to her final and most frightful offspring, a creature more terrible than any that had gone before. His name was Typhon.

'A flaming monster with a hundred heads,
Who rose up against all the gods.
Death whistled from his fearful jaws,
His eyes flashed glaring fire'."

There were many, many men before I hit rock bottom. There was the nice guy from Hicksville, (there really is a place called Hicksville) who, I unexpectedly discovered one morning, taped our sex sessions. There was the club musician from the band "The Biggers" – I know, how could I go wrong there? He belonged to some mutant strain of man who lived a double life. He played the NY club scene and was an active part of all the partying that went with it – while his wife and kids lived in Suburbia. Bigger offered sex, nothing more, and I fucked him for the sake of my reputation. At one of my needier moments I agreed to a date. All through the date I just kept pretending that he was this really rich, nice guy who was wining and dining me, and – Lord save me – I even tried to hold his hand. After that I had to fuck him just to prove that I wasn't some pathetically needy woman desperately wanting a relationship. If that rumor had spread through the club, I would have been eaten alive. But all my one-night stand with Bigger actually proved was that Bigger wasn't really so much "bigger" after all.

There was my baseball player, a man who found me when I was walking by his hotel. This was a promising relationship. Ball players, after all, could offer a very nice lifestyle. My ball player was more superstitious than any person I had ever known – including my dad's mother, who would make me wear a safety pin at my lapel and would spit on me for good luck. But in addition to walking into a new room backwards, one of the superstitions my ball player had was to bed a new girl every time he was in a visiting city.

And then there was my artist, a man completely not my type. He was brilliant and poor – dirt poor – but I was sure that it was a passing phase. My artist fed my mind with a luscious buffet of the most tantalizing information; but he fed my body Ramen noodles cooked on a hot plate in his studio. Ah, my artist. Incredibly handsome, modest and well on his way to becoming famous. He even started a new genre called "Impressionistic-Modo." I decided I could be the girlfriend of a world famous artist. Why the hell not? Think of the parties, the trips, the life.

I met my artist at a gallery, it was the opening of his show. Somewhere along the way I learned that gallery openings are free and they serve you all the wine and cheese you can drink and eat – also for free. I became a regular. As I drank my third glass of cheap merlot, I stared at one of his paintings. He walked up to me.

"My fans say in my art you see who you really are," he said with a smile. "That beneath the surface image is the real you, dying to come out. And my critics," he ran his hand through his thick, black wavy hair speckled with paint and highlighted with grays, "my critics say the paintings are great globs of bullshit... Let me get this right... and the only thing hiding inside them is a blank canvas dying to break free." We both laughed. Between the talent and the green eyes, it was easy to understand why I was willing to settle for cup-o-soup. Besides, it was only a matter of time until he hit it big in the art world. And big in the art world is *big*.

My artist painted me on a shiny, porcelain canvas and gave me the picture as a gift. I was sure that I would look like some horrific rendition of a Picasso nude, but it was actually quite identifiable as me and really pretty great. I hung it on the wall opposite my bed, right next to a framed photo of Charlie. My artist and I spent whole days together, laughing, reading, having sex. I was so caught up in him I even fucked him in the back room of his gallery – regularly. "Babe, are you okay?" he asked me one afternoon, following me out of the back room and into the exhibition room.

"Mm-hm," I hummed, my mouth full of his cum.

"You want to grab some dinner?" He scratched the scruff on his chin. Dinner meant free peanuts and watery drinks at a nearby bar.

"Mmm!" I hummed again. Where the hell was my bag? I needed tissue to spit; the bathroom was all the way down the hall and I was in my bra and panties. I looked around frantically as the cum started to drip down my throat.

"What are you looking for?" he asked.

Oh come on, didn't he realize that I was trying not to speak? Too late. Drip, drip, drip. I swallowed, against my better judgment. I should have just spit on the floor. "My bag," I said, giving up, "my bag." Damn. I really didn't want to swallow him. I knew better. I was getting sloppy in my old age and as far as I knew my gorgeous artist hadn't been tested. For anything. That was a dangerous game. Too dangerous. Of course, the fact that I should never have had this man's cum in my mouth to begin with never entered my mind.

I spent so much time with my artist that I didn't bother with anyone else. I worked nights and then I ran to his place to hang for the day. Most days I packed up Charlie and brought him with me; after his initial resistance, he became a terrific traveler and he loved going to the studio. He would run back and forth in the wide open space and pounce on the brushes my artist would give him. Eventually, he'd find a sunny spot where he could pass out. I was feeling a little skuzzy (my artist didn't believe in daily showers and there wasn't always time for me to shower either) but very satisfied – who wouldn't with daily orgasms? My artist was more than just a great lover – he was my educator. I justified the relationship as my post high school formal education. The amount of information that man knew was staggering. Interesting facts about politics and travel, about Abbie Hoffman and Charles Bukowski.

My artist and I walked down a rainy lower Fifth Avenue arm in arm, laughing. As we crossed Ninth Street, two older women with opened umbrellas stopped to watch us pass. I was nearly thirty years younger than my artist, but he was still so hot other women would stop to stare at him. At us. I loved it. And believe me, no one mistook him for my father – the man oozed sex. Instead, people thought I was an art student fucking my mentor. I wished that I was, because despite the poverty, with him I was the woman that I wanted to be: smart, happy, purposeful. The rain started to come down heavily so I pushed myself closer to my demigod. He pulled his coat up over our heads.

"It's suede!" I said, pulling away. "Don't, you'll ruin it!"

"Can't ruin it," he said. "It's been with me my whole career. It just gets better and better the older it gets."

"Amen to that," I said, kissing him. He let his beloved coat fall to the street and we stood there, making out on Fifth Avenue like two teenagers in the back of a car.

I had been with him nearly five months and we had spent almost every day together. Most days he'd paint and I'd just lie around on the floor watching him. Inevitably, he'd lie down next to me and we'd make love, then he'd get an idea, jump up, throw on his jeans (sans underwear) and go back to painting. As far as I knew, those jeans had never been washed… but I didn't care. Standing there, naked except for that pair of torn, filthy jeans, he looked like a work of art himself. He painted with one brush and kept another tucked in his rear pocket. With every brushstroke, the muscles would ripple across his back. His skin glistened with perspiration from our lovemaking and his work. I watched, mesmerized, never bothering to get dressed because I knew that he'd soon be back for more inspiration. I thrived on being his muse. Then night would fall.

That day we were at my apartment. "Why can't you stay?" I said, whining. "Just today. Just for a little bit… Come on, I have the night off!"

"You know why," he said, consoling me.

"No I don't."

He grabbed me by the arms and shook me gently with each word. "Yes… you… do….." Long shake on the last word. I laughed in spite of myself.

"But we look so good together… we are so good together!"

"Yes," he said, still holding me by the hand. He bent down to pet Charlie.

"I don't get why you can't… you know…" I broke free and my voice trailed off.

He stood back up and looked me straight in the eyes. "Are you asking me to leave her?" No one had ever asked me that question before. I didn't know what to say.

"No, I'm not asking. But would you… I mean, ever consider it?" I didn't really want him. Not yet. He was just too poor, and I had no intention of working long hours to support my husband, the artist, and his new girlfriend, the tramp. But I was curious.

"How old are you, Victoria," he asked, his voice changing. He suddenly looked much older. In my dreary apartment on that day, he seemed all of his fifty-four years.

"Twenty-two." It was close to the truth.

"A baby. There's so much you don't know." He sat down on one of my two dining chairs. I walked to him and stood between his legs; he wrapped his arms around me and looked up at me while he spoke. "My wife has been with me for nearly twenty-five years. That is three years longer than you've been on the earth." My artist believed humans were descendants from another planet on a continual life cycle. He claimed he had proof.

"Uh-huh." I knew about his extraterrestrial beliefs; I didn't know he had been married for so long.

"You don't end something with someone who's been with you for twenty-five years," he said, letting me go. Then he gently pushed me away. He stood up and put on his rain-splotched jacket. He walked to the door and turned back. "Victoria, I think—"

"I know," I said. There was just nowhere left for it to go. He kissed me, for a long time, then he stroked my chin – and Charlie's head – and left. Watching him go, I felt emptier than I ever had before. "What an asshole," I said, staring at myself in the mirror.

I had to do better the next time. I was genuinely sad that my artist was gone, but I'd lost another half a year. Being with my artist was like being with Dr. Fifth Avenue; again I was devoting my existence to an older, all-knowing man who profited from my youth. Was it really possible that I had learned nothing in six-and-a-half years?

My blissful days of fucking for Ramen noodles were gone and reality was hitting me hard. Really, really hard. For one thing, I had a few anxious months when I waited out two separate HIV tests. I had repeatedly swallowed my gorgeous artist, whose wife knowingly allowed him to fuck for sport and inspiration, while she was busy working to keep him in paint and noodles. For another, bills were piling up. Little stacks of late notices had taken over my table and there was no one to turn to. Although it pained me, I decided that my previous instinct was right, and it was time to get a real job. The club was just too unreliable; some nights I made hundreds, some nights, tens. But what could I do? What else was I qualified for? I stared hard at myself again. Why was I so sorry that my artist had left? Probably because I liked the person I was when I was with him, even if it was all make-believe. I pretended that I was an artist; I pretended that he loved me; I pretended that I was his only muse, the reason that he could paint. I pretended that I mattered.

I was really hard up, even more than usual. I made the rent but little else. And forget about shopping. The only thing I'd purchased over the past year was black shoe polish to keep my boots from looking worn. My mail was always the same: late notice from ConEd; the gym canceling my membership for late dues; AT&T offering to set up a payment plan. My answering machine was riddled with nasty messages from the credit card companies. Worse of all, with the way business had been at the club, I was afraid that I might not continue to make the rent, and then Charlie and I could be evicted. There was just no way I would allow Charlie to end up back on the street, no matter what I had to do.

Nothing was as I had planned. I was supposed to be living the high life by this time, being supported by a man with my own house account at Bergdorf. I was *not* supposed to be slinging drinks and offering accidental peepshows in the hopes of an extra ten-dollar tip. The only time I drank champagne anymore was if one of my clients offered me a glass or left some behind. Sure, I had my regulars and their hundred dollar tips, but it wasn't enough. And frankly, I didn't want enough. I wanted everything.

So where was this elusive lifestyle? How could I pay my bills? I couldn't work any more than I did – my ankles were already permanently swollen – and I certainly wasn't going to snag a rich man sporting cankles. My credit cards had long been maxed. My mother didn't have any money to loan me, and I finally had to borrow some from Liz. She was really good about it, especially since she knew I had blown thousands of dollars on my breasts. But what could I do, return them? I also took a load of my designer clothes and bags to a local consignment shop. Unfortunately, they put one of the dresses in the window – an off the shoulder Michael Kors – so every day I would walk by it and be reminded of my failures. There may be nothing more depressing than seeing the representation of your hey-day hanging in a shop window with a half-off sticker attached to it. Every well I had was tapped completely dry. I even had to order Chinese food again. I had managed to avoid that particular restaurant since my dinner-and-a-show, so when I called and asked for my delivery guy I half-hoped that he was gone. Naturally he wasn't. When he showed up, I asked him if he remembered our deal. Boy did he. He immediately came inside and shut the door behind him.

"Peking Duck!" he said with a squeal. I couldn't help but laugh at him. This time, as I stood there with my shirt open, I saw him adjust himself.

"Hey!" I said, pulling my shirt closed. "No touching!"

"Yeah, yeah!" he said. "Thirty more seconds!" I reopened my shirt and he stepped closer. "Next time I bring you extra special secret dumplings too!"

"Thanks," I said, "but there won't be a next time." I buttoned my shirt and he limped out. Of course, there was a next time. Flashing the delivery guy made good sense; I was able to eat some real food and put my money to better use. This time I ordered a whole soy sauce chicken, beef with broccoli and my Peking Duck. If I had to humiliate myself, I wanted to make sure that I had enough food to last me for a few days. My friend showed up as planned, but this time he wasn't alone. "Oh!" I said when I opened the door. I was in my robe, ready for my free meal. I wrapped the robe tightly around me. "Uh, I thought you would be delivering alone."

"This my cousin. He deliver too. He help me. You order lots of food!" So there it was. I wasn't the only one who had upped the stakes. If I wanted my free groceries for the week, I needed to pay for it.

"Ah, what the hell," I said. At this point I was too broke and too starving to care. "Does he know the rules? Your cousin?"

"No touch!" my friend said, smiling that smile that made me laugh. His friend mimed me opening my shirt.

"Hold on there, mister," I said. I didn't like his cousin. He was at least ten years older than my friend with a hard face that never smiled. For a moment I considered sending them both away just so I could regain control. Then my stomach rumbled and I got a whiff of the food. "Make sure you two are the only ones who know about this," I said. Truthfully, I really didn't care. My boobs were always on display at the club, the only difference was that here they would see some nipple. "Okay," I said, "close the door." They both stood in the kitchen against the door but the kitchen was so tight they could barely fit. They elbowed each other, fighting for who would stand in front. It was clear that neither could see anything, and they began to bicker. "Fine, come in," I said. My friend put the bags of food down on the table and they hovered at the doorway between the kitchen and the living room.

"Extra special secret dumplings!" he said smiling.

"Thank you," I said and walked to the couch. I stood in front of it and opened the top of my robe.

"More please," my little friend said at his cousin's coaxing. It was clear neither man could see the sides of my breasts. I scowled at the older man and opened my robe more. Again the cousin grunted something to my friend. "Take off top please" said the younger one.

"What?" I said, covering back up. "Wait a second, you don't make the rules here, I do."

The older man said something in Chinese to my friend.

"Lots of food," my friend said. "More please."

"No," I said. "That's it." The older man was getting agitated now. "Tell your cousin he's getting a great deal. Tell him I'm a model and I make thousands of dollars. Take it or leave it." My friend translated to his cousin and the cousin turned to me. He said something directly to me and my friend translated.

"My cousin say if you hungry, we see more please." That was that. I was now at a standoff with my two delivery men. We each had something the other wanted, and did I want what they had. I decided that I would make their night, but this would really be the last time.

"Fine," I said. "You win." My friend broke out in a huge smile. "But just for today!" His smile left him. "I'm sorry but this will be the last time I call you." I hated to ruin his fun but it had to end somewhere. The older man walked to the couch and sat down and the younger one followed. "Oh great!" I said. "Just make yourselves at home." I walked closer to the two men who were staring so hard that I was sure they could see right through my robe. Slowly I slipped out of the top of the robe and let it fall to my waist, making sure that the belt was pulled extra tight. I began to fumble with my hands, not sure of what to do, and I started to perspire. I was uncomfortable in my own skin. I felt like a trashy stripper in a small, stale bar. Thank God Charlie managed to sleep through it all. The older one gave me a direction through the younger one.

"Turn please," he said, pointing. The older one wanted a profile. I did. "Other way," said my friend. I did. It was clear that they saw every freckle on me; either man would be able to draw my breasts with the precision of a police sketch artist. It was the longest sixty seconds of my life. When the minute was finally over, I pulled my robe back up, completely embarrassed. The older man still sat there.

"We're done," I said, goading them to get up. The man spoke to my translator.

"How much to touch?" asked my friend.

"All right! That's it!" I said pulling them up from the couch. "No touch, no more, it's over. I am not a whore." No, not a whore, just a flasher for Chinese food.

I slammed the door behind them and decided definitively that I had to get a man to support me. Even semi-support me, just until I got back on my feet – or off my feet – whichever the case may be.

I stored most of the food for the week, and as I ate my very expensive dumplings, I figured that my most probable option was to meet Price Charming walking down the street. Or better yet, cruising down the street in his stretch limo. I had as much of a chance of that as I did anything else. Great. My best option appeared to be standing on a street corner in my cocktail outfit, waving down limos. So, after some more thought and a few bites of an over-cooked chicken leg, I decided I would call my agent to see if he knew of any "available men." Although I wasn't thrilled about it, calling him sounded like a better plan than working the street corner. I would be dignified about branching out into this new – or very old – profession; I would do it on my terms and it would all be within my control. I would see only the most upscale men, and our meetings would be fun and sexy. And I would work only when I needed to. I could do this, because if I had to humiliate myself, it might as well be for six-figures and not for dried-out poultry. Desperate times call for desperate measures. I finished my dumplings and watched *Entertainment Tonight*.

My agent set up my meeting with Mario. I was told that he was about sixty, only five-foot-three, European (no one could pinpoint which part of Europe, exactly), and that he owned a major clothing company. My agent warned me that Mario wasn't overly attractive. Supposedly he was a legitimate businessman and all he wanted was a gorgeous date to a major function that he had coming up. I exhaled – probably for the first time since I decided to dabble in this business – realizing that I may not actually have to go as far as Libby. (I ignored the voice in my head who asked why a man who owned a major clothing company would need to solicit a date from a lower-end modeling agency.) I fantasized that there would be more to Mario than this one-time dinner; maybe he would be as easy to land as John and as generous as Michael.

Mario sent his limo for me and when it pulled up alongside my building my heart actually fluttered. It had been quite some time since I had been in a limo. Prince Charming, perhaps? I sat back, thoroughly enjoying the short trip... complete with champagne. Thank you to my agent! This was definitely the right man for me. Sure, I'd balked when Mario told me our rendezvous was to take place at a hotel bar about a week before his big function, but after my initial uneasiness, I decided it was no big deal. So what if the bar just happened to be in a hotel? He had set up this meeting to check me out – to make sure that I was worthy of attending this function with him – and to see if I matched the comp card that my agent had sent to him. Since I had nothing to do that night except serve flaming drinks to tourists, I walked into the bar with my head held high, confident something more – like some high-end modeling work – would come of this.

"What's in the bag?" Mario asked as I sat down.

"My stuff," I said, not fully understanding the question and trying not to stare in horror at my cocktail companion. Mario's English was pretty poor, so I wasn't sure if I completely understood him, but why did he care about my bag? Are large bags offensive in Milan? I glued my eyes to my bag, not wanting to face Mario.

He drank two vodka martinis but I had only one. It would have been way too easy to get loaded after the half bottle of Cristal. I had to keep my wits about me but a big part of me wanted to down one – or six – more martinis right there. Even with my agent's warning, I wasn't prepared. Not overly attractive? Not overly attractive is what you say about Will Ferrell, not about Mario. Mario was just... simply awful. If you think of the vilest creature you could ever imagine – something so hideous that the devil himself cast it from hell rather than look at it – then you would begin to understand Mario. And I don't mean he was simply ugly – ugly is no big deal. Mario was repulsive. To start, this man who owned a thriving clothing company was badly dressed by Salvation Armani. His jacket was at least two sizes too large and hung down, reaching almost to his knees. Smack in the middle of the right lapel was a large soup stain – tomato, I think. Dear God, how I hoped it was soup and not dried vomit. It was obvious that his jacket hadn't seen a dry cleaner in quite some time, "quite some time" meaning: ever. His mouth was slack and he very nearly drooled when he spoke. He had most of his hair – which he slicked back with the natural oils – but it needed to be cut and washed and it was chock-full of dandruff. My stomach started to burn. To ache, actually. For some time I thought that I might be developing an ulcer; the stomach pain that Mario caused me made me pretty sure of it. Was this really my only option for the night? I swallowed a big gulp of my martini and chewed an olive. It felt like there was a jackhammer attacking my stomach lining; my insides were on fire. Desperation was the only thing keeping me there. Okay, scratch him as boyfriend material, but this was work. And I needed work. I forced a smile. He leaned across the table and I caught a whiff of his body odor. Dear God. Then, in broken English he said, "I want you."

"What?" Even after everything I had been through these past six-plus years, I was still shocked by his impudence.

"I want you..."

"Oh, Jesus," I said. "I heard you. Look, can we talk about the job?"

"Job? I am," he said.

"For your company." I had abandoned all thoughts of being his escort, but I still tried to further my work objective.

"Oh. I don... hire model. But I like you. You – I get work."

"Lucky me."

"Lucky me..." he said, drooling. So I was stuck. I thought of my Chinese delivery guys. And the bills. If I got evicted, I would have to go back to Pennsylvania to live with my mother, who was allergic to cats. I thought of Dr.

Fifth Avenue, and Libby, and her Valentino wardrobe, and slicing cheese. I desperately needed money. I thought about Charlie and what would become of him. I fought back my disgust and pushed on.

"I need money," I whispered, "I need work. Call my agency—"

"How much?" he asked.

"Excuse me?"

"How much money?"

"They do all my bookings for me... here." I reached into my bag and pulled out a comp card. I tried everything possible not to understand what he was actually saying.

"Nice," he said, pointing to the picture of me in lingerie. "You don understand," he said, taking another drink. "How much? How much money to be... for my girlfriend?" I understood just fine.

"A thousand dollars up front," I said, without flinching. "And then another thousand after." There it was. I don't know where it came from or how, but there it was. It might as well have been in huge neon lettering: "I, VICTORIA MESSING, HAVE NOW HIT ROCK BOTTOM." Blink, blink! Blink, blink! No matter how I disguised it and no matter what pretense I hid it under, I was in a hotel bar telling a strange man how much it would cost him to sleep with me. Suddenly, flashing delivery guys seemed blissful.

We went through the motions anyway. Two days later Mario called my agency. I had called first to ask if they knew of any other "available men" but they said Mario was one of their best clients so they needed to keep him happy. Later that evening, I found myself back in that same hotel bar. This time I had plans to show off my portfolio. I was going to wow him with my modeling potential, make him forget all about sex, and turn this meeting into my big modeling break. Up until that minute I never even knew I wanted a big break in modeling.

My hands were shaking as I walked toward the hotel lobby. My portfolio was wobbling in my grasp and the more I tried to steady it, the more it shook. I froze at the revolving door and looked around. People were on the street, the valets were parking cars, someone was laughing; life was carrying on as usual.

But not for me. For me, everything had changed and after this my life would never be the same. Sometimes when I was with Dr. Fifth Avenue I would imagine that I was a high-class call-girl, but imagining and being are two very different things. I caught sight of myself in the shiny revolving door and I understood that as of that very minute, I wasn't pretending anymore. Sleeping with some married men was nothing. Flashing a couple of guys was nothing, teen-aged girls do it on spring break. But this, *this* was something. This was real. From this point on there would be no turning back. After this, I would be a prostitute. And not a very high-class prostitute at that.

I pushed the door around and walked through. I looked into the lounge area and saw Mario, already deep into his second martini. He stood to greet me, and I kissed him quickly on both cheeks. Again he asked what I was carrying, so I showed him my portfolio. I forced him to look through it although no one was kidding anyone – he wanted sex and I needed money.

Mario leaned across the table and handed me an oversized envelope with what looked like a thousand crumpled, one-dollar bills. He must have spent the previous forty-eight hours standing on a street corner holding out a little coffee cup, begging for "fuck money." Even without the soup-stained jacket he looked – and smelled – horrific. Maybe my agent was mistaken about who Mario was. How could this ogre be wealthy and successful? I would never have given him the time of day without the limo and the company he owned. I wanted to get up, I wanted to run, but my agency would most certainly drop me if I did, and then I would truly have nothing. I was pinned to the seat.

My face got hot when I looked at the envelope. I told myself that all models do this at one time or another – that it's no big deal. But in my heart I knew the truth, real models weren't prostitutes. Resigned to this, I ordered myself a dirty martini – a fitting drink – and tried to convince myself that this was no different than a night with Dr. Fifth Avenue, and it had to be easier than a night with Michael.

While he got another martini, I racked my brain for any other last resorts for money. Who? Who? His martini arrived – gin, not vodka. Whew. That bought me a little more time while Mario tried to explain the mistake to his waitress. Money, money, money. My Olympian gods were pretty much all gone, well, all except Dr. Fifth Avenue, but I couldn't tell him how hard-up I really was. I could never admit how pitiable I had become.

I was ready for Mario, in theory anyway. I brought an entire box of extra strength condoms. I wasn't planning to use them all, but what if one broke? As I watched him dribble the martini down his chin, I wondered if I could get him to wear two at a time.

I felt like I was watching a movie starring me. There I was, sitting in a dark, quiet movie theatre, staring up at a giant-sized Victoria. Nothing felt real. I wondered if I would be able to stay detached all night, maybe being disconnected was the answer, the civilized way to get through it. Then Mario leered at me and I knew I could never be indifferent about this. I took another long sip of my martini and chewed another olive. I couldn't stall any longer so I polished off the rest of my martini, ready as I'd ever be to follow him upstairs.

We took a seemingly endless elevator ride to Mario's floor. I pushed myself to stay bubbly and chatty. We got off of the elevator and I followed him to his room. I stalled at the door. He looked back at me and then disappeared inside. I took a deep, labored breath and entered. Being drunk definitely helped.

I walked into the room slowly. The lights were off, but I could tell that it was a deluxe hotel suite, complete with a sitting room and dining area. Mario was nowhere to be seen. "Hello?" I asked. Nothing. I flicked on the lights and waited for my eyes to adjust. "Hello?" Still nothing. I scanned the room, and the bed was nowhere in sight. A glimmer of hope ran through my mind. Maybe we could just sit and talk and do some business! I put my bag and portfolio down on the couch.

"Victoria?" I heard him call from the bedroom. "Victoria?" Startled, my body turned in the direction of the call. "Victoria!" he said in a menacing tone. My legs were frozen. I just couldn't move. Try as I might, I couldn't free my feet from the floor. "What are you do-ingk?" he asked.

"I'm coming!" I said. I didn't recognize the sound of my own voice. Hell, I didn't recognize myself. I cleared my throat.

"If you shoot up... don do too much drug! You pass out... you make sleep."

Oh God, how I wished I was shooting up. Or snorting, or puffing, or huffing, or anything that could fuck me up even more. I wished I were back with Spike Jansen. Partying on his face with a little crystal meth seemed like a dream right now. I pried my feet from the floor and marched into the bedroom.

Lit by only a small glowing bedside lamp, the room was mostly dark. Despite the fact that it was a four-star hotel, the atmosphere reeked of a dingy hotel where the rooms were rented by the hour. My mind jumped back to that one random morning with Dr. Fifth Avenue when he wanted to do the crossword and I wanted to have sex. How I wished Mario would pull out a Sunday *Times*.

Mario was lying on the bed, his pants loosened, waiting for me. I swallowed hard, knowing it was now or never. I had no idea what I was doing and half-expected the police to barge in and arrest me because, aside from everything else that was wrong with this, I was also *breaking the law*. I had tried to pocket the thousand dollars at the bar downstairs, but it was all such a mess of bills and anxiety that I told him to give me the money when we got upstairs. Mario and I called a lot of attention to ourselves during those few moments and someone – anyone – may very well have seen the exchange.

With two condoms in my pocket, I walked to the bed with all of the enthusiasm of a convicted man walking to his execution. I unbuttoned my blouse and sat next to him. Eagerly, he squeezed my nipple. Needing this to be over as soon as possible I reached down and grabbed his dick. He was very small and already hard. His slack mouth moaned from my touch; his hot body emitted a strong, foul odor. I would never be able to have intercourse with this man without vomiting. While I stroked him over his underwear, I thought of all the myths that I'd heard: the models who fuck to become famous, the Hollywood casting couches. Somehow, they didn't help. So I ran the realities through my mind as well: I desperately needed money. That was the only reality and the one ugly truth.

Still moaning, Mario told me to reach inside his underwear. I did. For a brief shining moment, I thought that I could get away with giving him nothing more than a hand job. He got harder and harder and more and more excited. Then suddenly he yelled, "Bite me!" He was already on the verge of an orgasm. "Bite my stomach!" He pulled my head forward, toward him. "Bite me!" he said... and I did. I bit his stomach as hard as I could, over and over, until he came in my hand. I would have bitten a hole in that disgustingly flabby belly if I had had the chance. I ran to the bathroom and scrubbed my hands up to my elbows. I gargled using an entire hotel-sized bottle of Listerine. I went back to find him lying there, his tiny dick already limp and done. I wanted to rip that dick off; I wanted to spit in his eye, to punch his soft, fleshy, smelly stomach which I had bitten only moments before. I wanted to vomit all over him ... but then on second thought, I would never want to be that personal with him again.

The room was still dark and it smelled like a combination of bleach and sweat, that unmistakable odor of a man's cum. My chest tightened, it was becoming impossible to breathe. Gasping, I sprinted to the sitting room, grabbed my bag, and then caught sight of my money lying on the table. Two thousand dollars. It was strewn on the table in the same way that Michael used to leave a tip for his household staff... for the woman who scrubbed his toilets. I stopped dead and stared at it. I needed that money and the hard part was already over. But if I did... *if I did*...? Shit! I thought the decision was whether or not to go through with it, not whether or not to take the money! What the hell was wrong with me? Why did I just stand there?

"Victoria! Victoria!" Mario yelled, while I stood frozen, staring at my money. I waited for my survival instinct to kick in, but it didn't. My gut wouldn't respond. But my mind... my mind just kept shouting "Whore!" over and over again. It was a step that could never be reversed. It could never be erased. A mere moment in time would brand me forever. I knew I would never be able to live with myself if I took the money. So I didn't.

I left Mario in the bedroom still yelling for me and I took off. I couldn't get out of there fast enough. I waited for an elevator, but I was terrified he'd come looking for me, so I took the stairs instead. My eyes were blurry from tears as I went down floor after floor... sixteen, fifteen, fourteen, twelve.... I went faster and faster and began to jump the stairs, three, four at a time, running like a criminal fleeing the scene of the crime. Was that, in fact, what I was?

When I reached the ground floor I just missed setting off the fire alarm when I tried to open an Emergency Door. Luckily, a smoker from the second floor was there at exactly the right time to show me which door to exit. I was a mess of tears and guilt. I crawled out of the hotel and slunk to the bus, wishing I had taken at least enough money for cab fare. I boarded the bus, cowering from the other passengers' stares. I felt all eyes on me. I walked to the back, sure everyone knew exactly what I had just done. An elderly lady with tired but piercing blue eyes nodded to me. I forced my gaze away from her and out the window.

I finally made it home but I felt like the most despicable creature ever to walk the earth. I knew if I ever told anyone my story, they would never believe

I'd left the money behind... but I did. I thought about Libby and how she seemed so content. I also wanted someone to pay, literally, for all the fucking and being fucked I'd done, but I couldn't do it. I looked at myself in the bathroom mirror. I was a failed whore. How could anyone fail at *that?*

I didn't answer my phone the next day when my agent called to find out how the meeting went. I didn't answer my agent's call ever again. Not even when he called to say I was being let go from the agency due to a lack of initiative on my part.

My days as a second-rate model booking some catalog jobs were over, and I didn't care one bit. Cocktailing became my life. I went to work and kept to myself. I had lost my soul when I bit Mario's stomach and I had no real desire to even try to get it back. I was more despondent than ever, and I went through my twenty-sixth birthday alone.

After another month of complete loneliness, I knew there was only one option for me – I made an appointment for a breast checkup. Soon after, Dr. Fifth Avenue and I were heading to the quaint West Village to Babbo for dinner. During dinner I broke down and asked to borrow some money. It killed me that after seven years I still needed to ask him for help. But I did. And he lent it to me a little at a time, making sure, of course, that his wife didn't catch on. Believe me, over those next few months, I paid it all back, in trade. With interest. Through those months of rekindling our romance, Dr. Fifth Avenue and I became short with each other, even bored with each other. Somewhat back on my feet financially, and scared that we would ruin what was once perfectly okay, I ended it again.

PART IV:

GODS VS. MORTALS

CHAPTER 10: GODS AND MORTALS

"For the most part the immortal gods were of little use to human beings and often they were quite the reverse of useful: Zeus a dangerous lover for mortal maidens and completely incalculable in his use of the terrible thunderbolt...."

On my way to Penn Station one afternoon, late as always, I ran into Dr. Ass in the lobby of my building. "How are you?" he asked. He really seemed to care how I was, but I knew I couldn't believe him, no matter how much I wanted to. I was in a self-induced hypnotic trance brought about by a lack of good sex and the impending visit to my mother's. I stared at him long and hard, telling myself over and over that if he had really cared about me, he wouldn't have been such a horrible lover. But despite my resistance, his eyes had me. One look at his wavy salt and pepper hair made me soften.

Maybe I was being too harsh, maybe I'd judged him too quickly. I smiled back, grateful that I was wearing a cute T-shirt and lip gloss. I'd catch the next train. I dropped my overnight bag and adjusted my shirt. Finally, I stopped grinning and spoke. "I'm okay, how are you?" Back to smiling.

"You know," he said, "partying in the Hamptons, it's become like a college town out there. I'm having a blast!"

So maybe I wasn't too quick to judge after all. I stopped smiling and caught my train.

I sat across the table from my mother in her kitchen, cutting coupons from the newspaper. I had to strain to see what I was reading through the fog of cigarette smoke that surrounded us. Liz was at the stove baking an apple pie.

Without looking up, Mom spoke. "Liz, honey, make sure you put a pat of butter right on top of the apples before you put it in the oven."

"Uh-huh," Liz said, not sounding like herself. I watched as best I could, but my eyes were burning from my mother's tiny inferno. Liz stormed to the fridge, yanked open the door and grabbed the butter. "Butter," she muttered under her breath. "God forbid I forget the butter. Disastrous. Maybe my arteries would be spared." She laughed a soft, deranged laugh.

"What's up with her?" I mouthed to my mother as I leaned across the table to point out a dollar off Steak-Ums.

Mom shrugged. "This was what she was like right before Megan," she whispered.

"Pregnant?" I whispered back.

"Stranger things have happened," my mother said and lit another cigarette off of the one she already had going. She offered me one.

"No, thanks. Jeez, Mom, don't you worry about your health?" Mom shrugged again and flipped through a *Redbook*. I stared at Liz. A pregnant Liz would never stand around in so much smoke.

"Shit!" Liz yelled, when she burned her hand putting the pie into the oven. I snickered at my sister, the PTA mom, cursing. But she wasn't through. "Goddamnit! Shit! Goddamned Motherfucker!" Liz screamed and kicked the oven door closed. My mother nearly dropped her cigarette.

"Hey, Liz," I asked, "you okay?"

"Fine," Liz said and left the room holding her burnt hand in front of her like she was clutching an egg.

Our mother chuckled. "Little Miss Perfect burnt her hand...."

I grabbed an ice cube from the freezer and followed Liz. I walked to the guest bathroom and could hear Liz crying through the door. I tapped softly. "You okay, Liz?" There was no answer. I knocked, louder. "Liz? You okay?"

Liz yanked the door open. "What?" she asked. "What do you want?"

"Nothing." I said, surprised by her reaction. "I just want to know if you're okay." Liz had tears streaming down her cheeks.

"Don't I look okay?"

"Fine. Uh, beautiful." I said.

"Jesus, Victoria. Go away." Liz tried to slam the door, but I blocked it with my foot. "What? What do you want?" She was at the end of her rope.

"I want to help." I felt the ice freezing my hand. "I have ice." I held it up as it dripped onto the floor.

"My hand is fine," she said. "Go away. If you need a bathroom, go upstairs."

"Is Megan okay?" I asked.

"Megan?"

"Yeah."

"What do you care about any of us?"

"I care very much. You know I love Megan." I was a little hurt.

My angry sister softened slightly. "I know."

"Are you pregnant?" I asked, approaching the subject hesitantly.

"Pregnant?" The question made Liz laugh out loud. She covered her mouth with her hand. Until that moment, I had forgotten how beautiful Liz really was. "No!" she said, still laughing.

"Whatever it is... they say it helps to talk."

"It helps to talk?" Liz asked, sitting on the closed toilet seat of the tiny bathroom, staring up at me. "Okay, let's talk."

I didn't recognize the tone in Liz's voice and I wasn't sure what I had started. "Look, Liz—"

"No, let's do it. Okay. A heart to heart. Sister to sister. What do sisters talk about...? I know! Let's talk about men. Maybe the birds and the bees, how's that?" I tried to walk away but Liz grabbed my arm. "Hey!" she said. "You started this! You asked me to talk and now I'm going to." I had never seen my sister like this. Her words came so fast they vomited out of her.

Liz began like she was reciting a soliloquy. "Well, it starts with you doing everything right: go to the right college, get a good job, meet a man and fall in love. Two years later, you have a daughter with him. You stop working, you let him support you...." She picked up speed. "And then five years later you find out that the whole Goddamned thing has been a lie anyway." She turned to me and somewhat pleadingly said, "Don't ever rely on a man, Victoria. Not ever. No matter what they promise you. You'll play by his rules, and you'll be terrified to break them because then you may lose him. You'll raise your children just like he remembers his own childhood – which really wasn't so great, but try telling that to a man going through a mid-life crisis – and he..." she looked dead ahead and stared at the sink when she said this, "and he will break you." She paused. Then softly she said, "Because to survive as part of a couple, one of you needs to die. And guess which one it will be?"

"What are you talking about?"

"Martin's cheating on me." She said it with less emotion than when she ordered a Happy Meal from the drive-through.

"What?" I asked. "What? No way. You have a baby together. That's impossible. I don't believe you." But Liz just smiled, stood up, and walked past me. I threw my last few words at her back. "Liz! No one gives you up for some stupid piece of trash!" And then I realized what I had said. Liz walked out the front door.

I left my mother's house realizing my needy, demanding, cavalier lifestyle wasn't all about me and the men that I fucked – it was about someone else too. Someone who had made a commitment and a life with the man I branded my meal ticket. Sure, once in awhile I had thought about Mrs. Dr. Fifth Avenue or Mrs. Michael M., but only out of curiosity, never out of consideration. I realized I could never talk to my sister about any of it – her situation or mine – because, inadvertently, I'd become her enemy. We'd never been close, but we grew to be on opposing sides; we were separate warring factions and I felt lousy about it. After that one afternoon I tried over and over to convince myself that my relationships were different – that my men weren't Martin, and that their wives weren't at their mothers' houses, crying over burnt hands and failing marriages. I told myself that they didn't have beautiful, freckled, wide-eyed little girls at home who would most certainly get hurt. I tried hard to convince myself, and sometimes I even believed it.

I wanted to tell my mother about Liz, but I didn't dare. If Liz wanted her to know, she'd tell her. I kept my sister's confidence – it was the very least I could do – and my mother and I spoke like nothing had changed. And in many ways that was the truth. Mom would say things like, "Why aren't you modeling?" or "That club!" – whichever part of my life she felt like criticizing at that moment. That night she went one better. "You're wasting your life!" she told me. "You should be out man shopping. You're not getting any younger you know, it's time for you to think about settling down. Like your sister." I couldn't believe my ears; my mother brought up the idea of marriage after she had spent twenty-five years telling me to avoid it.

This time I was annoyed with her. Like my sister, I was floundering, and she was our mother. Maybe, just once, she could offer some real advice. "I hope you're not looking for a grandchild from me," I said. "I'll never get a husband. All I date are married men." I was fed up.

"If anyone could make a married man remarry, it's you," she said, wheezing violently.

"Mom, are you okay?"

"I'm fine," she said, "but what about you? Are you okay?" I hung up.

I was always confused after my mother's calls. In her way, telling me that I could get a man to leave his wife and marry me was meant as a compliment. But why couldn't she recognize that everything was so much bigger than that right now? Why couldn't she comprehend that I didn't want to be the one who pulled Martin away from Liz and Megan? And why would a married man leave his wife for me anyway? He had his dinner and his dessert. The mother of his children and the twenty-year-old fuck-buddy. As long as I was willing to play the game, he had no reason to change anything.

"Whatcha doing?" Dr. Fifth Avenue asked while I sat on the examining table, gown open in front.

"Not much," I said.

I knew this showed true weakness, but I just needed some guidance, and he was the closest thing to a father that I had. I would have preferred to run straight into Michael's arms, to have him fix everything, but Michael was nowhere to be found. Dr. Fifth Avenue was safe. And solid. And reliable. And I knew, no matter what, he would always love me, right?

I felt guilt toward Liz, but I justified my visit by telling myself that I wasn't sleeping with Martin. My relationships were different. Mrs. Dr. Fifth Avenue wasn't Liz. Mrs. Dr. Fifth Avenue did just fine for herself... she had my Mercedes. I was convinced that Mrs. Dr. Fifth Avenue knew what was going on with her husband but didn't care. Why would she? She had her own tennis lessons four days a week. Come on, I knew she wasn't Venus Williams, so who plays that much tennis? Someone who likes her thirty-year-old tennis pro, that's who. So what did she care who was sleeping with her husband? It probably gave her some rest; a night off. And besides, I wasn't sleeping with Dr. Fifth Avenue at that point... or anyone else for that matter.

"I'm super busy with work," I said while he squeezed my breasts.

"See," he said, "I told you modeling was your ticket!"

"Mm-hm!" I said, covering my melancholy with too much enthusiasm. "You sure did!" I didn't want to tell him that the work I was talking about involved a completely different type of "shots." When he squeezed again, my eyes brimmed with tears.

"Sorry," he said, sounding concerned. "Did that hurt?"

"It's fine." I smiled at the female nurse who was required to be at every check-up.

"Well," he said, "you look great. Everything checks out."

"Great!" I said, again sounding much too perky, like a cheerleader on amphetamines.

"Come back if you're worried about anything else," he said with a wink.

"Uh-huh." He scribbled some notes on my chart and handed it to the nurse. Panic began to overtake me. He couldn't leave! I had used up the excuse of a medical visit and I couldn't call him to schedule another appointment. What could I do?

Then it hit me in the pit of my stomach. I knew why he wanted out of there so fast. Once I realized it, I couldn't wait to throw on my shirt and get out of there myself. Dr. Fifth Avenue had a new mistress. I could feel it. Something about him had changed; he seemed sheepish around me. He was not the usual fiery god that I knew, wielding thunderbolts and inflating bosoms. Then just as quickly as that feeling arrived, it left and I changed my mind. I needed him. No matter what else was going on, just seeing him and watching him leave was not enough for me. Despite my better judgment I had to do something. A bogus check-up was not what I had come for.

I stalled. "My telephone number has changed. Do you need to have it on file at all... for any reason?" The nurse's eyes darted up from my chart. "Or should I just call again when I need an appointment."

"Oh no!" said Dr. Fifth Avenue, smoothly placing his marbled Mont Blanc into his white jacket pocket. "Of course we should have your number. You never know if and when those things might get recalled."

"Oh..." I said, looking down at my breasts, scared.

"That rarely happens," he explained, winking. "It's just a good idea. Just leave it with my receptionist. Goodbye," he consulted the chart, "Victoria." I prayed he was only pretending he didn't know my name.

"Wow!" said the receptionist. "You change your number a lot, honey! But you always seem to remember to keep us up to date." She smirked and copied the number into my chart.

Changing my number was a luxury that I couldn't really afford, but this last change had been a necessity; I heard Mario was back in town and searching for someone with good teeth.

The very next day, Dr. Fifth Avenue called. Despite so many things, like the fact that he thought I was stupid, I eagerly anticipated his call. Huh, maybe he had a point about me being stupid. Anyway, his call made me feel somewhat better. At least it made me feel more desirable than I had been feeling. To handle my six-nights-a-week work schedule, I was living on free coffee from the deli and it was taking its toll – I had a constant slight vibration coursing through my body from all the caffeine, I was perpetually groggy, and my insides felt itchy. I also had permanent dark circles under my eyes.

Two days after Dr. Fifth Avenue and I had made a date, John called. "Hello?" I said, my voice cracking. It was noon, and Charlie and I were sound asleep.

"Hey!" said John. "Remember me? Four Seasons in Beverly Hills?" He lowered his voice: "The Upper West Side apartment?" Normal voice: "Marylou's?"

"Yes, yes, yes," I said not wanting to be reminded of any of those things. "Of course I remember you." I yawned and rubbed my eyes. John was the only Olympian who'd flat-out dumped me, and I would just as soon forget all about him. (I didn't count Ivan returning to his wife as being dumped.)

"Were you asleep?" he asked. I didn't want to explain that noon was the middle of the night for me.

"Out late."

"Good for you. Man, I miss being young. How old are you now?" I was way too tired to remember.

"Twenty-something...?" I said more as a question than a fact. "How old do you think?" I just couldn't keep the lies straight any more. "Oh you know what? Who cares." Then it dawned on me. "Hey," I asked. "How did you get this number?"

"From Dr. Fifth Avenue," John said, with no apology. "I'm the president of his tennis club. He traded your number for a couple of better tennis games." He said this like I should be pleased. "You know," he said in all seriousness, "you're still a commodity."

"What?" I asked, shaking the sleep from my brain.

"A couple of tennis—"

"I heard you," I said. "I just don't believe this."

"What?" said John. "You're hot! You think you wouldn't rank a tennis game for him? And, he tells me you still look great, despite the fact that, you know, you're kind of old! Come on, tell me.... What are you, like twenty-three or something by now?" There wasn't the slightest hint of sarcasm in his voice.

I slammed the phone on John and called Dr. Fifth Avenue on his cell. For the first time ever, I didn't give a flying fuck if his wife was there or not. He answered with a cautious, "Hello?"

"Are you kidding?" I asked.

"Who is this?" His voice became lower and more focused.

"Victoria."

"Oh!" he said. "Listen, you should always say it's you right off the bat, otherwise, I can get a little panicked! And you have to be careful when you call me on the cell...." I was beyond furious that he was still trying to teach me mistress etiquette. "Hey," he said, "is this important? I'm on my way to a tennis game."

"Yeah, I know!" I said. "Thanks to me!" Then I drew in a deep breath and asked, "Are you kidding me? You traded my unlisted number for a tennis game?"

"I gave it to John," he said. "I didn't think you'd mind."

"You didn't think about me at all," I said. "And what, now he gets to fuck me so that you get better matches?" Charlie crawled under the covers to hide.

"Victoria, I don't think I've ever heard you speak like this," he said, sounding disenchanted. I was livid; *now*, after he had traded me for a tennis game, he was going to act like my dad?

"You've never heard me speak like that," I said, "because you've never done anything that completely insensitive before!" I paused to consider if that was actually true, then the anger took over once more. "Don't you ever, *ever* do anything like that again! You violated my privacy. I gave that number to you. Not to that asshole. Do you understand me?"

"Yes."

Then I became calm. And quiet. And seconds went by. Maybe even a whole minute. Then I spoke. "How would you like it if I violated your privacy?" Despite my anger I was clear-headed enough to know that if I went down this road he would be gone forever.

"What are you saying?" Dr. Fifth Avenue asked and I could hear genuine fear in his voice. And there I had it, my answer. The only true power that I possessed over any of my men was with regard to their wives. And love? The one man I thought would always love me traded my unlisted number for a tennis game. He never really loved me at all. "Victoria? Kiddo?" My silence frightened him.

"Don't call me that." My heart was pounding and I was sweating.

"What are you talking about?"

"You know what? Don't ever call me again." I slammed the phone down on Dr. Fifth Avenue for good. I took a step back and stared hard at the phone. How could it be that after all those years with this man, I meant nothing to him at all? Hours later I thought about what I had done and I wondered if I had the luxury to be so proud. But it didn't matter, it was over. The next day, strictly out of curiosity, I dialed his cell. Sure enough, he had changed his number.

It was time to put away my rose-colored glasses once and for all. Clearly, nothing was working for me. Over the past few months I had dabbled in prostitution, been traded by a man whom I thought loved me to a man I loathed, found out that I had become my only sister's enemy, and had succeeded in getting even further into debt. The only positive was a smitten young guy at the membership office of my old gym who let me sneak in for daily workouts. It would be fun while it lasted.

As I dressed for work, I flipped on the TV. There were the usual early evening news shows, all of them trying to scoop the latest celebrity gossip. I normally tuned out the reporters, but that night, for some reason, I kept listening. I was applying mascara when I heard it. My hand stopped. My breath stopped. My heart stopped. I turned slowly in the direction of the television, sure I was mistaken. I wasn't.

I rushed over and turned the television as loud as it would go. "A shocker here, Brad," the chipper newsperson said. "After being in police custody for only minutes, reputed mob boss Michael M. was shot." I turned the channel. "Picked up by police as he returned from Italy... head of the M. crime family, Michael M. has been shot." I turned to another station. "This just in, Michael M., head of organized crime in our area is feared dead." I stood in front of the television with my hand clutching the remote. I shook my head. They had to be wrong. Nothing would ever happen to Michael, nothing could ever happen to Michael. He was untouchable!

"No," I whispered. I repeated it over and over until that solitary word became the mantra I chanted to help Michael stay alive. The one word that I could never say to him was now the only thing keeping me breathing. The newscasters had to be wrong. They were making it up.

What I remember of that night is standing up and sitting back down, standing and sitting, standing and sitting, over and over again. I tried different channels, flip, flip, flip, but there he was, channel after channel. Despite the best efforts of his team of attorneys the camera caught his face; his black eyes stared up at me, hungry, angry, and trapped. He shouldn't have been there. Michael was a wild animal – a strong, powerful, uncontrollable god. Didn't they understand that? I clicked off the television and paced my tiny apartment. If they hadn't arrested Michael, he would never have been shot. It was all their fault.

I had to find out if Michael was okay, but I didn't know which hospital to contact. Even if he wanted to get in touch with me, how could he? Nick couldn't call me; I had changed my number so many times. And Michael was in no position to hunt me down. I was frozen with indecision. I traced the scars on my wrist as a widow twirls her wedding band at her husband's funeral. I completely forgot about work, and by the eleven o'clock news there was an update. "Reputed crime boss, Michael M., is reported in stable condition but remains in the ICU. There is no word on the shooter."

Thank God. He was okay. But what would happen now? Why was Michael arrested? Would the police come looking for me? I nearly jumped out of my skin when the phone finally rang. It was work, wondering where I was. I didn't answer.

I must have fallen asleep because the next thing I remember is the phone ringing again. It was three in the morning and it was work again. I told Michigan's new assistant that there was a death in my family and I'd call them when I could come back. She tried to sound compassionate, but I knew if I was absent more than a few days my job would be gone. I just didn't care. Michael's life was on the line and I had to know how he was. I spent the rest of that early morning praying, to God or to anyone who might listen. I explained to God that Michael was a better person than He may think. I prayed for myself as well. I prayed that Nick would come by. That Michael would want me. That he would need me. That there would be a knock on my door. A quick, purposeful, needy knock. But that knock never came. Not that night, nor any of the long, lonely nights which followed.

Day after day went by. I went back to the club eventually, but I was a shell of my former self. I delivered drink after drink barely having the energy to make small talk for tips. Michigan told me that I had to step up my game or be out. I tried, but I was too depressed. The only man I had ever really loved was lying half-dead in a hospital room and there was nothing I could do about it. There was no way I could see him. There was no one who thought to contact me. Why would they? I was a secret in his life. Although he had been my entire life, I had never really existed in Michael's world at all. There were no children to comfort together, no Sunday dinners to enjoy with the family, no dog to walk in the park, there was nothing real. The last seven years of my life weren't grounded in anyone's reality but my own, and I had never had a terrific grasp on reality. I wondered who would come to see me if I were lying in a hospital room: my mother, Liz, Megan, that's all I could come up with. I had devoted one-third of my life to a battery of men, and not one of them would come see me if I were dying. I was alone. I had never before known what the true cost of being a mistress could be.

Dr. Fifth Avenue called on a particularly low evening. It was as if he had spies planted in my apartment and knew when I would be my most vulnerable. Then, and only then would he swoop down from Olympus – in the form of a beautiful white bull – and strike. This was one of those times. Although I protested seeing him, he said it was important. I just didn't have the energy to fight anymore.

As I let him in my apartment that night, I felt a profound sadness. He didn't look any different than he ever had, and for the most part, neither did I. It could have been any night, seven years earlier. He dropped the Armani overcoat and leaned down for the kiss.

I turned just in time for him to catch my cheek.

"You okay?" he asked holding me at arm's length.

"Mm-hm," I said, nodding.

"Well, will you be ready soon?" he asked, looking at my torn jeans and dirty zip front sweatshirt. "How about some lobster rolls at Chin Chin, huh?" he asked, thumbing through a high-end lingerie catalog. "You love those!"

"Okay," I said, heading toward my closet. Charlie woke up, saw it was Dr. Fifth Avenue, yawned, and went right back to sleep.

"Hey," Dr. Fifth Avenue said. "I did these." He pointed to a model in the catalog. "You're in pretty good company, wouldn't you say?"

I stripped, right there in front of him, and pulled a little black dress out of the closet. He stopped reading his magazine. Forgetting about panties or a bra, I threw on the dress and slicked on some lipstick. I let my hair out of its knot and tossed it.

"Wow!" he said. "I like this just-got-fucked look on you!"

I forced a smile.

At Chin Chin, I really had to concentrate to keep the conversation going. My mind kept drifting back to Michael. I picked at my lobster roll, and Dr. Fifth Avenue stroked my hand. He told me about business, about his son, about the fact that he had no girlfriend, and of course, about John and tennis. Just to keep things interesting, every fifteen minutes or so he'd try to sneak a peek up my dress. As coffee was delivered, Dr. Fifth Avenue finally got to his point: he was buying a house in Monaco. That was the news. That was why he called, to have a wide-eyed twenty-something stare in wonder at how magnificent he really was. I nodded along, pretending to be interested, but the truth was that I was long past Dr. Fifth Avenue and his dinners. I had been sucked in over Monaco – Monaco for his wife and him, that is. I barely even touched my dessert.

Back at my apartment I pulled off my dress and waited for him in bed. It was what he wanted, what was expected of me, and I just didn't care. He looked at me oddly. He came over and sat next to me.

"You okay?" he asked.

"Sure, fine." But I wasn't fine. I was far from fine, but would that really matter to him?

"Tell you what," he said. "Business is a little better... frankly it's a lot better. That's why the little chalet in Monaco." Could he mention "Monaco" one more time? "What do you say I help you out?"

"Okay," I said knowing that he would renege on his offer just as soon as he got laid. "Thanks." He must have understood my tone.

"No, I mean it. Actually..." he was sitting up straight, looking excited. "Actually, there's an apartment available in the brownstone next to my office. I was just talking to the owner this morning. It's two floors. With a private garden in back. Why don't I hook that up for you?"

"That's very nice," I said, "but I just can't afford anything more than this place."

"I mean, get it for you... as in buy it for you to live there. You and that cat of yours. A thank you for all the years of ... well, you." He smiled, and wrinkles formed around his bright blue eyes. "Look, business was too good for me this year and turns out I'm quite the investor! Anyway, I need to dump some money and my accountant says real estate is the best bet. I would own it, of course, but you could live there. All you'll need to worry about is maintenance, something like two hundred a month."

Not long ago, I would have been thrilled. Wasn't this what I'd been waiting for? What I had wished for all those Christmases ago, the brownstone on Fifth Avenue?

He went on. "It'll need a fresh paint job so I'll send my decorator over... I'm thinking something with a safari feel... that'd be nice for a love nest, right? Of course, you don't owe me... you know, sex, but I figured we're heading back there anyway. Oh! And I want to plant some organic tomatoes in the back. They're so expensive at the market! Have you ever noticed that? It'd be nice to have a garden. I'm also thinking the downstairs front room could be my second – or third– office, I need to store some extra paperwork there...." His voice was high and rushed, caught up in the whirlwind of his thoughts. Then he said it. "Sounds way better than John's place, right?" And there it was. He was doing this – all of it – to impress John. I wasn't sure that I needed to be in the equation at all.

Naked in my pullout bed, I thought about what that apartment would truly cost me. It would clearly be his; it didn't even sound like I would have a say in the decor. I would always have to worry that he would just show up – hungry and horny. And there was no way that I could ever bring another man there. I would be thirty-years-old fairly soon. Could it really be possible that I would have amounted to nothing more than being the mistress of Dr. Fifth Avenue? I would live abiding by his rules; following his wishes. That would be far worse than when I screwed my various gods for rent money. At least then no one but the landlord could evict me. I gasped when I realized that I had achieved my life goal; I would finally be "kept." I had just never realized what being "kept" actually meant. Suddenly, I understood that I finally had a chance at everything I had ever wanted, and they were all the wrong things.

I sat up and pulled the sheet around me. I thanked Dr. Fifth Avenue for his offer and walked him to the door. He was still babbling as I closed the door on him. Charlie woke from the clamor and threw himself onto his back, purring. I could tell he approved.

Suddenly, I had clarity. My whole life I had been chasing shortcuts, and the fact was, there just weren't any. After all the time spent with and on my gods, I had developed my own god complex. I mean, who did I think I was? How was I exempt from the rest of the world? Why did I expect to have everything handed to me? Sure, my men were all rich, but what made me think that they were anything all that special? Deep down I finally realized that having penthouses and charge accounts handed to you may be a nice thing, but they weren't real. At least not for me. And they don't define you as a person. All that really matters is what you think of yourself, and I didn't think very much of me. It was time to change. On that one particularly nondescript night, my life as a mistress was bookmarked by Dr. Fifth Avenue – it began with him and it ended with him. That was the night that it became painfully clear to me, no matter what I may have believed, I had been sleeping with mortals for all of those years.

I barely slept that night. Possibility kept my brain buzzing and my body pacing. I gave myself permission to get past who I was and to focus on who I wanted to become. I sat down to get to know myself. I told myself that I matter, and that I was capable of getting the life that I wanted, for myself. It took me almost a decade but I learned that I didn't need a man to make it all happen. I swear I heard "I Am Woman Hear Me Roar" coming through the vents in the floorboards of my apartment. I imagined my cockroaches standing up in unison and applauding me; hoping that I'd get out, and someone would move in who stocks her house with more than dry bread and Diet Coke. For once, if I saw Gloria Steinem on the street, I wouldn't cross to the other side.

I got out my trusty journal which had become worn through from years of tears and abuse. I made a list of everything I would and would not do. Starting that very moment.

1. I will cut back on my drinking.

2. I will not consider my self-worth based on the size of my breasts and the man they conquer.

3. I will realize all men who are conquerable would be so by any woman. Being a mistress is not a talent; in fact, it requires someone who is otherwise talentless.

4. I will go back to school and find a career that doesn't require blowjobs, butt plugs, or twine.

5. I will find out what my interests and gifts are.

6. I will get over my own god complex and start being an active member of society.

7. I will get out of debt and otherwise clean up my person.

8. *I will not sleep with any more married men.

9. *I will forgive myself for the married men I have slept with.

10. *When I have achieved the above, I will be open to a man, not based on wealth or status, but based on mutual respect and interests.

11. *I will go get a life.

*The most important of my new commandments.

I knew it was a tall order, but it was about time.

In an effort to get healthier, I became a vegetarian. It was surprisingly easy; sure, I loved my burgers and fries, but I wanted a clean break from who I was and needed to do that from the inside out. Charlie didn't love being a vegetarian, so a couple of times a week I grabbed him a burger at the McDonalds around the corner from the club.

Over the next few months, I tackled the rest of the list. Although I truly believed that it was my partner and not me who had committed adultery, I still felt incredibly guilty about my past. But did I have to be bound forever by the things I did at nineteen? Like Prometheus, would I be chained to my past sins for all of eternity? It was Zeus who punished Prometheus; could I let Dr. Fifth Avenue control me... even now? Now that I was gone? Prometheus was ultimately freed of his cruel destiny, couldn't I free myself? What did I know then, at nineteen? I didn't excuse my past, but I tried to let it go.

I went to a better modeling agency. A real agency. Much to my surprise, they welcomed me with open arms. I was too old to work high fashion, but I did the occasional print work, more catalog jobs, and most importantly, I became a regular showroom and fit model working ten to twelve hours a day and making between six hundred and a *thousand dollars a day*. For me, that was real money. These jobs were fulltime during the season and they expected professionalism. No drama was tolerated. I went to bed early, woke up early, and arrived early. I appreciated the opportunity and I let them know it by my diligence and grace. I was astounded that I had the ability to make that kind of money on my own.

Naturally I quit the club as soon as the other jobs came along. My good-byes weren't exactly tearful. When I tried to say good-bye to Michigan, he wouldn't even acknowledge me, and when I told Libby I was leaving, she said "Whatever" and walked off. Obviously, I hadn't forged lifelong relationships. And I decided Charlie and I needed to move out of the apartment. I had to remove myself from the place where I could be accessed by my past lovers. All my past lovers. Even him. But because my credit was horrible, it wasn't easy.

It took months. I turned twenty-seven at my old place, but I finally found someone who would rent me an apartment – in their brownstone no less – on a month-to-month basis with no credit check. Just first and last month's rent up front. I jumped at the chance. The apartment was clean and nice, a small one-bedroom with a tiny kitchen (not much bigger than my old kitchen) in the middle of Chelsea. With the exception of the bedroom, which was a deep red color, the rest of the apartment was painted a soft white. Those bedroom walls screamed at me; they reminded me of the cheap motels Michael used to take me to. As part of my plan to get a life, I couldn't tolerate anything that reminded me of Michael, so I repainted the bedroom white to match the rest of the apartment. With every brush stroke, I forced my thoughts away from Michael. Of course, I forgot to prime the walls, so when I stepped back to admire my handiwork, I saw a nice shade of pink. But pink was okay. Besides, no one but Charlie and me saw my bedroom. I did leave one tiny spot of red paint behind a dresser. My brain told me it was a reminder spot, that I could look at and see how far I'd come. My heart told me that it was a Michael spot, and in my weakest moments I would look at it and think of him. I can't tell you how many countless nights I spent masturbating up against that wall, staring at the red spot behind the dresser. Michael. The news had lost track of him, but that, I assured myself, was a good thing. If Michael had died, they would surely report it. Although I tried not to become a news junkie, I did sneak peaks every morning before I left for work, every night when I came home, and any chance I had in between.

Sadly, my new apartment didn't have much of a view. It was a back apartment, so it overlooked a large cement block bordered by a chain fence and patrolled by a yappy dog. That was our backyard. I was worried that the dog might bother Charlie but it didn't even seem to faze him. He sat right in the windowsill and looked down at the dog just to torture him. There were so many reasons to love Charlie. And, as the universe loves a good joke, guess what my landlord grew in our backyard? Organic tomatoes. But this landlord left me alone. Living month-to-month didn't offer a huge sense of security, but I was used to living month-to-month, if not day-to-day or hour-to-hour. And the rent was great — $1900 a month. For the first time in my life, I was making considerable money. I was grateful to use so little on expenses and I stashed the rest away. It was the first time my bank account was on the plus side in I didn't know how long. It thanked me with every deposit. Like a starving alley cat it ate up my offerings heartily, but then it would arch its back and hiss at me if I even thought about a withdrawal. So I couldn't think about a withdrawal. Ever. Even this glorious modeling job couldn't last forever.

I was feeling pretty good about myself. As a sort of penance for my past life, I volunteered on Saturdays at an animal shelter which kept me busy cleaning cages until I worked my way up to adoptions. I was great at helping families find their perfect match. How funny, since I never could find mine. Trying to find a hobby that kept me out of trouble, I joined a pottery class at the Y. The class was filled with people there for their own therapeutic reasons, including recovering drug addicts and alcoholics. I felt strangely at home. After listening to their stories, I found it much easier to cut back on my drinking. School was also on my mind. Remembering that I once had a full ride to a state university, I decided I couldn't be a total idiot. So every Saturday I took English and creative writing classes at a city college and then ran to my volunteering job. Things were looking up for me. Thanks to me. And when I did let myself spend some money, I had newfound fulfillment in buying things for myself and getting exactly what I wanted, not just lingerie or what the man-of-the-moment wanted to see me in. Sure it sucked that I wasn't sporting next season's Prada, but at least I was dressing the way that I wanted to dress.

During my change of lifestyle, I learned a tough lesson. I learned that although I was willing to shoulder the guilt, I wasn't the sole reason my men cheated on their wives. I wasn't anything all that special. I wasn't so incredibly beautiful they couldn't keep it in their pants. I didn't ooze intoxicating pheromones that brought them to their knees. And I wasn't Aphrodite. I was just available. Spike Jansen had said those very words to me so many years before, but I didn't believe him. Back then, I wanted to believe that my beauty, my allure, my sexuality were the reasons that my men cheated; it made me feel powerful, smug. But that just wasn't the way it worked. Do you remember I said I have some ideas on why a man cheats? A man cheats because he's a cheater. That's the best answer I have.

I won't say that it was completely smooth, the fall from Mount Olympus. Like a junkie I still craved my drug. There were many days when I still longed for Michael and his lifestyle, and shallow as it sounds, I found it hard to imagine having a boyfriend who didn't make real money. Sure there were lots of opportunities to meet men through work, but most of those men reminded me of John. And that was a complete turnoff. (I never figured out why I disliked him so.) I knew that deep inside me, I would find it hard to love a mortal man. Also, I wasn't particularly in love with my Chelsea apartment. It was much better than what I had, but it wasn't what I'd always dreamt about. I still wanted the penthouse; the classic six; the loft… and I certainly wanted the view.

One morning while I was doing my make-up for work, I was startled by the phone. I poked myself in the eye with my liner. Cursing and dabbing at my tearing eye, I just beat the machine. "Hello?" I said, out of breath and aggravated. Charlie looked up, turned around, and went back to sleep.

"Hello?" Liz said, she had obviously been crying. "How are you?" Her tone was friendly but forced.

"Okay," I said, wondering why my sister was calling me at 7:45 a.m. on a Tuesday. "How's Megan?"

"Great. Thanks. Honor roll again."

"That's pretty amazing," I said. My eye started running again.

"Can I ask you something?" Liz said.

"Sure."

"Uh, Jesus, listen to me," Liz said. "I can't believe that I'm saying this. I can't believe I'm asking you!"

"It's okay," I said. "Ask me."

"Well, you need to understand. I don't mean to bother you but I can't exactly talk to any of my friends about this."

I figured she called for reasons other than to remind me of our mutual dislike for each other. I swallowed and pushed on. "Ask me. I'll try to help if I can."

"Well, uh...." This was obviously very difficult for her. Finally, she blurted it out. "Do you think Martin buys her things?"

I could hear the desperation on the other end of the phone. It had been a long time since Liz first suspected Martin of cheating. She must have been certain by now. I proceeded carefully. "Buys her things? Like gifts?"

"Like anything," Liz asked.

"No," I said without missing a beat. "No, I don't think he does."

"Are you just saying that?"

"No."

"But how can we know, right? And I know money isn't supposed to matter... but it does. We struggle too, you know? We have bills and debt and tuition and I think the one thing that bothers me more than anything...," she took a deep breath, "is the idea that he throws our money at that stupid little *whore!*"

"Liz," I said, "I promise you that Martin is not spending any significant money on his mistress... if he has one. He is not buying her an apartment, or expensive jewelry. After all this time, he's probably not even buying her expensive dinners. If he has a mistress, it's costing her more than him in the long run. I promise you that. You may not see it or understand it, but I know it." Then I said these words, slowly and deliberately, "I know this, Liz." It had taken nearly a decade for Dr. Fifth Avenue to offer me an apartment, and we all know that it was never really going to happen.

There was silence on the other end. After what seemed like an eternity, Liz asked, "Did he ever love you? I mean... really love you?"

"Never," I said and I didn't even need to think about this one. "Never," I repeated to both myself and Liz. "Not even when he said he did. Never."

"Okay," was my sister's only response.

We sat in silence for a few more seconds. Then Liz asked, "Was it that doctor, the one that I went to with you?"

"Yeah," I answered.

"Yeah," said Liz and she hung up the phone.

That was the last time that Liz and I ever spoke. The differences that divided us had finally become so great that they separated us permanently. I was sorry that she would be gone from my life, but I owed her enough not to lie to her. She was my sister, after all.

CHAPTER 11: PAN

"Pan was a wonderful musician. Upon his pipes of reed he played melodies as sweet as the nightingale's song. He was always in love with one nymph or another, but always rejected because of his ugliness. ... Sounds heard in a wilderness at night by the trembling traveler were supposed to be made by him, so that it is easy to see how the expression 'panic' fear arose."

I had met Norman long before I was in my new apartment, but I didn't see him until after. I was meeting Norman at Lespinasse – a regular place for executives to lunch. We were getting together to discuss plans.

Let's catch you up to speed. I'd been living in Chelsea, and without a man, for about eight months. That meant a lot of free evenings. Not wanting to get sucked back into a life ruled by men, I mostly stayed home with Charlie. Really. Sure I longed to go out – I missed expensive dinners, expensive wine and expensive cars. But I considered myself something of an addict, so I gave myself a mandatory period of time that I would avoid it all. There were many long, lonely evenings. On those nights, after I had visited my Michael spot, I would gravitate toward my journal, rereading what I had written and what I had felt. I couldn't shake the idea that my experiences would make a book, a book that might actually help some other nineteen-year-old thinking about a life with a married man. At the very least a book that might make someone laugh, or maybe make someone else appreciate what she has. I figured there was a good chance that someone might read it and hate me and who I was. That was okay. But there was also the chance that someone else might read it and realize that the story of a man and his mistress was not what she had thought. For whatever her reasons. Maybe that person might even be Liz. And then I thought, hey, what woman wouldn't want to read about Michael? To know Michael? To experience Michael? That, I figured, was reason enough to write.

Night after night, store-bought coffee in a paper cup poised by my laptop, I wrote. And wrote. Until I had this book. Well, most of it. I felt like I had such purpose in my life – such a reason to breathe. It was the closest I ever came to being the person that I wanted to be, a person like that mysterious woman I saw all those years ago in the village shop – the artist who hurried out to buy coffee and then home to create her masterpiece. That was me.

That's why when I ran into Norman at Blockbuster, I agreed to a meeting. It was kismet. Norman was a publisher.

I'd originally met Norman at the club. He was always a nice guy: he tipped well and he was never crass. He told me about his business and his wife to whom he had been married for twenty-three years, and how his oldest son was heading off to Villanova that coming fall.

Getting ready for lunch, I was a bit nervous. It was a Wednesday, but I had the day off; there was no market week, no fittings, and no buyers. I dressed as close to professional as I could: fitted black skirt, heels, black stockings and a white shirt with pearls. I agonized over those stupid pearls all morning, I couldn't decide if they said confident or trying too hard. They were also from Michael, so then I couldn't decide if that meant that they were lucky or unlucky. Finally I decided it was all too silly to fuss over. The pearls looked nice and they fit the image of the woman in the book, so the pearls stayed.

Norman was late. I waited in the lounge area, my elbows resting on my knees, playing with my pearls. I tapped my foot anxiously and a man looked over his paper at me.

"Sorry," I said. He went back to reading but I saw him glance at my legs. I decided to get out of his line of vision and walk off some nervous energy. I looked around to see if Norman was coming from another direction. That's when I realized Lespinasse was in a hotel. A hotel. For a second, my heart jumped into my throat. I had seen too many hotels in my day. Frankly, I was amazed that I hadn't previously visited this one. But rather than stressing over it, I decided to look at it positively – it was destiny that I would meet my publisher in a hotel… a hotel was the perfect backdrop for my story.

I concentrated on my sales pitch. "Victoria Messing is an unlikely heroine." Too rehearsed. "Every word in my book actually happened!" Too animated. How excited could I be about having flashed delivery men for food? Then

Norman arrived. He walked directly toward me and I gasped, despite myself. He was much sleazier looking than I had remembered him from the club or that brief encounter at Blockbuster. Norman wore pleated polyester pants, a vest to cover his protruding stomach and a full beard to try to camouflage his triple chins. He was bald on top of his head but he tried, in vain, for a comb-over. I told myself to relax. Who cared what Norman looked like? He wasn't my date; he was just a Good Samaritan, willing to pass on some information about the book business.

Norman smiled. "Victoria!" he said and pecked me on both cheeks while he slid off his coat. He took off his glasses and cleaned them with his tie. We sat down and he ordered the Wild Scottish Hare and a mimosa. By this time, the thought of eating any animal, let alone a bunny, revolted me, so I ordered a small veggie salad and an iced tea. "Watching your weight, huh?" he asked, and I would swear – under oath – that he looked me up and down.

"No," I said, "not at all, actually. I'm just a vegetarian."

"Really?" he asked, sounding surprised. I assumed he was going to apologize for eating Thumper in front of me. Instead, he said, "Vegetarians are usually so skinny!" I was 5' 9" and about one hundred and fifteen pounds. I was, in every sense of the word, skinny. He could only have been referring to one thing: the size of my breasts. I shifted in my seat and squeezed lemon into my tea. I took a deep breath and tried to let the uncomfortable feeling pass. Well, what did I expect? This may have been a business lunch, but Norman was still a man. I could forgive this one tiny indiscretion, but I would surely mention it if it ever came up again.

Eager to get to the point of the meeting I cut through the bullshit. I dug into my bag to gather my book proposal and pushed my plate out of the way. Norman stopped eating and looked at me.

"Oh," I said, "please. I'm sorry. Finish."

"No, no. I'm done," he said, smiling at me. He had a dab of sauce clinging to his beard. I tried to ignore it, but it was just too obvious

"You have, uh… sauce," I said, rubbing my own chin.

He wiped his beard, not the least bit embarrassed. Then he gulped his mimosa and ordered a second. "Well. I bet you're eager to get down to business!" Was I ever. I exhaled. "First," he said, "let me explain how this works." He sipped his second mimosa while I got out a small pad and pen to take notes. He watched me, seemingly puzzled. I looked up again to see that the sauce on his beard was replaced by orange pulp on his moustache. I didn't even bother. "I am a very busy man, but I will help you whenever I can. For instance, I can give you an advance up front."

I felt a rush of adrenaline pulse through my veins and I rode the high it gave me. It wasn't a good high by any means, but it was a high that I was familiar with. An advance? What was he talking about? I knew established authors often received advances, but what was he basing this on? The short query letter I had sent to his assistant to prepare for this meeting? I bit my lip, a habit I thought I had abandoned long ago. The whole scenario sounded a bit too much like Dorian and his Cover Model Contest. I looked around frantically for a scale. "The book business is crazy," he said, "so in return, I ask that you be available whenever I need you."

I wasn't sure what was going on. I was marching in Norman's parade but I was out of step with his beat.

"Now, I will do this on good faith... giving you an advance up front." He handed me an envelope. "It's a thousand dollars," he said with a wink. That was it. What the hell was going on here? Why was he handing me money in an envelope... in a restaurant... in a hotel? He hadn't even read the book yet. And why a thousand dollars? Suddenly, I remembered Mario and his thousand dollars. I knew exactly what Norman wanted. I came off of my high and watched as every friendly balloon animal in his parade turned into a terrifying clown with fangs and long, sharp nails. What an ass I was. Just because I had changed, why on earth would I assume the men I encountered would have changed too?

Stunned and needing answers I said, "But, you haven't even seen my material yet."

Norman looked me up and down. "I've seen enough to know that what's underneath has to be spectacular." He sipped his mimosa.

With that one sentence he had cut through me. I finally understood and it all made sense, but I had to ask anyway.

"What are you talking about?" I asked in a whisper.

"You," he said. "You came highly recommended by a mutual source."

"A mutual source? Recommended? You're making me sound like a whore!" I said this a little too loudly and he leaned in to quiet me.

"I apologize," he said. "I didn't mean—"

"Who?" I asked.

"What?" He was worried I might make a scene.

"Who recommended me?" I spat these last words at him.

"Michigan... from the club. I hope that's okay," Norman said, breaking a sweat. At least it wasn't Dr. Fifth Avenue passing on my unlisted phone number again. Let's rejoice in little victories.

"Michigan doesn't know anything," I said. "I was a cocktail waitress... but I left that ages ago. I was a cocktail waitress, nothing more. Understand?" He nodded to tell me that he did. At that moment I was eternally grateful that I had left Mario's envelope and that I had never branched out to join Libby in her profession of serving more than drinks. For once, I had a right to be indignant about someone's accusation. I was never a whore. Not by my definition anyway, and that's all that matters.

"I'm sorry," he said, "but, please let's put that behind us, okay? Let's concentrate on other things." I softened slightly, assuming that he meant my book. Then he said, "I would expect to see you on Fridays, when my wife is away."

"Wait, are you hearing me? I'm not interested in—"

"Let me finish," he said. "I also have a daughter whom I love dearly and I wouldn't want to be affected by any of this, so if she's in the city, you'll have the night off."

"Are you for real?" I felt my cheeks burn. To decide to be a mistress and pick a man was one thing. To be recommended from one man to another, and then be told what I could and must do, was something else entirely.

He rambled on about "taking good care of me" and "making me very happy," and somewhere mid sentence, I cut him off.

"Listen, Norman," I said, still trying to be businesslike because we were in a public place, "I have no interest in being your or anyone else's play toy. I have turned down many more powerful and more important men than you. You don't even have a chance, got it?" I stood, leaving his envelope on the table. God, did it feel good that for once I didn't even have to consider what was in that envelope. I grabbed all two hundred and sixty pages of my book and stuffed them into my bag. I'd get it published somewhere else.

As I was leaving, I heard Norman mutter to himself. "I wish Michigan got his stories straight. Fucking lunch cost me over a hundred bucks. Fucking little AIDS fag." I turned back.

"What did you just say?" I asked.

"I was talking about Michigan," he said, not looking at me.

"I know. I mean, the AIDS part," I asked.

"Haven't you heard? I thought it was all over the club by now." It probably was, but I wasn't. I thought of the Bare-Assed Blowjob Girl. "Who cares anyway," Norman said. "He's a fucking little cocksucker." He laughed at his own pun.

CHAPTER 12: PHOEBUS APOLLO

"He is the beautiful figure in Greek poetry, the master musician who delights Olympus as he plays on his golden lyre; the lord too of the silver bow, the Archer-god, far-shooting; the Healer, as well, who first taught men the healing art. Even more than of these good and lovely endowments, he is the God of Light, in whom is no darkness at all, and so he is the God of Truth. No false word ever falls from his lips."

For those of you who like happy endings, here it is. Another year and a half passed, I was twenty-nine, and had yet to get my book published. But I kept working on it. I decided that the original ending had been premature. It had concluded with Charlie and me in Chelsea, but something inside me told me that there was more. I couldn't shake the feeling that something else was going to happen, and that I'd know when these chapters of my life were complete. Then, I would get it published.

I also moved again. Thanks to the glut of available modeling jobs and my eagerness to work, I made enough to stash some money away and to buy Charlie and me a nice apartment on the Upper East Side with an incredible view and an equally incredible mortgage. No, it wasn't an entire brownstone, and it wasn't on Central Park West or Fifth Avenue, but it was better. Truly. And not just because I bought it myself with my own money and all that crap. It was just a beautiful apartment, a one-bedroom in a new building on Lexington Avenue. There was a small entryway which just fit a round cherry table on which I used to keep a vase of calla lilies, until I found out they were toxic to cats. Off the entrance to the right was the kitchen with new appliances, including a dishwasher. (A dishwasher!)

There were windows on three sides of the apartment, including the kitchen. The entryway unfolded into the living/dining area which had picture windows overlooking Manhattan. The view from the living room was spectacular – it was the reason that I bought the place. Looking downtown I could see as far as the Chrysler building, and to the left I could see a sliver of the East River, if I really craned my neck. But night was the best. At night I could see New York glistening, twinkling, all shined up and ready to be stared at – a lot like the old me.

I converted one part of the bedroom into an office, and the other was, of course, where we slept. The furniture was all white but somehow Charlie didn't shed on it. The apartment looked clean and new. I never really knew what my taste was or what I wanted my apartment to look like until I moved here. Prior to that I was always told what was beautiful by someone else. But I found what I actually liked, all on my own. I never even knew that I had my own style. My own opinions. I never knew I was a real, live person.

And I never believed that I'd be able to take care of myself, that I would buy myself my dream apartment, that I would be a success all on my own. I always thought my worth could only come from the importance of the man that I was with. I never considered myself anything more than eye candy, so that's all I ever was.

So what about all the other stuff? Well, for those of you who kept reading because you like fairytale endings, you'll probably want to stop reading now. For the rest of you, here goes. Mom couldn't believe that I achieved this level of success on my own. She still believed someone bought the apartment for me – someone like Michael. Liz and I still didn't speak, but I remembered Megan on every birthday and every holiday. I just hoped she remembered me. Mom told me that Liz gave Martin another chance. And another. He promised to stop cheating. Three times now.

And for the big question, what about men? I was dating. Just dating. Sadly, the single ones were just as messed up as the married ones. Maybe even worse. I had a date with a reporter from the AP who thought I should pay for my own movie ticket. Then there was the out-of-town businessman who – on the first date – asked me back to his hotel to sleep with him… and his sister. At the same time. Not to mention the lawyer with hair plugs so bad they looked like tiny bunches of flowers sprouting from the top of his head. He had once been a correspondent for a top-rated TV news show, but all that was left of his former glory was an insatiable cocaine habit and his desire to "fatten me up" by always buying me pasta dinners (that way, he would still look camera-thin in comparison). Then there was the wealthy, closeted businessman who just wanted me around as his beard. That was okay. We had nice dinners and fun trips to Martha's Vineyard and Fire Island and we saw a lot of operas and musicals. Unfortunately, he eventually thought that he had to get it up, and when he couldn't, he blamed me.

There were some normal ones too. Regular old nice guys. Like Guy. Guy was a stockbroker, about 6'2" and fortyish. He'd been divorced for a long time, and he had no kids. He was nice. We met at the gym (a new gym where I actually paid my own membership) and after several weeks of talking he finally asked me out. I said, "Okay – sure." Actually, that's exactly what I said, "Okay – sure." Maybe it wasn't the, "I-can't-live-without-you-I'm-so-excited-that-you-finally-asked-me-out!" response that he was looking for, but it was just dinner.

We were heading to Nobu, a good choice, and all I was hoping for was some friendly conversation and a great dinner. I dressed in a simple black spaghetti-strap dress with sling-backs. I threw a wrap around my shoulders and doused myself with perfume. What the heck, it didn't matter anymore, I could wear all the perfume I pleased. I also added a coat of MAC lipglass – again – just 'cause I could. I slicked my long hair back into a low ponytail. I smiled at myself. I liked how I looked. More refined than when I was younger, classier. I looked a lot like Liz. Huh. Dr. Fifth Avenue had said that very thing to me all those years ago. Well, I guess he had to know something – his profession was based on aesthetics.

Guy called me from the car to apologize profusely. He was stuck in traffic coming uptown. He was so, so, so sorry. Really. So very, very sorry. He usually accounted for things like traffic and this was an egregious mistake on his part. He really said, "This is an egregious mistake on my part." Then he apologized some more. He hoped I wasn't angry, and he wanted me to know that he understood that he should never keep a woman "like me" waiting. What that meant, I wasn't sure. But I think it was meant as a great compliment. After a few more apologies, I squirmed a bit, a little uncomfortable with how, well, wimpy he sounded. He said he'd call again when he got close, and I told him not to bother. It was a beautiful night; I'd wait for him in front of my building.

Guy was the best prospect that I'd had in awhile. He was a good mix of success and niceness, of wealth and normalcy. I was certainly going to wait for him. Besides, Nobu was sounding better by the second. Guy was completely average, but he was trying desperately to be more. His effort was endearing. One day quite innocently he asked me, "I drive a Beemer. Have you ever been in a Beemer before?"

"No," I said, truthfully. "No I haven't." Guy seemed so genuinely happy I didn't have the heart to tell him the reason I had never been in a BMW was because my dates normally drove Ferraris or Bentleys. Even Dr. Fifth Avenue's "Summer of Chrysler" was meant to be whimsical – like wearing costume jewelry – but his real cars were Mercedes.

I smiled at my doorman as I glided through my beautiful lobby brimming with exotic plants. I had achieved this – all of it – for myself. Okay, I didn't build the darn building, but you get the point. I stepped out onto the sidewalk and was swathed by warmth. It was a glorious early summer evening; I slid my wrap off and inhaled deeply. Nice. It was all so nice. I had gone through a lot to get to this place: a beautiful apartment, expensive clothes, nice Guy taking me to Nobu. I smiled, proud of myself, and decided that I would take a bit of a stroll, gazing – not longingly, but curiously – at the boutique windows.

It was in the middle of all this polite niceness – looking at Italian leather handbags with my back to the street – that I first heard it... well, felt it is more accurate. It was a vibration that sprinted across the sidewalk and up through my body. Initially, I shook it off. I laughed at myself, sure my brain was playing tricks on me. (Italian leather was just too ironic, no?) My mind was fooling me. It had to be. But the sound intensified. "Let me in!" it whispered, first lovingly, and then, "LET ME IN!" it roared.

I lifted my shoulders, trying to block out the noise, but the sound snuck past my every defense. The hum buried itself deep inside my brain – there was no escape. I pinned my gaze to the handbags, terrified to turn or to look directly at its reflection in the window for fear I might turn to salt. Again and again I heard the engine rev; it was the unmistakable growl of a Ferrari. I closed my eyes and prayed that Guy was here to surprise me, to pick me up in his newest purchase. Stockbrokers get huge bonuses, right? That had to be it. It must be Guy.

But you know me better than that. That wasn't the real prayer I prayed. In truth, I prayed that Guy would be stuck in traffic just a bit longer.

"Purrrrr… Purrrrrr…" there it was again. Didn't anyone else hear it? I glanced from side to side, but people were hurrying along. No one else seemed to notice. Everyone but me was oblivious to the hypnotic, gentle soothing sounds of the Italian automobile, the *deus ex machina*. I opened my eyes and forced them to look at the reflection in the glass. That's when I saw them: the car… and *him*. Dear God. Or maybe more accurately, Dear god. Michael had returned.

Time froze. Then Guy pulled up right behind him.

"Victoria!" Guy said bounding out of the car. But I couldn't move. I couldn't turn around. They could both see my reflection in the glass. I had to do something, but if I turned to them, I would have to react. Like a child, I stood there waiting for direction. I just didn't know what to do; even breathing had become impossible.

And then he got out. Dear God and Dear god. I felt the rush of emotion; the vibration from his car morphing quickly into my own slow, steady quivering. He was still feet away from me but I could feel his hands on my body; my own hands trembled. He was heavier than he was all those years ago, but he was still as strong… still as powerful… still as dangerous. In the reflection, I could see that his hair was graying – beautiful silver streaks lined both sides of his temples.

I must have started breathing again because I felt my breath catch in my throat. He stood next to his Ferrari, and even standing still he had so much charisma, so much wild sexuality that he *took up all the room in the universe*. I'm sure neither the earth nor the sun would mind getting out of his way. The planets would gladly realign for him. The oceans were already under his control.

His mere presence made Guy cower. Guy looked at the Ferrari and then back to his own car. He had probably never before been on the losing side of a competition. Especially one that dealt with money. Poor Guy.

I stared at the handbags in the window in an inane attempt to look as if I hadn't noticed them or the pissing contest that was about to ensue. Once again, poor Guy; not only would he be the loser, but he would also be the only one competing. Guy was measuring to see who had the bigger one but a deaf, dumb and blind dog could tell that. Michael never even looked Guy's way. "Victoria?" Guy said again, now fully emasculated. His tone was more of a question than a statement. Both of these men were here for me and I was required to do something.

Finally, I turned. As if my whole future were on that street, I turned. As if the next fifty years of my life were mapped out in chalk on the asphalt, I turned. To my right was nice Guy, with a nice car, with a nice evening planned. To my left was *Michael*. Why now? I couldn't look directly at him but his reflection was successfully burned into my retinas. Forever. Why did his gray look so alluring; his body look so strong; his scar look so dangerous; why was I dizzy? After all this time! After all this progress. Why? I looked at Guy. Nice. Nice Guy. Guy was confused.

"Victoria?" he asked again.

Then I turned to Michael, but my eyes couldn't meet his. I was angry with him. Why hadn't he contacted me? What happened after the shooting? Did he go to jail? Was I in danger just being near him? But my anger was melted by the adrenaline running through my body. I could no longer hear the car… now all I could hear was my own heartbeat dancing to some wild rhythm.

Finally, my eyes met his. I let them rise slowly, hungrily, up his face, lingering at the scar, the teeth and up into the two black pools which for me were made, I was now sure, out of pure kryptonite. I was breathing so heavily that I could have had my own 900 number; if only I had thought of that for a job all those years ago. I felt the tears well up in my eyes and I fought them back—hard. I wanted to run to him, to press my body against his, to feel his arms of steel wrap around me, to feel the steel that was bulging from inside his jacket push against me. But I knew that I had to get away. I had worked too hard to turn back now.

Guy made one more lovely effort. "Victoria?" he asked once again. I knew I owed Guy some words but none came.

Silently, Guy got back into his Beemer and drove off, watching us stare at one another. I shook my head slightly. I needed to fight every feeling that I was feeling. I needed to turn my feet toward home and go there, but they wouldn't obey. Instead, I bit the inside corners of my mouth. I felt my chest rise up and down. There was nothing I could do. I let my eyes ask him. Ask him why. His eyes answered back with a long blink and a single tilt of his head. Then he opened the passenger door and said simply, "Bella, get in."

I smiled.

So, that's what happened in my life as a New York City mistress. There was a lot of glamour and a lot of money – just not always for me. There was also a lot of unhappiness and very little normalcy – mostly for me. And there were always a lot of men. What I tell you is truth. Every bit. Was it as you expected? Probably not. But I think that if we've learned anything together, it's that nothing ever is. Oh, you're wondering if I got in. …Well, what do you think?

"First there was Chaos, the vast immeasurable abyss,

Outrageous as a sea, dark, wasteful, wild....'

From darkness and from death Love was born, and with its birth, order and beauty began to banish blind confusion. Love created Light with its companion, radiant Day."

CPSIA information can be obtained at www.ICGtesting.com
Printed in the USA
BVOW021708050412

286983BV00002B/103/P

9 780974 547664